ISBN-13: 978-0615494739
ISBN: 0615494730

This is a work of fiction. Names, characters, places and incidents either are the product of the author's imagination, or are used fictitiously. Any resemblance to actual persons, living or dead, business establishments, events, or locales is entirely coincidental or satirical.

Published 2011 by Pulpwork Press, New York. Information for bookstores and web retailers available at PulpWork.com.

Portions of this book were previously published as follows:

Point of Destruction, **Electronic Tales** © 1994. Electronic Tales.

Plight of the Achilles, **Electronic Tales** © 1996. Electronic Tales.

The Ikarian Connection, **Mystery Adventure Tales**, Hidalgo Publishing © 2000. Hidalgo Publishing Company.

Dead Beat in La Esca, **Thrilling Tales**, 86th Floor Productions © 2007. Joel Jenkins and Derrick Ferguson. 1st publication.

Dead Beat in La Esca, **Four Bullets for Dillon** © 2011. Joel Jenkins and Derrick Ferguson. 2nd publication.

The Gantlet Brothers Greatest Hits

Joel Jenkins

The Ikarian Connection

Prologue:
1982 Los Angeles, California

The sun had long set and the blistering heat of the day began to subside. Though daylight had long passed, the tar roofs of the suburban maze still held stubbornly to the warmth they had gathered during the day. Tank-topped teens loitered on cracked asphalt driveways, collecting around hydraulic-jacked cars that hopped to the thumping bass reverberating through the neighborhood.

A sleek silver Jaguar cruised slowly, deliberately, through the winding streets that curled like snakes through the endless tracts of housing. Massive, scarred black hands encompassed the steering wheel as though they were guiding some child's toy. Hiding in plain sight, mused the driver. That was what they were doing.

Finally he spotted what he was looking for and glided the car to the curb opposite. Number 7431. The house certainly didn't appear to be anything out of the ordinary—white weather-beaten siding and peeling trim, and a lawn that hadn't been watered in recent memory, now little more than dried tufts of brown grass.

The huge hands moved to the glove compartment and removed a gold-chromed Smith and Wesson automatic. He flipped the release catch and a magazine loaded with .45 caliber cartridges dropped into his palm. A faint smile flickered across his broad features and he jammed the magazine back into place. With a practiced movement, he pulled back the slide and let a bullet pop into the chamber. Releasing the safety catch, he slipped the gun into a holster secreted in the small of his back. He shrugged a blue satin jacket on over his huge shoulders as he stepped from the Jag.

"Hey, mister," called a curious boy from the seat of well-used tricycle. "Is that your car?"

"I'm just borrowing it." He put a hand on the boy's shoulder and pulled a twenty dollar bill from his jeans' pocket. "I want you to do something for me. You take this… and I want you to go in the house and tell your Momma that she needs to call the fire station. And to earn this twenty I want you to stay in the house until after the fire trucks have left. You got it?"

The boy nodded, brown eyes wide. "But mister, where is the fire?"

He motioned at 7431. "Right there."

The boy pedaled urgently toward his home bent on fulfilling his errand.

The man turned and strode evenly across the hot pavement, moving lightly for someone so large. His style of dress was not nearly as ostentatious as the vehicle he drove. The denim jeans he wore were stretched to the point of bursting, barely able to contain his massive thighs. The satin jacket had seen better days. The silk-screened New York Yankees logo had faded and peeled. However, he could have been wearing nothing but rags and still have been impressive. He stood four inches over six feet and his shoulders were nearly half again, as broad. His head was shaved clean except for a thick Mohawk, which was offset by a full beard and a gold hoop in his left ear.

By his relaxed gait it might have appeared that he was on a friendly errand, but as he neared the porch his demeanor showed otherwise. He bounded lightly up the sun-scorched steps which squeaked beneath his weight despite the softness of his tread. Setting his teeth in a grimace, he laid a scarred fist to the wooden door panel and rapped quickly, three times.

Time crawled interminably. Finally he could hear the footfalls approaching the door. A small sliding hatch about the size of a hand opened up at the height of an average man's eye-level. He looked down into the bloodshot eyes of the guard behind the door—the pupils dilated so they looked like black marbles.

"What's the word?" asked the man behind the door.

"I need some crack."

"You got some green?"

The big man reached into his pocket with his left hand and pulled out a crisp bill that showed Benjamin Franklin's portrait. He put this directly in front of the view hole as he reached down with his left hand and retrieved the gold-plated .45.

The hundred dollar bill seemed satisfactory to the guard, but the eyes narrowed momentarily, as if suspicious. "Who sent you, man?"

"No one sent me…are you going to sell me some rock or not?"

"Who are you?"

The big man was getting impatient now. The guard behind the door would be in charge of screening out any undesirables…like cops, informants, or people without cold hard cash. He'd be holding a shotgun to the door about waist level in case there were any problems.

The man on the porch had hoped for easy access to the crack house, but it looked like he was going to have to do things the hard way.

"I'm Blake Hawkins, you piece of nothing crap. Now let me in!" He shoved the Smith and Wesson up behind the hundred dollar bill as he twisted to the side of the door. The gun jumped three times as Blake pulled the trigger. Blood sprayed sticky across his hand, confirming that he'd made at least one hit.

A shotgun roared, blowing through the door in a geyser of splinters and lead. Blake figured that it was the guard's dying shot. He'd scored a hit to the head, and most people weren't going to get up from that. Gambling on this fact, Blake plowed through the door, ripping it from its hinges. Throwing it aside, he took a quick inventory of his surroundings.

The guard lay dead on the floor. Every bullet Hawkins had fired hit its mark. Next to the dead man lay the hundred dollar bill—three bullet holes in Benjamin Franklin's powder-burned face. The interior of the house was dark and dingy, smelling of sweat, vomit, and the harsh chemicals used to manufacture the crack.

A worn and stained rust-colored carpet covered the floor. Directly in front of Blake stairs rose to the second story of the house. Breaking off to either side of the steps were entry halls that pushed further on into the garbage strewn house. What he was looking for would be in the basement of the place, hidden away from the prying eyes of the neighborhood.

Blake figured that the boy had reached his house by now. In another minute or so he would make the call to the police about a fire. He had maybe three minutes after that to start one. Time to get moving.

He took the right hallway around the stairwell and found a doorway in back of the stairs. Blake quickly tried the handle. The knob turned but the door wouldn't open. It was barred from the inside. Blake lifted one massive leg and slammed his foot against the door. Two blows was all it took to remove the door, frame and all, from the surrounding wall where it had been moored. The door slid with a shriek, down a metal staircase that descended into the basement.

A man appeared at the bottom of the stairs holding an enforcer style pump shotgun with a magazine of ten rounds jacked into it. He wore a bulletproof vest over his t-shirt, and Blake realized that the upstairs was where the rinky-dink appearance of this outfit ended. It was a put-on—a sham. This was a pro operation all the way. One that pumped hundreds of thousands of dollars worth of crack cocaine out onto the streets every year. Not that he cared. It was all business to him.

Blake fired off four rounds for the head. The man below had reached his station at the bottom of the stairs a few seconds too late. Probably he had wasted precious moments putting the vest on after he heard gunshots upstairs. These were moments that had allowed Blake the advantage. Only one round hit, the others ricocheted off the cement wall behind. One round was all it took to put the gunman in a permanent coma.

Bounding down the stairs, Blake leaped over the door and past the body at the bottom. Gun smoke mingled with the scent of chloroform. Many crack labs were enterprises of small-time gangland entrepreneurs. In order to obtain the chemicals they needed for producing the crack cocaine they would buy off the shelf items in the grocery store—spot remover for the chloroform; safrole for the sassafras oil; asthma medication for ephedrine, starting fluid for ether. This place didn't deal in such small time manufacturing. Cases of industrial grade chemicals lined the walls, flanked by tanks of ether. This stuff was difficult to get, but they had big time connections.

Rounding the corner, Blake entered the central portion of the lab. Halogen overhead lamps lit the near pristine working conditions. Four street chemists scattered, looking for cover beneath work tables and behind stacks of boxed chloroform bottles. There was really no where for them to go. They were sitting on a literal powder keg.

A gunshot went off and Blake felt a bullet tug at his right ear. He turned, firing more by instinct than knowledge, aiming in the direction that he had heard the gunshot. The gunman had crept in behind him, standing on the stairs above. Blake's bullet struck home and, gurgling, the man slumped over the rail and fell heavily to the hard tile floor near Blake's feet.

He looked up at Blake, pain and anger etched into his face. "You don't know what you're messing with," he croaked, crimson dribbling from the corner of his mouth. "My boss has a long memory. You won't get away with this."

Blake laughed harshly. "Then you tell your boss that Blake Hawkins trashed your crack house. This is the third one by my count!"

"Why?"

"As I'm sure you are aware…life is all about money. And your competitor is paying me plenty."

"My boss will hear about this…I'll see to it," he coughed out.

Blake cocked an eyebrow and reached into the pocket of his blue satin jacket, producing a Russian made grenade. This make was especially danger-ous because the fuses were made with varying lengths. Some would explode immediately upon release. Unscrewing the core and checking the fuse mark-ing was the only way to know how many seconds before detonation once the pin was pulled and the handle let go. This one had a long fuse…ten seconds.

Grinning maliciously Blake pulled the pin and released the mantle. "And while you're at it…you tell your little nothing piece of crap boss that Blake Hawkins killed you!"

He gently rolled the grenade across the floor so that it came to rest next to a rack of highly flammable ether canisters. Then without saying another word he turned and sprinted up the stairs, down the hall and through the front door.

As he got halfway across the front lawn he heard the muffled thump of the grenade. Mere moments later the canisters of ether erupted, belching out fiery destruction that blew out every window in the house and sent tongues of flame licking out across the lawn. The shock wave hit Blake with a tangible force, scorching heat washing over him. He stumbled forward as the force of the blast momentarily lifted him several inches from the ground.

Shingles and shards of lumber rained down from the sky as a chain of explosions ripped through the house. As Blake stepped into his Jaguar, the ex-plosions settled and what remained standing of the house became a seething inferno. Thick black smoke spread an ominous pall in the sky. Briefly Blake watched a crow wing its way across the graying sky.

Feeling a dampness at his ear, Blake reached up. His fingers came away wet with his own blood. He ran the events of the last few minutes through his mind until he recalled being clipped by a bullet. Shrugging, he inserted the ignition key and started the Jag. He maneuvered the car through the debris in the roadway, and at a reasonable pace—so as not to arouse attention—he left the area.

Chapter One:
1987, Shasta Trinity, California

The sun was setting, the sky ablaze with reds and pinks that spread, ribbon-like, across the horizon. Matthias Gantlet paused a minute to enjoy the view before pulling his red Corvette out of the small gas station at Lakehead, and eventually back onto I-5, where the weekend traffic was surprisingly light.

Warm wind whipped through his long brown hair, twisting it into a hopelessly tangled mat. The evening air was warm and Matthias decided to leave the convertible top down for now and take full advantage of the welcome heat. He slipped a Condemner cassette into the stereo and listened to the rasping vocals mesh with intertwining beds of lead and rhythm guitars.

The freeway cut smoothly through the rugged terrain on either side, which was forested thickly by oak and pine. Now and again, on either side of the highway, vast expanses of blue breeze-rippled water appeared from behind the cover of towering conifers. It seemed as though he were driving through country that was spattered with many magnificent lakes, but Matthias knew that they were are all connected. Lake Shasta was the largest man-made reservoir in California, with more shore line than even San Francisco Bay—where Matthias was headed.

A protuberance in the small of Matthias's back caused him to shift uncomfortably. It was an annoyance that he had grown accustomed to—he carried the pistol with him constantly. It had grown to be his permanent companion and most trusted friend. He had made a lot of enemies since his escape over the Berlin wall five years earlier and beside his four brothers, the only thing he completely trusted was his Desert Eagle .44.

He temporarily slipped it from its holster and laid the gun, its chrome gleaming under the red skies, on the leather passenger seat beside him. With a ten-inch barrel on it, it was truly a massive gun and boasted nearly twice the stopping power of a .45.

Pushing past the speed limit by twenty miles an hour, Matthias made good time towards San Francisco. The Corvette's eight cylinder engine thrummed smoothly beneath the hood, the wide tires sticking to the road like glue.

Eventually dusk fell and in the twilight Matthias could make out an older model van pulled to the side of the road. The shoulder was fairly ample and the nose of the van was pointed towards the highway. Matthias could see someone working under an upraised hood. He slowed the car and pulled in behind the van, raising a cloud of dust as he came to a stop.

He concealed the .44 magnum beneath a half folded road map and stepped from the Corvette. As he approached the van, a woman peering beneath the hood extricated herself and came toward the 'Vette. As they approached each other he nearly lost his train of thought. She wore a pair of form fitting blue jeans and a white tank top, smudged with grease where she had leaned in to get a look at her engine. The tank top did little to conceal, and everything to accentuate, the proportions of her fantastic physique. Her bared shoulders and arms exposed sun-darkened skin with a sprinkling of light freckles emerging from beneath the straps of her shirt. Raven black hair was confined behind her head with a blue tie, then it fell in a pony-tail to the center of her back.

Feeling that his admiration might become too obvious, Matthias focused on the deep blue eyes that gazed at him with a mixture of skepticism and hopefulness.

"I saw the van broken down and thought I'd stop to see if I can help out," he offered.

She bit her lower lip and Matthias took notice of her full red lips and wide, sensual, mouth. Matthias was worried that his appearance might have scared her. He stood six feet tall and a very solid two hundred ten pounds. A rigorous body building regimen had added thick slabs of muscle to the lean body of his youth. His hair was almost as long as hers, and although his features were handsome he sometimes intimidated people with whom he came into casual contact. He pushed up his custom Gargoyle sunglasses to the top of his head so she could see his eyes.

"The power gave out. It jerked a couple of times, and that was it. I had to coast to the side. Lucky for me there was a shoulder. You much of a mechanic?" Her voice was vibrant with just a hint of huskiness.

Matthias shook his head. "I'm afraid I'm not. If you like I can take a look, but if it's anything beyond the obvious I'm not going to be much help…unless it's giving you a ride to the nearest service station."

She shrugged. "If it was anything obvious I would have caught it. My brother's a bit of a grease monkey. He taught me how to change oil, install alternators, and stuff. If it was anything easy I would have caught it."

"Can I offer you a ride then?" asked Matthias. "It might be quite a walk to the nearest town."

He could sense her hesitation. She needed the ride but didn't know if he could be trusted or not. "I don't know," she answered falteringly. "It's not that I don't appreciate the offer…but I don't really know you."

"I understand," said Matthias. "But what are the chances of someone swinging by that you know? You live in the area?"

She shook her head. "No. Oregon."

"Where you headed?"

"San Francisco."

"Me, too." He extended his hand. "I'm Matthias Gantlet."

She took his hand and shook it with a firm grip. "Courtney Johns. You're name sounds familiar."

"I sing for a band called Gantlet, maybe that's where you've heard the name?"

"The band's named after you?"

Matthias smiled. "Well, in a manner of speaking. My four brothers are also in the band so I can't take the entire credit."

"Yes, I have heard of the band…" Courtney said, but Matthias's attention was distracted as a black luxury sedan approaching from the north slowed. Two dark-suited men peered intently through the front and rear passenger side windows as they cruised by. Matthias watched the front passenger reach for a CB receiver and pull it to his mouth.

"Courtney," interrupted Matthias. "Why don't you grab your stuff and get in my car. I'll give you a lift."

Courtney looked up and followed the line of Matthias's gaze. She turned and saw that the black sedan had pulled to the shoulder and was wildly backing toward her van, as though it were going to plow right into it.

She looked back toward Matthias.

"I don't like the looks of them," he said. "Get your stuff, quick!"

She jumped to the back of her van, threw open the double doors and reached in and grabbed a pair of suitcases and a garment bag. Burdened by the heavy baggage, she began making her way back to the Corvette.

The black sedan lurched to a stop, sending clouds of dust billowing from beneath its wheels. Immediately two men disgorged from the right side of the vehicle. One circled around the back of the van and the other came from the front.

Matthias figured that they were trying to outflank him. It was a classic maneuver but one that wasn't often put to immediate use. It showed Matthias two things. These people were professionals and they weren't here for a friendly conversation. They planned to do harm.

Normally Matthias would take the fight to one of them in the hopes that he could overpower or out maneuver him before the second opponent circled in from behind. In this case, if he left his current position, he would risk exposing Courtney. One of them would have a free path to her.

Matthias fell into a kung fu stance, his body turned sideways to present a narrower target, his fists raised to block attacks, his head lowered slightly so his face wasn't an easy target, and his weight resting slightly on the rear leg so he could facilitate easy movement. In many ways Matthias came from the school of street brawling, but he had spent the past year studying Jeet Kune Do with a student of Bruce Lee's. He had learned to take what was most practical from street fighting and what was most practical from the other combat arts and combine them into an effective offense.

The first suit came around the corner of the van. He was a stocky six foot two with a face reminiscent of a bulldog. The moment that he reached inside his suit jacket Matthias knew that he was in trouble. These guys were packing heat and they intended on using it. Traffic was extremely light. A few well placed bullets could finish him and Courtney off and these men could be back in their sedan and on their way before anyone passed by. Matthias leaped forward and grabbed Bulldog's arm as it emerged from beneath the tweed jacket, connected to a nine-millimeter pistol.

"Get the girl!" Bulldog croaked to the second thug, apparently thinking that he could keep Matthias occupied long enough for the man to accomplish whatever they were trying to do.

Bulldog was strong and immediately tried to wrench his arm away from Matthias's grasp. Matthias wasn't going to give him a chance. He drove his left knee hard into the man's groin and, as the thug doubled over, smashed his right elbow into the man's pug face. The gun spun loose as Bulldog crumpled to the ground.

Matthias could hear the crunch of gravel underfoot as the second thug, looking for an easy blow, ran up behind him. Since Matthias had made short work of the first man, evidently the second had temporarily abandoned his aims on Courtney. Pivoting, Matthias lashed out with his left foot, cracking ribs as he connected with the man's torso. The thug reeled to the ground and Matthias followed up rapidly with several more kicks to the face and body.

With two opponents down on the ground, Matthias quickly surveyed the situation. The chauffeur of the sedan was popping the driver's door open now. He would have to be dealt with.

A screech of tires alerted Matthias. He cast his attention to the north bound lane of I-5. A blue sedan of similar make and model to the one that his attackers drove skidded to a stop in a cloud of blue vapor, leaving black trails of smoking rubber on the pavement. Recklessly, they began bouncing across the uneven median toward the south bound lane and the site of the melee. Things were suddenly looking worse.

Courtney had thrown her suitcases and garment bag behind the Corvette's seats with Matthias's guitar and hockey bag. She was leaping into the passenger side when Matthias turned and sprinted toward her. It seemed as though the best course of action might be vacating the general area.

Bounding up over the shiny red hood and rolling over the top of the wind shield, Matthias managed to ensconce himself in the driver's seat of the Corvette. He had left his keys in the ignition. Giving them a quick twist, the engine roared to life.

Courtney turned to him, frantically. "What are we going to do?"

"Drive real fast," answered Matthias.

Squirming, Courtney tried to settle into the seat and belt herself in. Matthias reached beneath her shapely posterior and pulled the Desert Eagle free.

She looked at him in shock. First because she thought he was taking liberties with her, and second because of the gun he brandished.

"That ought to be more comfortable," he said as he jammed the gun between the seat cushion and the upholstered hump where the emergency brake rested between the bucket seats. It was a place where he would have easy access to the pistol, should he need it. Right now he was going to need both hands to drive.

Gravel spit from beneath the rear wheels of the 'Vette as Matthias gunned it out into the roadway. The acrid scent of burning rubber drifted to Matthias's nostrils as the blue sedan screeched to a halt in front of them. In mere seconds Matthias had accelerated to forty miles an hour. Now he had no where to go but straight into the side of the sedan. Unless...

Matthias braked hard and spun the wheel to the left. The Corvette's rear drifted to the right as Matthias made the turn. It impacted hard with the left passenger door panel of the sedan. Broken plastic, and fiberglass sprayed out from the point of the blow but the 'Vette was clear. Matthias gunned it across the small opening in the freeway median and toward the north bound lane. With a sickening grinding noise, the car bottomed out several times as Matthias took it across the uneven median. Fortunately they had enough momentum to make it across. Once they hit pavement, Matthias immediately braked again and spun the wheel to the right so that they sat facing south in the north bound traffic. He accelerated.

Courtney slid down in her seat so that she could barely peer across the dashboard, afraid to look. "You're going to kill us!" she gasped out.

"If I don't they will," answered Matthias, nodding in the direction of the two sedans that were shadowing them in the South bound lane across the center divide. Both had been unprepared for Matthias's sudden and unexpected maneuver and were several hundred yards behind on their parallel course. That wouldn't last for long of course. Matthias was keeping the car to the side of the highway, half on the meager shoulder of the road and half in the actual lane.

The Corvette slipped by a blue pickup truck approaching from opposite direction. A blast of wind buffeted them as rear-view mirrors came within inches of colliding. Matthias looked ahead for an opening in the median that might allow him back onto the other side of I-5. Finally he saw an area that gradually dropped into a gentle ravine and sloped back up to the roadway. If he eased his sports car across he might be able to negotiate it. If he miscalculated they would become hopelessly stuck at best; at worst they would plant the front of the Corvette into the side of the ravine and flip end over end. Matthias didn't ponder the ramifications for long. Sometimes you didn't have the luxury of thinking over a plan of action. And one of the worst things you could do was take no action at all.

Giving the engine a little more gas, Matthias pushed the car into the median. He worked the car deeper, branches scraping the undercarriage as the Corvette roamed over small shrubs. Then they were up the opposite side of the ravine and back on solid pavement. Their maneuver had cost them about a hundred yards and the blue sedan was hoping to close that distance with bullets. The thugs didn't stand a chance of catching them in an all out contest of speed. The Corvette had them hopelessly outclassed. However, they hoped to stop the chase short with a few well-placed pieces of lead.

Matthias heard the pop of a .32 pistol and his right rear view mirror disintegrated into a haze of fiberglass and reflective shards. There was only one thing to do…fight fire with fire.

"Take over driving," said Matthias.

Courtney looked hesitant at first, then understood his request. She slid across the center hump of the car and put her left foot on the accelerator, taking the wheel as she did. In turn, Matthias slid over the back of the seat and into the well behind it.

Now Matthias could see their assailant, a thug with slicked-back hair and pinched face leaning from the passenger side window. Matthias hoped that the wind in his eyes would keep him from making the shot.

Kneeling in the well and steadying his .44, Matthias wished he had some different cartridges in his gun. Ideally he would have liked some solid ammunition for penetrating power, or better yet some jacketed bullets for armor piercing. Either of those bullets would be more suited for stopping a vehicle. A couple of those in the engine block could do bad things to an engine. The Desert Eagle that Matthias carried was loaded with magnum shells. On impact they were designed to collapse and mushroom into a wider piece of lead. They were meant for human targets, creating a bigger exit wound than entry wound.

Two bullets punched into the fiberglass about six and eight inches from Matthias. Now it was his turn. The gun rocked in his hand as the hammer fell three times in rapid succession, empty cartridges spewing from the gun to fall on the pavement. The sedan's windshield shattered and the driver pitched back in his seat. Driverless, the vehicle swerved across the highway and careened violently into a side railing where it came to rest in a mass of twisted metal. At the impact, the gunner pitched from the window and struck the ground fifty feet away, instantly breaking his neck.

Briefly, Matthias regarded the carnage he had wrought and felt a grim sense of satisfaction in his gory handiwork. The black sedan pulled up behind the tangled wreck and the driver leaped out. Adrenaline still surging through his veins, Matthias turned to Courtney.

"Keep going. Let's not give them the opportunity to change their mind and come after us. One of their cars is still running." He pulled himself into the passenger seat.

"Did you hit their car?" asked Courtney, whose attention had been focused forward on the task of driving.

"Yes," answered Matthias, omitting the rest. He didn't want to burden her with the full brutal reality of what he had done. This was far from the first time that he had taken a life and he didn't feel any reason to make her an accomplice to these additional deaths.

With some satisfaction, Matthias noted that Courtney appeared to be quite a competent driver. That fact had probably saved their lives. She had held her composure while bullets were flying thick in the air. That wasn't an easy thing to do.

She slowed the Corvette from one hundred thirty to about ninety miles per hour.

"You okay driving for a while?" asked Matthias. He was coming down from his adrenaline high now and could feel fatigue edging in.

"I'm all right. I don't want to stop and switch until we're a long ways away from those guys."

Matthias had an eerie feeling that was all too familiar. If that feeling once again proved to be correct, their troubles were just beginning.

Chapter Two

Even under the stark sunlit skies, the looming maze of monoliths jutting towards the heavens look somehow sinister to Matthias. Most people lived their lives dealing with the surface matters of every day existence; concerned with paying the rent and putting food on the table. But there is a darker more sinister under belly on which all this is built. A world of Machiavellian machinations and power games where all the world served as playing pieces for those who pulled the strings. Somehow, unwittingly, the Gantlet brothers had peeled back the veil of secrecy and seen some of the clockwork evil that moved in shadows beyond the obvious. To Matthias, San Francisco was a haven for such. A city so huge was bound to have secrets. Matthias hoped that he wouldn't uncover too many of them while he was here.

A police siren wailed behind the Corvette. Matthias looked back and saw that he was the target of this policeman's attentions. He slipped over to the shoulder of the highway.

Courtney glanced at Matthias nervously. "Do you think this is about the car you shot?"

Matthias shrugged. "More likely it's about our smashed tail light. But they might be on to us about that incident back at Shasta Lake."

"What are we going to do? I told you we should have stopped and reported it to the police."

Courtney was visibly disconcerted and Matthias didn't blame her. A policeman, just on a revenue run, could make the average citizen's life hell by waiting on deserted roads with artificially low speed limits and handing out bogus tickets. It was just fact of life. Cops had their quotas if they were going to fill the government coffers. Now, Courtney had something serious to hide and she was concerned about what might happen to her.

Matthias leaned over and touched her on the knee. "Trust me when I tell you we don't have anything to worry about."

"Sir," interrupted the doughy-faced cop appearing on the driver's side. "I need your license, registration, and proof of insurance."

Complying, Matthias noticed the rather pasty complexion of the policeman, despite the sunny weather that generally graced the San Francisco area.

"You realize that your right tail light is out?"

"Yes, sir."

"I notice your driver's license is from Florida. What are the two of you doing in the area?"

"I'm here to judge a fitness contest," answered Matthias.

"This car is registered in your name. Did you drive from Florida?"

"No. I drove up from Seattle where I was working."

"What kind of work do you do, Mr. Gantlet?"

"I'm a musician."

"So, what were you doing in Seattle…making a drug run?"

Matthias was starting to get annoyed now, but this was the kind of behavior he had grown to expect. "As if there were no drugs available in California? No. Actually I was doing some recording at London Bridge Studio."

"I see. And you Miss…?"

"Johns," answered Courtney.

"Miss Johns," repeated the policeman. "What are you doing in the area?"

"I'm competing in a fitness competition."

The policeman raised an eyebrow. "I see. This is becoming more interesting by the minute."

"Believe me when I tell you that it's purely coincidental," offered Matthias. "It's a long story and you probably wouldn't believe it any way."

"You're probably right about that," muttered the lawman. It was plainly obvious that he was skeptical of their entire story.

"Are you carrying any drugs or weapons?"

"No we're not," answered Matthias.

"You mind if I search your vehicle?"

"Yes, I do mind."

"You know, you ought to cooperate with me. I can make things very difficult for you."

"I'm sure you can."

"You wait here. I'll be back in a few minutes."

The policeman walked back to his patrol car to run a check on Matthias's license and registration. Once he was in the car, Matthias sighed.

"We're home free now," he told Courtney. "I'm just glad he didn't notice the bullet holes. That would have been a little more of a hassle."

"What makes you so sure that he is going to let us go?"

"My brothers and I have a little agreement with certain powerful people in the government. They leave us alone and we don't tell the general public about certain government activities.

"Like what?" asked Courtney, her curiosity piqued.

Matthias shook his head and laughed. "Really, it's better that you don't know."

Courtney smiled. If anyone else had told her this story there would have been no way she'd believe them. There was something about Matthias, however, that inspired trust. And after the events of the past few days, she wasn't about to discount anything as impossible.

"So what are we going to do about the Ms. Fitness contest?" asked Courtney. "I've spent years preparing for this. If I do well here, I'm in the National Event. I can't back out because I know one of the judges."

"I wouldn't be concerned about it," said Matthias. "Just keep things quiet. Don't go bragging to the other girls about having an in with the judges and I'll do my best to remain impartial."

"Do you think you can do that?" she asked. She half-hoped that he would say no. Not because she wanted to win the contest unfairly. On the contrary, she had worked hard for this and wanted to win it on her own merits. But if Matthias answered that it would be impossible for him to remain impartial then that would show that he might be interested in her.

He had been nothing but a gentleman on the drive down. They had stopped for the night at a Motel Six and he had even offered to pay for the second room. Initially, she had been worried. After seeing him brutally dispose of the two men that had attacked them by her broken down van, she thought that he might be equally brutal in all facets of his life. He was obviously strong enough to take what he wanted.

On the drive down to San Francisco, however, he had proven himself very kind and thoughtful. Still, she had reservations. He was a rock musician after all, and she knew that her mother would never approve. Still, there was a certain dangerous allure to him that she found attractive.

Matthias never got to answer her question. The police officer came back to the Corvette shaking his head in bewilderment. He handed the paperwork back to Matthias.

"I don't know what it is," he said. "You came back squeaky clean and with instructions to keep my hands off you."

Matthias smiled at him. "I'd tell you all about it…but then I'd have to kill you."

"It looks like I'll be letting you off with a warning. Do get that tail light fixed as soon as possible, though."

"I'll do that, Officer."

Carefully, Matthias eased the Corvette back into traffic and continued into the heart of San Francisco. As they approached they looked out across the gleaming waters of the bay, dotted with both pleasure and commercial craft.

"I'd like to get out there and do some Jet-skiing before I leave," said Courtney.

"If you can find a hole in your schedule, I'd like to take you," said Matthias.

Courtney smiled. "I think I can pencil you in. How about the day after the competition?"

"Perfect. I'll pick you up in the morning."

"You ever been Jet-skiing before?" she asked.

"A couple of times. I'm no expert, but I had a lot of fun."

Matthias pulled the Corvette up to the glass double doors of the Red Lion Inn. A large parapet sheltered the burgundy carpeted steps where the doormen were stationed. Uniformed bellhops stood by, waiting to unload guests' luggage. A lot attendant greeted them as they pulled forward. Matthias gave him a copy of the car key and began unloading Courtney's bags.

"This is quite a place," said Courtney, stepping from the car. She watched the glass elevators ascending crystal tubes alongside the hotel. "This is the outfit the contest committee recommended. They're sending a shuttle tomorrow morning to take us to an orientation. The hotel is a little fancier than I expected."

"It's not Motel Six," answered Matthias. "But then again, these guys charge a lot more, too."

"Where are you staying?"

"Here," said Matthias. "The committee is covering my room. They aren't paying me anything else, so I figure it's the least they can do."

"I'm afraid I'm stuck with my hotel bill," said Courtney.

Matthias threw his hockey bag over one shoulder and carried one of Courtney's suit cases in each hand. Courtney was shouldering her garment bag when a couple bell hops descended like a swarm of birds and began plucking the luggage away. One young bell hop with cropped fire red hair began tugging at Matthias's hockey bag, but Matthias failed to relinquish it— instead strengthening his grip upon it.

"I'll take that for you, sir."

"I can handle it," said Matthias.

"But this is our job, sir."

"I prefer to carry this bag myself," he said very firmly. "If you'd like you can grab my guitar case out of the back of the car."

"Yes, sir." The bell hop lifted the guitar case from the back of the car just before the lot attendant squealed off in it.

"Did you see that?" asked Courtney incredulously as she watched the Corvette disappear into the vast parking lot.

Shrugging, Matthias smiled. "I can hardly complain about it after the way we've been driving it."

"Speak for yourself!" retorted Courtney, humor in her voice. "I'm not the one who rammed it into the side of car.

The doormen of the Red Lion swung the sparkling portals of the hotel inward for them, opening a path into the posh lobby.

"Who was the one who let it get hit by bullets? That wasn't me. For that, I'm deducting points from your routine tomorrow. I think those bullets were dodgeable."

They came to the polished oak clerk's counter where they each received the keys to their rooms. They faced each other for a moment before going their separate ways.

"Well, I guess this is it," said Courtney.

"Yeah," said Matthias. "I'll see you for dinner."

"Remember though. I'm on a strict diet. Absolutely no fat, and I'm also depleting my carbohydrates."

"We'll talk to the chef. I have a way of convincing people to cooperate."

"That's true" said Courtney, suddenly recalling the way Matthias had disposed of her assailants at the van.

Her deep blue eyes gazed up at him and Matthias bent down and gave her a kiss. Her lips were soft and full. It was over far too soon.

Matthias's face grew serious. I think those guys were after you…not me. I need you to think about what you said earlier."

"I can't think of any reason why someone would be out to get me."

"If you think of anything let me know. But don't worry about it too much. Concentrate on the show tomorrow. I have a few angles that I'm going to work on."

Once in the hotel room, Matthias threw his hockey bag onto the king size bed. He unzipped and began unloading a portion of its contents, carefully laying them out on the expensive bed spread. Satisfied that he had everything he needed, he sat down and made a phone call with the bedside phone. He dialed the number from memory.

The phone rang four times, then was answered by a deceptively docile voice. "This better be good."

"Otto," Matthias greeted his brother, the bass guitar genius of the band Gantlet. "I need a favor."

"Of course. Do you ever call me for anything else?"

Matthias ignored the jab. He and his brothers were about as close as any family could expect to be. Not only did they create music together, they often depended upon one another…putting their lives in each other's hands. "I need you to run a license plate for me."

"Not a problem."

Not only could Otto lay down a mean bass line, he was awfully handy with computers. His other hobby was hacking into government mainframes and looking for interesting tidbits of information. It was the challenge that motivated him. If someone told him it couldn't be done he had to give it a try just to prove them wrong.

Matthias pulled a scrap of paper from the pocket of his Levi jeans. "It's a black Lincoln, California license plate FGE763."

"What's up?"

"Somehow I got myself in the middle of an attempted kidnapping."

"How many did you kill?"

"Two or three."

"Matthias! You're getting old. A year ago you would have killed five or six!"

Matthias let out an unamused laugh. "You're just jealous."

"You know it. If you need any help I'll be happy to fly over and help you shoot a few people."

"Thanks for the offer. I'm just doing the leg work now, though. If I need any extra guns I will let you know."

"Hey, did you hear about my latest stunt?"

"What did you do this time?" questioned Matthias.

"I cleaned out some Ku Klux Klan bank accounts and spent all their money for them. About four hundred thousand anti-racist pamphlets should be arriving at their headquarters tomorrow."

Matthias laughed. "Who's your next target?"

"I'm working on something that will top any prank I've ever pulled. You'll have to wait and see…"

"Okay. In the meantime, get me something on the plate."

Matthias gave his youngest brother the phone number, hung up and turned his attention to the equipment lying on the bed. He began loading an empty magazine from a box of ammunition. He slid the hollow point bullets into place and depressed them with his left thumb while he shoved another in after. Each magazine for the Desert Eagle held nine rounds. Matthias liked to keep several full magazines at hand. In case he needed them.

A pounding on his hotel room door woke Matthias from the deep slumber of violent and passionate dream. Groggily he threw aside the covers and rolled from the bed to his feet. He wore a pair of gym shorts and nothing else. He had stayed up late. Dinner with Courtney had ended early with a good night kiss at her hotel room door. She was on a strict regimen that included special dietary requirements, exercise, and plenty of rest. She would need to be sharp for the contest today.

After they had said good night, Matthias hit the hotel gymnasium and, heaving around tremendous weights, managed to scare away the few casual exercisers that were actually using the place. After that he spent longer than he meant to practicing the guitar.

Matthias threw open the hotel door and found Courtney, wearing a halter top and jeans, standing with her left hand on her hip. At her feet lay her gym bag that contained the posing outfits that would be required for her contest.

"I thought you were going to get up and say goodbye to me this morning." Her tone was half question, half demand.

Matthias ran a hand through his tangled hair. "I'm sorry," he mumbled. "Come on in. I'll throw some jeans on and walk you down to the shuttle."

Courtney stepped into the room, eyeing Matthias's physique with an appreciative glance. "Nice outfit."

Matthias smiled and began to pull on a fresh pair of jeans. "I am sorry. I really meant to be up."

"With a physique like that you should be entering contests yourself."

"Thanks," said Matthias. "You should see my brother, Sly. He looks like Schwarzenegger. He just steps into the gym and packs on the muscle. Comes easy to him."

"Steroids?"

Pulling on a tank top, Matthias shook his head. "Pure genetics. Mama Gantlet taught her boys to stay away from the drugs." He ran a brush through his hair a few times.

"Okay. Let's roll." He took Courtney's arm and escorted her from the room and to the glass elevator which took them directly to the lobby. From their vantage point in the elevator they could see across the rolling cityscape. The morning sun peeked through the smog and caught against the undulating waves on the bay.

"So are you ready for the contest?" he asked.

"I'm a little nervous," she admitted.

"Don't worry. By the time the first song is over the stage fright goes away."

"Thanks a lot, Matthias, you're a big help. You do realize that my dance routine is only one song long?"

"Oh, yeah," shrugged Matthias. "Well, I hope you get over stage fright quicker than I do."

"So do I," muttered Courtney. "So do I."

Matthias pulled Courtney close and looked into her eyes. They kissed long and hard. He felt the warmth of her body as she melted against him.

"What was that about?" she asked playfully, as they parted.

"It wouldn't do to have you seen kissing one of the judges in public. This might be my last chance for quite awhile."

"You do realize that we are in a glass elevator?" she asked.

The elevator doors slid open and they stepped onto the carpeted floors of the lobby. She turned to him, seriously. "Remember, don't do me any favors when it comes to judging. I want to win this fair and square."

Equally serious, Matthias responded. "I'll judge you on the same criteria I judge the rest of the girls. No special favors."

"Good."

"Courtney!" called a voice from across the lobby.

Matthias looked up and saw a black woman approaching them from the other side of the spacious room. She was dressed casually in a pair of Lycra shorts and a baggy t-shirt that was tied at her waist. Her long black hair was caught up in a tie. She was equally stunning as Courtney and, by the firm and proportioned shape of her legs and hips, Matthias figured that she was also a fitness competitor.

"Vera! It's nice to see you," exclaimed Courtney, giving her a big hug. "I didn't know if you'd be competing this year."

"I almost didn't make it."

"I'm glad you did. You know, I'm planning it on making it to the Nationals this year," said Vera.

"You and me both," responded Courtney. "This year maybe we will both have better luck."

Matthias had read over the ground rules and judging criteria for the fitness competition between recording sessions in Seattle. He knew that only the top two competitors would go on to the Nationals. The contest included both physique and dance rounds both of which contained a specific set of criteria.

"How did you two place last year?" asked Matthias.

"Vera placed third and I placed fifth," answered Courtney.

"Who is this fine man?" asked Vera, with a wink at Courtney. Matthias shook the hand that she extended to him. He detected the faint scent of the jasmine perfume.

"This is Matthias Gantlet. He's one of the judges for this year's contest."

"I see! Working the contest from all angles, are we?"

A reddish tinge appeared beneath Courtney's tanned cheeks.

Seeing her discomfort, Vera mercifully changed the subject. "Courtney's one of the few fitness competitors I actually like, you know."

"Most of the others are two-faced stuck ups," agreed Courtney.

Vera muttered under her breath, "Speaking of which…" Her sidelong glance directed Matthias's gaze to a pneumatic blonde that was approaching them. Her shoulder length hair just brushed the designer jacket that she wore over a tight black dress. Brightly manicured hands clutched the strap of her leather bag.

"Veronica, Corrine! I was worried that I wouldn't find you. I so much enjoyed your company last year I was worried that you might not be here again this year."

"Hello, Donna," greeted Vera through gritted teeth.

But Donna had already brushed by her and Courtney. "Oh, you must be Matthias Gantlet. I just love your music. I must have every single album that you've done."

Matthias occasionally ran into enthusiastic fans and he didn't mind so much when they truly enjoyed the music that he and his brothers made, but he questioned this woman's sincerity. Maybe it was the high-pitched tone of her voice that she carried on in. Maybe it was because it sounded like mock enthusiasm.

"Really, which was your favorite?"

"Oh," she paused scarcely a heartbeat. "Why, your newest one of course!"

Matthias was about to ask her the title of the album, but she put her hand on his right arm. "I'm Donna Dawson. I'm so excited to meet you." Then she lowered her voice and breathed out her next words through her dark red lips, quiet enough so that only he would be able to hear her.

"Maybe we could get together this evening and I can show you a good time."

"We'll see about that," he answered unenthusiastically. He nodded toward the front door. "It looks like your ride has arrived."

Indeed, as Matthias spoke a blue and white shuttle van drove up through the circular drive and pulled to the curb. Shortly thereafter, a thin man in a blue driver's uniform opened the passenger door.

With a special smile for Courtney, Matthias bid the three women good-bye and watched them pile into the shuttle bus and depart. Shaking his head, Matthias turned and headed for the elevator. Being a musician he'd met more than his share of Donna's type. The beauty was skin deep. They were attracted by the fame and, in this particular case, by what he might be able to do for her career.

Now, Courtney—she seemed different. She wasn't sucked in by the rock star media personae. If she was, she was doing a good job at hiding it and Matthias had to admit to himself that he was attracted to her more than just a little.

A shower and breakfast later, Matthias was back on the road. The contest was taking place that evening at the Central Plaza Theater. Of course, preparations began much earlier than that and even as a judge he was expected to go through an orientation of sorts. Officials of the Ms. Fitness Pageant would go over the judging criteria one last time while the girls underwent their preparations and the stage and lighting crew did their part.

Matthias found a parking spot several blocks from the theater. He paid the attendant extra to keep an eye on the car and walked the remaining distance. Conflicting scents of various eateries intermingled in the open air as Matthias walked the busy streets. Small shops peddled their wares in colorful window arrangements that lured a trickle of the passing humanity into narrow door wells and through decorated portals.

Letting himself through an unlocked rear door of the theater, Matthias found his way through dim back stage hallways until he emerged through thick blue curtains onto the stage. Here the girls had gathered in a group to do a run through of that night's proceedings. The order of appearance would be set and details ironed out.

As Matthias approached, however, he could sense anxiety in the air. Something was wrong here.

A mature women dressed conservatively in a blue blouse and blazer took roll call for a second time. "Has anybody here had contact with either Miss Donna Dawson, Miss Vera Jackson, or Miss Courtney Johns?"

"I have," answered Matthias, striding up behind her.

The woman appeared to recognize him. "Mr. Gantlet," she said. "I'm Anna Southeby."

"Yes. I believe that we've spoken several times."

"Which of the girls did you see?" she asked.

"Aren't they here?" asked Matthias.

"No, they haven't arrived yet. They were due here over two hours ago."

"I saw all three of them board the shuttle bus this morning at the Red Lion."

"Are you sure?"

"Yes, I'm sure," answered Matthias, not understanding why he was being second guessed. "But you're right. They should have been here well ahead of time."

A dark-skinned man with neatly manicured stubble and perfectly coifed hair stepped from side stage. There was a shocked look on his face. He held a still receiving cellular phone in his hand.

"What is it, Armand?" Anna asked, her voice brittle.

"The police have found the shuttle bus. The driver has been shot in the head and the girls are missing!"

Chapter Three

Anna Southeby cradled her head in her hands. "Those are all top contenders. Without them the show is ruined!" She looked up suddenly, as though she had an inspiration strike her. She turned her attention to Matthias with hope glimmering in her eyes. "Isn't this the sort of thing that you do sometimes? Bodyguard work, finding missing people and such?"

Matthias hesitated. There was no way that Mrs. Southeby could even know the extent of it. Most of what he and his brothers were involved in was covered up before it ever got to the press. However, there were a few highly publicized incidents.

"That's not the sort of thing we get involved in anymore," answered Matthias. "But I'm not one to turn my back on anybody that might need my help." He was understating his feelings on the matter. The fact was nothing could have stopped him from going after the girls. He prayed that they hadn't been harmed. Whoever had taken them was certainly a vicious person. There was a dead shuttle driver to attest to that.

"Don't worry," said Matthias with more assurance then he felt. "I'll find them."

Anna Southeby caught Matthias by the arm. "Thank you," she said. "Remember, the show starts at 7:30."

"Mrs. Southeby," said Matthias. "There's more at stake here than your show. I'm concerned about the lives of three women." He brushed her aside and addressed Armand.

"When did they find the shuttle?"

"About half an hour ago," he answered.

"I'm going to need your cell phone to make some calls."

"Absolutely."

Matthias took the proffered phone and retreated to a prop room back stage. When the reception proved poor, he opened up the back door and made a call to Otto.

On the seventh ring Otto picked up the phone. "I'm busy. What do you want?"

"Hey, it's Matthias. You got some information for me?"

"Sorry I didn't connect with you sooner. It took me a little longer than I expected. The DMV put in some new security measures that I had to circumvent."

"What did you find?"

"I got info on the plate but it doesn't match the car you described. The license goes with a catering truck owned by La Hacienda Pier Restaurant. The kicker is that there have been no license tab renewals for four years. The ownership records show that the vehicle was scrapped…sold to Bill's Wrecking for fifty dollars."

Matthias scribbled a few notes down on the back of a business card. "Have you got a location on these businesses?"

"I sure do. Both are in the LA area."

"Thanks, Otto. Looks like I'm going for a drive."

Matthias took 580 from I-5. It took him four and a half hours to drive the nearly three and ninety mile distance to Los Angeles. His radar detector helped him avoid several speed traps but the traffic was far too heavy for him to get up a steady speed for more than a few minutes at a time.

Bill's Wrecking was situated in a rundown area of the city. The barbed wire fencing and dead cars strewn and heaped within didn't seem incongruous to its surroundings. It was late afternoon and the surrounding tenements threw long shadows across the street. Situated in one of these shadows was a mobile home that served as the office for Bill's Wrecking. Its peeling paint and dirt-powdered exterior fit the general theme of the junk yard, thought Matthias as he climbed the sagging wooden steps.

The door was ajar to provide for some ventilation in the afternoon heat. The interior wasn't much better organized than the yard outside, consisting mainly of a few filing cabinets, a desk, and piles of assorted car parts. Behind the desk, a medium built man in blue grease-stained coveralls fiddled with a catalytic converter.

The man looked up from his project. "Can I help you?"

"I'm hoping you can," said Matthias. He shifted his sunglasses to the top of his head and gazed around the dim interior. "I'm looking for a 1973 Chevy truck that was sold to you about four years ago by La Hacienda Pier Restaurant."

Scratching his head, the man pursed his lips as he thought. "I do seem to recall that. The engine had blown a gasket and they didn't figure it was worth replacing."

"You still have it here?"

"Yeah, I parted out what was decent in the engine. I managed to sell a couple of body panels. The rest of it is still sitting on the east side of the lot. Why all the curiosity about an old catering truck?"

"My interest is in what became of the license plates, more than anything else."

"Hmm. Come to think of it, I don't believe there were plates on it when I towed it in. It's been a few years, so I could be wrong. You can check if you like."

Matthias and Bill, whom the junk yard owner introduced himself as, found their way through stacks of twisted metal and scrap. After about ten minutes they located the Chevy Truck—although somewhat worse for the wear—the La Hacienda Pier Restaurant logo still on the door. The engine compartment was bare and the front fenders were missing. The front and rear bumpers were intact, but both devoid of license plates.

"Well, I guess that answers your question, Mr. Gantlet. There are no plates here. I don't ever recall there being any but, like I said, I could be wrong. I don't sell plates to people, but it might be possible that somebody came in here and nicked them from me. I've lost parts before. I know this junk yard pretty well and I know where things are kept. If you steal something from me I might not notice right away, but someday someone would need that part and I'd coming looking for it. Eventually I'd realize that it was missing."

"Have you had a lot of problem with theft?"

Bill shook his head and pointed to the fences. "That's not only barbed wire up on top, but there's razor wire up there, too. It does a pretty good job of discouraging petty theft."

"I bet that it does," said Matthias.

The sun had set by the time Matthias crossed town and got into Santa Monica traffic. La Hacienda Pier Restaurant extended over a small sea wall for a particularly magnificent view of the Pacific Ocean. Matthias pulled the Corvette into the parking lot. He flipped the headlights off and walked to the front of the car where a wood rail discouraged people from falling thirty feet to the beach below. The half moon effectively illuminated the night, and momentarily Matthias watched the frothing waves lap at the sand.

He thought of Courtney and prayed to God that she and the other girls were all right. The trip to the junk yard hadn't shed that much light on tracking down the sedan from the first kidnapping attempt on Courtney—the one that Matthias had foiled. It seemed obvious that the first and second incidents must be connected. If he could track down the sedan he should be able to figure out who was behind this.

Bill, the owner of the junk yard, appeared to have a pretty good if not nearly photographic memory when it came to pieces of junk in his custody. Matthias was betting that Bill was right, and there hadn't been plates on the catering truck when he bought it. It seemed possible that there was some connection with La Hacienda and the kidnappings. How or why, Matthias didn't know.

Following the wooden plankways, Matthias entered the restaurant through large double wooden doors—each of them set with a large brass rimmed porthole. The sea motif continued inside, as well. The lobby was liberally sprinkled with seafaring paraphernalia. An ancient spy glass in a glass case overlapped a ragged nautical map, and even a brass gilded captain's wheel was prominently displayed behind a square of velvet ropes.

A suited man at the reservation desk stopped Matthias as he ventured forward. "Ahem...Your attire is hardly suitable, sir. Do you have a reservation?"

"No, I don't," answered Matthias as he opened his wallet. "However, I am counting on you getting me one." He laid two hundred dollar bills on the reservation book. Quickly they disappeared into a pocket in the clerk's vest.

"I think that we can overlook your fashion error this one time. Are you here to meet someone?"

"Just me," said Matthias.

"Follow me then, sir."

Following the clerk through an array of tables and sharply-dressed patrons, Matthias was eventually seated at a small table to the rear, beneath a stuffed swordfish. The booths were high-backed, and Matthias had little view of the other diners.

Shortly, an attractive waitress wearing a white blouse and a brief black skirt that showcased her long slender legs came to the table. She flashed a row of perfect teeth in a winning smile and handed Matthias the menu.

"I'm Susan, your waitress for tonight. Were you supposed to meet a friend here?" she asked.

"No," answered Matthias, curious that he had been asked the same question twice in as many minutes.

Matthias glanced at the menu.

"I'll give you a minute to look the menu over," she said.

"No need," said Matthias. "The Salmon Special with the pasta sounds good."

"Would you like anything to drink?"

"I'll stick with the water, thanks Susan."

"Anything else that I can help you with?" she asked.

Matthias took advantage of the invitation. He pulled a folder of promotional photos from his leather jacket. "As a matter of fact, you can." He spread the three 'head shots' on the table. "I'm looking for three girls that disappeared and have reason to believe that they may have visited La Hacienda. Do any of these women look familiar to you?"

Susan carefully looked over the photographs before slowly shaking her head. "I'm sorry. I don't recognize any of them."

"Thanks for looking."

"Sure," said Susan. "I'm sorry I couldn't be of more help."

Dinner came rapidly and was quite delicious, but Matthias couldn't bring himself to enjoy it. As Susan brought him the bill, she shoved a scrap of paper into his hand, leaned down and whispered into his ear. "I may be able to help you, but I can't say anything here. Call me after 1:00 tonight and we'll talk."

Matthias nodded and watched as she strode off without a backward glance. Sure enough, a phone number was written on the paper scrap. He checked his bill and wasn't surprised to find out that it was outrageous. He dropped two hundred dollar bills on the table. As he left the restaurant the clock on the wall read 7:42. The Fitness Contest would be starting about now and, Matthias figured, Mrs. Southeby would be pulling her hair out, fretting about how the contest had been ruined.

A cool wind struck him as Matthias came down the plankway and into the parking lot. The air was strong with the scent of the sea. Matthias found it invigorating after the stuffy air of the restaurant. He hoped that Susan might be able to give him some sort of lead later that evening. It appeared as though she was scared of telling Matthias anything where she might be overheard.

As Matthias put his car key into the door of the Corvette, he heard foot-steps on concrete over the roar of the surf. Turning, he saw a very large black man approaching him—a grim look of determination set on his face. The sea breeze hardly rippled the closely trimmed Mohawk and full beard. The man's neck was as thick as a small tree trunk, merging with powerful trapezoids that sloped down to shoulders as wide as a doorway. He wore a leather Forty-Nin-er's jacket unzipped to his waist and beneath that a blue tank top.

"I've got some questions to ask you!" the words were spit out like projec-tiles.

"About what?" Warily, Matthias backed up a few steps. The man was approaching like a charging bull and Matthias was caught in a narrow space between two cars. He didn't have any where to go.

"About some missing girls!" One massive hand reached inside his jacket. Matthias had seen that same movement several days earlier. This time Mat-thias was wearing his Desert Eagle and his trusty back up gun, a .454 Cassul. However, Matthias wore both of them underneath his leather coat which was zipped to his chest. By the time he opened his jacket the man would shoot him four times.

As he had done two days previously, Matthias dove forward and grabbed hold of the man's arm as a gold plated .45 emerged. Though this tactic had been effective before, Matthias hadn't reckoned on this man's superhuman strength. His sheer size should have given Matthias a warning, but Matthias was no pushover either and, where other men would shrink and hide, he recklessly leaped in, counting on his strength and wits to see him through.

Matthias went for a knee to the groin, but the giant had already antici-pated such an attack and shifted to a side stance, resulting in a bruising, but ultimately harmless, blow to the outer thigh. The attack had been enough to distract the man's attention, though, and Matthias was able to slam the giant's hand against the Corvette driver's side window. In a spray of glass, the gun spun loose from the big man's grip and fell to the pavement with a metallic clatter.

Glancing briefly, Matthias tried to follow the trajectory of the falling pistol so he could determine its location. This proved to be an error in judgment and he felt himself lifted bodily from the ground as a blow landed heavily in the center of his chest. More punches fell in rapid succession, pounding Matthias unmercifully.

Lowering his head and trying to duck beneath the big man's arms, Matthias felt a fist impact with his skull. Although the blow was jarring, the damage to the rock musician was superficial, but the big man cursed in pain as the blow fell. Matthias waded in at close range. There wasn't enough room to throw a meaningful punch so he used his forearms as weapons, lashing out with snapping blows that threw the big man against the black Mercedes parked next to Matthias's Corvette.

The giant was only stunned for a moment though. Breathing heavily, Matthias shook his head. He was throwing the best that he had at this guy and couldn't take him down. He was doing damage, but the guy just kept shaking it off. Briefly he wondered who this man was and how he fit into the scheme of things.

It was only a fleeting thought that raced through Matthias's mind, because the next moment he was leaping to avoid his opponent's charge. Dodging to the left, Matthias hoped to clear the hood of his Corvette and roll to the other side of the car, but the big man moved with an amazing alacrity and caught Matthias in the midsection with one massive shoulder. The momentum of the charge carried them both against the wood railing which splintered and gave way as the two of them plummeted towards the sand thirty feet beneath.

Plunging through the nothingness, the two hurtled in a violent embrace. The moment the two of them smashed through the rail, Matthias twisted, using the giant's momentum to force him to the bottom. Scarcely had he succeeded in doing this and they struck the beach, sand spraying at the heavy impact of their bodies.

The big man took the brunt of the blow, landing on his back. Matthias was thrown some six feet from the point of their impact—shaken and a little disoriented, but still in fighting shape. His opponent had not been so fortunate. He got up slowly, sand cascading from his jacket as he emerged from a small crater of his own making.

Matthias could scarcely believe that the man was alive, let alone standing.

"I'm not through with you yet, you little piece of nothing crap!" He pointed a finger at Matthias to emphasize the point.

Snatching up a piece of driftwood, Matthias thought it best to respond with force. "Eat this!" He slammed it across the side of the giant's head, the force of the collision breaking the impromptu club into a half dozen pieces.

The man laughed. "You're going to have to do better than that, boy!"

At that moment the entire complexion of the fight changed. Matthias saw a half dozen gouts of sand erupt from the beach in a ragged line that started near his adversary's feet and crossed rapidly toward him.

Reacting with quick twitch speed that saved his life, Matthias hurled himself behind a bank of jumbled logs that had been thrown up on the shore by the sea. Bullets stitched across the sea-whorled timber, some completely penetrating and narrowly passing by Matthias's head and right shoulder..

Though he couldn't hear the sound of gunshots, Matthias could hear bullets striking the wood in a sickly staccato that resonated hollowly along the grain of the logs. As he dug into the sand, a forked limb split off above his head and vomited a shower of wood chips across his back. Reaching inside his jacket, Matthias found what he was looking for. Now he needed a target.

Peering through gaps between the jumbled logs Matthias was surprised to see an Achilles inflatable boat storming through the surf in their direction. Two men kneeling in the bow section of the craft held machine guns. The muzzles lit up their faces with stuttering bursts of flame, but only a faint popping was discernible and that was often drowned out by the crash of the waves. Matthias had no way of seeing, but he knew that the guns were silenced. Besides the sound suppression, the flash from the guns were smaller than that of an unsilenced weapon.

Matthias could also make out two other men in the boat. One was stowing a set of oars, which he was apparently abandoning now that the element of surprise was gone. The fourth man pulled on an outboard motor, which roared instantly to life. All the assailants were dressed in black knit ski masks that were pulled across their face to conceal their identity.

It wasn't difficult to decide, thought Matthias, on where to put the first bullet. There was absolutely no silencer on the .44 magnum and it spoke loudly in what had been an oddly muted fire fight. The shell punched through the front tube of the boat and emerged through the other side, utterly shredding the Hypalon hull. Almost immediately the craft faltered in the wash of a wave and was sucked beneath the water leaving its occupants to fend for themselves. The machine gun fire, too, came to an almost immediate halt as the assailants abandoned their weapons and began to swim.

Suddenly the big man came diving across a gap in the timber from the log jam where he, too, had taken cover. For a moment Matthias thought that the giant had been in cahoots with the assailants from the ocean and, that now, he was coming in to finish Matthias off. But the giant skidded to a halt on his belly, coming to rest next to Matthias's position.

"There's more of them," he warned.

At first Matthias didn't spot them. They came from the blackness of the night's ocean, swathed in black rubber wet suits that kept them concealed until the last moment, when they emerged from beneath the waves and the moon's telltale light reflected, gleaming from slick, midnight-dark pates. Each of them carried a wicked-looking spear gun—jagged pikes against the crescent light in the sky.

"What's going on here?" asked Matthias, incredulously.

"I don't know, but you're the one with the heat. My piece is still up in the parking lot so you'd better start popping these suckers before they skewer us with those things."

Matthias could see at least a half dozen of these dark divers ascending from the sea. He made a split second decision that he hoped he wouldn't regret later. He slipped the big man his back up pistol—a five shot revolver that fired the most powerful handgun ammunition in the world.

Matthias liked the Desert Eagle. It was a very powerful gun that, with a round in the chamber, could hold ten cartridges…and it was magazine fed. That made for easy and quick reloading. The .454 Cassul did have certain advantages, though, when it came to sheer back-breaking firepower. The disadvantage was the fewer rounds it could hold and even with a speed-loader, a ringed apparatus that held the five rounds in position so they all could be slipped into the revolver simultaneously, it couldn't be reloaded as quickly.

As one, the new found allies rose from behind their makeshift fortress of logs and began to shoot. Their tandem fire took down divers left and right, the gunshots booming in a rapid fire rhythm of destruction. Then, as the surviving divers ascertained their two targets, the sharp popping of the spear guns' CO_2 canisters replied, frost forming on the capsules and blasts of intense pressure hurling their razor sharp spears through the air.

A harpoon punched a foot deep into a log near Matthias's shin. The divers' shots came under pressure; they were hurried and inaccurate, striking nearby but not hitting the mark.

The big man's gun was long empty now and Matthias fired off his last few shots at a diver who plunged recklessly across the sand toward them, shark knife in hand. The gleaming diver twisted and rocked at the impact of the shots. He died in mid-leap, his momentum dropping him at the log behind which they stood.

The final survivor clambered back into the surf at break neck speed. Methodically, Matthias let the empty magazine of the Desert Eagle drop into his left palm. Reaching into his jacket pocket he let it fall and pulled free a full magazine. He slammed it into the handle of the gun, put the safety on and, pulling back the slide, jacked a round into the chamber.

"You just gonna to let him go?"

Matthias turned to him. "Any idea where he might be headed?"

The giant carefully looked out across the waves. "I don't believe it. I see the conning tower of a submarine out there."

Only because of the fortuitous moonlight, beyond the surf and protruding from the deep waters after, Matthias could see it too. Barely discernible on the shadow-cloaked tower was an empty circle with sharp jagged spokes radiating outwards—the stylized rendering of a sun.

"Those divers came from the sub," said Matthias. "And I'll bet you he's headed back there."

Matthias flipped on his laser scope.

The big man grinned. "I like your style."

"I'm not so sure that I should take that as a compliment," answered Matthias.

"Shoot for the tank."

"That is the idea. I don't know who wants us dead but I plan on doing maximum damage until they succeed."

As he finished speaking those words, he saw a dark form pulling himself from the water and up a short ladder to the conning tower hatch. Matthias sighted in. Even with a laser sight, a pistol shot at this distance was a marginal bet, at best.

"I can't make out the laser dot," said Matthias. "Can you see it?"

"I see it. You need to pull slightly up and to your right."

Matthias followed his directions.

"You got him! Squeeze that trigger, baby."

Gently. Matthias pulled the trigger. What resulted was a cacophony of explosions. Two hundred forty grain gunpowder sparked off, pushing the bullet from the gun at twelve hundred feet per second. Moments later the oxygen tank on the diver's back erupted. Flesh and bone was pulverized and the small sub shuddered, the top hatch spinning erratically a hundred feet into the air.

Slowly the sub began to sink beneath the waves.

The big man laughed triumphantly pumping one scarred fist in the air. "You nailed him."

Matthias laughed, despite himself. "It was a team effort. Much as I hate to admit it, I couldn't have done it without you. Whoever you are."

"Blake Hawkins." He shook Matthias's hand.

"So does this mean we're calling off our little altercation or do you still plan on killing me as soon as we get back up to the parking lot?"

"I may have misjudged you," said Blake. "Now that I've seen you in action I've changed my opinion."

"I'm glad to hear that," said Matthias. "Because I've had enough crap beat out of me for one night, and if you started anything I might just have to shoot you."

"Wait until we get back to my car," laughed Blake menacingly. "That's where I keep my real firepower."

Chapter Four

The night seemed uncharacteristically quiet as they reached the parking lot of La Hacienda Pier Restaurant. Maybe it was merely the stark contrast between the loud and violent conflict that Blake and Matthias had just taken part of, or maybe it was something more sinister.

"We'll take my car," said Blake. He spoke in a tone that showed he was used to calling the shots and giving the orders.

He must have realized the way he came across, thought Matthias, because the big man quickly added an explanation.

"It's less damaged than your wheels." He looked over the Corvette and noted the missing rear view mirror, smashed tail light, shattered body panel… and now a broken driver's side window. "It looks like it's been through some sort of war. Are those bullet holes?" Blake came closer and inspected.

Matthias followed him, looking through the broken rail that he and Blake had crashed through, and out over the bare beach below. For a moment, the very normalcy kept him from registering the jarring wrongness of the scene. Everything was gone. Every body had been removed from the beach, harpoons and ammunition shells had disappeared, and even their footsteps had been swept from the sand. Minutes ago, the beach had been a vista of carnage. Now it appeared as though the event had never transpired. A chill ran through him.

"Blake. Take a look at this."

Coming up alongside of him, Blake looked down on the beach. His eyes grew wide with disbelief. "I don't get it."

"Something else is wrong, too," said Matthias. "We fired off an awful lot of rounds and blew up a diving tank. Don't you think that the police should be here by now? Or that we should at least be hearing their sirens?"

Blake nodded slowly, his mind scrambling to put together the pieces of the puzzle, but nothing seemed to fit. "I don't like this at all. Let's get out of here."

"I can go along with that."

Moments later, a deep blue Ferrari sped from the parking lot. The interior smelled of leather and jasmine. The scent of jasmine seemed familiar but wouldn't quite bring recollection to Matthias's mind. He struggled with it, then let it go—hoping that the brief moment of recognition would come back to him later and that he would be able to put his finger on that indefinable thing that his senses were trying to tell him.

Blake handled the wheel of the vehicle expertly. He spoke while he drove.

"I overheard you asking questions about some missing girls when I was in the restaurant. I was sitting in the booth behind you."

"So is that why you tried to blow a hole in my skull in the parking lot?'

"I wasn't planning to kill you…unless I found out that you had something to do with Vera's disappearance. The gun was just incentive for you to answer questions."

Suddenly it all came back to Matthias. In the hotel lobby, Vera had been wearing jasmine perfume. She'd been in this car. "Vera Walkens?" asked Matthias.

"Yes. Vera is my fiancee. I'm trying to find the little puke that kidnapped her."

"So how did you end up at the same restaurant that I did?" Suspicion began working at the back of Matthias's mind. Blake wouldn't have had access to the same license plate that Matthias had been tracking. Either they were both on the right track or Blake was in on it somehow.

"Morty, a friend of mine, is fairly good at working the streets for information. He heard that the driver for the kidnapping heist has friends at La Hacienda. I was just hanging around and seeing if I could turn anything up. When I overheard you, I thought that I might have hit the jackpot."

"We hit something all right," muttered Matthias. "We touched a nerve somewhere. That much is clear."

"Have you turned up anything that might be useful?"

"Hard to say. The waitress at La Hacienda gave me her phone number and said that she had some information for me. I'm supposed to meet her tonight after she gets off shift."

"Did you ask anybody else about the missing girls?"

Matthias shook his head. "She's the only one. And you."

"Man, I did not breathe a word to a single soul. I was just listening. If you ask me, you're being set up. That girl told somebody about you and that somebody tried to have us both done. If you go meet that woman tonight you're going to end up D.E.D.—dead."

"I don't see that I have much choice. If I want to find the girls I'm just going to have to play along."

"So what's your angle? Why are you trying to find these missing girls? You some sort of undercover cop?" Blake appraised Matthias for a moment. "Nah, I don't think so. You don't look like a cop and you don't act like a cop. I've met enough undercover cops to know how they think. So what are you?"

Matthias chuckled. "A musician."

Now it was Blake's turn to laugh. "Yeah right. I'm Jimmy Hendrix, too. You know what my angle is. Why don't you come clean and tell me why you're in this?"

"I'm telling the truth. I was in San Francisco to judge the Ms. Fitness contest. I talked to Vera and the two other missing girls just before they boarded the shuttle bus for the theater. When I showed up later I found out that they were kidnapped." Briefly Matthias backtracked and told the story of meeting Courtney on the road side and the ensuing abduction attempt. He brought Blake up to the present with his attempts to track down the girls through the sedan's license plate.

Blake clenched his jaw as he absorbed the information. "Vera told me the day before the competition she had a man following her around. She thought that they were trying to hit on her. More likely they were trying to kidnap her."

"Maybe when the first couple tries at kidnapping the girls didn't work out they decided to hijack the shuttle bus. But why? What did those three girls have in common that would warrant their kidnapping?"

"They're all fine-looking fitness competitors," answered Blake, thinking out loud. "They are all expected to do well. You think someone's got it in for the Ms. Fitness organization?"

"Could be," said Matthias skeptically. "Still, that's a pretty indirect way of making a hit at them. No permanent damage is going to done to Ms. Fitness because three of their competitors disappeared."

Blake pulled the Ferrari into the parking lot of a small hotel. "We can get a couple of rooms to hole up in while I make some calls. I want to see if Morty has come up with anything new."

Matthias assented. "I'll need to call the waitress later and there are a couple other calls I need to make, too."

The hotel lobby was lit in a lurid blue neon that washed everything with a cerulean tint. The clerk was a tired looking man that appeared as though he needed a long vacation from alcohol. Blake got them adjacent rooms and Matthias questioned the clerk about the use of his fax machine, tipping him fifty dollars to ensure his enthusiastic cooperation.

Using the blank side of a flyer promoting some of the local attractions, Matthias sketched out a crude facsimile of the jagged sun logo that he and Blake had seen on the side of the submarine conning tower. With it, Matthias scrawled out a brief message and handed it to the clerk, who immediately began working the fax machine with his short stubby fingers.

"Notify me immediately when I get a response to that," said Matthias, "and there's another fifty bucks in it for you."

The clerk scratched at his thinning hair, wondering what was so all-fired important. Ultimately he decided that he didn't care as long as he got another hefty tip out of it.

"Yes, sir."

Matthias caught a whiff of alcohol on the clerk's breath. "I'll be in my room."

The small room was nothing to shout accolades about, but it was clean and not uncomfortable. Like everything else in the hotel, the decorating was done in a blue motif. The carpets, walls, blinds, and bedcovers were varying shades of aqua. Matthias shucked off his leather jacket onto the bed. Without it, he felt oddly naked. He had specially designed the jacket for hazardous situations. The lining was sewn with heavy Kevlar plates that brought the coat's weight to nearly thirty pounds. The panels were meant to stop bullets but they had helped this evening in padding some of Blake's power house punches. Still, lifting his shirt, Matthias could see an ugly black and blue patch over his left ribs.

Groaning, Matthias laid back on his bed. Three hours later a loud noise awoke Matthias with a start. He pulled his .44 from its holster before he realized the noise was only the phone. Laying the gun on his jacket, he reached over and picked up the receiver.

"Yes."

"Sir, this is Clyde in the lobby. You said that you'd give me fifty bucks if I notified you when you got a return fax."

"I remember."

"Well, you have a return fax."

"I'll be right down."

A few minutes later, and fifty dollars poorer, Matthias knocked on Blake's door. Blake opened it with his gold-plated pistol leveled at Matthias's head.

"Come in."

"I will if you put that thing down."

Blake raised his eyebrows and lowered the gun. "It's an old habit."

The room was a mirror image of Matthias's down to the requisite painting of a sea swept coast line. The musician brandished a piece of fax paper.

"I've got some interesting information."

Blake pursed his lips. "You and me both. I just got off the phone with Morty."

Matthias went first. "Well, top this. That sun symbol on the sub is a registered trademark—belongs to a company called Ikarian Enterprises. It's their corporate logo."

"Kind of like the moon and stars on the back of the Proctor and Gamble stuff?"

"Yeah. It gets better. La Hacienda Pier Restaurant is actually owned by Ikarian Enterprises. There's a paper trail of corporations in between but it all traces back to them."

"The name of the company sounds familiar," mused Blake.

Matthias consulted the fax. "Evidently they're big time ship builders. They seem to do a lot of military government work but they must keep a fairly low profile because I've never heard of them."

"The ship building gig would explain how they got a hold of a submarine," said Blake. "But I still don't get how they did that voodoo on the beach with the disappearing bodies."

"I've been trying to think of some rational explanation myself. I haven't come up with one yet."

"Who is the big man over at Ikarian? Satan?"

Matthias laughed. "That would explain a few things, wouldn't it? Actually, it shows Stephen Ikarian as the president and majority stock holder. Evidently he inherited a lot of money and the company from his father. His grandfather started the company back in the thirties. It says here, Grandpa got his seed money from rum running."

Blake furrowed his brow in thought.

"What?" asked Matthias.

"Nothing. I think we'd better get moving, though. Morty says he heard some rumors. He says he knows where the girls are being held."

"What are we waiting for then?"

"Just for you to shut your trap."

It was near midnight when Blake pulled his Ferrari up alongside a curb in a deserted warehouse district. Once the engine was killed they were met with silence. Even the black crow winging its way between buildings didn't sound a note of derision at the land bound vehicle below.

"So this is one of Ikarian's warehouses?" questioned Matthias.

Blake shrugged. "Morty didn't say anything about the Ikarian connection. Just that this is where Vera and the others are being held, but considering what we know it only makes sense that this belongs to him." He paused and turned to Matthias. "I've been thinking. This whole thing is my fault. My past is coming back to haunt me."

"How's that?" asked Matthias.

"I didn't recognize the Ikarian name at first but it sounded familiar. I've heard the name Ikarian. I didn't used to be such a nice guy and got on the wrong side of a lot of people."

"So you're telling me that you're a nice guy now?"

"Don't give me any crap, Gantlet," Blake responded. "I've done a lot of things that I don't feel so good about. You name it, I was in it—drug dealing, gang enforcer, pimp. I was working for a drug gang and I took down some crack houses run by a rival outfit. Later I heard that someone named Ikarian was the big man behind it all. I never paid that much attention, though. In those days I wasn't scared of nothing…and nothing worried me."

"So when did you put all this behind you?" asked Matthias.

"About two, two and a half years ago, when I met Vera. She wasn't impressed with my reputation like all the other girls seemed to be. But still, she saw something in me. She made me realize the kind of life I was living just wasn't right."

Finally pieces of the puzzle were falling together for Matthias. "Ikarian kidnapped Vera just to get at you. Courtney and Donna Dawson were just incidental… a smoke screen to throw the police off the track."

Blake nodded. "Like I said, my fault."

They walked several blocks of grimy storage buildings with grit-caked windows. An occasional street lamp cast a limpid pool of light across their path. Skirting these illuminated areas, they stuck to the perimeter shadows.

In the day this area was a hive of activity. At night it was little more than a morgue.

"This place is as dead as Elvis," whispered Blake.

Keeping to the umbra of the alleyway, the two of them peered across the street to the warehouse beyond. Despite the studied filth of the building, it stood out from the other structures in the area. It was set well back from the street in a large courtyard surrounded by fifteen-foot chain-link topped with rows of barbed wire. The most glaring difference was the cleanliness of the courtyard. No merchandise crowded the pavement and no fork lifts were to be seen. Not only was this odd, but it left a decided lack of places to hide. Fortunately the area was only moderately lit and strips of darkness criss-crossed the lot providing some meager concealment.

Quietly they crept across the street. Using a small pair of bolt cutters, Blake cut a vertical seam in the bottom of the chain-link fence. The sharp snap of the links being cut seemed unnaturally loud in the surrounding stillness. Slipping through the slit in the fence they crossed to the building. Matthias reached up and tested the handle of the side door. It was unlocked. A warning bell went off somewhere inside Matthias's head.

"There's something wrong here," he said as he pushed the door inwards. It swung silently into the darkened interior of the building.

"We've got no choice. If we don't check it out we'll never know if the girls were really here or not."

Matthias answered by drawing his gun and swinging low into the blackness of the hallway. Staying in a crouch, he took several short steps until he was completely enveloped in shadow. Here, he waited for his eyes to adjust to the minimal light. He was in a long corridor flanked by a half dozen doors to either side. The floor was nothing more than concrete laid with heavy linoleum, purely utilitarian. Banks of fluorescent tubes were imbedded in the false ceiling of acoustical tiles and Matthias caught a vague scent of decay in the heavy air. Running his left finger along the floor Matthias could feel a layer of dust that had gathered there. This place didn't get much use, he decided.

At the end of the corridor Matthias got the sense of a much larger room, probably the actual warehouse. Blake ventured in and as they crept down the hall they tested each door on their respective sides of the hallway. Each knob turned freely but no door would open to either their pull or push.

Something was not right here, but neither Matthias nor Blake could put their finger on it.

Matthias spoke in a low voice. "Throw me your penlight."

Blake reached in his pocket and tossed the small flashlight to Matthias who blindly grabbed it when he felt it strike him in the chest. Flipping it on, he ran the narrow beam across the linoleum, up the wall and to the ceiling studded with fire sprinklers. He moved the beam to the door nearest him. Everything appeared to be normal. The column of light crossed the brass hinges and Matthias thought he saw a glimpse of steel. Closer examination showed a ferrous ring behind the door frame, running around the entire portal's seam.

These weren't doorways at all, Matthias suddenly realized. The entire hallway was lined with steel plate. They had voluntarily entered what amounted to an elaborate mouse trap.

"Go!" yelled Matthias as he exploded into a sprint toward the exit. No sooner had he cried out when a steel plate dropped over the exit. A yellowish mist began to cloud from the fire extinguishers above. They'd walked into a gas chamber!

Blake had entered the warehouse after Matthias and stood fairly close to the exit. If he dove for the doorway, he knew that he could escape before the second steel plate dropped, trapping them in. For some reason there had been several seconds delay between the first barrier falling and the second. Recruiting all his strength Blake ripped loose a false door from its hinges and, turning, wedged it into the still open exit way.

The second plate dropped, splintering the wedged door and splitting it half way through…but still a two foot gap remained at the bottom. Blake quickly rolled beneath the plate and took in a lungful of untainted air. Seconds later Matthias came diving through, and rolled to his knees coughing.

"It's some sort of sedative," he hacked out. "I feel dizzy."

Blake pulled Matthias to his feet with one massive hand. "Shake it off, man. We ain't seen the last of it."

As if on cue, a motorized hum resonated through the air as steel pillars rose from the earth around the perimeter of the warehouse. Each had been camouflaged to appear as part of the surrounding concrete paving. Alarmed, Matthias watched as one rose a mere six feet away from them. The ugly snout of an automated .50 caliber machine gun began to rise from a declined position. Directly above the gun barrel was an infrared video camera protected by a sheet of bulletproof glass. They only had moments before the barrel leveled off and began to fire. Unscrewing the pen light that he still held in one hand, Matthias dropped a triple A battery between his thumb and forefinger. With one quick movement he rolled over to the gun turret and jammed the battery into the barrel. Moments later the machine gun sighted in on Blake and began to fire.

Matthias hit the ground as the gun barrel ruptured, and shrapnel sliced through the air overhead. The gun turret was a smoking ruin of bent metal. Somehow the feed mechanism kept functioning and bullets spewed into the air in a glittering trail that fell rhythmically, sounding like some demonic wind chime, against the pavement.

Furiously checking to his left and right, Matthias could see the other machine gun turrets slowly rotating. Crimson laser dots cut through the night as the blind eyes of the machine guns searched for their targets. Now was the time to make a break for it, before it was too late.

Blake and Matthias had one advantage. They were up against machines, and their robotic adversaries couldn't move with the swiftness that they possessed. Already, with lightning mental acuity, Blake had ascertained the situation and acted. Unlike Matthias, he was still on his feet and, galvanizing his muscles into instant action, he sprinted across the courtyard. One turret had already homed in on the gap that they had cut in the fence. It sat stock still, waiting for a target to cross its path and cut loose with a searing hail of molten lead.

Escape would have to lie in some other direction. The barbed wire that topped the fence was intended to keep people from entering the premises. It was slanted out over the sidewalk. Someone coming from the inside, if they gained the top of the fifteen foot fence, could leap out and over the barbed wire and never come in contact with it. This was Blake's plan.

With his momentum carrying him forward, Blake gathered his legs beneath him and leaped high onto the chain-link fence, his fingers closing around the cold wire. Using powerful legs and arms he quickly scrambled toward the top.

As excellent as progress that Blake was making, Matthias could see that he wasn't going to make it in time. Several turrets were taking aim at him. Rapidly, the musician once again unlimbered his gun. This time he chose the .454 Cassul. It was five pounds of destruction in Matthias's grip. Three shells vomited from the pistol shattering both the inadequately thin bulletproof glass, the camera behind, and cracking the gearing mechanism that allowed the turret to rotate.

Confident in his aim and the power of the gun that he was wielding, Matthias instantly wheeled and fired off two more shots at the second turret that was targeting Blake. The first bullet glanced off the glass, leaving an indelible web at the point of impact. The second bullet lodged somewhere in the gearing and the turret turned less fluidly and at a fraction of the speed, to be sure, but still deadly functional. Matthias hoped that his assault had been enough to buy Blake the time he needed to jump clear.

As Blake began to hoist himself to the top of the fence somebody, somewhere, threw a switch. Suddenly the fence was arcing with electricity and Blake's muscles seized as the current coursed through his body.

Matthias couldn't believe that they had missed the telltale signs of an electric fence when they had cut through it to enter the courtyard. Obviously, somebody had gone to painstaking lengths to conceal the fact. Now Blake was frying on the fence and there was nothing Matthias could do. Or was there?

Glancing up to the power lines overhead, Matthias found what he was looking for. The gray bulk of a transformer rested slug-like against a thick power pole. Dropping the Cassul into his holster, he drew his Desert Eagle. Quickly aiming, Matthias sent bullet after bullet pounding into the transformer.

It erupted in an orange waterfall of sparks and an explosion boomed through the air as a blinding flash painted the sky a pale yellow daylight hue. Matthias felt the pounding of the explosion in his chest and heard the perceptible buzz as the power failed around him.

Unable to reach the fence in time, Matthias watched Blake's grip slacken and his body fall heavily to the earth. Coming to his side, Matthias threw Blake over his shoulder. Matthias could smell the burnt flesh and scorched hair as he made his way to the hole they had cut in the fence. Blake was nearly two hundred sixty pounds, carrying him for any distance was a considerable feat, even for a strong man like Matthias. The musician fervently prayed that he wasn't carrying dead weight.

Despite Blake's past misdeeds, Matthias had a certain respect and admiration for the man. Not only was he one of the toughest men Matthias had ever met, but it took a certain willpower to drag oneself from life in the cesspool to something more honest.

Moving as rapidly as he possibly could, Matthias managed to pull Blake through the hole in the fence and get him back to his shoulders. Time was of the essence. A complex that was this elaborate was bound to have some sort of backup power supply.

No sooner had Matthias crossed the street when the lights began to flicker on at the warehouse and the gears of the turrets began to grind. Matthias ducked into the shadows of the alley and, running at a careful jog, managed to get Blake back to the Ferrari. Laying his large form in the passenger seat, Matthias quickly checked Blake. The breathing was shallow and labored, but the eyelids flickered and Matthias saw the fierce determination in the eyes beneath.

"Morty set us up," rasped Blake through singed lips. "I want you to find that little piece of nothing crap and beat the truth out of him. Find Vera…" In sporadic jumbles of words he told Matthias where Morty could be found, then Blake lapsed back into unconsciousness.

Blake was on death's door and, in a frenzied race against the clock, Matthias sped to the nearest hospital. Seven minutes and twenty broken traffic laws later, Matthias pulled the Ferrari up to the emergency entrance. He enlisted the aid of several male nurses who brought out a rolling stretcher. Matthias lifted Blake's limp form and laid him on the stretcher. The hospital staff rushed him into the emergency room, and Matthias stayed behind at the desk to answer a few questions and leave several thousand dollars in deposit money against the impending medical care. After this he excused himself to go to the bathroom and promptly left in Blake's Ferrari.

The longer he stayed, the more chance there was that the police were going to want to question him. Blake was in God's hands now. Matthias had done what he could for the man, now he needed to track Morty down and get some information or three more people were going to die—if they hadn't already.

A half hour later, Matthias found himself in a part of town that had seen better days. What were once elegant apartment buildings were now little better than run down tenements. Flickering neon buzzed in shops barred against intrusion, while the denizens of the night prowled the dirty streets on unholy business or mischief. The blue Ferrari that Matthias was driving stood out like a billboard shouting, 'Car jack me!' but that was a secondary consideration right now.

When he found the name of the building he was looking for scrawled in scratched gold writing on the smeared windows of a building even more worn than the rest, Matthias pulled the Ferrari up against the roadside, double parking because of the lack of spaces available. As he stepped to the sidewalk, a trio of ruffians immediately accosted him. They wore Raiders jackets, and their gang colors showed in bandannas tied on their arms.

"That there looks like Hawkins' wheels. What are you doing with it?" questioned a stick-thin teenager who stood several inches taller than Matthias.

It seemed that Blake had somewhat of a reputation around town, considered Matthias. Maybe he could turn that to his advantage. "They are Blake's wheels and if you let anybody put so much as a scratch on that car he's going to hold you personally responsible. You catch my drift?"

They nodded, suitably impressed or so terrorized that they didn't ask for clarification on what he was doing driving Blake's Ferrari. Cement steps with crumbling edges, led Matthias to the dirty glass doors. A security lock was meant to keep strangers out and friends were to call up to be buzzed in. This system had long since been broken and Matthias let himself into a lobby that smelled heavily of pine disinfectant. Deciding to take the stairs, instead of taking his chances with a dubiously-functional elevator, Matthias climbed to the eighth floor and followed the threadbare carpet to apartment 814.

The door jamb was splintered and the door ajar. Matthias stopped and listened. No sound came except for the crying baby four apartments down. Using the barrel of his Desert Eagle, Matthias shoved the door open and slipped in to the dim interior.

The apartment was nearly devoid of furnishings. A pile of bedding lay in one corner on the bare wood floor. To its left was an antique-style lamp, knocked over, pieces of shattered bulb forming a halo around it.

In the center of the room was the person Matthias had come looking for. Someone else, however, had been here first. Morty lay contorted, face down in a pool of blood, his throat slit from ear to ear.

Chapter Five

Matthias kneeled down beside the body and turned it over. The flesh was still warm and the blood still wet. The killer had been here only moments before. Peering into the shadows, he wondered whether the perpetrator might still be in the same room with them. There was little place for a skulker to conceal themselves, though, and Matthias's examination satisfied him that he and the body were alone in the one room apartment…unless the murderer was hiding in the bathroom.

He was about to rise and check the washroom when he heard a clanking on the fire escape outside the window. Quickly Matthias leaped to the sill and threw up the window. A half dozen flights below, Matthias could see two darkly clad men clambering downward, the black metal escape swaying drunkenly.

Stepping out onto the rickety platform, Matthias pressed himself up against the decaying brick wall, hoping that a combination of partial conceal-ment, darkness, and stealth would keep him from being discovered by the two men in flight. Apparently, both of the murderers were more concerned about escape than the possibility of someone following them down the rusted narrow ladders and across the grime covered landings, because neither of them offered more than a cursory glance upward.

Matthias's need for concealment kept him from gaining any ground on the men, and moments later they leaped the last ten feet to the top of a Dumpster below, each landing with a bang, the heavy impacts denting the already battered lid. They vaulted to the ground and each began to sprint down the trash strewn city canyon toward a dented and scratched van that was parked toward the mouth of the alley.

Seeing that his stealth was going to cause him to lose his quarry, Matthias moved down the escape with remarkable agility. Reaching the last landing, he leaped free of the teetering scaffold of metal and bolts and dropped to the pavement. His bent knees cushioned the majority of the drop, but the momentum pushed him forward head over heels. Using the impetus, Matthias rolled to his feet in one smooth motion and burst down the alley at tremendous speed.

Ahead of him, the van's engine roared to life and the wide tires spun. For a moment Matthias closed within feet of the van, then a chasm opened up between them as it leaped forward at a speed Matthias could never hope to match on foot.

Rounding the corner now, Matthias saw the vehicle speed down the street, past the Ferrari still guarded by the two gang-attired teenagers, and down the blocks of hulking tenements. Hardly slackening his speed, Matthias continued his sprint until he reached the Ferrari. Breathing heavily, he halted at the gleaming blue roof of the sports car, reached into his pocket. Quickly folding a couple one hundred dollar bills, he flicked them in the direction of the two gangers.

"Blake appreciates the effort." Matthias didn't wait for a response. He slid behind the wheel of the car, slid the keys into the ignition and careened off in a cloud of dust and exhaust fumes. The van had quite a lead and was lost from Matthias's view now. He wasn't worried about the van outrunning him. The pace of his quarry's vehicle could hardly match the cornering ability, acceleration, or high end speed of the Ferrari but Matthias couldn't catch what we couldn't find.

Rapidly accelerating to a recklessly breakneck speed in a narrow road that was crowded with parked cars to the left and right, Matthias caught sight of the van less than a minute later. No sooner had he seen the vehicle when it made a right turn at a narrow intersection and once again disappeared from sight.

Reaching the corner, Matthias slackened the Ferrari's speed and hung back from the van. His goal wasn't to catch the murderers…not yet. First he wanted to see where they went. If all went well there would be time for retribution later. While Matthias drove, possible scenarios played out in his head. The most likely, he decided, was that Morty had been made a lucrative offer to feed him and Blake some misinformation that would lead them into a trap. When the trap didn't work as planned, Ikarian had sent some of his company men to keep Morty permanently quiet. There was one way to be sure that Morty didn't tell Blake or Matthias about the men who had bribed him…and as the saying went, 'Dead men tell no tales.'

The longer Matthias dogged the van the more he became concerned about them realizing that they were being followed. The Ferrari was about as conspicuous a car as one could drive, so Matthias kept it well back. Only the headlights, and no other distinguishing characteristics, would be evident to anyone in the van.

Once they got to the highway, Matthias turned on the halogen fog lights that sat low on the vehicles frame. He hoped that this would change the look of the Ferrari's night profile and that it wouldn't be so obvious that the same vehicle had been following them for the last half hour. Even this early in the morning traffic was moderate and there were enough vehicles that Matthias could stay out of sight by keeping behind the other cars.

Matthias followed the van on 405 until it intersected with I-5, arrowing through Laguna Hills and back toward the coast where especially turbulent waves were throwing themselves up against the sea walls. The van slowed and began to coast through a commercial district that lay along the water front. Keeping the sports car reined in, Matthias followed suit and slowed to a veritable crawl. Finally he turned off the Ferrari's lights as the van ahead rounded the corner. He counted on the feeble illumination from the business park's overhead lamps to keep him on the road.

Morty's murderers slowed as they passed a particularly secure piece of ocean front land to the right. Granite, steel, and glass combined to form the jutting monolith that loomed darkly against the ocean sky. Needle-like spires and long awkward curves combined in a synergy of mass and the avant-garde to form a sinister looking structure that inspired both fear and awe.

A forbidding granite wall of fifteen feet in height circled the grounds, topped with jagged iron spikes. The roadway to the entrance curved gracefully to meet a manned guard booth that rested behind a single electronically-operated gate. A brass placard at the gate read 'Ikarian Enterprises.' Matthias remembered the electric fence at the warehouse and decided that the visible defenses of the grounds were probably not nearly as deadly as the defenses that he couldn't see.

The van cruised by the main entrance and Matthias coasted past far behind. As he went by he could see the uniformed guard behind the thick glass windows of his booth. He sat reading a magazine and didn't look up as Matthias rolled past in the half light thrown out by the spotlights above the gate. By his brief glance beyond the gates, Matthias could tell that this building was intended to be a central hub for the Ikarian empire. The perfectly manicured lawns were a far cry from the cluttered ship yards that made Ikarian his money. This was the sanitized version of Ikarian Enterprises where everything was prettified to conceal the gritty reality. Ikarian was nothing more than a high rent drug dealer—one that was petty and vindictive. A few years back, Blake had the nerve to cross him and now Vera, Courtney, and Donna were paying the price for it.

Making a right turn, Matthias's quarry disappeared into a triple level parking garage that appeared to be unattended. Pursuing them into the unlit corridors of its interior, Matthias was forced to turn his headlights on to avoid colliding with the curved walls of gray cement that twisted around in tight hairpin turns, winding upward like a corkscrew. At the second level of the building, he thought he had lost the van for good but the coned beams of the Ferrari's headlights caught on a most peculiar sight as he delved deep down a dead end turn he had mistakenly made. An entire slab of concrete was shifting back into place, as an unsegmented garage door would fall back into a vertical position when closed. Briefly, Matthias caught sight of a dark wedge of space existing beyond the wall, but it quickly narrowed and disappeared.

Intuitively, Matthias reached up and flipped down the gray leather sun visor of Blake's car. His garage door opener was clipped to the visor. Taking a long shot, Matthias pressed the button. For long moments nothing happened. The rock musician was about to give up and try another tack when slowly, miraculously, the wall began to slide along well oiled tracks and lift upward until a space fully ten feet high and a car and a half in width was revealed.

Matthias had known that many automatic garage door openers worked on identical radio frequencies and that sometimes an opener intended for one door might open another. By sheer chance he had discovered the one small flaw in Ikarian's defenses.

Deciding that the Ferrari would be far too conspicuous, Matthias resolved to go on foot from here. He parked the sleek blue sports car next to a Ford Fiesta. Matthias pocketed the opener from the visor and opened up the glove compartment. Just as Blake had hinted on the beach, what seemed eons ago, he kept his real firepower in the car. Nestled firmly in the back were two grenades each the size of a child's Jawbreaker candy, but these shells were gleaming steel, a clip and a ring the size of a silver dollar protruding ungracefully from their mirrored surfaces. They didn't quite pack the power of their full size counterparts, but still could be very effective in confined areas. Matthias added these to his arsenal, and stepping from the car, he once more triggered the radio frequency that would open up the wall passage.

The massive slab of concrete moved inexorably upwards and Matthias entered the shadowed recesses beyond. Sloping downward, the hidden tunnel spiraled earthward and plunged into dank depths below. Flickering blue luminescents cast a hazy aura on the dripping moss-covered walls. Matthias walked quickly, wary of the palpable menace of his surroundings. Finally the tunnel straightened into a shaft that curled northward—back toward the Ikarian complex.

Four hundred yards later, he emerged into an underground parking lot that was starkly lit in contrast to the dim excavation from which he came. Fully half a hundred cars dotted the massive room—everything from the most nondescript to the most attention grabbing vehicles. Matthias figured that this was the land transportation center for Ikarian's private army. Vans and busses were outfitted to serve as incognito troop carriers. A fleet of cars were at his soldiers' disposal to carry out whatever mercenary activities that Stephen Ikarian deemed necessary to further his goals.

At the center of this array of vehicles, rested an armored Rolls Royce, buffed to a black-hole sheen that seemed to devour light instead of reflecting it. Matthias took note of it, realizing it might be the ideal vehicle to make an escape in.

Rounding a dog leg turn in the room, Matthias heard the sharp report of car doors slamming, amplified by the echo of the chamber. He saw the van he had followed for so many miles. The men he trailed waited for an elevator at the distant end of the room, nearly half a football field away. They were still dressed in black, though the ski masks had long since been stripped away, revealing the smooth-shaven features beneath. The first paused to punch a security clearance code into the key pad at the elevator door.

This caused a potential problem for Matthias. Without the code there would be no way to follow them up the shaft. He would be at an effective dead end. Briefly, Matthias wished that his brother Otto were here. He was the electronics expert of the family and often carried gear that would be perfect for unscrambling a coding sequence. However, Matthias would have to rely on his own talents here.

A desperate sprint across the room would only make him a moving target. He would be discovered long before he made it to the elevator. Seizing upon a third option, Matthias crept up behind the front wheel of a box-shaped white Volvo. He eased his Desert Eagle out and flipped on the laser sights. Resting the .44 on the hood of the Volvo, Matthias carefully adjusted his aim until the red dot of the laser rested between the shoulder blades of the second man who was entering the now open elevator.

The pistol boomed like thunder and the man went down, a hole torn through his spine. The closing elevator doors caught upon the lifeless body, retracted, and tried vainly to close again. As the first murderer desperately tried to drag his cohort into the elevator, Matthias rose from his hiding spot, running rapidly—hair streaming and his black leather jacket flapping behind him like the wings of an angry crow. Flame belched, bullets burst from his gun in angry rapidity, puncturing the elevator door and several finding their mark in the last murderer's body.

Moments later, Matthias picked up the corpse of the man that blocked the elevator door. The corpse landed wetly as Matthias threw him to the pavement outside. The elevator door closed and, with a cold gaze, Matthias surveyed the dead man he shared the car with—the eyes protruding and mouth agape, slumped against the blue suede interior in a dark pool of blood.

With some satisfaction Matthias noticed the flashing button of the elevator panel that indicated that the first floor had been their planned destination. Now it would be his destination.

Gun barrel still smoking, Matthias took this opportunity to feed his pistol a fresh magazine. His gunfire was sure to have attracted some attention and he didn't want to be caught running short on ammunition.

The elevator doors retreated as soon as the rising car came to a smooth stop. Matthias was surprised to find himself released into some manner of indoor terrarium. Treading outward onto a cobbled walkway, he was immersed in humid air, rank with the scent of rotting vegetation. He could hear the sound of water running nearby, yet the thick plant life closing in on either side of the path blocked out all view of anything that might be hiding to his left or right. Fifty feet above, a massive dome structure of curved panes showed that the night sky was brightening with the hint of dawn.

Matthias had gone the night without sleep, yet the adrenaline pumping through his veins kept him alert. He brushed aside long-bladed ferns that reached out as if to bar his path. Tropical blossoms lolled invitingly on draping vines that fell from skyward reaching palm trees.

Soon the path intersected with another from the east. This stone walk was broader and curved gently toward massive double steel doors set in a flora-shrouded concrete wall that appeared to be the foundation for the soaring steel and glass geodesic above. Matthias doubted if even a Light Anti-Tank Weaponry rocket would take down those doors, but if he had one handy he certainly would have given it a try.

He could see another number pad by the door. Without the codes he wasn't going to be getting out of the dome by that exit. Turning to the west, the trail led him to a broad wooden bridge that arched over a channel of dark green water ten feet below. On the opposite side, cement steps led down the walls of the channel to five Jet Skis that were tethered there, rocking gently from side to side. The scent of the sea was strong in the air and Matthias figured that the dark tunnel mouths on either end of the channel led out to the Pacific Ocean, at the edge of which the lavish Ikarian building rested.

Crossing the bridge, Matthias saw a man reposing on a polished brass seat. This throne sat atop a three-tiered dais of chiseled basalt that abutted the far wall. As he came closer the man hailed him.

"Welcome, Mr. Gantlet. I do so hope that you've brought some of your renowned brothers with you. Just one Gantlet brother seems pitifully inadequate…not much of a challenge, if you can understand what I'm getting at it."

Matthias continued to approach the fellow. As he came into closer proximity he could see the man was dressed impeccably in a double-breasted gray Armani suit. He leaned, as if bored, on one fist, a quizzical expression on his sallow and hollowed features. He sat upright and Matthias noticed the aquiline nose and jutting jaw that combined to give him a predatory and arrogant appearance.

"I'm guessing that you're Stephen Ikarian."

"Yes," responded the man, raising one long-fingered and bony hand to acknowledge the acquaintance.

The other hand, Matthias noticed, rested firmly in place on the left arm rest of the high tech chair. He suspected that Ikarian's seat was wired into the buildings computer system and that even now he was sending out an alert to his security force. Even at this moment, Matthias decided, he could be surrounded by a half dozen men. The lush foliage could easily conceal that many assassins from sight.

"Welcome to my Fortress of Solitude, as it were," proffered Ikarian conversationally. "This is my little hideaway, where I ponder the problems of the world and decide the best ways to solve them."

"I've seen how you solve things," spat Matthias. "Let me get right to the point. I'm offering you a deal. You give me the three women you kidnapped and I'll let you live."

"Ah yes, the women. It took me a while to understand why you pursued me with such vigor, but I have come to realize that it has to do with this Courtney Johns woman. It was purely incidental. She was not central to my plot, merely an innocent bystander. Such is life."

Matthias leveled his gun so the laser dot rested in the center of Ikarian's forehead. "Let's cut the chit chat. Where are they?"

"I don't suppose it would do any harm to tell you. They are now heading out to sea on one of my many yachts. Shortly the boat will rendezvous with a group of business men from Singapore who will purchase them to be prostitution slaves. I know it may seem bizarre to you, but this sort of thing happens all the time. My main motivation was to hurt Mr. Hawkins as he hurt my financial dealings in the past. However, I am a business man and there is no reason I shouldn't profit from my little game of revenge."

"You can end the game. Blake's not alive to enjoy your little mind trip anymore."

"On the contrary," Ikarian answered slyly. "Mr. Blake has remarkable vitality. He's pulled through and is resting comfortably at the hospital. Of course, that won't be the case for long. One of the nurses is on my payroll. She will inform Mr. Hawkins what is to become of his fiancee. After that she will see that a fast acting poison is injected into his body. Then…this game will be complete. Not that you didn't, both, play admirably well."

"I think you've given me all the information I need," said Matthias.

He pulled the trigger, but Ikarian had anticipated the timing of the gunshot. Moments before, he had depressed a button on his chair's arm console. At lightning speed the seat pivoted and receded into the wall behind. Bullets ricocheted off metal, whining through the air.

"Scum sucking pig," raged Matthias. He whirled and sprinted back down the path he had come. He didn't move a moment too soon. A burst of automatic fire sent bullets splaying from the cobblestones where he had stood moments before. As he reached the bridge, only seconds later, the distinct pop of a mounted grenade launcher sounded in the dense, imitation tropical air.

Chapter Six

Matthias had heard that sound before and he knew he'd better get cover quick. He dove head long into the channel, cutting deep into the briny water. Overhead, a grenade exploded in a ball of flame that licked across the water's surface in yellow-red roils.

Eyes open beneath the water, Matthias saw the flame diminish as quickly as it had come and, though distorted by the water, he saw the forms of two gunmen rushing to the peak of the bridge, hoping to find his lifeless form floating face down upon the water.

He wasn't going to give them the satisfaction. Kicking upwards, Matthias burst forth from the water and took a deep breath of the scorched air. As he emerged, he snapped the Desert Eagle upwards, casting the water from the barrel as he sighted, and fired. By the time he had once again submerged in the water he had punched one bullet through the head of the first and two through the chest of the second. A falling corpse splashed down near him and Matthias could see a gaping red wound where the bullet had emerged.

Yet, there was little time to admire his handiwork. The dome was swarming with men who would gladly rush to their death in the hopes that they could bring Matthias Gantlet's head on a platter to one of the most powerful men in the world.

The grenade had utterly decimated three of the Jet Ski's, leaving shattered fiberglass and scorched engines that drunkenly floated half submerged. Matthias pulled himself onto one of the other charred, but apparently operable machines. He hit the automatic starter and it roared to life. Seconds later Matthias rocketed into the tunnel, a hail of bullets skipping through the churning wake of frothing white that marked his path.

It was too much to expect, that he might have already eluded his attackers. Already two of the more foolhardy of Ikarian's employees had fired up Jet Skis and ventured to follow him into the tunnel. They came, spewing tails of brine behind them, engines roaring like demons as they sped through dim caverns washed in coalescing light, filtered from water-proofed illumination set in the rocky sand below the waves.

They took courage in the fact that it would be far easier to fire a gun forward in this twisting tunnel than it would be to fire at a target behind while still trying to steer. Matthias, too, realized the precarious position that he was in. An ill aimed burst of lead scattered against the granite wall ten feet behind as Matthias guided his Jet Ski around a sharp twist. Reaching into his pocket he pulled loose the first of Blake's mini-grenades. Hooking the ring on the right handle of the Jet Ski he pulled the pin free, released the handle, waited two seconds and hurled the grenade into the turn behind him—just as his first pursuer reached it.

A blast of superheated air rushed past Matthias, but the storm of fire and shrapnel had done its work far behind him. The second pursuer couldn't slow his Jet Ski in time and jounced across the wreckage of the first and into the stone wall, crushing skull and bone.

Ahead, the light of day filtered promisingly down the tunnel. Increasing his speed on this straight away, Matthias burst from the mouth of the cavern and into the dawn's light. The rasping of metal cut through the roar of the engine and Matthias turned to see a sharpened portcullis falling across the exit just moments after he had emerged.

Laughing triumphantly at his narrow escape, Matthias plowed into a large swell and hurtled into the water some ten feet from his Jet Ski. Spitting out a mouthful of tangy sea, Matthias observed that the weather, if anything, had gotten progressively worse. He struck out in a powerful crawl stroke that finally brought him up alongside the Jet Ski, which now sat dead in the water, the engine throbbing steadily.

Once again mounting the Jet Ski, Matthias looked out at the horizon. The wind had whipped the waves into a churning cauldron of whitecaps. Low clouds scudded heavily across the sky, dark with rain. In the distance, barely more than a marble of white in Matthias's vision, a yacht headed out to sea. Without further hesitation, he set a course for the boat, hoping that he would be able to reach it in time.

The Jet Ski was small and fleet in comparison to the yacht and Matthias felt that given enough time he should be able to close the distance between the two. The mounting swells, however, limited his speed, but the rolling blue-green waves did give him the advantage of concealment. Despite the earliness of the day the air was already warm and the sea, heated by warm summer days, was not so cold as to cause Matthias discomfort. As the hours passed, the margin between him and the yacht narrowed and he rode down the heavy troughs, hidden by massive walls of swelling ocean, until he was able to cut into the boat's churning wake and creep up from behind.

Speeding along in the shadow of the stern, he was merely a speck along-side the gleaming white hull that arced gracefully upward to ivory decks and the superstructure that grew from it like spired crystals. Briefly, upon his approach, Matthias could see the bold black letters etched upon its prow—The Connection.

As he wondered how he was going to get on this yacht, a rhythmic pounding intruded over the deep thrum of the boat and the high whine of the Jet Ski. Looking to the north, Matthias saw a small helicopter cutting through the air. Hoping that at this distance he would be mistaken as a mere bit of froth in the wake, he moved the Jet Ski to the other side of the boat where he would be hidden from the view of the copter's occupants.

The stroke of the rotors grew louder, overwhelming the senses in a cacophony of sound. Wash from the blades swept across the deck and, even tucked away near the hull far below, the air currents tugged at Matthias. Even as the copter lowered itself onto the yacht's deck and the blades slowed to a stop, the boat slackened its pace and an anchor went down, chains clanking as the massive iron hook dropped beneath the waves.

As the yacht engines died, Matthias shut down the Jet Ski, dove off and let the swells take it away. Bobbing now, in the water, his heavy jacket threatened to pull him under, but striking out for a short distance he reached the anchor and began to pull himself up the chain. The rocking of the boat and the slick bottoms of his wet shoes made the climb difficult and only by main strength and determination was he able to attain the railing and roll over onto the deck.

Gaining his feet, he crept along the walkway peering through port holes and trying to stay out of sight. A shout went up as an engine sounded in the distance, growing louder as the minutes passed. Peering from a hiding place behind a lifeboat, Matthias could see a motor craft approaching. They came up alongside the yacht and a half dozen men scurried over to toss them mooring lines and throw down a rope ladder. Shortly, four men came up over the side. Peering through a gap in the tarp that covered the lifeboat, Matthias discerned the men were of Asian descent. They spoke in broken English with heavy accents. One wore a rain jacket but the others were attired in stained tank tops and loose fitting pants. They were earringed and tattooed with serpent designs that snaked up their forearms and across wiry biceps. Each openly wore a holster and pistol and several, additionally, carried knives at their side.

Ikarian's sailors were better dressed, but Matthias saw that many of them also sported guns. He pushed the idea of a frontal assault down a notch or two past his other options. He would use stealth until stealth failed him, then he would resort to force.

A jumble of voices welcomed the sailors aboard, but when one man spoke the others immediately quieted. Matthias recognized the voice as Ikarian's. Evidently he had flown in on the helicopter to personally supervise the transfer of the girls. Matthias had an urge to roll out from beneath his hiding place and fill Ikarian full of holes, but he restrained himself. If Matthias ended up dead he wasn't going to be a whole lot of good to Courtney, Vera, or the stuck-up one. He would wait. Maybe an opportunity would present itself later.

"Is everything in order?" asked Ikarian.

"The heroin is in the underground warehouse beneath the restaurant," said the largest of the smugglers in barely recognizable English. "We're here for the usual payment. Plus, you say you have pretty American girls for the return trip?"

"That is correct. Let's go to the captain's lounge to discuss the details while my associate brings the money from the helicopter."

The gathering of men dispersed in various directions—some to the captain's lounge and others to their assorted duties.

The exchange in front of his hiding place had cleared up several things in Matthias's mind. Number one, the girls were definitely on board the yacht. Number two, Ikarian didn't trust his men enough to handle the exchange of cash for drugs by themselves. Number three, the disappearing bodies on the beach could be easily explained. La Hacienda was merely a front for an underground drug warehouse. They had opened up some hidden entryway in the cliff side and spirited the corpses away while he and Blake took the long way back up to the parking lot. Probably the warehouse dated back to Ikarian's grandfather and his rum running days. Now it was being used for a different sort of illegal drug.

Matthias slipped from his hiding place and began to methodically comb the deck area, hoping to find the place where the girls were being held captive. It took some time because of the sailors that occasionally crisscrossed the deck on various errands. One side of the yacht was a hive of activity, a half dozen men busily securing the helicopter to the deck.

The rock musician realized that his time was running short and that if he didn't find the girls soon they were going to be hauled out and thrown into the bottom of the smugglers' motorboat. From there they would be transported to the smugglers' ship where they would conveniently disappear forever.

Finally, his search paid off. Peering through the barred window of door he saw the three girls trapped in a small storage room. Courtney and Vera stood at the center of the room speaking in hushed conspiratorial tones, while Donna sat slouched against a wall between cases of toilet paper. They all wore the same clothing that Matthias had seen them wearing in the hotel lobby before they had taken the shuttle bus. By now the outfits were bedraggled and worn. The girls had no benefit of makeup and their hair no benefit of styling, but each still radiated a natural beauty. Of course, Matthias had eyes only for Courtney and he focused in on the raven tresses and the line of her strong, yet somehow delicate features.

Breathing a prayer of thanks for their safety, Matthias ducked back from the window before alerting them to his presence. He examined the door and found that it was latched with a heavy padlock. Matthias hadn't yet learned the art of lock picking, so the only remaining avenue was force. A few well-placed bullets would break the lock free or he could try to rip the hasp out of its moorings by sheer physical strength. The second option would be the quietest but the hasp appeared to be firmly anchored into a solid oak frame and might resist his efforts. The first option would be much quicker and surer. It would also attract a load of attention. Unless, thought Matthias, the kidnappers were already preoccupied by some sort of distraction.

Leaving the girls in their confinement, Matthias moved swiftly to the below deck engine room hatch that he had spied earlier. Opening the bulkhead hatch and creeping down white-washed wooden stairs he slipped into the gloomy bowels of the ship. The engine's throbbing grew in volume as he descended into the oil-scented and strangely still interior. The ship's sailors appeared to be occupied elsewhere and Matthias found the massive engine unguarded.

Without wasting a moment of precious time the rock musician found several barrels of diesel fuel stored in the far corner of the room. Taking a barrel opener that hung from the wall, he twisted the cap of the bung open and kicked the fifty-gallon container over onto its side. Fuel splashed out in erratic spurts that soon washed the deck in inches of the foul smelling stuff. To ensure that maximum damage would be done, Matthias removed the interior fill cap from the engine's fuel tank and tossed it into the sloshing mix of diesel and oil.

Retreating up the stairs, he carried the mostly emptied barrel with him, letting the last seven or eight gallons pour a trail to the top deck where he left a clear pool of the stuff at the mouth of the hatch. On the other side of the deck he could hear the kidnappers engaged in heated conversation. He kicked the barrel back to the bottom of the stairs and briskly returned to the storage room where the girls were held captive.

Withdrawing the Desert Eagle, he stood back and fired two shots that sheared the hasp and lock away from the door. He threw open the portal and stepped inside. That's when Vera nearly brained him from behind with a length of two by four. Matthias staggered forward hitting the floor and Courtney leaped upon him with a wrench held high, ready to finish the job. Her jet black hair formed a wild halo around her head as she tensed to deliver the blow. Dazed, Matthias held out a hand to fend off the attack.

"Matthias!" exclaimed Courtney, barely holding her blow in check.

He grunted out an agonizing affirmation. "I'm here to rescue you. If you two don't kill me first."

Courtney moved from her position astride Matthias and he dizzily regained his feet. He recovered the pistol that he had lost in the assault and briefly checked the back of his head and found his hair sticky with blood. Donna was cowering in the corner. Whether this fear was real or feigned she had done an excellent job serving as a decoy while Vera and Courtney carried out their plan. Matthias looked at them with a new found respect and, albeit somewhat painful, admiration.

"They'll have heard the shots," he said. "We need to get out of here."

As they left the small storage room, they could hear shouts. It was evident that the gunshots had been heard. Fortunately their source hadn't yet been located. Matthias quickly shepherded the girls along the walk way until they reached the tarpaulin covered life boat that Matthias had hid beneath previously.

The rope ladder had been pulled up but was laying in a heap near the rail. Matthias hastily snatched it up and, after pushing one end over the side, secured the other to the rail.

The wind grabbed the ladder and it twisted to and fro in a spiraling motion over the open smugglers' motor boat below.

"You three get into the boat. See if you can get the motor started. I'll keep guard here."

At Courtney's urging, Donna climbed over the rail and nimbly down the ladder. Her weight gave it stability and she soon dropped to the fiberglass bottom of the craft. Vera followed directly after and Courtney paused for a moment before descending. She gave Matthias a kiss.

"Thanks for coming for me," she said.

He smiled. "Thanks for not bashing my head in with that wrench."

A bullet ricocheted from the rail, and Matthias turned in the direction of the shot, simultaneously laying down a screen of bullets that forced the gunman back behind the engine room bulkhead.

"Get in the boat!" Matthias ordered Courtney, but she had already dropped below the lip of the ship's deck and was rapidly descending to the sea-tossed vessel below.

Switching his pistol into his left hand Matthias reached into his right side jacket pocket and found the last grenade. Still gripping the pistol, he hooked his left index finger on the pin and pulled it free.

It was tricky throw, but Matthias managed it perfectly, dropping the gleaming metal sphere mere feet from the bulkhead and the glistening puddle of fuel. Mounting the railing in two quick steps, Matthias pushed himself free from the boat as a ball of flame mushroomed outward from the bulkhead and across the Connection's deck. A rush of hot wind pushed Matthias through the air, the white caps glinting like some insane kaleidoscope as he spun toward them and finally plunged into their suffocating embrace.

Desperately kicking with his powerful legs, Matthias tried to find the surface but the sea clutched stubbornly and wouldn't let him rise. Holding the Desert Eagle in his teeth, Matthias struggled free of his heavy jacket and slowly the ocean relinquished its deadly grip. He emerged from the waves and saw black smoke rising from the deck of the ivory-hulled yacht.

At the base of the ship the girls had loosed the motor boat and he could hear the sound of its engine. He was a good hundred feet from the boat but, over the swells, he could see Courtney gesticulating wildly as she pointed out his location. Vera was at the wheel, as if she were immune to the elements; she stood like an ebony goddess. Ignoring the spray and wind she guided the boat toward him.

Glancing upward Matthias saw a disturbing sight. Three gunmen moved to the rail, a wall of black smoke billowing up behind them. They hadn't yet spotted Matthias bobbing in the waves, so they rested their guns against the rail and leaned over to fire upon the helpless girls.

Rolling upon his back, Matthias lifted his .44 magnum and for a moment he caught the fleeting glimpse of a red dot passing across the central man. The gun rocked in his hand as he fired the last four shots in his magazine. Two men pitched backward in a mist of crimson gore. The third man got off a burst from his submachine gun peppering the boat below. A half dozen holes appeared in the hull of the motor boat and the engine casing burst open as a hail of lead utterly destroyed their chances of escape.

Matthias opened his hand and let the Desert Eagle sink into the water. It was a fine gun and he felt a twinge of regret at irretrievably losing it. He still had the Cassul in a holster strapped to his chest. In it, he had five cartridges. All his back up ammunition had been lost in his jacket.

The surviving gunman who had been at the yacht's rail ducked for cover. Kicking hard to tread water in the chaotic ocean, Matthias drew out the .454 and waited for the man to reappear. Evidently the demise of his two friends had discouraged him though, and before the gunman could gather enough resolve to once again come to the rail, the yacht's prop began to churn the water. The large ship moved away from the boat and the girls as though it were fleeing the area.

Matthias couldn't believe their good fortune, and reholstering his gun he struck out for the motor boat. Long minutes later, Courtney reached out to him and helped pull him aboard.

"For a while there, I didn't think you were going to make it," she said.

"I'm a little light-headed," admitted Matthias. "I think I'm losing some blood."

"I'm sorry about that," said Vera, looking up from the ruins of what had once been a functioning motor. "I thought you were one of the kidnappers."

A silence fell on them as the Connection slowly began to turn in an arc until the prow was facing them. It gathered speed as it came. It appeared as though the captain intended to ram the smaller craft. Matthias grimaced. Evidently the flames from the grenade hadn't reached the engine room. Apparently, the grenade had done a large amount of superficial damage on the deck, but nothing to the motors below. He shook his head. Diesel was a slow burning fuel; not as volatile as gasoline. He should have taken that into account and tried to drop the grenade right down into the hatch instead of trying to kill two birds with one stone and take out the gunmen who had been behind the bulkhead at the same time.

Vaguely, Matthias could make out the wheel house on the superstructure of the Connection. It was obscured by drifting smoke and he doubted his ability to actually strike the pilot of the boat, especially firing from the low angle in the small craft that they were in. Long odds were something that he was getting used to, though. Unlimbering the Cassul, he aimed and began firing the hand cannon. Glass shattered and wood chips flew but the mammoth yacht continued on unhindered.

Matthias was the last to abandon the boat. The girls leaped free from the stern of the boat a moment before Matthias jumped from the bow and the Connection rode up over the top of the motorboat and buried it beneath the swells. Matthias took anxious strokes which pulled him beyond the sweep of the yacht.

As he turned to watch, the Connection faltered momentarily as its prop ground through a portion of the boat it had crushed beneath its titanic weight. It continued on and once again began to methodically circle back toward them. Matthias knew that at least one of them would die on the ensuing pass. There was no way that they could avoid the ship for long. All efforts would eventually be futile, and they would be swept beneath the ship and ground to pieces in its propellers.

Matthias yelled across the foam-capped waves to the girls whom he could see bobbing up and down in the ocean swells. "Split up! It will be harder for them to spot you!"

He knew, however, that it would only prolong the inevitable. Ikarian would never tire of this deadly game. It would go on and on until all of them were dead.

Making no effort to escape, Matthias let himself be targeted as the next victim, hoping this would give the girls a moment of reprieve. The boat swept inexorably toward him when a sudden explosion rocked the vessel, blowing out a chunk of the hull just above the waterline. Red flame billowed out the side of the ship as the engine room burned.

The rock musician let out a shout. The diesel had finally done its work. Now the yacht was little more than a floating hulk, and even as he watched the fiery conclusion of his handiwork, it began to take on water and heel to the side, the helicopter breaking loose and sliding off into the depths. Screaming men flung themselves, burning, from the ship, charcoal black billowing behind.

Against this backdrop of destruction, Matthias struck out to rejoin girls. Finally, he came upon them treading water in a loose semi-circle.

"How did you do that?" asked Vera incredulously, as she watched the *Connection* sink beneath the waves, an oily slick marking its passing.

"I meant for it to happen a lot sooner," answered Matthias. "My timing leaves a lot to be desired."

"I thought for sure we were all dead," breathed Courtney.

"I was beginning to think the same thing," admitted Matthias.

"I don't give a rip how you sunk that thing," interrupted a bedraggled Donna. "I just want to know how I ended up floating in the middle of the ocean when I should have already won the Ms. Fitness preliminaries, and be toasting my victory with a glass of wine by the fire right now!"

Vera and Courtney exchanged glances and Matthias chuckled.

"You're presuming an awfully lot, girl," Vera fired back.

"I'm afraid that you're all going to have to wait until next qualifier," said Matthias. "The first thing we need to worry about is getting back to shore."

Donna didn't care to argue with this assertion and as they struck out at a slow, steady pace a current grabbed them and began to carry them away from the slick of charred timber and oil. Matthias sincerely hoped that Ikarian had been one of the many casualties on board.

They were many miles out. The girls were all very athletic and, in fair weather conditions, Matthias figured they probably could have eventually made it back to shore. But the weather was poor and it took twice as much effort to go half the distance. Matthias's head wound had finally clotted, but he was weak and found that he had a difficult time keeping with the others.

Courtney dropped back to stay with him.

"This isn't quite what you had in mind when I said we'd go Jet Skiing, was it?" asked Matthias.

She laughed. "I didn't have any of this in mind when I came to California."

"How are Vera and Donna holding up?"

Somewhere in the distance lightning struck and moments later thunder came rolling through the air.

"They're fine. Although Donna is extremely unpleased with this whole situation. She thinks that all this is somehow our fault and she's told us as much, several times."

Matthias took a side stroke and lifted his ear from the buzzing water. He smiled. "There's a boat coming," he said.

Cutting the frothing waves that, at times, completely enveloped it, a small fishing vessel made a beeline toward them. As it came along side of them, Matthias saw the black giant, soaked to the bone, who sat at the motor.

His skin still charred and his head shaved bald, he leaned over and plucked Vera from the waves as though she were a child.

"Well, are you going to gawk or are you going to get in?" questioned Blake. After Donna and Courtney had climbed into the craft, Matthias followed and sat, exhausted, in the bottom of the boat. He stripped off his shirt and began ringing the water out of it.

"I'm glad to see you're up and around," said Matthias.

"It takes more than a little bit of electricity to put me down for the count."

"How did you find us?" asked Vera, concern over her fiancee's condition showed in her eyes.

"Matthias, here, was driving my car. It's been stolen a few times so I put a radio transmitter unit in it. Once I found the Ferrari, all I needed to do was put the pieces together. I came across a few of Ikarian's employees and convinced them to tell me what was going on."

"How do you two know each other?" questioned Vera.

Matthias motioned to the hideous black and blue bruising across his torso. "You see this? This is what happened when we met. Between you hitting me in the head, and your husband-to-be throwing me off a cliff, I can't say I've been pleased to make your acquaintances."

"Ah, that's nothing," dismissed Blake. "You gave me worse than that.... and then you electrocuted me on top of it!"

"I electrocuted you? I saved your sorry hide."

"Then you stole my car and my grenades..."

Courtney and Vera exchanged glances. Despite the verbal sparring, they could tell that the two men were awfully pleased to see each other. They had a feeling that they might be seeing a lot of each other in the future.

As they neared shore, lightning crackled long jagged ropes in the sky. It would be good to get back on dry land.

Point of Destruction

The waves of heat shimmered, hanging over the runway in spectral ribbons. Parched sand blew in on the occasional gust of wind—gusts that gave fleeting relief from the blistering sun hanging red in the sky. Beyond the control towers and the vast jumble of airport buildings and tin hangars, Cairo rose on the bank of the Nile River. Level upon level of steel and gleaming glass, its modern Goliaths grew among the mud-brick huts with thatched straw roofs that clustered at its far edges and distant suburbs. The scream of yet another plane pierced the dusty air and a Leer jet arced from the sky, settling smoothly onto the runway where it slowed and taxied toward the rusting hangars at the far edge of Cairo's international airport.

The plane stopped on the hot tarmac. Waiting Egyptian attendants in jump suits pushed up a rolling set of large metal stairs to meet the side of the plane. The hatch came open and a figure appeared in the hatchway. Though many Egyptians of the city had adopted some of the more conservative European dress and styles, few would mark Matthias Gantlet as anything but an outsider. Long brown hair fell midway to his back. He wore a black leather jacket partially zipped at the waist. Beneath was a shredded red Adidas shirt that had long ago seen better days. To finish the extremely casual ensemble he wore a pair of Levi's and a belt which buckle was engraved with an ornate G. As he descended from the plane the hot wind whipped his mane back revealing a strong jaw line, a mustache and a pair of Gargoyle bulletproof sunglasses.

A short Egyptian man rushed forward to shake Matthias's hand. Though his clothing was European in all respects he still wore the traditional Islamic skull cap over his wavy black hair.

"Matthias Gantlet, I presume?" He spoke in English, his thick accent soaking the words to a point that they were nearly unrecognizable.

"You presume correctly," answered Matthias, resting his guitar case and hockey bag on the tarmac beside him as he shook the man's hand.

"I am Moustapha Fahmy, envoy for the Cultural Minister Marsum Heikal. I am to show you to your hotel room and fill you in on certain…ahem… details of your endeavors while you are here."

"Of course," answered Matthias. "We're anxious to get started. I understand that the financial end of things has been all squared away?"

"Yes it has," answered Moustapha. "Your offer has been considered and accepted." He glanced nervously around for a moment. "I assume your brother is in the plane?"

Matthias nodded. "He's just shutting down the Leer. He decided he wanted to make the flight over himself. You know, he used to fly jet fighters for the US Navy."

Moustapha searched his memory. "Yes, I do recall that from the files I reviewed. His tour in the military was fairly brief and rather tumultuous."

Chuckling, Matthias turned back to find Sly Gantlet coming down the stairs, guitar case and gym bag in hand. If Matthias might have caused a spectacle by his non-conservative appearance, Sly took it a step further. He towered over Matthias's nearly six foot frame by another four inches. His black beard and mustache were offset by long, flowing blond hair. He wore a pair of cheap swap-meet sunglasses with mirrored lenses. Dressed in pink jeans and a garish Hawaiian-style shirt buttoned halfway, he came across with the same haphazard ostentation that he was known for on stage. He was also attired with a belt buckle similar to the one his brother wore.

Moustapha introduced himself to Sly and ushered the two musicians toward the terminal as several photographers broke across the tarmac to get a few shots of them. One of the reporters held out a microphone and shouted a couple questions in broken English that neither Sly nor Matthias could decipher.

Sly posed for a few pictures, grimacing wildly in rock star fashion while Matthias picked up his bags. Publicity was part of the terrain when it came to being a rock musician; you give the paparazzi a few shots and in turn they put you in the paper and help you sell a few more records. They had a legitimate alibi for coming to Egypt, but Matthias was still reluctant to encourage the press. If reporters started following them around they were going to have a more difficult time accomplishing their real mission.

Turning his back on the reporters, Moustapha urged them toward the terminal. "Let's get checked out through customs," he said.

Matthias eyed him suspiciously. "You're not going to turn us over to the wolves, are you? Because let me assure you that either Sly or I could kill you bare-handed before you took two steps."

Moustapha was taken aback. His eyes grew wide, and then he laughed nervously. "Please. I have some authority here with the custom's agents. Your bags won't be searched. I'm afraid, however, that a search of the plane is unavoidable. You and your brothers do have somewhat of a reputation among certain circles."

"The plane is clean," answered Matthias.

Moustapha, though, was still visibly shaken by his previous comment. There was a slight tremor in his hand.

"Don't take it personally," said Matthias. "If you're straight up with us you don't have anything to worry about. It's a nasty business were in and we've been double-crossed before."

Sly had finished his mugging for the cameras and caught up to them, overhearing the last portion of the conversation. "The only business that's more cut throat is the music industry," he growled.

A hot blast of air tugged at them. Moustapha smiled beneath his thick mustache. "It's the khamsin," he said. "For fifty days we get this warm wind."

The airport bustled with tourists and business travelers. Mingled liberally with the European dress were the traditional long galabiyah shirts and the light-colored Islamic gowns and skull caps that heavily bearded men wore. Robed women, veiled to cover their hair, ears and arms, drifted with the crowds.

Moustapha ushered them past the long lines at the custom counters. A heavyset guard moved to block his way as he attempted to lead the Gantlets past the counters. He spoke to Moustapha in Arabic and Matthias recognized the challenging tone.

Producing a packet of papers, Moustapha handed them to the custom's guard who briefly examined them and handed them back. He gestured to the Gantlets and, this time, spoke in English. "Come here."

Matthias came forward and handed the guard his passport. The man rapidly stamped both his and Sly's passports and waved them through. In a few minutes they were clear of the airport's mass of humanity and comfortably ensconced in the back of a mud-colored limousine with Moustapha. The

Egyptian made a motion to the driver, who raised the privacy shield between him and his passengers.

Once the shield was firmly in place, Moustapha leaned forward. "As you know, we've got two agendas to accomplish. First we'll start with the official reason you're here—to meet with local musicians and give them advice on selling their product in US markets. You and your brothers have been very successful at doing this in a very short period of time after you escaped over the Berlin Wall. I think you will legitimately be able to offer some valuable counsel to some of these musicians. We have a rather informal dinner party set up this evening that around a hundred of Cairo's talented musicians will be attending. This will serve as a forum for them to approach you and discuss marketing tactics and such. Many of these musicians are not rock and roll musicians, but I do think the knowledge you have will apply equally to other sorts of music."

Matthias frowned. "I thought we were going to be jamming with a local band."

Moustapha nodded. "Tomorrow morning you're scheduled to enter the studio with a band called Iron Camel to collaborate on a song with them. They're hoping that this will give them a marketing boost in the US so that they can pick up some distribution there."

Sly grinned. "Hey, as long as we're getting royalties on it, I'm all for it."

"With what we're paying you, you'll hardly need them," said Moustapha. "The first half of your payment has already been wired to your Swiss bank account. Upon arriving at the hotel you're welcome to confirm that fact."

"You've lined up our social agenda, nicely," said Matthias. "How about the anti-social portion?"

"That is well in hand," answered Moustapha. "We want you to destroy one of our own military outposts."

There was a brief silence. The limousine came to a halt as a vendor with an overturned cart righted the wagon and began replacing armfuls of oranges that had escaped onto the cobbled road. As a force of habit, both Matthias and Sly warily surveyed the surrounding buildings and alleys. They were sitting ducks in the case of an ambush.

Moustapha read their eyes. "Don't worry," he said. "The car is both bulletproof and bomb resistant. It's on loan from a wealthy oil man who is sympathetic to our endeavors.”

”As you know, the Middle East is a boiling cauldron of political ideologies and sometimes it is difficult to strike a balance. And when one does… well, there is always someone who comes along and is ready to upset the balance that you have worked so hard to achieve.”

“Let's cut through the crap,” said Sly. “What is it, exactly, that you're getting at?”

“Sadat was too friendly with Israel. He made too many concessions for the Islamic fundamentalists' taste. That's why they assassinated him, but by that time Egypt had already lost its status in the Arab League. The other Arab nations didn't look kindly on our efforts for peace with the Jews and they ousted us from our seat of membership.”

“Now President Mubarek is running things. He's maintained a good relationship with the United States but he wants to rebuild ties with the other Arab nations. In order to do this he has agreed to do some things for influential members of the Arab League.”

“Like what?” asked Sly.

The street vendor hitched his donkey back up to the wagon and moved aside. Traffic began to flow again.

“We have some missile sites on the Sinai peninsula near the Israeli border. The Palestine Liberation Organization is providing us with some nerve gas warheads to be fitted with these missiles. Mubarek's price for allowing this is readmittance into the Arab League.”

“So where do we come in?” Matthias leaned back and relaxed a little now that they were moving again.

“There is profit in maintaining peace with Israel,” answered Moustapha. “The Israelis have the best intelligence department in the world and sooner or later they are going to find out that they have an array of chemical weapons sitting on their border aimed at their major cities. The Israelis are high strung. It could mean risking war. There are factions within Mubarek's cabinet which don't want to see this. That's where you come in.

“As I have said before, the Gantlet brothers have a reputation in certain circles as a mercenary group as well as a rock group. You are a third party and, if it is ascertained that it is you who destroyed the missile sites along the border, it is not a large leap of logic to assume that the Israelis hired you to do their dirty work in a preemptive strike, so to speak. At the same time, Mubarek's reputation with the Arab League remains intact and we still can gain re-admittance."

"We will require certain equipment," said Sly.

The hotel lobby smelled faintly of curry. Sly and Matthias followed Moustapha across thick red carpeting to the polished mahogany counter. A studious clerk with a voluminous beard and a skull cap greeted them politely in Arabic. Sly answered him in the same language and quickly procured a pair of keys—one of which he handed to Matthias.

"I guess our rooms both overlook the gardens below," he said.

Matthias hadn't understood a word that the clerk had spoken, but Sly was fluent in the language—claiming to have 'picked up' Arabic in one of his wanderings. Sly was the golden child of the five Gantlet brothers. Things often came easy to him. Where another person might expend an enormous amount of time and energy to learn something, Sly would seem to pick up the skill almost effortlessly. He hid this ability well, behind a flamboyant exterior that blinded most to his considerable and varied talents.

"We will be holding our festivities with the Egyptian musicians in the garden tonight," said Moustapha.

"A party!" said Sly exuberantly.

Moustapha looked uneasy. "Let us call it a social gathering," he said. "To serve as a forum for sharing your knowledge."

"It's a party," said Sly.

Matthias looked wryly at Moustapha. "He's made up his mind. You can't talk him out of it now."

"The Islamic tradition does not look favorably upon alcoholic drinks," said Moustapha. "Although, there are those who choose to ignore this admonition of Muhammed."

"You and Matthias can hang out together then," said Sly. "He got drunk one time when he was a kid and swore it off completely. Me…however, I've got a beer named after me. What kind of hypocrite would I be if I collected royalty checks for Sly Beer and I didn't even drink?"

"You'd be a sober hypocrite," answered Matthias. "I have a feeling we're going to need every edge we can get."

Sly smiled. "Don't worry. I'll keep it under control. I'll relax tonight… have a few beers, but that will be it for the rest of the trip."

They took a cage-style elevator to the seventh floor and the elevator man opened the door into a golden hall artfully adorned with statues from the pantheon of Egyptian gods. The torso of Isis guarded the elevator's entry, her form arched in a feline manner: the head of a cat resting upon the shapely human shoulders.

The spacious rooms were decorated in a similar manner; sculptures flanking draped divans and cushion strewn beds. The walls were decorated with framed papyrus and crossed scimitars that were bolted firmly into place. On the south side of the room a wall of glass permitted a view of a lush garden below. Palms arched gracefully over a stone tiled gallery. Tables were nestled into stone alcoves hanging thick with ferns and ivy.

Shortly, Sly joined Matthias in his room. He threw his guitar case on the bed and after rapidly ratcheting a four digit combination into the locking mechanism, popped the lid open. A red Gipson Flying V electric guitar gleamed in the black velvet lining of the case. With a reverence that only a musician would understand, he carefully laid the instrument aside and nestled it in the throw pillows of the bed.

Reaching into the case, he ran his finger along an impression in the dark lining until he found a secret catch. He pressed this and flipped the lining upward as though it were a second lid. Beneath, a brace of .44 Desert Eagle pistols were snugged into the false bottom of the case.

Now, Matthias did likewise with his guitar case. He set aside his pearl white four string Peavey bass guitar and opened the false bottom of his case, revealing a brace of UZI machine guns flanked by eight magazines of forty rounds apiece. He jacked a magazine into the handle of the miniature machine guns. Meanwhile, Sly checked the laser sights on his Desert Eagles. These were a handy bit of equipment, but in stressful situations there wasn't always time to check and make sure that the crimson dot of the laser was resting on the target. That's where accuracy, instinct, and luck took over. Sometimes it was better to be lucky than good. Luck, however, always runs out sooner or later.

Leaving behind their machine guns, Matthias and Sly holstered their Desert Eagles so that the grip lay within easy reach on their left side. They were big guns and weren't easily concealable so, despite the heat, they both shrugged on their biker style leather jackets. Matthias had commissioned these jackets and gave them to his brothers and a few close friends. They weighed fully twenty pounds, lined with heavy-duty Kevlar and pockets for ceramic plates that could stop a lot of firepower. It was good insurance but hardly a guarantee. There were plenty of bullets out there that could punch or slide through these suckers, but the important thing was that most couldn't. Later on, Sly had reciprocated the gift with the unique belt buckles he had given to his brothers and that he himself often wore.

In the enclosed garden below, Matthias and Sly noticed a variety of people filtering in and taking seats among the greenery. Some wore traditional Islamic garb, and some conservative suits and ties. A few of the more radical musicians came in jeans and t-shirts and a couple rockers dared come in spandex and leather pants with ratted hair hanging in bleached mops.

"Looks as though the musician contingent is here," said Sly.

A knock came at the door. Stepping to the side, Matthias opened the door to find Moustapha fidgeting in the doorway. "If you are ready, many of the musicians are arriving."

A few minutes later, they strode into the gardens and were quickly surrounded by musicians eager to learn the tricks of promotion in the American music market. They represented the gamut of musical styles; everything from the harpsichord to disco. As the evening wore on they answered many questions and settled into a long discussion about studio recording techniques with several members of the band Iron Camel. A *tajir*[1] swung by on a regular basis and supplied those interested with a steady stream of alcohol. Matthias abstained, but the rest availed themselves of the liqueur.

Abn Fahd, the burly Iron Camel drummer, settled across the table from Sly and Matthias, next to his band's guitar player. Sly and the guitarist were speaking back and forth in rapid fire Arabic, but Abn also spoke French, a language which Matthias had learned, along with English, when he was a child.

The *tajir* made another pass at their table and poured another round of *khamr*. Sly looked up a bit blearily.

---

1 *A merchant; often synonymous with those who sell alcohol*

"Who's paying for this?" he asked curiously.

The *tajir* nodded obsequiously and motioned to a table across the gardens. It was growing late and much of the initial crowd had filtered away and gone to their homes, but a group of about a dozen turbaned men unconnected with the musicians had slipped in and appropriated an empty table. They were laughing and making jokes and downing prodigious amounts of *khamr*. The smell of hashish drifted through the dry desert air.

As the *tajir* gestured in their direction, a very large man whose face was crisscrossed with scars bawdily raised his glass in acknowledgement of his donation. He smiled—a grimacing, broken-toothed grin—and turned back to his party which was being made somewhat livelier by the appearance of a half dozen belly dancers, who began writhing seductively to the accompaniment of several musicians, and the clattering of their own cymbaled fingers.

Sly raised an eyebrow. "You think they'll share their dancers, too? Who is that guy anyway?"

"That is Yasser Banhiron," answered the *tajir*. "He is a very important man."

Matthias got a translation from Abn who seemed a bit skeptical of the *tajir*'s description. "He is a thug," said Abn in French. "Word is that he is a bad man to cross."

"At least we seem to be on his good side now," digested Matthias. "Though I have no clue why."

A bevy of dancers glided over to their table. Their faces were concealed with brightly colored veils and as the whirled they trailed gauzy scarves. Shaking their hips they moved closer, their sleek bellies moving in ways that, until now, Matthias had thought impossible. Though typically dusky-skinned, one of the dancers was quite fair. Her strawberry blonde hair cascaded out the back of her veil and to the small of her back.

She singled Sly out and began dancing for him, swaying suggestively and letting her long fingers brush his face and chest. At the end of her dance she leaned over and whispered something in his ear.

As the other dancers retired and began to disappear from the gardens, Sly stood up and took the blonde girl by the hand. "I'm going to catch up with you guys a little later," he said. "We're going to go somewhere quiet and talk for awhile."

Sly followed the blonde dancer into a dark portal in the stone wall at the back of the garden.

Matthias turned to Abn Fahd. "Tell me what else you know about this Yasser Banhiron."

Abn shrugged his broad shoulders. "I know that his party must be over."

Matthias looked to the table across the garden and found it completely empty. Only the empty mugs of wine showed evidence that the men had once been there.

As the girl led Sly into the darkness, he grabbed her arm and wheeled her back so that she was facing him.

"Let me see who I'm sneaking away with," he said. He reached up and, with a tug, pulled the veil from her face. He was pleasantly surprised by what he found. Framed by dark lashes, her crystalline blue eyes appraised him. Her nose came to a point, slightly upturned, her full red lips barely parted. A few light freckles crossed her high cheek bones.

Sly's limbs felt heavy and his mind felt like molasses. He must have had more to drink tonight than he thought. "You're obviously not a local," said Sly. "What's your name, girl?"

She took his hand again and began leading him further down the alleyway. Sly reeled along. Above the walls of the surrounding buildings he could see Cairo's gleaming skyscape. A cat yowled and leaped from a garbage pile where he had been feasting, shooting into the darkness. The warm khamsin wind gusted through the mazes of the alleys.

"My name is Tatiana," she said. "I came here from Russia several years ago."

"So you're a Commy!" concluded Sly.

She laughed lightly. "Why do you think it is that I left Russia? Perhaps Egypt is not much better, but it is some better. I make a very good living dancing in the clubs here. The Arabian men love blonde women and since I am one of the few, they tip me very well."

Sly peered at the diaphanous scarves that scarcely concealed her charms.

"I can see why," he stated matter of factly. "Where are you taking me?"

Tatiana smiled. "Somewhere quiet where we can be alone." They rounded the corner of mud brick and came to a halt in a dead end alley. Tatiana unzipped Sly's jacket and ran her hand along the hard lines of his chest. She stopped suddenly. "What was that?" she asked.

Sly wheeled. "I didn't hear anything."

Her hand tugged at him as she removed it from his jacket and slowly backed away from Sly, her hands clasped behind her back. He was about to pursue her when he heard a voice at the mouth of the alley.

Yasser Banhiron stood a glowering shadow back-lit by the glow from the city. "Good work, Tasha," he rumbled. "Karim has your payment. Now scat!"

Tatiana skirted Sly and ran gracefully along the wall past Yasser. As she turned the corner she glanced back at Sly, her eyes hard and cold.

"You want a piece of me?" slurred Sly. He moved forward with leaden steps.

"Yes," said Banhiron. "There are certain parties that want you removed from the picture."

Sly grinned. "So what are you waiting for? Come and get it!" Sly reached into his open jacket for his .44 and found nothing but an empty holster.

"Did I mention that, as well as being an accomplished dancer, Tatiana is also an expert pick pocket?"

"No you didn't," growled Sly. "But I don't need anything but my bare hands to snap your neck."

Banhiron made a motion with his finger and three robe-clad figures stepped into view, curved blades thrust through the girdles at their waists. "That is an admirable goal, but first I have someone else for you test your mettle against."

One of the men stepped forward and threw aside his blade. Shedding his robe he moved forward, clad in nothing but a pair of shorts. The city's aurora gleamed from his olive skin, accentuating the huge muscles that rolled beneath. He towered over Sly by several inches, his chest big as a barrel and his arms thicker than most men's legs. Sly was no pushover, either. His massive frame had dished out and absorbed more damage than most men survive in an entire life time, but each step was a supreme effort and only by force of will did he raise his fists.

Banhiron spoke again. "It shouldn't be too difficult for Kalhid to crush the life from you. Probably not even a challenge, since you're lucky to be standing after drinking all that *khamr* we served you...not to mention the sedative we managed to put in several of the bottles."

Sly snarled with bravado. "It'll take more than a little wine to put me down. Send your lackey over and let me show him why I got booted out of the Navy."

"Yes, I understand you're something of a kickboxer. Kalhid, here, happens to be the local champion. He remains undefeated to this day."

"Enough talk!" yelled Sly, rushing recklessly forward.

Moustapha came over to the table where Matthias and the two members of Iron Camel sat. "Where is Sly?" he asked.

"He went off with one of the dancers," answered Matthias.

"Dancers?"

"A fellow named Yasser Banhiron sent them over. Have you heard of him?"

A look of concern crossed Moustapha's face. "We must find him now. Where is he?"

Matthias jumped to his feet. Abn Fahd struggled to a standing position. "I don't feel well," he said. To his left, Iron Camel's guitar player tried to rise, but slumped suddenly—passing out on the table.

"There must have been something in the wine," said Matthias. He dashed to the exit at the rear wall where Sly had left with the blond belly dancer. In the half light he found his way through the alleys, but quickly slowed to a stop at an intersection, not sure which way to proceed. At this point Moustapha and Abn Fahd caught up to him. Matthias stretched out his hands to halt them.

"Quiet," he said. "I thought that I heard something."

Suddenly a pale form scampered around the corner. Matthias leaped forward and caught the girl's arm in his hand.

"It's the dancer," breathed Abn Fahd.

Caught completely by surprise, the girl let out a yelp of fear. In that instant Matthias saw her raising a gun in her free hand. Before she could level it, he grabbed hold of her wrist and twisted hard. She cried out and the gun fell to the cobblestones of the alleyway.

Abn Fahd, with a decided effort, retrieved the gun. "This is an awfully big gun for such a little woman," he said.

"That's Sly's gun," said Matthias. He twisted the girl's wrist again. "Tell me where he is, right now."

Wincing in pain, she quickly divulged the information. Matthias let go of her and went barreling down the alleyway to the right. In about a minutes time he found the dead end alley where Sly and a hulking Egyptian were pummeling each other with devastating blows. Matthias's approach had, however, been far from silent and as he moved toward the boxed alleyway two robed men stepped forward to meet him; one to his right and one to his left. They both reached for their blades.

Before either scimitar could be drawn, Matthias altered his headlong rush so that he rammed into the assailant on his right, crushing him between himself and the wall. As Matthias impacted, the man's head snapped forward then back so that he cracked his skull against the bricks. His assailant's form went slack still pinned between him and the wall.

The second swordsmen stepped toward Matthias and unsheathed his blade, bringing it high above his head. Matthias knew that by the time he reached into his jacket and withdrew his .44 magnum he would be dead. However, the fingers of his right hand now rested on the pommel of a sword. He had knocked the first swordsman unconscious before he could withdraw his blade and now that sword was readily available.

The man had worn his blade on the left. Normally Matthias would draw from the right side, but he had little choice in the matter. In one smooth motion he withdrew the blade and swung it upward, pushing the palm of his right hand against the hilt for extra impetus. The blade caught the swordsman in the neck underneath the left side of his jaw, cutting through spine and vertebrae so that head spun free in a crimson spray.

As Matthias regained his bearings, Abn Fahd rushed by him and toward the scarred figure of Yasser Banhiron. He aimed a powerhouse punch at the man but the sedative in his system had done its work and the swing was wide.

Yasser returned the favor more effectively and drove Abn Fahd to the ground with a mighty blow. With this, he slipped back into the shadows. Matthias withdrew his Desert Eagle and considered firing off a few shots into the darkness, but decided against it. He couldn't see his target and thus far no guns had been fired. The brawl might go unreported until someone found the bodies later. Firing a gun would bring the police down on them, so better to let Banhiron go for now.

Sly let loose a spinning kick that snapped Kalhid's head back and sent him reeling, but as Sly came to the ground he went down on one knee. His head pounded with unabated fury that had only grown worse. His battle with Khalid had gotten his blood going, circulating the sedative he had consumed to all parts of his body. Any moment now he was going to keel over to the flagstones and Khalid was going to kick him to death.

Khalid was bruised and bleeding, but seeing an opportunity to finish Sly, he advanced on the bearded musician. Matthias saw what was about to happen and moved in behind the hulking brute. Sly raised his head and saw Matthias coming up to blind side the huge Egyptian kickboxer.

"No!" bellowed Sly. "He's mine!"

Even drunk and drugged, Sly's strength and skill far surpassed those of a normal man, but Matthias couldn't believe that Khalid possessed anything less than superhuman skills, himself, and he was unhindered by alcohol and drugs. Sly was fighting with a proverbial mill stone around his neck. Still, he backed off momentarily as his brother rose to his feet and fiercely grappled with the Egyptian.

Sly slammed his knee into Khalid's side over and over but the big man fairly shrugged off the weak attacks. The Teutonic guitar player pushed a palm up against Khalid's neck and began to squeeze his thumb into the Adam's apple. Khalid sputtered and choked before throwing Sly free.

The Egyptian turned and saw Matthias standing behind him with drawn gun. He glanced down at his opponent who was desperately trying to stay conscious, still up on his hands and knees.

Matthias could see what the Egyptian was thinking. "Touch him again and I'll put a bullet through your eye," he told the man.

The Egyptian turned and fled, half naked, into the nighted alleyways and Matthias let him run. As Matthias approached his older brother, Sly finally lapsed into unconsciousness. Matthias stooped and threw all two hundred forty inert pounds over his shoulder like a gunny sack. Taking measured steps, Matthias retraced his path back to the hotel.

Abn Fahd had consumed less alcohol and less sedative than Sly and regained a groggy consciousness that enabled him to stumble back to the hotel with, latecomer, Moustapha's help.

"Wipe my prints off the hilt of that blade," Matthias ordered Moustapha before they left the scene of the crime. Careful to leave no prints of his own, Moustapha used the hem of the dead man's robe to wipe the telltale impressions away.

"They do have two witnesses," said Moustapha.

"Yes," said Matthias. "But I'm gambling that they aren't the type to let the law handle things. We may end up seeing them again before this is all over."

"This is very bad news," said Moustapha. "Yasser Banhiron is a Bedouin who often serves as an enforcer for Minister of Defense Idi Kabhul. Idi Kabhul is the one who lobbied Mubarek for the placement of the nerve gas warheads on Egyptian land. The appearance of Yasser Banhiron in all this means that he must suspect the real reason you are here and decided to make a preemptive strike against you."

"They play dirty. I'll give them that much," said Matthias. "They went for Sly's two weaknesses—alcohol and beautiful women. It nearly worked."

"Beautiful women," mused Abn Fahd. "Isn't that a weakness that most men have?"

"Almost all," agreed Moustapha. "It is the women that have the real power in this world. The men? Well, we just scramble for whatever is left over."

Sly awoke late the next morning, his head throbbing and body aching. A sharp rapping sounded at the door of his hotel room. He rolled across the silken sheets and plodded to the entry.

"Who is it?" he called.

"It's Matthias," came the voice.

Sly unhooked the dead bolt and opened the door. Matthias entered, dressed in sweats and a tank top that revealed his muscular arms and shoulders.

"You ready for your morning workout?" Matthias asked.

"Not likely," grumbled Sly. "I feel like someone took a sledgehammer to my head. Who won that fight last night, anyway? I can't remember much of anything toward the end of it."

"I think it was officially a draw," said Matthias. "You both beat each other up pretty good."

Sly unwrapped a protein bar and bit into it. "Next time that guy is going down. Man, my head is killing me."

"So you sure you don't want to hit the gym?" cajoled Matthias.

"I'm sure," replied Sly. "I got in once earlier this week. It only takes me a couple workouts a week to maintain my size."

Matthias was a bit chagrined by this reminder of how much more easily things came to Sly. "If I don't get in at least five times a week I shed weight like I was on a crash diet or something."

"What time are we supposed to be in the recording studio?" asked Sly.

"Right now. I came to get you. Moustapha's got a limousine waiting for us outside."

Sly nodded half-heartedly. He looked at his scabbed and blood-stained knuckles. "Let me clean up a little. I'll be ready to go in about five minutes."

Salmiyya Street was crowded with shoppers. Tourists and residents mingled in shifting masses, their colorful garb combining to form a kaleidoscope mosaic. This was one of Cairo's poshest boulevards. Saudis, Kuwaitis, and Egyptians rubbed shoulders in the frenzy to part with their hard-earned cash.

Secreted in an alley off Salmiyya Street, a small recording studio was nestled in the back of a shopping complex. The limousine pulled to a stop at a small green door lettered with white Arabic characters.

Matthias and Sly popped open the doors to the brown limousine and went inside. The interior had a low ceiling. A fan hummed, serving more to circulate the smoky air than to cool the studio, which amounted to little more than a sweat box. The recording studio was separated into two main rooms. The musicians for Iron Camel had their instruments set up in one area. The other portion of the room was walled off with a window to observe the performers and an intercom to communicate with them. Inside this room rested a thirty-six channel mixing board and a reel to reel recording machine as well as a rack of effects boxes.

Abn Fahd sat behind his drum set, hitting the toms while the sound engineer checked the recording levels to make sure they wouldn't distort during recording. Sly and Matthias had met the majority of the band the previous night so they said their hellos. Moustapha had yet to arrive, though he had promised he would be by later in the day to fill them in on the location of the military bunker they were to clean that evening.

Several new faces graced the studio. A weasely looking engineer fiddled with the sound board. His face was narrow and pocked. His curly hair grew in a wild tangle that protruded for about eight inches on either side of his head, emphasizing the thinness of his features and giving him a certain resemblance to Bozo the Clown.

In stark contrast, behind him stood a woman so beautiful that Matthias had difficulty taking his eyes off her. Her almond eyes were a deep brown and her nose small and straight. Her lips were very full, and when in repose turned down slightly, giving the impression that she was often in deep contemplation. Her flawless complexion was a light olive; her carriage proud, but delicate and doe-like. Mocha-colored hair cascaded in a glossy river across her shoulders.

"What do you think about that?" Matthias asked rhetorically.

"What do I think?" asked Sly. "What do you care what I think? You can't take your eyes off her."

The engineer had finished getting the drum levels and had moved onto the guitar player. "Who's that?" Matthias asked Abn Fahd, jerking his head in the direction of the recording booth.

Abn Fahd grinned. "Abu Razek is our sound engineer. We've had a couple different bands recommend him to us."

"Actually, I was referring to the girl," said Matthias.

"I know," said Abn Fahd. "Her name is Aisha Kabhul."

"Kabhul? Isn't that the name of the Defense Minister that Moustapha thinks sicced those guys on us last night?"

Abn Fahd nodded his head. "She's his daughter. She's cool though; been hanging out with the band for about a year now, helping us do promotion work and bookings."

"She seeing anybody?"

"No. Her father is super strict. He already has her promised to some rich Saudi oil guy. She's never met him, but they are supposed to be married some time next year."

"How's your head?" Sly asked Abn Fahd.

"It hurts every time I hit the drum heads. How's yours?"

Sly squinted behind his mirrored shades. "It hurts to be alive."

The intercom squawked. "Don't worry about running your guitar sound through the amplifier," said the engineer. "We'll run a line right into the mixing board."

Sly waved his hands over his head and strode over to the guitarist. "No. No. No. No. No. You want to release this in the States, right? The guitar is going to sound fuzzy and thin. What you want to do is mic the amplifier directly. It'll give you more crunch."

"I'd better get in the sound booth before your engineer ruins everything," said Matthias.

Sliding into the sound room, Matthias introduced himself to Abu Razek and Aisha Kabhul.

"Hmm," grunted Abu after the introductions. "I have twenty years of experience in the sound recording industry. Who is this guy that comes into my studio and begins changing recording techniques that I have developed for twenty years?" He motioned toward Sly who had disconnected the line running straight into the mixing board and was adjusting the amplifier knobs.

"I understand that you've got a lot of recording expertise and we're going to rely on you to pull things together. Sly doesn't mean to take over, he just wants to help out. We were asked to come in and cut a song that might have a shot at getting some US airplay, so we're going to do a few things today that have worked for us in the past. If our techniques are a little different than the ones you usually use, just roll with it and consider it an experiment."

Abu's discomfiture seemed to ease. "Very well, then. Let me set up a microphone for the guitar amplifier." He selected a microphone from a cabinet and hurried out into the sound room.

Aisha flashed a white smile at Matthias. "That was very smooth. I didn't know that the Gantlet brothers were so diplomatic."

Matthias chuckled. "We're not always and Sly is never real big on diplomacy. He almost exclusively prefers the direct approach, but I find that sometimes it's easier to get what you want by using a little honey. You catch more flies with honey—that's what my mom used to say."

"I'll keep that in mind," she said in a fashion that hinted at the suggestive. She regarded him quizzically. "I thought you were German, but your English is flawless."

"Your English isn't so bad either. I am German. Only Sly was born in the United States. Of all of us only my oldest brother Fritz still has an accent. Don't get me wrong, he speaks English fluently, but I think he's too proud to let go of his accent. He wants everyone to know that he escaped over the Berlin wall or something…"

"By himself?"

"No. All of us were there, except Sly was already on the other side."

"Wow. I'm impressed."

Matthias's brow furrowed as he remembered how his mother and father were brutally killed in the prisons of communist East Germany.

"I bet you have a lot of interesting stories to tell," said Aisha.

"Some happier than others," said Matthias forcing a smile.

"Maybe you wouldn't mind telling me some of the happier ones sometime."

"How about tomorrow afternoon? Maybe you can show me a little of the city."

"It's a date," she said. "And maybe I can pick your brain about some methods for promoting Iron Camel. They're a good band. I think they have a lot of potential."

"I'd love to hear a few cuts," said Matthias.

"I just happen to have some." She presented him with a demo tape.

Iron Camel was a nice tight band. They played through their song with practiced precision, layering the guitars together in blistering harmonies. Abn Fahd was a wild man on the drums, making some amazing tempo changes mid-song and winding up the cut with somber back beat. Perhaps due to the Eastern influence, they had a unique sound that both Matthias and Sly agreed might make a dent in the charts if given a chance. The spoiling factor, however, was a nasal vocalist who often wandered off key in an original but hair-raising crescendo of shrieks.

Sly contributed a lead guitar track to the song and Matthias worked with the vocalist to tone down his singular style into a hummable melody line, for which Matthias cut a back up harmony track. After the tracks were recorded, the band gathered around the console for a mix down session with Abu.

Moustapha entered the studio and motioned Matthias and Sly to follow him to the back room. It was little more than a storage facility for master tapes. Racks of reel to reel tapes lined the walls. Matthias pushed aside a stack of dusty recording industry magazines and a small black purse, then sat down at the coffee-stained card table at the room's center. Sly followed suit while Moustapha laid his briefcase on the table and flipped it open. He retrieved a sheaf of papers and rolled out a map on the table top, pinning the four corners with magazines.

"This is the latest information we have from our source in the military." He pointed to an area in the Sinai Peninsula. "A mobile installation of two short range ballistic missiles will be moved to an underground bunker here in the southern mountainous region. Later this afternoon warheads, equipped with sarin nerve gas canisters donated by the Iraqis, will arrive. We want you to compromise the site and destroy the warheads, remotely, with incendiary bombs that we will provide."

"Incendiary bombs will take care of the sarin?" asked Sly skeptically.

Moustapha hesitated. "Sarin gas is highly volatile so it should go up with little risk, however, to be on the safe side we are providing you with the option of remote detonation after you have placed the bombs."

"Very thoughtful of you," said Matthias. "But what happens if we're exposed?"

"The effects range from a mild headache to cardiac arrest, depending upon how concentrated the dosage is. Exposure is primarily through the respiratory system or eyes, although in strong concentrations it can be absorbed through the skin, also. It is colorless and odorless so these symptoms will be the main indicator of exposure."

"That's reassuring," said Matthias. "Besides getting a headache or dying from a heart attack, what are some other signals that we're being exposed?"

"Symptoms include miosis—watch for the contraction of the pupil. That's one indicator that you're being exposed."

"What about antidotes?" asked Sly. "I understand there are some treatments available."

"We will provide you with some syringes of atropine sulfate. This has proven a very effective treatment if injected soon after the exposure. Also we'll give you some diazepam—an anti-spasmodic drug. This is all worst case scenario. As a preliminary precaution we will provide you with protective equipment."

"How many troops will be stationed there?" asked Sly.

"Approximately ten men. They will be heavily armed so you need surprise on your side."

"You have the equipment that we requested?" asked Sly.

"Yes we do."

"That nerve gas scares me," said Sly.

"All the more reason to take it off the market," said Matthias.

Twin beams of light cut a swath in the night as the Jeep bounced across the rutted road that wound deep into the mountains of the Sinai. The sky was coal black and the darkness seemed to suck at the headlights, devouring the illumination as quickly as it could be produced.

Matthias was at the wheel. Sly had insisted that his brother drive so that if they encountered any trouble, his own hands would be free to do some shooting. Matthias reluctantly agreed, on the condition that Sly would do the driving on the way back.

Each of them wore a complete set of Kevlar body armor. The suits were bulky and rather cumbersome, but well worth wearing when doing something drastic like attacking an Egyptian military installation. Their helmets lay on the seat beside them, vibrating as the Jeep rattled over a section of washboard-textured road.

"This place is desolate," said Sly, looking forward across the dusty cascades of rocks and barren hillside populated only by scrub bush.

"I wouldn't vacation here, if that's what you mean," answered Matthias. He slowed the Jeep to a stop and consulted the topographical map by flashlight. There should be a depression off the road up ahead. We'll pull up there and conceal the Jeep…go the rest of the way on foot."

"I'm way ahead of you, little brother." Sly reached into the cargo compartment at the back of the Jeep and pulled loose a sand-colored tarp to drape over the Jeep.

Matthias found the depression and carefully steered the Jeep down the precipitous slope where he pulled it between two vehicle-sized boulders. With a planned precision and few words between them, they unloaded the desired weaponry from the Jeep—strapping and pinning it to their bodies in an outlandish display of lethal force.

"Checklist," said Sly

The two brothers took turns running through their gear to make sure they weren't missing anything.

"Ditch the Light Intensification goggles and bring that modified Night Owl infrared monocular," said Sly. "It's way too dark tonight for the light goggles. You need at least a little light and it's so overcast that you can't even see the stars or moon."

Matthias grunted an affirmative and picked up the Night Owl unit— which resembled an oversized camera lens. This could be hand held or attached to a mechanism on his helmet which he could lower in front of his eyes and allow him to look through the lens while using his hands for something else. The unit was modified from the factory specifications with a heavy-duty power supply and a more powerful infrared lamp which cast a beam just over two hundred yards long. This beam shed a light that was completely invisible to the naked eye, but was able to illuminate heat sources for someone who wore the infrared lens. Heat sources included everything from a human body to a car. The monocular was especially good for ferreting out people in concealment.

"I'm good to go," said Matthias.

"Remember," answered Sly. "Leave all the shooting to me. I'm clearly the better shot."

"You want to place a bet on that?"

"You're on. Loser buys the person with the most kills a steak dinner tonight."

"I hope you remembered your wallet," replied Matthias.

They climbed from the ravine and blazed a trail along rocky ledges and over steep slopes, using the brush to haul themselves upward when sandy purchases gave way. In about forty minutes time they overlooked a small valley. It was little more than a crevice between mountain slopes, but, at the bottom, they knew there was a concealed entrance large enough to drive a truck into. Inside that underground bunker two missiles with nerve gas warheads lay temporarily dormant.

Matthias flipped down the infrared monocular over his eyes and looked down into the ravine below. "We've got a heat source toward the center," he said. "Probably the hidden bunker is running a generator."

"Any sentries on the perimeter?"

Looking from mountain to hillside Matthias began to pick out the telltale red glow of men and vehicles. "We've been set up," said Matthias. "There are soldiers crawling all over the place. I'm guessing that there are forty or fifty of them. They're expecting us to show up at the bunker."

"And then they're going to put a few hundred well-placed bullets in our bodies," finished Sly.

"Yeah," concurred Matthias. "As soon as we set foot down there we're dead meat. We're just lucky that they haven't spotted us yet."

"Maybe they don't have any troops equipped with infrared, or maybe they see us and think that we're part of the ambushing forces."

"There's a third option," said Matthias. "They know we're here and they're just waiting for us to leave cover before wiping us from the face of the earth."

"I say we pull out. If we were making a surprise attack we might have an outside chance, but they're perched in the hills waiting for us."

Keeping low, Matthias started to slide back in the direction that they had come.

"I can't resist at least taking a pot shot at that bunker, though," said Sly. He unstrapped a LAW rocket and snapped out the front and rear barrel sections. Normally these were collapsed into the central chamber for portability, making the light anti-tank weapon less cumbersome.

"I don't think that's a good idea," said Matthias.

Sly ignored his brother's advice, lowered his infrared monocular and sited in on the bunker. He squeezed the trigger and a 66 millimeter shell burst from the muzzle, flame and smoke billowing from the rear vent of the LAW.

For a brief moment the valley was lit by a blinding explosion that illuminated every nook and crevice of the surrounding landscape. A ball of flame leaped from the bunker; shattered concrete rained from the sky. Sly doubted that he'd actually penetrated and done damage to the missiles which were supposedly housed within, but he couldn't help laughing at the destruction that he had wrought.

Even as the laugh left his lips it was cut short by the staccato of a machine gun. An instant later, bullets ricocheted from the boulder behind which he hid, whining as they scattered. Sly turned and ran down the declining trail which Matthias had already started along. A burst of bullets spattered along the cliff face above his head.

They made better time on the way back to the Jeep. Partly because they had traveled the path once and knew the way and partly because they took desperate risks on the dark and treacherous slopes—leaping and sliding down steep rock falls and across gaping chasms that yawned hungrily beneath.

Halting breathlessly at the Jeep, they heard the sound of gunfire punctuating the night.

"Maybe," said Sly, "They figure if they put enough lead in the air some of it is bound to hit us."

Matthias climbed into the Jeep's drivers seat. Fumbling with the keys, he finally turned the ignition and the engine roared to life. "You might want to jump in back," he told Sly. "I have a bad feeling that we're going to need some heavy fire power before the night is through."

Sly scrambled in. "Don't you mean a good feeling?"

"I guess that all depends on who's getting hit by the bullets."

As Matthias rocketed toward the steep slope that would take them back up to the roadway, Sly crouched low and began uncrating a machine gun.

The huge thing was at least sixty years old but it had been kept in flawless condition in some Egyptian warehouse. It was a heavy machine gun produced in the US in the 1920s and it was still one of the nastiest guns around. Before he could even think of hoisting into place atop the mounting tripod bolted in the back, the Jeep careened up the slope, throwing loose slabs of shale from its massive tires as they spun their way upward.

With no warning, an Egyptian military Jeep careened around the corner of the dirt road. At the speed they were going they would reach the exit from the ravine and be able to block it before Matthias could pull onto the road. Matthias saw them coming, and knew that if he slackened his speed now that his own Jeep would slide down to the bottom of the ravine and they would be a sitting target for whoever was in the Egyptian vehicle.

The military Jeep roared to a stop, dust roiling up and over them, momentarily obscuring their vision. Matthias lurched his own Jeep onto the road, slamming it into the enemy vehicle—tossing it up and over so that it crushed its screaming occupants beneath. One machine gunner had been standing at the time of the impact, waiting for the dust to clear so he could get a clean burst off. He was thrown clear of the vehicle, splaying the glass of the Gantlet brothers' windshield as he impacted and lay, momentarily stunned, on the hood.

It took the strength of both Matthias's hands to keep his vehicle on the road after the impact, but finally he managed to straighten the sloughing jeep. The uniformed soldier on the hood still held a Russian made AK-47 assault rifle in his hand. Slowly, the man began to regain his senses and Matthias could see the fingers on the trigger hand beginning to twitch. Quickly he slammed on the brakes and the soldier flew off the hood and tumbled to the rutted dirt road.

As Matthias accelerated, the soldier sat up and began to raise his rifle. The frame of the Jeep shuddered as Matthias barreled over the top of the Egyptian, grinding him beneath the wheels.

Only now, was Sly able to mount the M1921A1 machine gun. He snapped it into place on its rotating mount and quickly fed a belt of .50 caliber cartridges into it—each shell as long as a full grown man's index finger.

"How much ammo do we have for that?" Matthias yelled back.

"Only about a thousand rounds," answered Sly. "Unless there is another crate of shells wandering around back here somewhere."

"There might be. I felt the weight load shift when I hit that Jeep."

"That was me," said Sly. "You almost threw me clean out the back."

"Well, I'm glad that you could hang in there."

"With your driving, I'm not taking any more chances." He snapped himself into a harness that was linked with the tripod mount. The only way he would be leaving the Jeep now is if the machine gun and tripod were blown from the sheet metal to which they were bolted. Sly swung the .50 caliber machine gun to the rear as distant head lights came over a rise and began pursuing them. Machine guns clattered, but the bullets didn't strike anywhere near them. Carefully, Sly lined up the sights of his machine gun between the headlights of the chasing vehicle.

"Slow down a little bit," said Sly. "I'm having trouble keeping my target."

Matthias complied and slowed to about thirty miles an hour. Sly let off a burst of about a hundred rounds. With satisfaction, he saw one of the headlights extinguish and then the vehicle veered off the road.

"Now that's what I call shooting," exclaimed Sly.

"We've got company at twelve o' clock," yelled Matthias as the Jeep's headlights suddenly illuminated a blockade of two Jeeps pulled across the roadway that cut between two barren hillsides. A half dozen soldiers were ensconced behind the vehicles. As they saw the Jeep, they opened fire. Matthias saw the flashes of muzzle fire just before the windshield shattered and bullets pounded like sledgehammers across his chest. The ceramic plates overlaying his Kevlar body armor stopped the slugs from penetrating but the impacts pushed all the wind out of Matthias's lungs and he struggled to retain control of the Jeep.

A slug caught Sly in the shoulder, ripping loose a chunk of Kevlar and jerking him backward, only the restraining harness he wore keeping him from being knocked out of the Jeep. Matthias kept the Jeep going forward. The road block was complete and there was no gap to shoot through, but Matthias knew that stopping would mean dying. The banana-magazine AK-47s that the soldiers were using were a heavy enough gun to possibly punch through the armor that they wore. Only the angle of their fire and the fact that it was punching through glass and metal before reaching them had kept the bullets from penetrating the Kevlar and ripping them to shreds.

Gun trained forward now, Sly let loose with a torrent of lead from the

.50 caliber. It ripped through the Jeep's metal walls and punched out the other side virtually unimpeded. Blood and flesh sprayed the ground as four of the soldiers went to their gory death. Matthias swerved from the road and up the slope on the right side of the road. He tried to keep the Jeep as vertical as possible, knowing that due to the steepness of the incline and the notoriously narrow wheel base of most Jeeps, any miscalculation would roll them down the hill into the vehicles below.

As the Jeep climbed the precipitous hill, Sly was able to get a line of sight on the two remaining soldiers who had scrambled for cover behind the engine block of one of the Jeeps. Almost parallel to the ground and held in only by his harness, he laid down a sheet of lead that cut down the remaining soldiers.

As their momentum began to slow, Matthias realized the futility of trying to make a turn on the slope and backed his way slowly down, turning just enough so that he lowered the Jeep onto the opposite side of the road block. Flames licked along the bullet torn Jeeps, throwing a flickering light on the ghastly carnage. Gasoline poured in steady streams from punctured tanks. The smell of it hung thickly in the air.

"Let's get out of here before they go up," said Sly, viewing the grisly scene with a callous eye.

Matthias quickly shifted into gear and left the wreckage behind. Several minutes later two explosions rocked the night and Sly could see the plumes of flame rising against the stark night sky—celestial signals that marked the passing of a few more souls.

They dropped off the battered Jeep at a ramshackle warehouse located in the back streets of Suez, just across the canal so vital to the worldwide oil trade. Inside the weather-beaten building, Moustapha waited in the cluttered interior, sitting on top of a rusting barrel. He no longer wore the conservatively cut suit of their previous meetings. Tonight he wore a pair of jeans and a red button-up shirt. As Matthias drove the Jeep into the warehouse, two burly warehouse workers shut the sliding amalgamated aluminum door behind them and locked it into place.

Moustapha leaped from his perch and apprehensively surveyed the damage done to the vehicle. He wasn't so much concerned about the Jeep sustaining some wear and tear as he was that this might be an indicator that the Gantlet's mission hadn't gone off as planned.

"How did things go?" he asked immediately.

"Not as well as anticipated," frowned Sly.

"We're dealing with one of two possibilities," said Matthias. "Number one: you set us up. Number two: someone else who knew about this leaked the fact that we were going to raid the missile site."

Sly grabbed Moustapha by the collar and lifted him up one-handed. "We were ambushed two separate times. The first time by about sixty men and the second time by about six, but that's the one that nearly proved fatal for us."

Moustapha raised his hands in a gesture of peace. "Do you think I'd be here to meet you if I'd had anything to do with that?" he asked. "Did you even have a chance at the destroying the missiles?"

Sly dropped the emissary, and Moustapha composed himself.

Matthias shook his head. "Sly nailed the bunker with a LAW rocket, but it was probably just superficial damage. We don't even know for a fact that there was anything in the bunker. We couldn't get within a couple hundred yards of it."

"They knew everything," said Sly. "They knew when and how we were going to attack."

Moustapha sank back down to take a seat on the same rusted barrel he had been warming earlier. He put his head in his hands.

"This is very, very bad for us," he lamented. "If this information is being leaked, it means that my boss, Mr. Heikal is exposed. If that is the case, however, why hasn't President Mubarek removed him from the office of Minister of Culture?"

"Sometimes it's politically expedient to leave some one in office because of their popularity or political connections…even if you don't care for what they are doing behind your back."

Moustapha considered this for a moment. "No. Marsum Heikal is almost an invisible politician. He is not well known with the people and he is tied with no one person that is very powerful. I think that Idi Kabhul is behind this again. As Defense Minister he is powerful enough to order the kind of troop movement that it would require to lay the ambushes that you speak of. For some reason, which I do not understand, he is not informing President Mubarek of our treason."

"Maybe he has a little treason of his own cooking," said Sly. "Either way, it's not our concern any more. As soon as we get back to Cairo we're getting on our plane and getting out of this country."

"You can't do that," cried Moustapha. "You haven't accomplished the mission we hired you for."

Sly smiled. "We acted on good faith regarding the information that you gave us. The reality of the mission turned out to be quite a bit different than the one we contracted for. We've finished what we came here to do."

Frowning, Moustapha turned away and paced several steps along the cracked and dusty concrete before turning back. He was over a barrel, and he knew it. "You will be paid in full," he said. "However, I do request that you stay for at least one day while I see what our information sources can uncover. We may have further work to offer you."

Matthias narrowed his eyes skeptically. "I don't know, Moustapha. It's usually not a great idea to stick around the scene of the crime and if the Minister of Defense decides he doesn't like us…well, we've seen what he can do."

"We'll put you in a new hotel under assumed names," said Moustapha. "We'll give you an extra hundred thousand as a retainer fee just to stay and consider our next offer, should we have one."

Matthias and Sly both raised an eyebrow and glanced at each other.

"One more day," said Matthias.

"You've got the number for our Swiss bank account," said Sly.

Matthias slipped out of a steaming shower late the next afternoon. His muscular frame ached from the adventures of the evening before. Upon reaching the hotel, he had dropped, exhausted, into a deep slumber, awakening only a few minutes ago. Where a machine gun had done its work, massive purple and blue bruises stitched across his chest in an ugly pattern. It looked a lot worse than it was, but it still hurt like crazy. For whatever reason, after the pounding of the initial impact had worn off, he had barely felt the bruises. Now, however, the lingering adrenaline was long gone and the deep bruising was not.

After carefully drying off, Matthias pulled on some clean Levis and a t-shirt. He brushed the tangles out of his long brown hair. After lacing up his tennis shoes and throwing on his jacket, he left the room, but not before strapping on the Desert Eagle that had become as habitual for him to wear as a pair of pants.

Matthias met Aisha outside of the recording studio at Salmiyya Street. Her mocha hair was pulled back with a black band, but fell loosely down her back. The strap of her small black purse was passed over one shapely shoulder. In contravention of Sharia Law she wore Western-style clothing that packed her graceful figure into an enticing package. Briefly, Matthias wondered if he was playing with fire. Hadn't Abn Fahd told him that this was Idi Kabhul's daughter? If the Defense Minister was really the one behind the ambush of last night, Matthias figured it might be wise to stay as far away from his daughter as humanly possible. Still, he rationalized, Abn Fahd seemed to have a high opinion of Aisha and she had, evidently, been working with Iron Camel for some time, trying to help them break into the big leagues. So, it was unlikely that she had been planted there for the sole purpose of getting information on the Gantlet brothers.

"I was worried that you weren't going to make it," she said glancing at the miniscule gold watch strapped to her slender wrist. "You're about ten minutes late."

"I apologize," said Matthias. "I didn't get to bed until very late last night and I just woke up about half an hour ago."

"You up late checking out the Egyptian night life?" she teased.

"In a manner of speaking," answered Matthias.

She put a hand on Matthias's shoulder and laughed. "Did you have too much *khamr* last night?"

"No, not me," answered Matthias. "You must be thinking of Sly. I steer wide of that stuff. So where are you taking me today, my beautiful tour guide?"

She smiled at his compliment. "Have you ever been to see the sphinx?"

"No I haven't. I was hoping I'd get a chance to take a look at it while I was here."

"I've got a cab waiting. Let's go." She took his arm and led him out of the alley onto Salmiyya Street where a dusty cab was pulled up to the curb.

The day whirled by as Aisha treated Matthias to a cavalcade of exotic sights—the least of which not being her own spectacular form. As a resident of Cairo, she was familiar with a variety of places that were off the beaten tourist track and they visited back alley bazaars where the booths were tented with gaudily colored cloths and attended by turbaned Moslems who proffered everything from pomegranates to black market clothing and fist-sized blocks of hashish.

Matthias bought Aisha a black Calvin Klein dress that she was wishing she could afford and spent a wad of Egyptian pounds on a razor edged tulwar that a knife vendor produced from beneath his table. Aisha did the bargaining for him and soon Matthias discovered that the prices suggested by the merchants were often five to ten times more than they were willing to accept for the product. Evidently haggling was an integral part of the art of a bargain. Finally the merchant wrapped the blade up in a cloth and handed it to Matthias. He had a few swords at home and had undergone years of intensive study under several masters of various forms of martial sword arts. He appreciated the craftsmanship that went into a fine blade—especially now that he had seen firsthand what a good sword could do to somebody.

As the afternoon wound up, Matthias and Aisha found themselves sitting at a polished teak table looking through plate glass windows at the sparkling Nile, while steaming bowls of exotically spiced food were placed before them.

"So do you regret it?" asked Aisha.

"Regret what?" asked Matthias.

"Spending the afternoon with me."

"Not at all," said Matthias. "It was a very instructive afternoon and I couldn't have asked for a more beautiful tour guide and instructress."

"I bet you say that to all your teachers," she teased.

"Believe me, if you'd seen some of my teachers you wouldn't say that. In fact, some of my grade school teachers in communist Germany were downright scary."

She grinned. "Do you want to shoot a few games of pool after dinner?" she asked.

"I'd love to, but I have to warn you. I'm not very good."

"Maybe, I can hustle you out of a few pounds or...," she looked at him slyly. "Maybe you're trying to put the hustle on me."

"I guess you'll just have to wait and see."

"We've got a competition size pool table at home that nobody ever uses."

Matthias shifted uncomfortably. "I don't know if that's such a good idea. I'm getting the feeling that Moustapha, the guy that arranged for our little seminar in Egypt, and your father might be at opposite ends of the political spectrum on a few things. Right now might not be the best time for me to meet him."

She shook her head. "I know that my father doesn't hold him in the highest of esteem. I really have no idea of the reasoning behind it, but my Father won't be home, anyhow, so it won't be an issue at all."

The Kabhul estate was set back from a wide paved road that wound up a hillside overlooking most of Cairo. A ten-foot-tall wall ringed the grounds, wrought iron gates offering the only egress or ingress. Above this gate a flag-pole displayed the Egyptian colors: three equal horizontal bands of red, white and black in the center of which a shield was superimposed on an eagle. Aisha reached into her purse and pressed a button on a small remote device. Immediately the gate began to roll back allowing the turbaned cabby entrance to the broad drive that led to the pillared steps of the palatial residence.

The cab driver left the estate and Aisha led Matthias into a huge entry room that was decorated with expensive tapestries and gold-scrolled cornices. Taking Matthias's hand, she pulled him past grand dining chambers set with silver chalices and golden serving platters and down thickly-carpeted stairs into a plush gaming room below. One wall consisted entirely of a massive aquarium of exotic fish.

Aisha racked up the balls into a tight triangle and picked out a pool cue while Matthias put their packages on the floor. After examining the rack of sticks mounted to the far wall, Matthias picked the heaviest cue stick he could find and lined up the white ball. With a long swift stroke he broke the rack wide open, dropping three balls into various pockets.

Standing in front of the draped double French doors with her hands on her hips, Aisha looked skeptical. "You say you're not very good at pool?"

"Give me a chance," he said, "and I'll prove how bad I am." Matthias began lining up his next shot. He glanced up at Aisha and saw a shadow pass across the curtains of the doors beyond.

"Get down!" he yelled as he dropped the pool cue and reached inside his jacket for the Desert Eagle.

Aisha hadn't often lived a life of danger and was a bit confused at Matthias's warning. Instead of dropping to the ground she turned around to see what was the matter. At that moment a half dozen robed men burst through the doors. Two of them immediately took hold of Aisha's arms and a third grabbed her mocha hair and pulled her head back, putting the edge of a wicked looking knife against her throat. By the time Yasser Banhiron showed his scarred visage, Matthias's pistol was out and the red laser dot was targeted between the knife wielder's eyes.

Matthias was about to pull the trigger when Yasser Banhiron spoke. "I wouldn't do that if I were you." Matthias glanced over and saw that the burly man was wielding a Mac-10 automatic machine pistol and had it leveled at Matthias. "On second thought," he continued, "do pull the trigger. It will give me a good excuse for emptying a magazine of thirty-six bullets into you and then, after that, we'll still kill the girl."

After thinking about it for a second, Matthias slowly put his .44 magnum down on the slate of the pool table.

Banhiron sneered cruelly. "A wise decision," he said. He glanced at his knife wielding cohort. "Kill her," he said.

"My Father will see you die for this," Aisha threatened as the knife man lowered the blade.

Banhiron laughed. "No he won't my dear, Aisha. He has already given his permission. His heart is broken that you would take up with this foreign dog and he says that he would rather see you die than disgrace him in such a manner."

"No!" screamed Matthias. His hands were below the level of the pool table and he grabbed hold of it, heaving it forward with all of his strength. It crashed into Yasser Banhiron's legs and he reeled back, flame flashing and lead spurting wildly from his miniature machine gun. The fish tank webbed and cracked where a few of the bullets struck it. A fine spray of salt water sprang from several hairline cracks.

Unfortunately for him, Matthias's Desert Eagle was now out of reach. An attempt to grab it would end up getting him skewered by several of the Egyptians that had drawn their swords from their sashes. However, he knew that his newly purchased tulwar was only a few paces behind him. Matthias went into a diving roll, snatching up his blade at midpoint and coming to his feet. Momentarily abandoning their restraint of Aisha's arms, swordsmen closed in around him. With one swift movement, the rock vocalist plucked the wrapping cloth from his blade and cast it in the face of the nearest Arab. The swordsman was but momentarily hindered by the cloth, reaching out with his blade and whipping it aside so that it would not obscure his vision. Matthias used this slight lapse of defense to rip his blade across the man's belly, effectively disemboweling him.

Barely able to get his blade back to the fore, Matthias found himself hard-pressed by two other of Yasser Banhiron's thugs. Steel met steel; the blades rasped in deadly communion. In mere moments, Matthias spotted his opening and sheered through the knee of his first assailant. The man went down with a howl, a sticky puddle forming on the carpeting around him.

The broad tip of his tulwar dripping red, Matthias pressed the attack as the second swordsman retreated. Yasser Banhiron staggered to his feet angrily. He whipped his machine gun aloft and shouted. In the confusion, Aisha slipped from her captor's grip and headed out the open French doors. Yasser sprang to grab her, striking her a heavy blow on the side of the head with the Mac-10, felling her before she could escape. She lay unconscious, so Yasser turned his attention to the lone figure that was holding off four of his men.

Matthias saw that he was being outflanked and rapidly retreated to the foot of the stairs that he and Aisha had used to enter the game room earlier. He backed up the steps so that the Egyptians could come at him only one at a time. This also gave him the advantage of having the high ground. Any opponent's upper body would be slightly more vulnerable to his attacks, while they would have more difficulty striking a vital area.

The main disadvantage was the lack of swinging room in the confined space of the stairs, so even as the boldest of his foes crossed the threshold of the stairs, Matthias continued to back up until he stood at the top of the stairwell. Here, he had plenty of space to swing the tulwar, but his opponent suffered the space restrictions.

The first man lifted his blade above his head and it lodged in the ceiling above, plaster dust filtering down. Matthias cut the Egyptian open and wrenched his fallen opponent's blade loose from the ceiling with his left hand. He stabbed it into the floor beside him in case he might need it later.

The second Arab up the stairs approached more cautiously, thrusting noncommittally as if testing Matthias's defenses or as if he were merely a… delaying tactic! This thought whirred through Matthias's mind with startling clarity. He didn't see anyone else at the bottom of the stairs. They were probably circling around the house and using the front entrance to come up behind him.

Thrusting deep into the well of the stairs, Matthias forced his opponent to retreat rapidly in order to avoid his blade. Dodging back several steps, the man slipped on the blood of Matthias's previous victim and tumbled to the bottom of the stairs in a tangle of limbs, forcing him to drop his blade in order to avoid skewering himself. Matthias leaped down the stairs after him, leaping over the still-twitching body.

At the bottom of the stairs, still not having regained his feet, the thug desperately cast around for his blade, but Matthias was there before he could recover the weapon. A well aimed cut with the tulwar's razor edge sent the man's head rolling across the carpet. The room was empty of life. The bodies of the dead were strewn about in gory testament to Matthias's fighting ability. The prostrate form of Aisha still lay near the double glass doors.

Practicality forced Matthias to attend to Aisha second. First, he found his Desert Eagle on the floor near the upended pool table. He brushed aside the fallen billiard balls and snatched it up. Coming to Aisha's side, he set aside the blade that had served him so well and checked her pulse. It still beat strongly, but there was a massive bump forming on the side of her head where Yasser had struck her.

Matthias expected to hear the sounds of pursuit from the stairway at any moment, but he still heard nothing. It was a large house, maybe it was taking awhile to circle around the building. After holstering his gun, he gathered up Aisha's limp form in his arms and stepped through the double doors and onto the patio beyond.

Immediately he felt the warm barrel of Yasser Banhiron's Mac-10 pressed up against his temple. "Don't move," rasped Yasser.

A scowling Arab with rotting teeth quickly disarmed Matthias.

Yasser cursed, his scarred face crinkling grotesquely. "After what you've done to my men, you don't deserve a quick death. I'm going to see that you and the wench die very slowly and, God willing, very painfully."

Aisha's eyelids flickered and her eyes opened. She looked dazedly about until she recalled the events that led up to her unconsciousness.

"Why?" she said weakly.

The Arab with the bad teeth grinned and sputtered convoluted French, "The question should be how." He held up Aisha's black purse. "A bug and a tracer are sewn into the lining." He turned his attention to Matthias. "Didn't you wonder how we knew everything that you were going to do?"

"You and the girl played right into our hands," said Yasser. He looked at Aisha. "There's nothing like having an unwitting accomplice, eh?"

Aisha spat at him and Yasser wiped away the moisture with one massive, yet misshapen hand that appeared to have been broken several times and poorly set. "You will regret that," he said with calm assuredness.

Sly paced back and forth in the small hotel room as Moustapha stared apprehensively at the telephone.

"It's not like him to be this irresponsible," said Sly. "I'm betting this has something to do with that Kabhul girl that he was seeing this afternoon. I told him that she couldn't be trusted, but would he listen to me?"

"Kabhul girl?" questioned Moustapha.

"You know, Idi Kabhul's daughter. She was at the recording studio the other day when we were doing that work with Iron Camel."

Moustapha's eyes widened. "That was Idi Kabhul's daughter? We are in trouble then. I didn't recognize her. I hadn't seen her since she was a little girl."

"Well, she's all woman now," said Sly. "And a beautiful woman has ways to make a fool out of even the smartest of men. I should know," Sly finished ruefully.

"The fact that Idi's daughter is involved in this confirms my suspicions that he commissioned the attack on you by Yasser Banhiron. They weren't able to get to you and so they took a different tack with your brother."

"Although the bait is very similar."

"I've also received some disturbing information through one of our intelligence sources. We are waiting for confirmation through another avenue, but

I fear it may be tied into the situation that we're involved in here."

"Well, spit it out," demanded Sly.

"A Chinese military warlord has been jailed in connection with three missing nuclear warheads. The PLO has been named as the buyer. I have a bad feeling those nuclear warhead are on their way here… and I have a worse feeling that the Arab League will settle for nothing less than the extinction of the Jews and the commencement of World War Three."

Sly barely seemed to register Moustapha's comment. "Yasser Banhiron was the guy who tried to take me out of action in the alley the other night. I'm thinking there is a good chance he is involved in Matthias's disappearance. Where can we find Banhiron?"

"We don't have time for that," said Moustapha. "We've got three nuclear warheads wandering loose out there somewhere. If I'm to have any chance at putting a discreet cap on this situation I'm going to need your help."

"Correction," said Sly. "You're going to need my and Matthias's help. I'm not doing anything until I find out what happened to him. You help me find Matthias and I'll do the rest of the job for free. No charge. Is it a deal?"

Moustapha nodded. "It is a deal."

"So where do we start?" asked Sly.

"Yasser Banhiron is little more than a Bedouin thug who prospers because he is willing to do the dirty work of more prosperous and powerful citizens who don't want to muddy their hands. His people are wanderers with no place to call home."

"You're going to have to do better than that," said Sly. "I'm offering you a million dollars worth of free bloodshed to help me find Matthias."

"Yes, of course. As I was about to say, I hear that Yasser keeps a flat in the Muhandisin quarter; a place where he can hold court with prostitutes."

Sly holstered his Desert Eagle and strapped on his Cassul revolver. "That sounds like a good enough place to start." He shrugged on his leather jacket. "You show me the way."

"Let me make a few calls. From what I understand, the location of his flat is well known by the local women of ill repute. With the proper motivation, I think some of the madams may be willing to part with his address."

Kalhid flexed his thick fingers and wire-like tendons writhed beneath his bulging forearms. The room was dim and cool compared to the blistering heat outside. Still, Kalhid's tank top was soaked with sweat. Matthias and Aisha were tied to heavy oak chairs that sat about a dozen feet apart. Matthias's jacket lay in a crumpled heap beside his feet. His shirt had been torn away, revealing the punctuation of bruises across his broad chest.

Laughing, Kalhid uttered a few cruel words in Arabic and then spoke to Matthias in a thickly accented French. "I see that someone has already started to do my work for me."

He balled his fist and slammed it into Matthias's rock hard abdomen. The musician had seen the punch coming so he had a chance to tighten up. The blow stung, but it wasn't the devastating strike that it would have been if he hadn't been prepared. Matthias acted as if the blow hurt worse than it did. He slumped forward gasping for breath, all the while keeping an eye on Kalhid so that he might prepare for the next blow.

The next punch came, followed by another and another—all to the body. The kickboxer was softening him up, figured Matthias. This was just the preparatory stage for more painful things to come.

Yasser Banhiron stood by the door of the apartment with a broken-toothed leer. Beside him, his Arab accomplice with the rotting smile seemed to be enjoying the spectacle as well.

"So," said Yasser. "Are you ready to tell us what need to know? This is just the preliminary beating; Kalhid has barely even gotten warmed up yet."

"You haven't even asked me any questions yet," answered Matthias through gritted teeth. He made a show of being in pain, though he was far from being incapacitated, yet.

"How much does Moustapha know of our plans?"

Matthias wasn't sure what the point of this question was. They must have already surmised that they knew of the nerve gas warheads and the missiles being placed along the Egyptian-Israeli border. He didn't see any harm in answering the question either. "He knows that you're putting missile batteries along the border with nerve gas warheads, but that should have been obvious even to a moron like you."

Yasser raised an eyebrow. "Nerve gas," he hissed. "I think that you lie."

He motioned to Kalhid who swung a haymaker at Matthias's jaw. Matthias leaned his head forward and the blow caught him in the side of the skull. Kalhid yelped in pain and jumped back cradling his fist. The rock musician felt a wetness creeping out of his scalp and matting his hair. The blow had drawn blood, but crushed the wrestler's knuckles. Matthias figured that it was a fair trade.

"Enough of this," roared Yasser. "We have a limit to our time. Perhaps he will be more cooperative when we work on the girl. She is a brazen and shameful woman, to go in public with her face uncovered. She deserves to be punished."

Matthias was perplexed. They weren't buying the truth, so maybe there was more going on here than he knew about and if the truth wouldn't satisfy them, how was he going to stop them from hurting Aisha?

While Kalhid wrapped his bloody knuckles with a cloth, the rotten-toothed Arab stepped over to Aisha. She cursed at him and struggled futilely with her bonds as he took hold of her tank top and ripped it down the seam, revealing her smooth olive skin and the white lace bra that she wore beneath.

"You're oh so delicate," said the Arab. "I don't know how much punishment you're going to be able to take. Kalhid is as strong as a bull and he often underestimates his strength. One blow might fall too hard and snuff out your frail life."

"I would rather be dead than be in your company," she replied fiercely.

Matthias could only admire Aisha's courage in the face of such adversity. He could see the ugly bump on the side of her face where Yasser had struck her and decided he could not allow her to suffer any more pain on his account. He must do everything in his power to prevent her from being hurt any further.

Though his calves were tied to the chair legs, Matthias had enough mobility to stand if he rocked his weight forward and onto his feet. Another coil of rope was lashed around his chest and upper arms and a third rope was tied painfully tight around his wrists—which had been forced behind the chair. While Kalhid finished dressing his broken knuckles, Matthias rocked forward so that he stood on his feet, albeit in a hunched position and carrying the chair on his back. With all the force that he could muster he propelled himself backward so that the chair smashed against the wall. He heard the chair creak as one of the legs buckled. Before Yasser Banhiron could reach him, he slammed the chair against the wall again. This time the structural integrity of the chair gave away and Matthias found himself able to stand upright, still tied to the ruins of the seat.

Yasser leaped at him, telegraphing a right-fisted blow. Matthias ducked under the punch and put his shoulder hard into the Bedouin's chest, driving forward with powerful legs. They both went down in a jumble. Matthias tried to roll off the man and to his feet, but his bonds tripped him up and he fell heavily into the wet bar, breaking glass and spilling ice. In seconds, Yasser was standing over him holding a knife blade.

"We weren't going to get any information out of you, anyway," he said as the blade plunged downward.

At that moment the door crashed open and Sly strode in, .44 magnum in hand. The gun spoke, a bullet entering the left side of Yasser Banhiron's head and exploding out the right in gory ribbons of flesh and gray matter. The knife skimmed over Matthias's shoulder and stuck firmly in the floor.

"The cavalry's here," said Sly., "saving your sorry hide, once again."

The rotten-toothed Arab reached for a pistol that lay on the nearby coffee table. It was too far away and Sly put two bullets in his back, sending him reeling into the glass table which splintered into crimson-stained shards.

Kalhid stood holding his white wrapped fist, in shock at the sudden turn of events. Sly waved his gun at him. "You stay there," he said in Arabic. "I've got a bone to pick with you."

With one eye on Kalhid, Sly bent down and helped haul Matthias from beneath the corpse of Yasser Banhiron. He quickly sliced the ropes and the splintered chair fell free.

Sly handed Matthias the magnum. "I want you to hold this. Ugly and I are going to go a few rounds. I have something to prove to myself."

Matthias knew it was pointless to argue, so he accepted the warm magnum pistol and stepped over to free Aisha from her bonds, while Sly taunted the Egyptian wrestler in Arabic.

"Come over here, little girl," beckoned Sly to the huge man. "Let's see how you handle yourself when you fight someone that isn't drunk, drugged, or tied up."

Kalhid hesitated, shooting a glance at Matthias.

"Don't worry," said Sly. "If you beat me, he'll let you go without even shooting you once."

"What about twice?" mumbled Matthias under his breath as the last rope confining Aisha fell slack. "Thanks," she said as she stood up and rubbed at her numbed limbs. He handed her his jacket and she slipped it on.

"What's in this thing, lead?" she asked, as the full weight of the jacket closed upon her shoulders.

"Kevlar with ceramic plates," answered Matthias.

Sly and Kalhid circled each other warily. Though Matthias could see that Sly was chomping at the bit, anxious to enter the fray, each of them respected the abilities of the other and was reluctant to rush in haphazardly. As if on cue they moved forward and grappled, massive pillar-like arms locked together as they strove to throw the other down. Sly almost looked small compared to the gigantic boxer and Matthias could immediately see that the Egyptian had the upper hand. Slowly he was bending Sly backward, relying on sheer strength to subjugate the blond musician's will and break his bones with brute power.

This was the wrestler's mistake. Sly loved to match his strength against another's strength and very rarely was he equaled, but here he was outclassed. The Egyptian, in his zeal to prove his superiority, wanted simply to crush Sly instead of relying on his skills and training. When Sly saw that he could not match the giant in strength, he resorted to guile. He used the big man's strength against him and suddenly reversed his efforts, pulling the giant forward as he swept the man's feet from under him.

The floor trembled as the Egyptian went down, Sly on top of him. For one moment, the wrestler rebounded from the floor and his head snapped back. Sly drove his fist into the giant's exposed Adam's apple, crushing it. Kalhid began to cough, but he could take no air in through his shattered larynx. He waved his hands frantically, desperately trying to take breath into his starving lungs. His lips began to turn blue.

Sly came to his feet and watched impassively as Kalhid struggled for air. "Maybe there is something to be said for sobriety. He's a lot tougher when I'm drunk."

"You arrived just in time," said Matthias. "I was about to get a knife shoved in me."

"The pleasure is all mine." He looked at Aisha. "How are you doing? It looks like you took a nasty hit in the side of the head."

Embarrassed, she put her hand to the bump to hide the ugly bruise. "I'll live through it," she answered. "I'm lucky you got here when you did, though. A few minutes later and I don't think I would have looked even this good."

Sly smiled wanly. "Well, I'm sure Matthias would agree with me that it would take more than a few bumps and bruises to make you look anything less than beautiful."

Aisha beamed back at him.

"I think Moustapha is in the car wondering if I'm even alive anymore," said Sly. "Perhaps we'd better get out there and let him know that everything worked out okay…at least so far."

"So far?" questioned Matthias.

"I'm afraid that the arms race has escalated. We're no longer dealing with nerve gas. The PLO has gone nuclear. They plan to wipe Israel off the face of the earth."

Moustapha let out a sigh from behind the wheel of his Lincoln luxury car as he saw the three of them emerge and descend the flight of stairs between apartment buildings. He was a little perplexed to see Aisha with them, but as soon as they piled into the car, he pulled the already running vehicle away from the curb. Sirens wailed in the near distance.

"We need to see about picking you up silencers for your guns," he said. "I could hear the gunshots from the car and, evidently, I wasn't the only one that noticed them."

"In New York City it wouldn't have been a problem," said Sly. "People mind their own business."

Matthias laughed and found that it hurt to do so. His entire torso was a mass of bruised muscle and flesh. "I think I need a few days off," he groaned.

"Didn't you hear what I said before?" asked Sly. "We're in the middle of a nuclear crisis. We've got no time to rest."

Moustapha shot a warning glance at Sly, his eyes motioning in Aisha's direction. It was clear that he didn't have any trust for the woman.

"How did you two get in that mess, anyhow?" asked Sly, changing the course of the conversation.

Matthias quickly related the story of their capture and the revelation that Aisha had been carrying a miniature microphone and transmitter in her purse. He slowed only when Sly pressed him for more details on his sword fight in the Kabhul mansion.

Sly scowled as the story was finished, but didn't say anything more. Moustapha found a parking spot near the hotel and ushered them inside, staying at a payphone in the lobby while the rest of them went upstairs and congregated in Matthias's room.

Finding a shirt that advertised a brand of guitar strings in his hockey bag, Matthias offered it to Aisha who seemed relieved to be able to shed the heavy leather coat that she had been wearing. She stepped into the restroom and emerged a minute later with the oversized shirt tucked into the waist of her jeans.

"I'm not going to win any fashion contests," she admitted, "but at least I'm modest again."

"How are you holding up?" asked Matthias.

Aisha shrugged. "I can't honestly say that I'm doing that well. I mean, I get attacked in my own home by a business associate of my father, and find out my father would like me dead. I really have nowhere to go right now." She looked down at the floor.

"This is my fault," said Matthias. "If I would have left you alone you wouldn't be in this mess right now."

"It's not your fault. I practically threw myself at you."

"Well, I'm not complaining," said Matthias. "But I am worried about you."

"Whatever you do, don't abandon me now."

"Why would I do that?"

Three rapid knocks came at the door. Sly answered it and let Moustapha enter the room. He glanced around the chamber and looked severely at Aisha. "I mean no offense," he said, "but because of your family ties I don't want you to hear any of the following. There may be a conflict of interest."

Aisha soberly returned his gaze. "As of today, my family ties are severed. In fact, I'd like to be able to help you bring down whatever it is that my father deems has more value than his own daughter's life."

Moustapha considered this. "Fine. But understand this: Once you've thrown your lot in with us there is no going back. You will not be let out of our sight until this mission is accomplished. I still consider you a possible liability to our success."

"I understand and I accept," Aisha answered evenly.

"Very well. I believe we've found the nuclear warheads. A rack of our short range ballistic missiles has turned up missing and we've traced them to a Bedouin tribe living in the Qattara Depression. The Qattara Depression is the roughest terrain of anywhere in Egypt, perhaps similar to the badlands of the Dakota's in the United States. The Bedouins are wanderers and in such terrain it is difficult to track down a small and mobile tribe. We have reason to believe that they will rendezvous with the PLO members that purchased the warheads and that they will be fitted to the missiles."

"The question is, what are they going to do with them after they are installed?" said Matthias.

"That's what I'm worried about," agreed Moustapha. "The first problem we have is that this tribe is very nomadic. There are at least a half dozen places that they frequent. Even if we check every single site there is no guarantee that they are going to be there. We may have some difficulty tracking them down."

"I think I can help there," said Aisha.

The three men in the room looked at her with some surprise.

"How is that?" questioned Moustapha.

"I can take you there. My father took me on a bit of a site seeing expedition several weeks ago. We went and visited a tribe in the Qattara Depression. My father said it was strictly a political trip to ease relations with the tribes that are often hostile to outsiders. Now I see that the motivation was a little more sinister."

"Maybe there is still a chance of keeping Egypt out of a war that we can't win," said Moustapha. "If, Allah forbid, those warheads are used, it will bring the wrath of the whole world down upon us."

Sand stretched for as far as the eye could see, broken only by an occasional ridge or depression that allowed the Jeep's occupants to feel like they were making some progress as they left wide tire tracks from one sterile landmark to another. This was the edge of the Sahara Desert which stretched into Libya and across northern Africa.

Sly drove recklessly across the dunes, casting up billowing clouds of sand behind. In the shotgun position, Matthias consulted the quavering needle of a compass and then compared the headings with a map he had spread out on his lap. Aisha crouched in the back, leaning over his shoulder as he pinpointed their position.

"We shouldn't be much longer now," said Aisha. "Once we're there I will help you find the Bedouin's camp site."

"And once we're there we're going to put you somewhere safe until it's all over," said Sly. "Things might get real nasty and we don't want you catching any stray bullets or getting in our way while we're trying to work."

Aisha rolled her eyes. "Believe me, I'm not going to be jumping in front of anybody's guns, if that's what you are worried about."

"Mainly I'm worried about three nuclear warheads," said Sly.

"Look up ahead," Matthias interjected. "The terrain is taking a turn for the worse."

The desert began a ragged slope into a region of small jagged hills, soon dropping into steep gullies punctuated by spires of rock and earth. This was the lowest part of Egypt, dropping to 436 feet below sea level. The land lay in tortured convolutions, dotted with salty marshes and occasionally a small lake reflecting glittering diamonds of sunlight through gaps in the hills.

Sly slowed the breakneck speed of the Jeep to match the terrain. Now the compass readings were absolutely vital to keep their bearings among the twisting trails that wound through the jagged mounds comprising the landscape.

"I can see how it might be easy to hide a few missiles in here," commented Matthias.

"We should be intersecting with an actual road up ahead," said Aisha, as she pored over the map. "Once we hit that and head west, I should be able to recognize some of the landmarks and point the way."

"We're counting on it," replied Sly gruffly. It bothered him to put this much faith in anybody besides his brothers. He didn't easily put his trust in those who hadn't proved themselves to him implicitly.

They followed a muddy gully and, tires throwing thick clots of mud, pulled up onto a rough roadway that wound erratically through the badlands. They had chosen to stay off the roads until now to avoid the possibility of an ambush along the way. Sly had kept a close eye on Aisha and she'd had no opportunity to pass any information of their foray to the Qattara Depression. Yasser Banhiron would have them believe that the prior information leak was due to the bug hidden in Aisha's purse. Still, there was always the possibility of some other source leaking information.

Moustapha had received intelligence regarding the location of the missiles and that the missing Chinese warheads had been purchased by PLO agents. This meant Moustapha wasn't the only one who knew this. If Idi Kabhul's people were aware that this information was known by Marsum Heikal and his associates, they might, rightly, assume that there would be some effort underway to undermine their activities. To prevent specific information of their operation from being leaked, Matthias and Sly had asked Moustapha not to tell anyone, even his superior, Marsum Heikal, anything about their plans. Bureaucracy had a way of being riddled with people who liked to talk. The fewer that knew of their endeavors the better.

Once on an actual, albeit rugged and rutted, road Aisha was able to recognize several landmarks from her trip with her father. After a half dozen miles she pointed to a barely recognizable side road that pushed further through the hills.

Since getting on the roadway, Matthias cradled a rifle in his arms and kept a sharp lookout for snipers that might be lurking in rocky crevices in the whorled peaks above.

"How much further do we have to go?" asked Matthias.

"Probably five or six miles," estimated Aisha. "We've still got another turn off to take before we get there. We're looking for a small oasis tucked away between peaks."

The sun was beginning to fall behind the ridges and long shadows spread across their path.

"We'd better find someplace to hide the Jeep," said Sly. "As much as I'd love to drive right into camp that probably won't be our best tactic, but I would like to be able to hike most of the way in before the sun sets completely."

"From the look of the terrain, it may take us awhile," said Matthias.

Pulling behind a peak, they managed to find an aperture between a jumble of boulders, which Sly was able to back the Jeep into. They broke into the gear packed tightly into the rear of the Jeep and garbed themselves in body armor.

Aisha pointed up the steep terrain. "Once we make it over that ridge, you should be able to look down on the oasis."

"What do you mean we?" asked Sly as he slipped the strap of an UZI over his shoulder. "You're staying here."

Matthias threw Aisha the key to the Jeep, which she snatched out of mid-air. "If we don't make it back in four hours, you leave without us."

"What will you do?" she asked.

"We'll either be dead or we'll find another ride."

Aisha pressed her body against Matthias and lifted her lips to his in a passionate kiss. "Goodbye," she said.

The memory of the kiss still fresh upon his lips, Matthias forged toward the top of the ridge with his brother following closely behind. Finally, the ridge came to a plateau and they climbed over the edge, Aisha and their Jeep no longer in sight. A few minutes later they discovered that Aisha had been mistaken about the Bedouin camp being just over the ridge. A rill that had once carried a stream, perhaps, led downward to a narrow path. This natural formation formed a stone catwalk, on either side of which plunged a hundred- foot chasm. On the far reaches of this catwalk was yet another, higher, ridge, which the Gantlets hoped would overlook the oasis.

The sheer weight of their body armor, weapons, and extra ammunition made crossing this catwalk a rather tenuous affair. Balance was critical and, though both very strong and able to carry their equipment with relative ease, they were not prepared to do a tight rope act. Freeing their hands by relegating their machine guns to their backs, they carefully stepped across, each managing to maintain their equilibrium until safely on the other side.

Climbing yet higher, they finally reached the lip of the ridge and, falling down on their bellies, pulled themselves forward so they could peer into the valley below without exposing little more than their heads and some of their shoulder. Though not particularly lush, compared to much of the surrounding area it was a tropical paradise. Several palms grew from beside a natural spring which was surrounded by a variety of scrub grasses. Pitched in this turf were more than a dozen tents, all of which had camouflaged tarps strung above them to prevent detection from air surveillance and satellite photography. In the failing light of dusk, Matthias could make out the hazy figures of Bedouin men moving about the camp. All of them appeared to be carrying Russian made AK-47 assault rifles, the telltale banana magazine giving away the make of the gun even at this distance.

The entire camp existed in a crevice between sloping cliff sides. To the east a large military truck was covered with a camouflage net. From where they lay, it was immediately evident that it was a portable missile launcher. The three rockets had a half dozen men working on the warhead installation. Off to one side a man was punching coordinates into an electronic device.

"It looks as though the warheads have arrived," said Matthias.

"Check for perimeter guards," said Sly as he, himself, began to search through his binoculars.

The only entrance was at the west side of the oasis between towering stone pillars. Putting his binoculars to his eyes, Matthias studied the formation of the pillars and found a turbaned man stationed among some rocks high in the closest tower. The Bedouin guard evidently hadn't seen the Gantlets and was paying close attention to something coming down the road. A few moments later two Jeeps crossed between the pillars and drove into camp.

Matthias trained his binoculars on the Jeeps. The first carried four Arab men and the second carried two more. Propped up in the back between crates was a woman bound in ropes. Matthias's heart sank as he saw that it was Aisha. They had found and captured her. In fact, the second Jeep was theirs—the one that they had left with Aisha.

Sly groaned. "Do you see what I see?"

"Yeah. They'll be expecting us now."

"Not if we don't give them time to prepare," he said as the Jeeps below pulled to a halt. Several of them grabbed Aisha by her shoulders and began dragging her struggling form toward a large, centrally-located tent.

"In a few seconds," said Sly, "they will be informing whoever is in command here that there are some intruders on the way. By the time they start giving commands we are already going to be there."

Without warning he vaulted over the edge of the cliff and began sliding down its steep face on his feet and posterior. Matthias realized that there was no turning back and began skiing down behind him. In a matter of seconds they had traversed a hundred yards and they rolled to their feet at the bottom, only a mad dash away from the center of the encampment. The deepening dusk appeared to have served them well and their reckless descent had gone unnoticed.

Sly signaled that he was heading to the east side of the camp, to check out the missiles, Matthias presumed. The younger brother gave the thumbs up and slipped into the encampment toward the tent where the bound Aisha had been taken. Once in among the tents he moved quietly and cautiously, slipping from shadow to shadow and avoiding the occasional Bedouin that wandered by. Any moment he expected an alarm to go up and once that happened stealth would be nearly impossible.

Matthias moved quietly to the flap of the tent. The place was nearly big enough to house a mess hall but the interior was dim as Matthias slid within. Suddenly the place blazed with light, temporarily blinding him. Someone behind him reached up and ripped his helmet off and two guns went to his head at either temple. At his left a familiar voice spoke.

"Despite all the trouble you've caused us, you Gantlet boys really are stupid." Matthias turned his head slightly and found that it was Aisha who held a machine pistol to his head. He immediately knew that he had been played for a fool. Inside he was hurt and angry, but he kept his cool. He knew that if he didn't he would be killed before he might have a chance for escape.

"You're an excellent actress."

"It's not acting. It is the principle of Al Taquiyya. Any action is permissible to snare the infidels."

"Is that so?"

"Slay the infidels wherever you find them, and take them captives and besiege them and lie in wait for them in every ambush," said Aisha. "So says the Koran."

In addition to Aisha, a Bedouin stood to his right, also holding a pistol to Matthias's head. In front of him a short but stolid man with iron gray hair and dressed impeccably in Egyptian military uniform approached from the opposite side of the tent.

"Violation of Sharia is overlooked, forgiven and even blessed when it is done in the service of the destruction of the unbelievers," he said, his left eye twitching involuntarily. "The eradication of the Jews takes precedence over the lie of the tongue or the sins of the flesh."

"So you must be Idi Kabhul. The one I've been hearing so many good things about."

At Idi's urging, the Bedouin began removing Matthias's armaments while Aisha, wisely, continued to hold her weapon to his skull. Aisha had watched Matthias when he strapped on his weapons and so, at her direction, they did a thorough job of disarming him. Once they had this accomplished, the Bedouin pushed him down into a corner of the tent while Aisha continued to train her weapon on him.

"Sarcasm," replied Idi Kabhul. "Yet another indicator of the decay of civilization."

"So you plan to set things right by launching three nuclear bombs into Israel?"

"Precisely. We have become weak. We have allowed too many concessions to the Jews; we have let them take too much when their very existence is a blight upon us. They steal our lands and expect us to roll over like a dying dog."

"And you agree with this, Aisha?"

Aisha nodded, venom flaring in her eyes. "Our leaders are weak. We need someone to take a stand."

"I take it President Mubarek doesn't know anything about this."

Idi Kabhul smiled thinly. "He thinks he is making a concession to have chemical warheads pointed at Israel. Unwittingly, he will become one of the greatest leaders of our age. In twenty minutes the nuclear missiles will be launched and he will be swept along by the tides of history."

"They'll never launch."

"So you think your brother is seeing to that?" asked Aisha, a smirk upon lips that not so long ago Matthias had kissed. As she spoke the tent flap was brushed aside and Sly entered, weaponless, and followed by two armed men. "We were equally prepared for him."

Once the older Gantlet brother was secure beneath the gun of the Bedouin within the tent, the two men that had captured him spoke.

"The technicians have asked us to inform you that two of the missiles are ready to fire."

Idi Kabhul smiled with satisfaction, then waved them from the room. "Tell them that I am pleased, but the third head of the snake must also be prepared for its strike."

Sly saw Aisha holding a gun on Matthias and sneered. "I thought there were a few too many holes in your story. The only thing that kept me from thinking you were an outright fraud was that lump on the side of your face."

"No sacrifice of the flesh is too great," Aisha answered, her eyes upon Matthias. "It was necessary to propagate the deception."

"It looked as though Kalhid was about to propagate the deception in even more intimate ways when I broke in and rescued you and Matthias. Do you think he would have gone through with it?"

"The man was dedicated to the destruction of the unbeliever."

"And could you have gone through with it?" asked Sly.

"Matthias knows not to question my dedication," she replied.

"We all must be convicted with fanatic zeal if we are to carry forth Allah's will," said Idi Kabhul. He drew forth a German-made Luger from his holster and walked toward Matthias.

"Germany has done some good work over the years. This gun is a prime example of craftsmanship and Hitler made some admirable inroads against the Jews, but you two have nothing admirable about you. You are just deluded pests—tools of the Western jackals."

He began to level the Luger to Matthias's head, but now that Idi was blocking his daughter's line of sight there was no reason for Matthias to stay put. He dove under Idi's aim, his hands reaching down to the gaudy belt buckle that Sly had given him for a birthday present. As thorough as Aisha's Bedouin henchman had been at disarming him, she hadn't known about the belt buckle. The thumbs on both of his hands flipped hidden catches that released two punch daggers from within the belt buckle. With one of these in each fist he punched Idi Kabhul in the right and left side as the Egyptian's gun went off, the bullet skimming down his back.

Sly's hands had also gone to his belt buckle. Suddenly two miniature one-shot derringers appeared in his hands. They were dwarfed in his massive grip, but the stubby barrel of each was fitted with a .44 magnum shell. His right-handed shot killed a Bedouin before he could react. His left-handed shot skimmed Aisha's shoulder, ripping open her shirt and gashing the surface flesh.

As each gun fired, Sly let them drop. He crouched down and reached for the Bedouin's AK-47, hoping he could bring it to bear on Aisha before she peppered him with 9mm slugs from her UZI. The Bedouin's finger was caught in the trigger guard and Sly fumbled as he tried to pull the thing into firing position. A few rounds plunged through the ceiling of the tent as Sly pulled the gun loose from the cadaver's clutch.

Just as Sly figured that it was all over, Matthias interceded. Holding Idi Kabhul off the ground by means of the punch daggers which he still held in the Defense Minister's sides, Matthias staggered through Aisha's line of fire. Slugs pounded through her father's back in a crimson spray and impacted weakly against Matthias's body armor, their impetus slowed by flesh and bone.

Aisha screamed in horror. "Father! I'm sorry!"

The reality of it, Matthias knew, was that she had only speeded his demise along. He would have been dead in minutes from the wounds that Matthias had inflicted upon him.

Aisha didn't wait around to hear this explanation. As Matthias divested himself of Idi Kahbul's leaking corpse, she spun and fled through a flap in the rear of the tent.

Sly rose, holding the assault rifle firmly in his grip. "The missiles," he cried. "They said that two of them are ready. I'm betting she plans to launch them now, ahead of schedule."

Matthias retrieved his UZI and a couple of spare magazines. "Let's go."

"There's one thing that I want to say to you first," said Sly.

"What's that?"

"Man, do you have bad taste in women!"

"I couldn't have done much worse, could I?"

"No. She's like the female Hitler or something—minus the mustache, and a lot hotter, but still..."

They burst out into the night, running low, dashing from tent to tent. Gunshots had been fired and the camp was in an uproar. Men dashed from their tents to the perimeter. Muzzles flashed like strobes, lead streaming toward shadows in the hills as they let loose with thick barrages from their assault rifles.

While the phantom enemy kept the Bedouins at bay, Matthias and Sly crossed the camp without being confronted. At the east end of the camp a core of missile technicians worked, frantically trying to install the third and final warhead. A hot wind gusted across the camp, pulling wildly at the robes of a ballistics specialist as he punched in the final specifications for the second missile.

Halting behind a Jeep, Sly and Matthias caught sight of Aisha sprinting toward the mobile missile array. Spasms of yellow light rippled across her lithe form, accompanied by the sharp chug of machine gun fire. Her dark hair billowed out behind her as she darted to her destination with gazelle-like graze.

Sly had but a moment to raise his gun and shoot, but by the time he was ready to fire she had leaped beyond a screen of palms and battered Bedouin vehicles. Matthias joined him behind the Jeep a moment later.

"You recognize this Jeep?" he asked Sly.

Slowly Sly turned and examined the vehicle. He broke into a broad grin. "I sure do," he answered. "We're going to have to thank Aisha for bringing our arsenal to us."

"I know just how we can thank her," answered Matthias.

A cordon of swarthy Bedouins had formed loosely around the mobile missile launcher, hoping to keep the site secure long enough to launch at least two of the nuclear warheads. For a precious few moments the machine gun fire quieted. The Arabs milled restlessly, their nerves strung tight as they peered into the night, wondering where the attack would come from. The buffeting wind blunted their senses and the darkness was alive with the gasps and whispers of the gushing air.

The idle of the mobile missile launcher's engine slowed as the technician pulled back the lever to raise the missiles into firing position. The hydraulics hummed as the noses of the missiles rose toward the stars in the black velvet sky. Aisha anxiously stood next to the controls.

"How much longer until the missiles are ready to launch?" she asked the technician.

The technician scratched at his tangled beard. "Inshah Allah, two minutes," he answered.

Aisha's almond eyes scryed apprehensively into the dark curtains around them, and she licked at her suddenly dry lips. She knew that Matthias and Sly were out in the camp somewhere. If they would bide their time just a little longer then nothing they did would matter anymore. The third warhead had not been completely installed and would not be launched, but the other two were targeted for major Israeli cities; cities that would be utterly annihilated by the nuclear weapons. The Arab nations would rally as one and join to sweep the Jews before them, reclaiming the holy lands that were rightfully theirs.

The cones rose into position, the hydraulics slowing until the humming came to a stop. Aisha breathed a sigh of relief. They needed only moments more.

The orders to launch the missiles were on her lips when the sharp chug of a machine gun broke the peace. A Jeep came roaring out of the blackness, the orbs of its headlights still extinguished. Flame spewed forth from the mounted .50 caliber, the chunks of lead that the monstrous machine gun hurled chewing through the Bedouin ranks. The cordon fell to pieces as screaming men were eaten to bloody pulp by the Jeep-mounted gun. Sly swept the snout of the gun toward a few standing men who were scrambling for cover, some firing blasts of hot lead from their assault rifles as they ran.

Bullets rattled against the Jeep and sliced through the windshield. Matthias cranked the steering wheel of the Jeep so that it sloughed around one hundred eighty degrees, throwing up pieces of grassy turf. Secure in his harness, Sly abandoned his grip upon the mounted machine gun and reached down into the well of the Jeep.

The technician lay face down on the crimson spattered control panel. A .50 caliber slug had caught him in the spine. Aisha pulled the body away, so that it fell to the earth. The launch button was smeared with blood. She reached toward it in, what she presumed would be, the act that would avenge her father's death and make his name live forever in infamy.

The Light Anti-Tank Weapon rocket was fully extended when Sly brought it up to his shoulder. He made sure that the rear barrel of the rocket, behind his head, was pointing clear of Matthias and pulled the trigger. The Jeep was heading away from the mobile missile launcher now, bouncing across the uneven terrain at breakneck speed. Still, the .66 millimeter shell slammed home against the hull of the first missile's nuclear warhead, ripping apart its skin and detonating a portion of the ball of conventional explosives within. Wrapped around a uranium core at precise distances the explosives were linked so that when properly detonated they would explode simultaneously, imploding the fissionable material within and causing a nuclear reaction.

The strike from the LAW rocket had upset this delicate balance, blowing uranium out the side of the warhead while triggering massive eruptions of the conventional explosives contained within.

At the point of destruction, Aisha's finger was on the launch button. The impact of the explosion ripped into her, mercifully ending her life in an almost instantaneous moment of white heat that vaporized every living thing within fifty feet. The blast tore apart the missile launch truck, throwing shrapnel two hundred yards.

Superheated air rushed past Sly and Matthias, buffeting the Jeep, blistering paint and charring hair. A chunk of torn sheet metal cut through the air. Sly ducked and it severed the machine gun mount just above his head, ricocheting off the front right post of the windshield and spiraled into the black.

As Sly glanced up he saw a tumbling shape obscure the moon and fall toward them. As it dropped closer, he recognized the cylindrical shape and the pointed cone. One of the warheads had been thrown into the air by the explosion of the first warhead, its interior explosives, as of yet, undetonated.

"Gas it!" he roared to Matthias.

The Jeep leaped forward, but Sly could never be sure if it was in response to his warning. At that moment the missile dropped a dozen feet away and crumpled into the earth, rolling after the Jeep until it lost its momentum and came to a stop.

Matthias flipped the headlights of the Jeep on and roared through the twin pillars that marked the gateway to the Bedouin camp. As he rounded the corner the night sky lit up in a brilliant white, the rocket that had fell so close to them finally going up, sending out a deafening concussion force that was barely contained by the valley oasis.

Sly slumped to the floor of the Jeep in exhaustion and relief.

"Do you think we got all the warheads?" called Matthias from the driver's seat.

After a moment, Sly called back. "We got at least two of them. The third one may still be intact, but at least we know they're not going to be firing it anywhere in the near future."

"That's good to know," answered Matthias.

They drove in silence for a few minutes.

"You know, we saved millions of Israeli lives tonight. For a couple of Germans I think we did pretty good."

"Yeah," answered Matthias, but his mind was on Aisha. "Pretty good."

"Maybe there is some cosmic balance."

To the Gantlet brothers' muted senses, the drive from the Qattara Depression was oddly peaceful. The explosions had bludgeoned their eardrums and they rang dully, as if they had foolishly stood in front of the main speakers at one of their own rock concerts.

Matthias frowned. His intuition about Aisha had been wrong. She had deceived and lied to him, persuaded him to compromise his own morals, all the while hoping to achieve an objective so horrific that Matthias could never have conceived of a creature as beautiful as her even imagining it. Sometimes, the ways of the world were beyond his comprehension and though he knew that Aisha was never truly the wonderful girl that he had thought, he couldn't help but feel like a little piece of him died tonight when Sly pulled the trigger of the LAW rocket.

Groaning, Sly slowly eased himself into the passenger seat beside Matthias. "I think you owe me a steak dinner," he said.

Matthias thought of the third, still unexploded, warhead. "I'm not hungry."

Reprieve of the Achilles

Prologue: October 3, 1985

The hull of the cruise ship Achilles Lauro rose up from the shadowed waters, a dark and imposing mass against the bleak blue sky of Egypt. Of the seven hundred fifty-five passengers that were booked aboard the six-tiered ocean liner, most had disembarked to tour the ancient city of Alexandria, which had been built in 332 B.C. by the order of Alexander the Great.

Warm winds blew in from the Mediterranean Sea, across the white sand beaches and over the ramparts of the city's great stone and mortar walls. Once Alexandria had been home to the Pharos Lighthouse, one of the Seven Wonders of the World, whose great fires and massive mirror had lit the way of many seafarers. The earthquake ravaged remains of the tower had long since been pulled down and a fort constructed from the remains, but Alexandria's seaport had continued to thrive, and it was the largest in all of Egypt.

The bay lay thick with freighters, barges, and pleasure craft. At this moment, the largest of those pleasure boats was the Italian registered Achilles Lauro; 23,629 tons of steel hull that proudly thrust its star-emblazoned double smoke stacks into the air. The eighty-nine passengers who remained aboard were blissfully unaware that their pleasure cruise was about to turn into a nightmare.

Built portside, the ticket lobby was unusually quiet when Carna Fahid and her friend Erena Matenapolous purchased tickets to board the Achilles Lauro. Four olive-skinned men dressed in dark suits, and uniformly bearing attache cases, stood in line ahead of them.

"Which are your least expensive tickets for the Achilles Lauro?" asked the first of them in flawless Arabic, which was Carna's first language.

"Our cheapest tickets are lower berths," answered the balding ticket attendant. "They cost 887 US dollars."

"Why US dollars?" demanded the man in a confrontational manner.

The ticket taker shrugged. "Mostly American tourists buy tickets for these cruises. I can easily convert the cost into the currency of your choice."

"Do that," scowled the man as he tugged at his thick black beard.

"Very well," answered the ticket agent amenably. "How many tickets do you need?"

"Four," answered the hawk-nosed man who stood second in line.

The ticket agent did his calculations on a calculator, and the final figure spooled out on a coil of white tape. While the four men ponied up for the cost of the cruise, the ticket
agent began to fill in the custom's information.

"Your nationality?" he asked.

"Norwegian," said their bearded leader. He quickly produced a passport to bear out this assertion.

Carna wrinkled her nose and looked at Erena who gave her a sidelong glance from her large almond-shaped eyes. Both were struck by the improbability of the man's statement, and Carna couldn't help, but to let a little laugh slip from between her darkly-rouged lips.

The traveler at the rear turned at her brief chuckle, and arched a thick eyebrow as he stared venomously in Carna's direction.

Most men might have been taken aback by the striking appearance of the two women; Carna was an Egyptian beauty in the mold of Cleopatra, dark basalt skin and chiseled features with flowing black hair; and Erena hailed from classic Greek stock, her figure full, and her face an intriguing combination of allure and determination. This bushy-browed traveler, however, was not deterred by their appearance, and continued to frown at them until the tickets were successfully purchased, and the four travelers on their way toward the terminal and docks to board the Achilles.

Carna and Erena momentarily purchased a shared room aboard the ocean liner, and they hoisted their numerous bags and made their way toward the ship. They could see the four travelers, who looked more like business men than tourists or pleasure seekers, board the ship ahead of them.

For Carna, this trip was to be a welcome reprieve from the misery of the recent year; a chance to relax, recoup, and think about what direction she wanted to take with her life. A recent break with her father had left her outcast from her family, jobless, and without much direction. The source of the friction had originated with her step-sister, Aaliyah, and her romance with a German rock musician, whom she had insisted on marrying. Her father, of course, had been dead set against it and went to extreme lengths to ensure that it would not happen. Carna had betrayed her father's confidence to help her sister, and from that moment she had been excommunicated from the family.

Carna had met Erena several years ago on a business trip to Greece, and they had quickly become fast friends. Her infectious sense of humor had a way of pulling Carna from the foulest of moods.

"There go our Viking friends," said Erena sarcastically. "They are about as Norwegian as you or I."

"Obviously," answered Carna wryly. "The PLO[2] has given up on ever taking Israel back, and have started immigrating to Norway instead."

"Yeah, that will happen…"

They climbed the long gang plank and boarded the Achilles. A few men and women lounged around the swimming pool, while others enjoyed a game of shuffleboard.

"I could use a swim," decided Erena. "Let's find our room and change."

"Sounds good," agreed Carna. "I'm looking forward to laying around in the sun and doing practically nothing."

They wound their way through narrow hallways until they came to their accommodations. The room was small, and not exactly luxurious, but when the ship engines started, and the Achilles Lauro left its docking and set course for Port Said, where it would meet with the disembarked passengers who were touring the city, the throb of the engine was not the overbearing presence that it was in rooms built lower within the hull.

The twin smokestacks of the Achilles leaked spiral plumes against the backdrop of the brilliant blue sky as it steamed toward Cairo to make the passenger pick up, and then the ship would turn its course toward Ashdod, on the coast of Israel. Carna and Erena emerged from their cabin about fifteen minutes later, draped in fluffy white towels and wearing one piece suits that left just enough to the imagination.

Erena wasted no time in pushing the reluctant Carna into the pool, and joined her with a resounding belly flop. Three and a half hours later they left

2 *The Palestine Liberation Organization*

the pool deck of the Achilles, sun-drenched and relaxed. They entered a low hallway that intersected with several flights of stairs, some of which descended deeper into the ship, and others which ascended to the higher tiers.

As they passed one of the lower stair wells, the sound of machine gun fire boiled up from below. Carna glanced down the steps and saw one of the ship's stewards stumbling up the stairs.

"They've got guns," he gasped. "I saw them…accidentally…in their room cleaning their guns."

As the steward finished his frantic pronunciation, one of the 'Norwegians' vaulted up the steps, a Russian-made submachine gun in his hands. He waved the gun, yelling. "Into the dining room or I will kill you all!"

Carna gasped and lurched forward, temporarily out of the line of sight of the terrorist. She was about to urge Erena to make a run for their room when they saw a thick-bearded terrorist herding a group of passengers down the stairs from above. He waved his gun at them, and barked. "Into the dining room, now!"

To emphasize the point, he sprayed a half dozen bullets over their head, punching dusty holes in the superstructure of the ship. The smell of gunpowder wafted in their direction, and the cacophony of gunfire erupted elsewhere on the deck. Perhaps, realized Carna dismally, this cruise wasn't going to be as relaxing as she hoped.

Erena frowned, surprisingly calm in the face of danger. "We should have known," she said simply.

Part One:
October 4, 1985 Fort Lauderdale, Florida

The air was thick and the heat stifling. Even the perpetual downpour that pelted the Fort Lauderdale streets with fat raindrops did little to cool the atmosphere. However, the torrential rain didn't stop Sly Gantlet from enjoying a swim in the outdoor pool of his penthouse apartment. The wounds of recent battles had begun to heal, leaving behind only scars and vague aches and pains as his muscles finally responded with the strength and vigor of old. He took deep strokes, plowing a momentary furrow through the water of the kidney-shaped pool.

Water vomited from the dark clouds above, spattering around him in an effervescent haze that served to invigorate rather than detour him. He had unadulterated Gantlet blood in his veins. He was an artist and a warrior and, like his brothers, his moods were vast and varied, swinging from somber meditation and sullen dejection, to the boisterous laughter and wild behavior that had become associated with his public persona. Now he enjoyed this moment, basking in the undiluted nature that enveloped him. The moment was not to last for long.

"Sly!" intruded a voice over the intercom. "I need to talk to you right now!"

Normally, Sly would have viewed this interruption sourly, but he knew the voice as that of his wife Aaliyah, and he also knew that she was not given to overstatement. This intrusion was not to remind him to pick up some milk at the store. Aaliyah was in her ninth month of pregnancy; perhaps she was going into labor.

He hoisted himself out of the pool and into the storm, rain pelted off his broad back, rolling over the diamond-shaped scars that were evidence of the tortures he had endured for love. He swept his long blonde hair away from his rugged visage and darkly bearded chin. Treading through the puddles of warm water on the wide patio, he took a moment to look out across the city that was cloaked in misty torrents, and then toward the rolling sea. With a few more steps he opened up the sliding glass door and stepped through into the dry interior of his home. The sound of the storm was dampened, the water beating against the wall of glass in muted rage.

Every window had recently been replaced with bulletproof glass. He hadn't thought it necessary until a helicopter had hovered over penthouse patio and began spraying hot lead. One learns from the tragedies, mused Sly.

He grabbed a towel and began drying off as he crossed in front of a long row of electric and acoustic guitars that were mounted on the wall. They represented his passion, and his profession. As the rock band Gantlet, he and his brothers had sold millions of rock albums. It was an amazing accomplishment, but the opportunity had been nearly snuffed out before they had a chance to begin. His brothers' escape from East Germany had been a brutal and bloody start to their careers. That day marked their escape from repression, but it was also the first time that any of them had killed another man.

Sly found his very-pregnant wife pacing in the sunken living room, clutching a portable phone in her white-knuckled grip. Several black leather couches and a couple matching side tables were all that furnished the sparsely decorated room. A guitar amplifier dominated the center of the room, with a Fender Stratocaster leaning against it.

Aaliyah nervously pushed back falling locks of long glossy brown hair and bit at her crimson lower lip. Her green eyes shone with frantic intensity, from beneath thick lashes.

Sly slipped out of his wet swim trunks and into some dry jeans. "What's going on?" he asked.

"It's Carna," answered Aaliyah.

Sly cocked his head. "Your sister? I thought that she was on her way here, so that I could set her up with that job at the record label."

"Yes, but first she was going on a two-week cruise with her friend Erena."

He shrugged. "I told the label about her qualifications. They were willing to wait a few weeks to see her."

"It's not the job," said Aaliyah, as she threw her phone on the couch. "It's the cruise ship she's on. The Achilles Lauro has been hijacked."

Sly pulled a tank top on over his barrel chest, his eyes narrowing as the gravity of the situation began to sink in. Instantly he began to gather information so he could make an analysis. "Where is the cruise ship? Who are the terrorists? Do we have any idea how many of them are there? What are their demands?"

Aaliyah just shook her head. "I don't know much else than what I've told you."

The rock guitarist could see the worry in her face and moved to her side, putting his arm around her and leading her to a couch. "Don't worry about things. I want you to take it easy, and let me do the worrying. I'm going to head over to Otto's and see if he can pull together some more information on the hijacking."

She nodded and a tear trickled down her cheek. Sly kissed her goodbye and walked toward the east side of the apartment. The penthouse covered the entire top floor of the building. At one time it had been the home base of all five of the Gantlet brothers, but as close as they were, they already spent an incredible amount of time together on tour and, needing some private time, everyone had eventually moved into homes of their own.

Taking a back hallway, Sly entered a game room. The walls were lined with framed tour posters and a full-sized pool table and foosball were the central furnishings. On the right side of the room a large bookcase dominated the wall. It was loaded with hundreds of cassette tapes, reel to reel recording masters, a dusty Grammy award, and a variety of books and magazines. Sly lifted a hinged piece of oak trim, and pressed a small stud beneath. This released a locking mechanism and Sly slid the book case back into the wall. Behind it was a huge double-door combination safe. He quickly dialed in the appropriate number sequence and opened the thick doors, revealing a weapons cache that would rival the armament of some small countries—anti-tank weaponry, grenade launchers, machine guns, rifles, pistols, and revolvers were racked along the walls. Sly walked into the safe and picked out an Israeli made UZI miniature submachine gun. He threw this into a gym bag, along with ten ammunition magazines that held forty rounds apiece.

For his personal armament, he slipped on a double shoulder harness. The Desert Eagle .44 magnum went on his right and the .454 Cassul revolver went on his left. To conceal these, Sly slipped on a Kevlar-lined leather jacket. An average man would accuse Sly of rampant paranoia, but since a young age he had found that staying armed was the equivalent of staying alive. He and his brothers attracted trouble like dung attracted flies.

After sealing the safe and sliding the book case back into place, Sly let himself through a steel door into an undecorated chamber. The floor consisted of the original cement slab, and the walls had never been framed in, the beams laying still exposed. A variety of tool chests were stored against one wall, and in the center of the room a battered Ferrari forlornly rested, with two tires deflated, and bullet holes stitching an ugly pattern along its cherry red side.

Sly ignored the car and went straight to the freight elevator, which was long enough to fit a full-size vehicle. This was a private elevator shaft that had cost a bundle to install. Sly pressed a button and began the descent to the sub-basement. Thirty-five floors later he stepped into a pitch black chamber. As he entered, motion sensors triggered bright lights that flickered overhead, revealing a dozen gleaming vehicles. Some belonged to Sly, and some to his brothers; all were high-end sports cars.

Choosing a yellow Corvette that was modified for higher speed and improved cornering, Sly set his gym bag in the passenger side foot well and slid behind the wheel. He pressed in a digital code on a small transmitter clipped to the sun visor, and a reinforced garage door opened up ahead, rain spitting through the opening as it rose.

In a moment the Corvette had ascended the rampway, and was on the water-drenched Fort Lauderdale streets. Traffic was light in the torrential downpour, and Sly sped along the slick boulevards, rows of flanking palm trees bending in the wind. The wet roads made it tricky to maintain control of the Corvette at the excessive speed which Sly was traveling, but he managed to rein in the fiberglass behemoth, and pulled up to a dilapidated warehouse at the edge of the city about seven minutes later. A massive transmitting tower rose from behind the warehouse, its steel frame stabbing into the sky. Also at odds with the ramshackle appearance of the building were the satellite dishes and microwave transmitters mounted atop the weathered roof.

The streets were empty here, few braving the storm. Sly ducked from the car, let himself in through a chainlink gate, and sprinted to the edge of the warehouse. Under the eaves he had some protection from the elements, and he followed the splintered wood siding of the warehouse around to the back, where he mounted an unsteady stairway that led to a door with blistered and peeling brown paint.

Before he could knock, a man nearly as tall as Sly opened the door. Besides height, there were other similarities between the men. The man at the door possessed the same prominent cheekbones, and the same piercing blue eyes.

"Otto!" greeted Sly, clasping hands with him in an overhand grip. "You must have seen me coming."

Moving his lanky frame back a few steps, Otto motioned Sly into the dim interior of the loft. "The storm is messing with my motion detectors, so I had to temporarily shut them down, but I saw you coming on the monitors."

Sly closed the door and shut out the storm. The air within the loft smelled faintly of creosote; some remnant from the timber that had been stored in the warehouse below in days past. Several twenty-four pin printers chattered away as they transcribed information that Otto was feeding them from a massive supercomputer that had been discarded by the government. The loft was a veritable hive of computer and electronics equipment. Wires were nested and strung in a bewildering maze that only Otto could track. A half dozen monitors were mounted from the ceiling that showed various views of the puddled streets and courtyard outside.

The back part of the loft was filled with metal racks stuffed with reel to reel tapes. Even now, Otto was taping several frequencies that he had picked up and found interesting. When he wasn't playing the bass guitar, Otto was an information junkie. He scanned the airwaves extracting tidbits of information meant only for other people's ears. When he came across a scrambled communication, he put his supercomputer to work to see if he could crack the code. Mostly he did it just for the thrill of it, but occasionally the information that he uncovered proved extremely valuable.

"So, are we going to get back into the recording studio, or what?" asked Otto.

"We're going to have to put that on hold for a while," said Sly. "We've got a situation on our hands."

A nasty grin spread across Otto's unshaven face. "Should I get my gun?

"Maybe later. What have you heard about the hijacking of the Achilles Lauro?"

Otto thoughtfully bit the inside of his mouth as he wondered why Sly had taken an interest in the event. "Quite a bit. A contact of mine in Egypt is monitoring the negotiations and relaying the translation to me. Something very fishy is going on there."

"What do you know about the terrorists?"

"Looks like a PLO offshoot called Force 19—a bunch of commandos that Arafat organized about three years ago. They're specifically trained for maximum casualty terrorist attacks. They were linked with the murder of two dead Israeli seaman that were found in Barcelona a couple of weeks ago, and about two weeks before that they were responsible for wasting three Israeli civilians taking a cruise on their yacht."

Sly furrowed his brow. He'd previously had encounters with the Palestine Liberation Organization, and plots hatched by their leader Yasser Arafat. Arafat's primary goal was to retake the nearly 8,000 square miles of the once Arab-inhabited territory that had been ceded to the Jewish people by force of a United Nations' resolution. Yasser was willing to go to any length to accomplish his aims. "How many of them are there?"

"At this point, it looks like there are only four of them. They turned the ship toward Syria last night, but Syria wouldn't let them land. They went back to Egypt and demanded that Israel release fifty political terrorists or they would start killing hostages."

"Have they killed any yet?"

"It's hard to say," said Otto. "They are telling Egyptian authorities that no one has been harmed, but I've heard there was a transmission to Syrian authorities where the terrorists claim to have shot at least one of the passengers. I haven't heard the actual transmission though, or seen a transcription of it. Supposedly a Lebanese radio station intercepted the signal."

"Aaliyah's sister, Carna, is aboard the Achilles. I want to see if we can do something to take out those terrorists."

Otto raised his eyebrows. He vividly remembered his brief introduction to Carna. She was a very attractive woman. "I'm on board," he said. "But we need to be very careful. Abul Abbas has conveniently contacted the Egyptian government and offered to do the negotiations with the terrorists."

Sly nearly choked. "The jackal?"

"Wanted by the US for terrorist acts. The one and the same."

"But he's about as tight with Arafat as anyone."

"Of course, Arafat is claiming complete ignorance," said Otto, "but Abbas's involvement leads me to believe that they are up to something bigger or more devious than just a hijacking."

"Maybe," said Sly. "If we're forced to retake the ship, it's going to take more than one of us to pull it off—at least, if we want to do it without the hostages getting injured. Can you get a hold of everybody?"

Otto shook his head. "Fritz and Matthias went back into East Germany to help extract Uncle Nickel. I'm not sure when they'll be back. I know that Mitz is in town coordinating a photo shoot for that clothing line that he's launching."

"See if you can pull him away from all those beautiful models. I'll meet you at the airport in an hour."

An hour and a half later the storm had slackened little. Rain pounded fiercely on the outer shell of the Concorde jet that sat positioned on a side runway of the Fort Lauderdale airport. As its engines warmed, an old paneled truck pulled up alongside the jet. Immediately a man with a curly mane of blonde hair leaped from the driver's seat and went around to the rear of the truck. Even amidst the downpour he moved with a confident swagger, and he wore a self-assured smirk upon his smooth shaven face. To those he met in passing he came across as cocky, aloof, and supercilious. He allowed only a select few to glimpse the person beneath. As drummer for the band Gantlet, Mitko—nicknamed Mitz when just a youth—was the backbone, the foundation upon which all the music was built. As a brother, he was always there when one of his four siblings needed a helping hand, so when Otto had apprised him of the situation, he had quickly handed over his duties to a trusted assistant and came running.

Mitz gave the door a shove, and it rattled upward. Inside, the rain thrummed against the tin roof, and he began shoving a variety of Otto's radio and communications equipment into the back of the truck. Otto came around from the passenger side, his shoulder-length black hair already plastered to his skull by the precipitation.

"You look like a drowned rat," said Mitz.

"…Said one rodent to the other," rejoined Otto. "Shove that transmitter over here."

Mitz pushed over the unit, and Otto easily lifted the heavy transmitter. Bending over it to shield it from the rain, he quickly pushed it into the cargo hold of the airplane. In a few minutes they had the contents of the truck transferred to the Concorde and tightly strapped down within the hold.

As the two brothers mounted the stairs, the front hatch of the plane popped open and Sly's massive frame filled the open space.

"Where were you?" asked Mitz. "We could have used your help out here."

"I was just saying goodbye to Aaliyah," answered Sly.

Now, between the daggers of rain, they could see Aaliyah standing behind Sly. Mitz saw the swell of her belly, and was reminded that the time was soon coming when a new life would be added to the Gantlet clan.

"How much longer?" he asked Aaliyah as he entered the plush interior of the plane.

She smiled, and Mitz could see why Sly had fallen head over heels in love with her.

"The doctor says seven more days," she answered. Her face quickly turned from the glowing pride of impending motherhood to somber meditation as she turned to Sly. "I'm really sorry to make you and your brothers do this," she said.

Mitz shook his head. "Hey, what are families for?"

"Ours just tends to be a little more bloodthirsty than most," commented Otto wryly, as he entered behind Mitz and stood in the vestibule of the aircraft.

"Make sure that he comes back to me in one piece," said Aaliyah softly, directing her request to Mitz and Otto.

"We'll do that," said Mitz with a cocky sincerity that few would doubt.

"Give Aaliyah the truck keys. She'll drop it off at the hangar, before heading home."

Mitz handed the keys to Aaliyah, and she pulled her rain coat around her tightly as she emerged into the storm and descended the stairs. Sly slipped back into the cockpit and ensconced himself in the pilot's seat. Though his father, Jacobbe Gantlet, had been an envoy to the US from East Germany, he had defected, and Sly had been born in the United States. He had served time in the US Navy as a fighter pilot, where his German appellation, Slatko, had been quickly changed to Sly by his fellow pilots. An unfortunate disagreement with a superior had led to fisticuffs, and Sly was dishonorably discharged, narrowly avoiding criminal charges.

The military was able to take away Sly's rank, but they had left him with a few valuable skills. Piloting was one of them. Receiving clearance from the tower, he taxied the plane onto the runway and began to power up the engines.

Though Mitz had no idea how to pilot a plane, he dropped his weight into the copilot's seat. Otto wandered up from the rear of the plane.

"I still don't believe it," said the youngest Gantlet. "You've got a hot tub back there—on a supersonic jet."

Sly chuckled. "The former owner was fairly extravagant."

"Was…is the proper term. I still can't believe the government let you keep the plane after you capped the owner. Usually they seize every asset they can get their hands on."

"The government and I have come to a mutual agreement," said Sly. "I don't kill anybody who doesn't need killing, and they leave me alone."

"…And we don't divulge information about certain government activities," added Otto. "I think that it is called blackmail."

Mitz waved a hand in a dismissive gesture and leaned back in his chair. "Whatever it is, it works in our favor. I'm all for it."

Otto strapped down and the hawk-nosed jet leaped into the slate sky, slicing through the bilious gray clouds that dumped their life blood upon the metropolis below. Lightning forked from the earth and leaped to the sky as a cold front moved in. The Concorde reached altitude, bursting through the sound barrier in a raucous boom that rivaled that of the thunder.

Captain De Rosa shuddered as the bearded Palestinian hijacker reappeared in the doorway of the Achilles Lauro's wheel house, waving the dark muzzle of his Soviet made Kalashnikov assault rifle. The waters off the Syrian coast were dark, but the bright lights of the civilization along the coast were clearly visible, yet unattainable to the hijackers.

At Syria's refusal to allow them entrance to port, the terrorist leader cursed foully and momentarily stepped outside the cabin to inform his second in command of the situation. Captain De Rosa understood a smattering of Arabic, and distinctly heard the words that followed. "Go execute the Jew! If that doesn't work we'll start shooting one hostage an hour."

Now the leader spoke in broken Italian to the captain, who sweated nervously, regretting ever choosing the naval industry as his profession. "Go to the place of eating," commanded the terrorist. "We don't have need of you."

Mopping at his bald head, Captain De Rosa complied with the terrorist's orders and ducked from the cabin, heading toward the cafeteria several levels below. As De Rosa left, one of the terrorist kneeled to the ground and opened up his attache case, revealing a variety of electronic equipment. With planned precision, he set to work on the ship's sonar.

As he descended toward the cafeteria, Captain De Rosa wondered if the Palestinians had meant they permanently didn't need him, or if they didn't require him at this moment. If the latter was true, that meant he was as dispensable as any of the other hostages aboard the ship.

He looked at the shoreline that beckoned, still several miles away, and briefly considered the idea of leaping from the Achilles and making a swim for it. He quickly passed on this thought. The swim was long and there was no guarantee he would win the battle with the tides. He was the captain of the Achilles Lauro, which meant he was morally obligated to ride out whatever threat or danger the Achilles Lauro and its passengers might face.

Hearing a scared cry from below, he stopped, peering over the railing to get a better view of the lower decks which were bathed in pools of luminescence from the ship's lights. He saw two of the terrorists emerge from the walkway near the cafeteria. One of the hijackers pushed a wheelchair, graced by a recumbent and bulky form. Captain De Rosa immediately recognized the man in the chair as Leon Klinghoffer, an American tourist. De Rosa had met Leon, a former New York business man who had been paralyzed by a stroke years earlier, and his wife Marilyn when they had boarded the Achilles Lauro. Leon was a Jew and he was an American, the perfect target for the Palestinian terrorists to vent their hatred on.

Captain De Rosa sucked in his breath, wishing that he could avert his eyes from the horrible scene that was unfolding below him.

The terrorists walked the crippled man up to the railing at ship side. Slowly, to heighten the terror that the man must be feeling, the hijacker at the left raised his Kalashnikov automatic rifle to Leon Klinghoffer's head. Leon was helpless. Maybe at one time, when he was younger, before the stroke had disabled him, he could have put up resistance, maybe even had a small chance against the terrorists; but now all he could do was bravely raise his head in token defiance.

The terrorist sneered, arching a bushy eyebrow as he pulled the trigger. The Kalashnikov belched lead, blood spattering against the feet and shoes of the killer, and the shots echoed eerily against the walls and bulkheads of the Achilles Lauro. The killer and his accomplice hoisted the bulky corpse of the retired New York business man from his wheelchair and, grunting, pushed him over the rail. The body plunged into the caliginous waters, followed quickly by the metal frame of the wheelchair.

Their dirty handiwork done, the terrorists turned with callous laughs on their lips and blood on their hands. Only now did Captain De Rosa turn away from the cold-blooded execution that he had witnessed. He ducked low, worried that the terrorists might see him and know that he had witnessed the horrific act. De Rosa sat in the shadows, breathing deeply to calm his nerves, then he turned and scrambled toward the dining room on Level A. If he could beat the terrorists there, they would not know that he had seen their cowardly murder.

They sliced across the turbulent heavens and over the heaving waves of the North Atlantic Ocean below, sticking to the 25th Longitude, only altering their course as they reached the verdant coasts of the African continent. To avoid crossing through Libyan airspace, they used the Mediterranean Ocean as an aisleway to the Egyptian coastal city of Said.

Here, Sly brought the plane in for a landing at a small private strip, which lay inland some ways. The owner of this private strip had, for copious quantities of cash, agreed to conceal their identity and falsify the necessary paperwork so they could avoid the unwelcome scrutiny of the Egyptian customs officials. Fortunately for the Gantlets, the Egyptian government was a system that had grown accustomed to corruption. Government officials expected to receive bribes to do the most commonplace of tasks, for which they were already receiving a wage to perform. Palms were greased, and a covert entry into the country was made possible.

Iron Camel drummer Abn Fahd stood next to his thirty-year-old flat bed truck as he waited for Sly and his two brothers among the cactus-studded desert land outside the beige stucco shack that served as the terminal for this pot-holed and cracked runway. He wasn't particularly tall, but his thick chest strained at the confines of his tank top, and his muscular arms would be considered impressive even by bodybuilding standards. His face was square-jawed and swarthy, studded with stubble that couldn't conceal his handsome features.

He greeted the three Gantlet brothers warmly when they emerged from the terminal after doing business with the proprietor.

"Good to see you," he said, clapping Sly on the back

"Likewise," said Sly. "Thanks for driving in from Cairo to pick us up. We would have rented a truck, but we needed to keep a low profile."

"I'm beginning to understand how things work with you Gantlet brothers."

"Speaking of which, these are my brothers, Otto and Mitz," introduced Sly.

Mitz smiled amiably without proffering a hand. Otto nodded, morosely noted the open bed of the truck. "Got any rope?" he asked.

"In the cab," said Abn. "We can tie down your gear so that it doesn't go anywhere. The roads between here and Said aren't much to brag about."

Between the four of them they had Otto's equipment safely secured on the dusty wood bed of the truck in short order. They packed themselves into the primer-spotted cab, and the engine coughed to life at Abn's persistent coaxing.

Ninety miles northeast of the gleaming modern skyscrapers of Cairo lay Port Said, resting at the junction of the turbulent Mediterranean Sea and the sun-dappled waters of the Suez Canal. Green spires rose from sphere-topped towers among the thriving metropolis that had become the gateway between the East and the West. Abn's truck rattled and jolted over uneven pavement as they closed in on the city. Finally the streets smoothed as they entered the boundaries of Said, and Abn drove them through a circuitous series of back roads.

"How are things going with Iron Camel?" asked Sly. "Did you guys ditch your lead singer yet?"

Abn winced. "It never came to that. His ego got so big that he decided to fire us…the rest of the band, that is."

"We have that problem with Matthias, too," said Otto with a tone of mock seriousness. "Every once and awhile we have to gang up on him and pound a little humility back into him."

Abn laughed. "I've seen him fight. If it were anyone else, but his own brothers, who told me that, I would have said that they were full of camel dung."

"Have you found another vocalist yet?" asked Sly. He peered through the dusty window of the truck at the glut of small European cars that lined the sides of the streets.

Abn Fahd shook his head derisively. "The whole band came apart at the seams. It was almost as though the only thing holding us together was our singer's giant ego. Once that was gone, we couldn't even play together. Finally I gave up on trying to drag everyone to practices."

"I know of some bands that need a good drummer. You willing to relocate?"

"You know it," answered Abn.

Mitz was sitting tightly against the door of the truck, and he glanced across Otto to give Sly a sharp look. "You're not trying to replace me or something are you?"

"If Mom hadn't made me promise to watch out for you, you would have been gone years ago," joked Sly.

"You see what we drummers have to put up with?" said Mitz.

Abn laughed, and then continued with his train of thought. "The big thing in Egypt is disco, which I can play—but who wants to? It's tough for a rock drummer to make a living."

"We've been there," said Otto. "When we first came to the States we had to sell our extra kidneys to buy food."

Abn gave Gantlet's bass player a sidelong glance, not sure whether to take this at face value or not.

Otto continued undeterred. "Originally there were six Gantlet brothers, but we had to sell one on the black market to buy musical instruments."

"I see," said Abn Fahd. "You are joking with me." He turned the truck down a side street and pulled up to the curb next to a cracked stucco building that had once been painted with a coat of whitewash. Now it was a dismal gray tone that blended with the fragmented cement stairs that led up through a dusty archway. The iron gateway was open and unlocked and several men sat chewing on bitter khat leaves. One of them spit out some green saliva onto the sidewalk and grinned, showing a mouthful of rotting teeth that had, over the years, been eaten away by the narcotic plant.

His eyes shone brightly as he reached into his sash and produced a bundle of the leafy drug. "Would you like to purchase some Khat?" he asked Abn, as the drummer passed by, carrying a load of equipment from the back of the truck.

Abn shook his head, and continued on into the shaded recesses of the archway, where he found a cement stairwell that curled upward to the second level of the building.

Sly, who spoke fluent Arabic, halted and spoke to the man for a moment. "We don't need khat," he explained, "but we will pay you well if you watch the streets for us. If you see any suspicious folks hanging about—whom you don't know—report it to us at the last door on the second level."

The man introduced himself as Mukhlis, and when Sly dropped a folded hundred dollar bill into his wrinkled palm, he readily agreed to help. "If you watch well, there will be much more of that for you," finished Sly.

Carna cradled the grenade tightly in her hand, the rest of the hostages gathered in a close circle around her. Erena sat with her bare back against hers, and she could see the fear in the faces of the men, women, and children around her; sense it in the air—so palpable that it was nearly a tangible thing.

The dining room of Deck A had become a prison. Heavy tables had been unbolted from the tile flooring and moved aside, forming a clear area to gather the hostages. On the starboard side of the Achilles, the room was lined with a wall of tinted glass that overlooked the sun-capped Mediterranean waves. Inside, however, the terrorists' Kalashnikovs cast ominous shadows against the floors. All joy and hope was consumed, leaving only abject terror in their place.

Being Egyptian born and bred, Carna could easily muster some sympathy for the Palestinian cause. She, too, felt that the Israelis had unlawfully encroached on Arab territory, yet she couldn't comprehend the point of hijacking a pleasure boat and terrorizing the passengers.

The Palestinians enjoyed a game with some of the women in the group, pulling the pin from a grenade and forcing them to hold it for hours on end. As long as the mantle of the grenade was gripped tightly, the fuse of the grenade would not be triggered. But if, through a moment of inattention, a slip, or a lapse into sleep, one's grip was loosened, the grenade would explode—its metal jacket bursting into a thousand pieces, to rip through the other hostages who had been forced to gather tightly around the deadly explosive.

The hijackers took a perverse delight in playing these potentially deadly games. Occasionally one would fire a burst from his Kalashnikov and into the ceiling overhead, to see if he could frighten some elderly prisoner into having a heart attack, or to see if someone would drop the grenade from their hand and incinerate their fellow hostages. The Europeans had been separated from the possible Jews and the American tourists and given slightly better treatment. Even though Carna was Egyptian and Erena Greek, because of their defiant attitudes they had been singled out to join the American group.

Erena was now regretting her defiant attitude. Though it had served her well in many situations, it had backfired on her this time, and had probably been the reason that Carna had also been assigned to sit with the group of Americans and hold the live grenade in her hand.

Carna, however, was not content to play the games of the terrorists. She watched them carefully. They were casual with their weapons, only training them on the hostages when they hoped to induce terror. Often they held them across their laps, or if they were walking, up over their shoulders. They were confident that the hostages were too scared to put up a resistance.

Though Carna had received very little formal training with weaponry, her father was an Egyptian warlord, and she had been exposed to weapons of many varieties—including grenades. By examining the markings on the grenade which she held, she ascertained that it was of Russian make, but that still didn't tell her what she needed to know. If the pin was in place, the core of the grenade could be unscrewed and a marking on the fuse would reveal how long, once triggered, the grenade would last before detonating. She knew for a fact that some grenades were made for setting booby traps, and that there was a zero second delay before the explosion. There was a good chance that she held a grenade that was timed differently, but just how long a fuse, she couldn't say.

Carna waited until three terrorists had grouped in the doorway of the dining room, smoking cigarettes and laughing. The leader of the group had previously left with the captain to turn the ship back toward Egypt…perhaps to find refuge there. For a moment the terrorists' eyes wandered toward the sea, and Carna lifted the grenade, hurling it toward the group. It bounced against the tiling of the floor and slid among the leather shoes of the Palestinians.

"Get down!" yelled Carna as she pushed down the heads of the nearest hostages.

The startled Palestinians cried out, one of them reached down and plucked up the grenade. The others scattered as he stepped through the door, and hurled the bomb out over the railing of the A Deck, over the glistening pools, and into the sparkling Mediterranean waters. The waves swallowed up the grenade, and something thumped beneath the ocean, the massive Achilles Lauro shuddering slightly, and water spraying in a massive gout that moistened the ship's great hull.

Once the shock of their near death faded, the terrorists began cursing profanely in a variety of languages. The man with the bushy eyebrows stormed over and picked Carna up, only to smash her savagely in the mouth with his fist. She went down, crimson spattering the tile floor, her mouth filling with blood.

He cursed at her wildly, but Carna did not dare look up. Glaring at Erena, he jabbed a finger at her and her Egyptian friend. "We have something special planned for you two," he spat. Then he looked directly at Carna. "Something we save especially for those who would betray their own kind."

Away from the window, across the dirty wood floors of the small apartment, Otto sat in a cubby hole of electronic and radio equipment that nearly concealed him from view. He worked the controls, constantly scanning the frequencies. Headphones concealed a large part of his skull, and the total concentration that consumed him left him nearly oblivious to his outside surroundings. Still, Abn Fahd noticed the 9 millimeter Glock pistol that rested on the table within easy reach of the youngest Gantlet brother. Though he was an information junkie absorbed in the wavelengths that fed him abstract bits of knowledge, he was not ignorant to the fact that the outside world might intrude in the most violent of ways.

Suddenly Otto grinned. "I've got it," he said. "Abul Abbas is in town, and the negotiations are about to begin. I'm going to need a translator, though. I picked up the name, but the language is like Arabic to me."

"That's because it is Arabic," offered Abn Fahd, picking up a pair of headphones.

Sly snatched them away. "He knows that," said Sly ruefully. "It was just a bad joke." He motioned to Otto. "Put the conversation on the speakers."

Otto slapped a button and thick Arabic began streaming out from the cones of several battered speaker boxes.

An unnamed intermediary handed the conversation over to the recently arrived Abul Abbas. "Maged and Manoli," he said in a rumbling bass voice.

Sly frowned. "What's he talking about?"

Abn shrugged. "He's got to be using a password or something."

The Egyptian drummer's surmise was instantly verified when the terrorists responded. "Commander. We are happy to hear your voice."

"Listen carefully," ordered Abul Abbas. "You will release the hostages, and the boat will continue on its way. All is not lost. I will ask for safe passage from the country in return for the safety of the hostages. A boat that is marked so that you will recognize it will come out to meet the Achilles Lauro. You will get on it, and be escorted to safety."

"We shall obey," came the terrorist's reply.

The negotiations ended almost as quickly as they had begun and the airwaves were reduced to static surges.

"You think that they switched frequencies?" asked Sly.

After Sly did a complete translation, Otto shrugged doubtfully. "It sounds pretty cut and dried, but Abbas is still going to have to get a half dozen ambassadors to sign off on the deal. If they don't like it, then we're in a holding pattern."

"I know just the thing to break them out of that pattern," mused Sly, "but it will take a little time to get things arranged."

The morning sun rose to its zenith in the sky. Otto continued to monitor the airwaves, but was able to come up with little of substance. Sly made some calls to high ranking officials in the Egyptian government that he had done favors for in the past, but he couldn't seem to get into contact with any of them successfully, and what little information he could glean indicated that the hostage release was being held up because of lack of approval from the ambassadors for West Germany, Italy, and the United States. Evidently there was a concern about whether the hostages were safe or not. If any of the hostages had been harmed, there was a general consensus that the hijackers should be prosecuted.

Sly was able to extract this much information from the people with whom he talked. If Otto had been correct about the transmission intercepted by the Syrian radio station, then the hijackers had killed, and they weren't going to be granted free passage anywhere, unless they could convince three governments that they hadn't harmed anybody.

Suddenly there was a rapping at the door. Sly jumped to his feet and stepped toward the brick wall. He drew aside a stained and dirty cloth that served as a curtain and discreetly peered through the grime-smeared window pane that it covered. He caught sight of Mukhlis's wrinkled profile.

"I see something," said Mukhlis urgently.

Standing to the side, Sly opened the door and let Mukhlis step through the arch, his long galabiyah shirt flapping wildly, and his tan-colored Islamic gown sweeping the ground. "Two foreigners," he said. "They have long hair like wildmen and wear leather skins."

Sly shoved another hundred dollar bill into Mukhlis palm. "Get lost," he said, using the Arabic equivalent.

Mukhlis professed his thankfulness, but wasted no time in getting clear of what he figured might be a dangerous situation. He scooted down the walkway, and headed for a back stairwell that would avoid the newcomers of which he had warned the Gantlets.

Mitz's hands went to the two holsters, one mounted beneath each arm. He slid two Colt Double Eagle .45s out, holding one in each fist. Meanwhile Otto reached across and casually flicked the safety to his Glock, spun in his chair and watched the only entrance to the room.

Abn was weaponless, and somewhat at a loss. He wisely backed out of the main firing line. The clap of footsteps climbed the mortar stairs and resounded in the enclosed walls of the staircase. Softer now, the tread approached the door of the small flat, which Abn had procured for the Gantlet brothers.

Mitz could hear the footsteps halt in front of the door, and he leveled the five-inch barrels of his twin .45s in anticipation. Sly reached over to the doorknob and flipped the door open. There was a sudden flurry of pulled slides and drawn weapons as the two intruders at the door, and the men within the room, burst into action with lightning speed and practiced precision.

The taller of the two men at the door wore a brown mustache, wild brown hair flailing out behind him as a .454 Cassul revolver jumped into his hand. The second man was a head shorter, curly brown hair falling to his broad shoulders, sharp iron eyes focusing behind a pair of round-lensed sunglasses. His hand leaped beneath his jacket and when it came out again, he held a grayed Colt Anaconda .44 magnum in his ruddy grip.

Sly recognized the guns as quickly as he recognized the intruders. With relief, everyone began putting their weapons away as the two newcomers were recognized as Matthias and Fritz, the remaining two Gantlet brothers.

Putting his gun back into his holster, Sly laughed out loud. "What brings the two of you here?"

Fritz, the oldest of the Gantlet brothers, scratched at the cleft in his chin. "We got a message from Otto. Once we got out of East Germany, we made a beeline for Said."

"How did you get in?" asked Sly.

"I made a call to Moustapha," answered Matthias, referring to a high-level advisor to Egyptian President Mubarek's cabinet. "I reminded him that if President Mubarek wanted to keep doing his balancing act between the Arab hard-liners and the West, that there were certain things he would want us to keep quiet about."

Mitz sat down on a wooden chair and leaned back against the brick wall. "Very bold," he said appreciatively. "We used the back door approach and sneaked in."

Fritz shut the only door to the flat. "It could work for us, or it could work against us. We didn't have a lot of time to set up anything covert."

"Mubarek could do one of a couple things," analyzed Sly. "He could co-operate with us and throw us a few tidbits of information, or he could decide that we're loose cannons and have us killed."

"I'm voting for the cooperation option," said Otto as he unwrapped a candy bar.

"How is Uncle Nickel doing?" asked Mitz.

Matthias threw a bag in the corner, and slumped down beside it, wincing as his back made contact with the brick wall. Several emotions played across his face, and it looked as though he were struggling with his words.

Finally, Fritz broke in. "It was a lure to get us back into communist territory. We've made some nasty enemies in East Germany."

"That doesn't answer my question," said Mitz. "How's Uncle Nickel doing?"

"He was in on the plot to trap us," croaked Matthias.

"Uncle Nickel shot Matthias right in the back. We never saw it coming. If Matthias hadn't been wearing his Kevlar-lined jacket, the bullet would have cut him in half."

"I had to shoot him," said Matthias quietly. "I mean, I remember him coming over and bringing us taffy when we were kids. I used to love him…"

A long moment of somber silence settled over the group like a dismal fog. Otto finally broke the quietude. "What a scum."

He was about to pronounce a further judgment, when he raised his hand in a signal for silence. "I'm getting something further," he said, and he switched the transmission to the speakers so that they all could hear.

Captain De Rosa sweated profusely as he answered the questions that were transmitted from shore, the hard muzzle of a Kalashnikov rifle pressed up against the back of his skull. Abul Abbas spoke again, the lower registers of his voice almost lost in the tinny speakers aboard the Achilles Lauro.

"The representatives of the U.S, West Germany, and Italy need to be assured that none of the hostages have been harmed. If they can be assured that this is the case, you will be guaranteed safe passage from the country," repeated Abbas.

"All the passengers are safe and unharmed," lied Captain DeRosa.

An hour later a battered tugboat chugged out toward the Achilles Lauro. Its black hull had seen better days, and its deck was littered with detritus. Two PLO intermediaries stood in the wheel cabin, while the tug's captain guided the boat up next to the Achilles Lauro. The tug was dwarfed by the cruiseliner's massive hull, an almost insignificant protrusion from the sea. Laughing and jeering, the hijackers threw down a rope ladder, and clambered into their escape craft, their assault rifles dangling from worn shoulder straps. They greeted the two PLO men aboard the tug with hearty embraces.

In moments the tug turned and cut a wake toward shore, leaving behind four bobbing forms that went unnoticed in the froth of the waves. Fritz swam to the edge of the ship, dragging a waterproof equipment bag that was supported in the water by a dull gray inflatable buoy. From a side pocket he withdrew a pair of rubber suction cups which he strapped to his wrists. He pushed these against the hull of the Achilles, forming a tight seal and suction. Using entirely the strength of his upper body, he slowly worked his way up the face of the metal hull, releasing the suction of one cup, while holding his weight with his other hand.

Finally he reached the dangling ladder that the hijackers had used to escape to the tug. He climbed up onto this, carefully knotted a rope around the last rung and dropped it to his three brothers who remained in the water.

After tying the rope to the equipment bag, Sly came next, walking along the hull as he pulled himself upward with muscle-knotted arms. Otto and Mitz agilely followed and soon they found themselves aboard the deserted lower deck of the Achilles Lauro, hunched over their equipment bag while Sly and Fritz stood watch with drawn pistols.

Once Otto and Mitz disseminated the submachine guns and ammunition, Fritz removed a Japanese katana from the equipment and strapped it to his back so that the hilt of the blade protruded past his shoulder.

Mitz raised an eyebrow. "You plan on using that thing?"

Fritz smiled. "You never know when the occasion might arise." He nodded toward Sly, who was strapping on a well-oiled bullwhip. "Besides, I'm not the only eccentric one here."

Fritz took the command which, as oldest brother, he assumed was his right and responsibility. "Otto and I will start by finding the wheelhouse and the captain. We'll see if he knows where Carna might be. If you find out anything, or run into any trouble contact us on our headsets." For emphasis he tapped the headphones and microphone that he wore, identical to the ones with which each of his brothers were equipped.

"Chances are that we're in no danger," growled Sly. "But maybe the terrorists left some surprises behind."

Mitz watched the tug as it shrank toward the shoreline of Said. "I can't believe we let those guys go. They didn't even know we were in the hold. We could have killed them to a man."

"Matthias promised the Egyptians we wouldn't kill them inside the borders of the country," said Fritz. "President Mubarek is trying to look good to both the Palestinians and the United States. If he promises the hijackers safe passage out of the country, and then we slaughter them right off the boat, he gets a whole bunch of his Arab neighbors up in arms over it."

"Mitz and I are going to look for Carna," said Sly as he headed toward the back of the boat. "Be seeing you."

In dripping t-shirts and tank tops, Otto and Fritz crept up white-painted flights of metal stairs, crossing by glistening swimming pools flanked by rows of empty lounge chairs. The Achilles Lauro was anchored firmly, but it seemed as though a ghost ship.

"Let's hope we find the hostages healthy and alive," said Fritz.

Looking out across the barren decks, Otto had to agree with his brother. "It's almost like all eighty-nine hostages disappeared off the face of the earth." He checked the Glock 9mm pistol that was tucked into a holster in the back of his pants. The Glock was well-known for its dependability, even when exposed to adverse conditions. Otto didn't want to worry about whether his gun would fire or not if he got into the heat of the action. In addition to extra magazines of ammunition for the Glock, Otto carried several grenades, which were clipped to his belt by their pins—a dangerous practice that sometimes resulted in soldiers blowing themselves up when the grenade caught on a projection and pried loose. The upside was this allowed him to pull the pin one-handed and throw the grenade faster than if he needed to use two hands for the process. It was possible to pull the pin of the grenade with one's teeth, but it often broke a tooth or two in the process.

A few minutes later they reached the summit of the Achilles Lauro and slipped into the wheel cabin. They found it as empty as the rest of the ship. The navigator's wheel was locked into place, and the instrumentation was turned on, but no member of the crew was there to read it.

Fritz checked over the two-way radio system, and found that it was now a mass of melted and fused wires. Someone had put a half-dozen bullet into it, effectively cutting the ship off from communication with the shore.

Briefly Otto looked over the instrument panels. "This is curious," he said. "Someone has messed with the sonar."

"Hmm?" answered Fritz, as he gazed through the windows of the Achilles and watched the tugboat transporting the terrorists dock. It was too far away for him to see any actual people, but he imagined the hijackers disgorging from the boat.

"The case of the sonar system is broken open," said Otto. "Either some-one was making some repairs, or someone was screwing with it. Whoever did it did a messy job of it."

"Why would someone alter the sonar?" asked Fritz.

Otto contemplated for a moment. "Maybe they wanted the ship to run aground, or…"

"Or maybe they didn't want the captain to know that there was a subma-rine dogging the ship," finished Fritz.

"It's possible," concluded Otto. "But what would PLO or Force 19 ter-rorists be planning to do with a submarine, and why would they be shadow-ing the Achilles Lauro?"

Years ago, Fritz had disappeared into the Far East for intensive training of his body and mind. He had studied obscure martial arts—disciplines that trained the mind in order to train the body. He emerged with a redefined sense of honor and obligation, and a mind that could rapidly dissect a prob-lem and examine all the angles without emotional interference, discarding the extraneous and putting the meaningful in its proper perspective.

"They were using the ship as a cover," said Fritz. "A submarine wouldn't be easily discovered if it stayed beneath a cruise ship. It would be concealed from satellite reconnaissance photography, and would be unlikely to be picked up by sonar or listening devices."

"That's all logical," said Otto, "but the question is what are they plan-ning?"

"What was the scheduled itinerary of the Achilles?"

"After Said, they were on their way to Ashdod."

"That's Israel," said Fritz. "Suppose Force 19 planned to drift into port beneath the Achilles Lauro and mount some kind of terrorist attack on the Israelis. Force 19 is a maximum casualty terrorist unit; some sort of suicide mission might not be out of the realm of possibility."

"Not at all," said Otto. While Fritz had been speaking he opened the cas-ing of the sonar and began to examine the components within. "In fact, what we have here is an extra component that feeds an alternate data stream into the sonar. If you're right, it probably corresponds with the standard marine lanes from Said to Ashdod—a feed to fool the captain into thinking that the sonar was in working order."

"So what's beneath the ship now?" asked Fritz.

Otto was easily able to bypass the added component. In a few moments he had the sonar functioning again, bouncing sound signals from below to see what dangers lurked beneath. The youngest Gantlet brother examined the view screen. "There's a sub beneath the ship right now," concluded Otto.

Sly and Mitz wandered through the desolate ship. They checked hundreds of staterooms for some sign of life.

"I'm starting to wonder if the hijackers killed all the hostages before they left," said Mitz. He and Sly were now working their way along the outside cabins, the brilliant sun hung fiercely in the sky, quickly drying their clothes, leaving a white dusting of salt residue on their shirts. Like Sly, Mitz cradled a miniature UZI submachine gun that was hardly much bigger than the twin Double Eagle pistols that were tucked beneath his elbows.

Mitz stepped into the humid darkness of yet another cabin. Standing quietly inside the doorway, he thought that he could hear the rhythmic sound of nervous breath. His eyes took a moment to adjust to the dimness, but when his vision clarified he still could not see the source of the sound. He lowered his UZI and called out in English, then again in German. "Come out and I won't hurt you!"

There was a stirring beneath the bed in the cabin, and a woman in her early fifties peered fearfully from beneath a cascade of sheets and blankets. "Please don't hurt me," she said in German, her voice quavering.

"Don't worry, you're safe now," answered Mitz. "The hijackers have gone."

"Thank God," said the woman, as she pulled herself up to sit on the bed.

Mitz could see that the woman had one of her feet amputated. He noticed a cane leaning in one corner of the room.

"A terrorist kicked me down the stairs," she said. "I crawled into this room and have been hiding here under the bed for three days. The only thing that I've had to eat for the entire time is two apples. "

Sly came in behind Mitz, and saw the woman. "Why don't you stay put here?" he said to the former hostage. "We're going to check over the rest of the ship and make sure that it is safe."

"We'll go up to the kitchen and see if we can find you something to eat," said Mitz.

The woman nodded feebly. "Thank you," she said.

Mitz shut the door behind them and noted the number of the room so that he could easily locate her on his return trip. He and Sly continued down the row of state rooms, and then on up the stairs to Deck A. Here they discovered the closed double doors of the dining room, the handles wrapped with wire, which were in turn hooked to the pin of a grenade, so that the slightest pressure from within would trigger the explosive.

"Simple," grunted Sly, "but effective. It would be nearly impossible to disarm this from the inside."

Circling around to the side of the dining room, Mitz walked along the glass wall, and saw the huddled men, women, and children within. As soon as he appeared, machine gun in hand, they shrank back in fear. Mitz grinned; he was a long way from the Gentleman's Quarterly image that he presented at parties and other high fashion social gatherings. His hair was a tangled mess of blonde curls encrusted with salt, and his disproportionately large drummer's forearms looked freakish gripping the UZI. "They could have easily broken out the windows on the side here," called Mitz.

"Maybe," answered Sly as he produced a notched boot knife. "But I don't think they have any idea what's going on. They probably still think that the hijackers are on board the ship."

Mitz tried to spot Carna amid the people within the dining room, but the glare of the sinking sun against the glass made it difficult to see anyone clearly.

They returned to the booby-trapped door. Gripping the grenade and its pin tightly, Sly used placed the notch of his knife over the wire and twisted, snapping the strand. Shortly, he was able to slide the grenade loose of the wiring and return the pin firmly into place. He hooked the mantle on his belt and finished cutting the wiring. Once he cut the handles free, he opened up the door to find scores of eyes staring at him fearfully.

"I'm looking for someone named Carna," he announced loudly.

No one dared answer, and an uneasy silence reigned, broken only by the stifled coughing of an elderly man who hid in the corner, hoping that his smoker's hack would not bring attention to him. Finally a sultry voice responded, a bathing-suit clad woman with dark skin and regal bearing strode through the parting crowd. "Are you looking for me?"

Sly scowled. "You've got a job waiting for you in the States. I came to see what the hold up was."

Despite her split lip and swollen face, Carna managed a genuine smile, and launched herself into Sly's brawny arms. "I've never been so glad to see anybody in my whole life!"

Mitz watched the reunion, a slight smile curling the corner of his lips. He turned and watched the fiery halo of the sun slip behind the rolling waves. A crackle came over his headphones.

Fritz's leaden voice boomed from the ear pieces. "Heads up," he called. "There's a hostile Russian-made submarine surfacing on the port side."

Within the cab of the flatbed truck Matthias shifted uncomfortably in the sweltering heat. He wore a white tank top that only partially covered the ugly and painful deep bruising that spread across his muscular back. Abn Fahd sat in the driver's seat across from him. They watched the waves roll into port, rocking the long lines of steeple-masted yachts, but barely affecting the ocean liners and cargo ships that parked their titanic steel hulls against massive bulwarks, which swarmed with forklifts and longshoreman. In the distance, they could see the Achilles Lauro; the stately Italian vessel showing no sign of the drama that was playing out aboard its blood-stained decks.

The tug transporting the Palestinian hijackers was chugging back into port, its speed slowing as it came into make the docking against a sun-bleached pier that was guarded by machine gun toting Egyptian military men.

"They're holding off on sending in the bomb sweepers," commented Matthias. "Probably they're waiting to dispose of the hijackers before they run a boat out to pick up the hostages."

"It may take them awhile to get the hijackers out of the country," said Abn. "The Achilles might be sitting out there by itself for a long, long time."

Matthias lifted a pair of binoculars to his eyes and watched as six Palestinians leaped from the tug to the splintered planking of the pier. They seemed rather pleased with themselves, mused the musician. Perhaps he could help wipe the smile from their faces. He watched as they strode proudly up the pier, past the uniformed Egyptian guards, and climbed into a Soviet-made BTR-152K, heavily-armored, transport vehicle that waited for them with its engine running. The rock singer noted that the twenty-three-foot vehicle had seen some action before, the rear plating of the vehicle was crumpled inward as if another military vehicle had run into the back of it. Along each side of the sand gray vehicle were three circular firing portals, currently in closed position. Unlike earlier models of this personnel carrier, the top was completely enclosed, and armored, to protect from aerial attack.

A heavyset man, clean-shaven but for a thick mustache as dark as his curly black hair, emerged from the truck and embraced each of the hijackers as they entered the vehicle. Matthias examined the newcomer's visage closely. The coal black eyes moved constantly back and forth, set back beneath a stern brow and on each side of a broad nose. The rock musician imagined that he could read a malign craftiness in the man's demeanor.

Matthias handed the binoculars to Abn. "Do you know this guy?" he asked.

Abn focused in on the terrorist. "That's Abul Abbas," he said. "He's the PLO bigshot that you've been hearing do the negotiations. He's also a former plane hijacker."

"Well, he's moved up in the world," said Matthias. "One minute you're a terrorist, the next you're a respected leader."

As the armored transport vehicle closed up its doors, Matthias watched one of the armed Egyptian military men take a place in the front passenger seat. "Not only do they receive an armed escort, but the hijackers are still armed."

"Why don't you just let them go?" asked Abn. "The hostages are free now, and Carna is safe. These guys are heavily armed; why don't you leave well enough alone?"

"That's a nice thought," said Matthias, "but we have to send a message."

"A message?"

"When someone messes with the Gantlets, their family, or their friends, we have to come down hard on them. Then people will think twice before crossing us. If we let people walk all over us, then it starts happening over and over again."

Abn started the engine of the flatbed truck, and slowly began to coast through the confusion of off-loaded shipping containers, crates, and the fully-loaded forklifts that weaved through the maze of cargo. By the time that he reached the narrow street that ran by the shipping yards, the transport vehicle was leaving a gate about a hundred yards up the road. Hanging back far enough so that he wouldn't obviously appear to be following the carrier, Abn shadowed the military vehicle through a maze of claustrophobic streets flanked by the chain-link fences of import and export companies.

The armored transport car stayed away from main thoroughfares, the driver choosing to discreetly travel the back roads, but these were often choked with people or cars. The going was slow, but eventually they left the limits of the city and, as the blazing sun sank in the west, they approached the broad hangars, low barracks, and shadowed towers of the Al Maza Military Air Base. The dying light reflected from rows of sleek gray fuselages—Russian-made MiG jet fighters that represented a small portion of Egypt's air power.

Abn slowed the flatbed as they neared the base, easing back even further behind other traffic. The transport truck pulled up to a gate guarded by a pair of soldiers toting assault rifles. Words were exchanged and the gate was rolled back, allowing the armored truck to enter the base. Matthias watched as it disappeared behind a row of bleak-looking barracks.

Abn pulled the flatbed over onto the opposite side of the road against a sand ridge, popped the hood, and went around front of the vehicle. He lifted the lid and propped it into place, making a show of looking for some imaginary mechanical problem. A warm wind rattled sand against Matthias's pant legs as he dropped from the cab of the truck and joined Abn beneath the hood.

"Did you see where they went?" asked Abn.

Matthias turned and watched the sun sink beneath the rim of the parched desert. "I couldn't see exactly where they went, but it will be dark soon and I'm going to go in and find them."

"That's a military base you're planning to sneak into," said Abn. "You know that you are absolutely insane, don't you?"

Matthias pushed up his bulletproof Gargoyle sunglasses as twilight slipped over the desert landscape. "Yeah, but life is a lot more interesting when you're insane."

"And shorter," added Abn. "How are you going to get in?"

"The guards for the air base are keeping an eye on us right now, but it will be getting dark soon. We're going to pretend that we've fixed whatever mechanical problem that your truck is having and climb back into the cab. Then I'm going to crawl out the driver's door and over that ridge. As soon as I'm out of the open, you head back to our flat."

"Got ya."

"Thanks for the lift."

"My pleasure," said Abn Fahd. He shook his head disbelievingly, and let the hood of the truck drop loudly into place. They both slipped back into the cab of the flatbed, and Abn restarted the engine of the truck, blowing a plume of black smoke out the exhaust pipe.

Matthias shrugged on his Kevlar-lined leather jacket, and hefted a suspiciously heavy gym bag that was resting on the worn rubber matting of the floor. He rolled the rubber mat up and leaned it up against the backseat, placing a baseball cap on top of the newly formed rubber cylinder. As he did this he ducked down beneath the level of the windows.

Abn raised his feet and Matthias crawled past the gear shift and pedals, slipping out the driver's side door to the warm sand. He reached up and Abn dropped the leather gym bag into Matthias's open hands. "May God be with you," he said.

"And you," said Matthias. He shouldered the bag as if it were a backpack, and he scrambled up the sandy ridge and into the yellowing grass that grew in scraggly tufts along its apex. When he had obscured himself in the sparse vegetation beyond, Abn gunned the truck, spraying sand as he turned back in the direction which they had come.

Matthias buried himself in the sand. He worried that waiting might allow the terrorists to make their escape, but he figured that it might take awhile for a flight out of the country to be arranged. If he tried to sneak past the perimeter of the air base while daylight persisted, it would be suicide. He needed the cover of night to aid him in his illicit endeavors.

Half a world away, Ronald Reagan received intelligence gleaned from a recording a Syrian radio station had made. With the news that an American hostage had been killed aboard the Achilles Lauro, the president of the United States was even less inclined to allow the hijackers any leniency. In his communication with Egypt's President Mubarek, he demanded that the terrorists be arrested and turned over to the United States for prosecution.

Mubarek officially claimed that the terrorists had already departed the country, and that the situation was already out of his hands. This official stance allowed Mubarek to retain his good standing in the Palestinian community, but even as he put on this public face his administration very obviously filed a last minute flight plan, indicating that the terrorists had yet to leave Egypt. An EgyptAir plane was scheduled to leave from Al Maza Air Base and fly to Algiers.

Immediately President Reagan made a call to Secretary of Defense Caspar Weinberger. "I want you to have the flight intercepted and force them to land in Italy," he said. "These hijackers must pay!"

Weinberger hesitated. "What if they refuse to comply?"

"Just do it," said Reagan.

During the conversation the scrambler aboard Air Force One lapsed, and the signal went out clean. A ham radio operator sympathetic to the Palestinian cause overheard the conversation. He quickly relayed the overheard message to certain acquaintances, who relayed it to contacts within the PLO.

Force 19's plans to infiltrate Ashdod had gone awry. The Achilles Lauro had been taken much too early, and now there was no hope that they could shadow the cruise liner into Israel and launch their terrorist attack. Still, they lingered beneath the ship awaiting their next command. When word came to them that the Americans were going to extreme measures to catch and punish their comrades, vengeance became the order of the day. Many Americans were aboard the Achilles Lauro, and their slaughter would send a bloody and unmistakable message to the United States.

Dusk was upon the Achilles Lauro when the dark conning tower of the Romeo Class submarine emerged from the waves in a frothing upheaval of displaced ocean.

Aboard the Achilles, Sly and Mitz heard Fritz's crackling warning over their receivers. Sly disengaged himself from his sister-in-law's embrace. "It looks like it's not over yet. I want you to gather up everybody and put them in the kitchen, then lock the doors. The dining room has too many windows to be safe."

Carna's relief turned to sick fear. "What's going on?" she asked.

"The hijackers are back," said Sly.

With a deep breath, Carna steeled herself and began shouting out orders to the unfortunate passengers of the cruise liner. While she began herding them back into the kitchen area, a stolidly built Italian man in a captain's uniform approached Sly.

"I'm the captain of this ship," he said. "What is going on here?"

"We've got a Russian-made sub emerging on the port side. Chances are that they aren't friendly."

"What can I do?" asked Captain De Rosa.

"Go into the kitchen and keep everyone calm," said Mitz. "We'll take care of it."

Captain De Rosa raised his eyebrows in disbelief. He wasn't even sure who these guys were. They looked like refugees from a rock video, but they had somehow showed up just after the hijackers had locked all the passengers in the dining room and warned them that leaving would result in immediate death. The newcomers to his ship were armed to the teeth, but they wore no military uniform of any sort. Still, these two fellows managed to inspire confidence in the shaken captain, and he was in no position to question the good intentions of men armed with submachine guns. The captain turned and did as the Sly and Mitz asked, doing his best to calm the renewed fear that was surging through the passengers.

Mitz and Sly didn't stick around. They cut through the narrow corridors of the ship, emerging on the port side moments later. True to their brother's warning, a shadow of a conning tower protruded from beneath the darkening swells. A mounted machine gun was being placed in the tower, and men clambered from the protruding spire, and into inflatable boats that quickly crossed the watery gap between the sub and Achilles Lauro. Already they could hear the popping of gunpowder charges, and watched as several lines snaked up over the rail and hooked their three-toed claws with a clank.

"These guys are good," whispered Mitz from concealment. "What do you bet they've already sent at least one boat around to board on the other side? There's got to be at least a couple dozen of these guys. If we let them get on board they'll outflank us and cut us to pieces in the crossfire."

"Not only that," said Sly, "but that is a Romeo class submarine out there. It's capable of carrying up to eight 533 millimeter torpedoes. Even if we manage to survive the human assault, they can blow this ship to kingdom come."

"We've got one advantage," said Mitz. "They don't know we're here. They're probably expecting minimal resistance, if any at all."

"But they're armed like they're expecting Armageddon," muttered Sly grimly.

From their vantage point in the steering house of the Achilles Lauro, Fritz and Otto could see the submarine emerge from the sullen waters of the Mediterranean. Soldiers rapidly deployed from the tower, inflating boats and starting the small engines that easily pushed them ship side. With their UZI submachine guns, both Fritz and Otto could have opened fire, but the distance was great, and though the UZIs were very portable and spewed a lot of lead in a short period of time, their barrels were short and they weren't very accurate at long distances. Likely, they would have been able to cut down a few of the boarders, and maybe even sink a boat, but the element of surprise would be destroyed and they still wouldn't have done severe damage to the enemy.

Fritz saw two of the four boats circling around the rear of the Achilles Lauro. He called down to Sly and Mitz. "There are two boats heading around the stern. Otto and I are going to see if we can intercept them before they get on board."

"Got that," answered Sly. "Mitz and I will hold the port side."

"What about the sub? We haven't got anything with enough firepower to take it out."

"I'll think of something," answered Sly.

"You better," answered Fritz. "Because if they start broadsiding us with torpedoes we're dead meat…"

"I realize that," interrupted Sly, impatiently. "Don't you have some boats to intercept?"

Fritz smiled calmly and motioned to Otto. Leaving the wheel cabin, they sped along the broad upper deck of the ship, finally climbing to the highest level and cutting past the star-emblazoned smoke stacks that lay dormant. They watched the waters and Otto spotted one boat coming around to the starboard side of the Achilles. "I've got this one," he called to Fritz.

The oldest Gantlet brother waved him on and continued his sprint to the rear of the ship. Here he looked down from the dizzying heights and saw that a group of terrorists had successfully moored their heavily laden boat against the rear of the ship. Several men had already climbed aboard and were busily hoisting crates up to the Achilles' deck. At this height he wasn't sure what the Force 19 terrorists were loading aboard the ship, but he had a sneaking suspicion.

After darkness fell Matthias waited for a lull in the traffic, scuttled across the highway and up into the scrub brush along the chain link perimeter of the El Aziz Air Base. The fence was twelve feet high and topped with coils of razor wire that could slice through a man's fingers with far too much ease. However, Matthias had no designs on climbing the fence. He pulled a pair of wire clippers from the pocket of his jacket and began cutting link after link until he had created a discreet seam through which he could slip. The guards who stood at the gate fifty yards away had still not seen him, and Matthias was anxious to keep it that way.

The headlights of a truck began to show in the distance, and Matthias quickly breached the fence. A sprint put him alongside the barracks within the compound. He slipped along the stucco walls avoiding the glowing windows, hearing the chatter of soldiers as he ducked beneath the panes and penetrated deeper into the air base.

Matthias realized that he was playing things fast and loose. He knew that the hijackers would be flying from the country, but there were hundreds of planes on the base, and even after eliminating the fighter jets from possibility, there were far too many aircraft to personally do reconnaissance on each of them.

It was becoming increasingly difficult for him to sneak about unnoticed as he crept toward the runways. Maintenance crews ran back and forth on battery-powered carts, busy despite the late hour. As he moved stealthily through the alley between two hangars, he found what he was looking for. A hundred yards out, a BRTR-152K armored personnel carrier sat on the runway next to an EgyptAir Boeing 737. Matthias recognized the crumpled armor on the back of the vehicle and he smiled.

A crew was fueling the 737, which had evidently been privately chartered to accommodate the hijackers escape. Matthias watched as the jumpsuit-clad crew unhooked the fuel hoses from the airplane's ports, clamped them down along side of the dusty tanker truck and began to pull off. As the truck's headlights swept away, Matthias plunged through the encroaching darkness, sprinting across the still-warm tarmac and coming to a halt beneath the silver belly of the jet, behind the great wheels of the plane.

Here in the darkness of the jet's shadow, not even the wan light of the rising moon was able to reach him. Within the hold of the plane he could hear a thumping as baggage was thrown toward and out the door of the cargo hatch. A luggage shuttle car rested on the tarmac, pieces of luggage being roughly tossed into the scarred cart that it towed. By the frequency of the bumps and the footsteps, Matthias gambled that it was just one man that had drawn the duty of removing the luggage. Probably the plane had been diverted from its regular duty in order to serve the demands of the hijackers, and just now the luggage of its previous passengers was being removed.

Matthias crept forward until he hid directly behind the unfolded wing of the 737's cargo hatch, and waited here until the last of the suitcases and packages had been tossed into the cart below. A short and rather stocky Egyptian leaped down from the plane and landed heavily atop a soft-case piece of luggage. Matthias heard the crunch of its breaking contents.

As the luggage handler's back was turned to him, Matthias used the rear corner of the cart as a step, and bounded into the belly of the jet. He tried to alight as softly as possible, and only a slight scuffing noise marked his landing before he rolled back into the shadowed recesses of the hold.

The noise of shifting luggage, as the handler clambered to the tarmac, had masked the sounds of Matthias's entrance, and oblivious to what had just transpired, the heavy Egyptian turned and closed the wing door, locking the lead vocalist into the inky bowels of the jet.

Matthias heard the whine of the cart's engine and the rattle of the luggage car as it departed across the seams of the runway. Then he heard the roar of the twin Pratt and Whitney engines as they sprang to life, and the wheels of the jet began to churn down the runway, gathering speed faster and faster. Matthias slid toward the back of the hold and braced himself against the back wall as the plane tilted skyward. Smiling grimly, Matthias hoped that the hold was pressurized and heated. Above him was a plane full of terrorists and below the baggage compartment there was nothing but empty sky.

Otto slipped down the railed steps of the Achilles Lauro. The moon shone in the reflection from the sloping swells of the ocean, and across these cut an inflatable raft that held five Force 19 terrorists, faces stern, and hands gripping Kalashnikov assault rifles as they embarked on a holy mission of slaughter. The youngest Gantlet brother reached the lower deck and hid from view, waiting for the terrorists to disembark from their wave-tossed craft.

He had assessed the odds, and knew that if the terrorists managed to board the boat, he would be severely outnumbered and probably wind up severely dead. However, he had no intentions of letting them board. With surprise, he could likely lean out over the rail and pick off a few of the terrorists before they knew what hit them, but they were five strong, and all armed with automatic weapons. It would be unlikely that he could kill them all without taking some lead.

The proper attack would rely on surprise and confusion to give Otto the upper hand. He waited until he heard a popping sound and watched as two grappling hooks arced over the rail of the Achilles. Otto smiled, now he could locate the approximate position of the terrorists below without poking his head over the edge. The slack lines of the grappling hooks went taut and the Gantlet bass player figured that several of the attackers were beginning to ascend.

Otto plucked two grenades from his belt and rolled them over the edge of the Achilles Lauro, one after the other. The first dropped into the waves a foot from the inflatable craft and exploded six feet beneath the surface. Flames lit the waves, etching their jagged, frothing lines in brilliant light for one brief moment. The sea erupted, shrapnel tearing through the inflatable craft and tossing the three remaining terrorists into the air.

Just as the first explosion subsided, the second grenade went off—before it touched the waves. A roiling ball of flame bubbled upward, scathing the great hull of the Achilles Lauro and consuming the three Palestinians who had been tossed into the air. Above them, miraculously escaping the spray of shrapnel, two terrorists frantically scaled the side of the ship, pulling themselves up the grapnel line as fast as their strength would allow.

Otto unsheathed a gleaming blade and quickly rolled over to the railing. The razor-sharp edge severed the nylon line of the first terrorist, and then a moment later, the second, sending them plunging back into the corpse strewn wash. Both emerged from the crimson waters, but Otto lay on the deck of the Achilles Lauro with his head and arms hanging over. As soon as they broke the waves, he began to fire. They made small targets, their heads and shoulders bobbing among the salty froth. He fired three quick shots, and one of the terrorists pitched back with a horrible cry.

The last Palestinian brought his rifle from beneath the waves and managed to squeeze the trigger. Water and lead erupted from the gun, strafing the hull beneath where Otto lay. But only a few rounds left the barrel before the gun went silent, the water causing a malfunction within the feed mechanism of the Kalashnikov.

The terrorist cried out, his curses echoing against the broad hull of the Achilles. Otto's breath came in adrenaline-spurred bursts, that urged him to empty his gun in the direction of the last man. His intellect, though, realized that the man was temporarily at his mercy, and steadying his nerves he took careful aim, then put a nine-millimeter bullet through the top of the would-be hijackers head with a sickening thud.

Sly and Mitz heard the dual roar of grenade explosions from the opposite side of the ship. They knew that in order to retain any element of surprise they would have to make their move now. Moving forward under cover, Mitz popped his UZI over the rail of the ship and sent out a spray of bullets. He emptied half of his magazine into the hijackers and their inflatable boat below. The terrorists screamed and pitched from the boat as bullets burst through their bodies, trailing crimson gouts. The boat was punctured multiple times and quickly collapsed into a shapeless olive-colored mass, surrounded by thrashing limbs and dying terrorists.

Assuming an undefended ship, a few terrorists had already begun to climb the side of the Achilles Lauro. Screams of the dying fought for attention over the din of metal against metal as Mitz emptied his machine pistol, sweeping them from the hull. They plummeted, dead and dying, into the suffocating embrace of the sea below.

Sly had also leaped from cover and into a position where he could fire. He kept his distance from Mitz, knowing it would be foolish to stand so near him that all the enemies' firepower could be concentrated on one small area. He stood back from the rail a bit so that the terrorists who remained in the second boat below could not target him. He focused his fire on the conning tower of the black Romeo class submarine.

Though Sly could make out no details, the moonlight revealed dark forms, bristling weaponry, on the tower. Among these was a mounted submachine that was being brought to bear in the general direction of the two Gantlet brothers. Sly emptied his machine gun, creating gory carnage on the tower. Terrorists slipped from the tower, sliding dead into the wet womb of the Mediterranean, and others slumped, leaking their crimson life blood down the dark conning tower, which had become a sinister grave marker.

Sly, however, knew that the submarine's danger was far from vanquished. If its silos were full, the torpedoes they contained could be emptied into the Achilles Lauro for wholesale death and destruction.

The rattle of Kalashnikovs boomed from the hull of the Achilles as a boat load of hijackers caught site of Mitz. The Gantlet drummer heard the whine of bullets as they ricocheted from the rail by which he stood. Heat lanced across his left forearm as a bullet creased the flesh, leaving a bloody furrow. Bullets clanked and sparked from the rail as Mitz fell back into momentary cover.

While Mitz was drawing fire, Sly decided that this was his opportunity to get into a position to do something about the submarine. Without rocket propelled grenades or an anti-tank weapon, they didn't have much that could put a dent in the submarine itself. He was going to have to close the distance.

Sly jacked a second magazine into his UZI, and with a running start, he leaped up over the railing of the deck and out over the open sea below. His flight into empty space gave him a sudden line of sight on the remaining terrorist boat below, and as Sly plummeted to the ocean he opened up with his UZI, slicing down terrorists and puncturing several of the boat's air compartments.

The miniature submachine gun thunked as the supply of bullets was exhausted, and Sly slapped hard into the ocean's waters, the UZI wrenching from his hand as he punched into the water. His back stung fiercely as he clawed for the surface in the inky black void that muted the screams of the men he had cut down.

One terrorist remained unscathed, and he perched himself on a still-in-flated portion of his raft, crimson washing around his legs. He had brought his gun to bear on the flying madman only a moment before he had plunged into the sea. Now he watched for the rock musician's head to emerge, his finger held tightly on the sweat-slicked trigger of his assault rifle. The dying screams of his cohorts had momentarily wiped from his mind the possibility of danger from above.

As Sly emerged from the salty waters that had momentarily entombed him, Mitz leaned out over the rail of the Achilles Lauro and caught sight of the sole terrorist that had put a death watch on Sly. Mitz's machine gun spewed forth, and he emptied his magazine, bringing down a fiery storm of death and destruction. The terrorist went down, his gun spraying awry bullets that spattered futilely against the waves, their momentum stolen by the blood-streaked waters.

Sly realized that Mitz had saved his skin and raised his hand in the hi-sign to signal that he was in one piece. He rolled over in the trough of a swell and struck out for the submarine, using powerful overhand strokes that made steady headway against the contrary pull of the ocean. As Sly worked his way to the dark shape that spread its hidden bulk beneath the waves, Mitz again reloaded his UZI. He saw some movement on the conning tower as someone poked their head out of the upper hatch, trying to ascertain the situation above. Mitz sent a short burst that scathed the tower, and sent the tentative voyeur scrambling for cover within the sub.

By sending regular waves of lead across the top of the tower, Mitz hoped to give Sly cover until he could reach the sub. Also, he hoped that it would keep the subs occupants from being able to close up the hatch. Only the fact that the Force 19 commandos within the sub were still trying to comprehend what was happening outside, Mitz guessed, was keeping them from ordering a torpedo attack upon the Achilles. Mitz figured they were still hoping that their hijacker force might prove victorious, and only that was delaying decisive action that would probably kill every man, woman, and child aboard the ocean liner.

Another burst of bullets rattled off the hull of the submarine as Sly hauled himself, dripping ropes of water, onto the mostly submerged craft. He pulled himself up the rungs that studded the conning tower, holding his .44 magnum Desert Eagle in his right hand as he crawled upward.

Mitz aimed high, but sent another stream of lead whirring over the top of the conning tower. His magazine was empty now, and he discarded the UZI, drawing his twin Double Eagle Colts. He knew that Sly was on his own now, but stayed at hand in case there was some way that he might give aid.

Sly rolled onto the conning tower, and immediately saw the dark curls of a terrorist's hair protruding from the open hatch. The rock musician could see a dusky hand gripping a miniature machine gun. Before the terrorist could move, Sly unloaded six cartridges into the opening. He heard a choking cry, and the terrorist's machine gun blew a gout of flame from its muzzle as it vomited metal skyward. Sly heard a thump, and the machine gun fell silent, but other cries came from within, and he felt the submarine move beneath him, water surging against the craft as it shifted its course.

The submarine was moving into position to fire its aft torpedoes, realized Sly. The Achilles Lauro and its passengers were only moments away from destruction. Sly turned his attention to the tripod-mounted machine gun that still rested atop of the conning tower. Its former owners lay about it in a gory tableau that was liberally splattered with sea water-diluted blood. The rock guitarist had little time to pay attention to such details as he grabbed hold of the machine gun. A long belt of wicked 7.92 millimeter shells drooped into a wooden crate, which Sly kicked into place as he turned the gun.

He recognized the mounted armament, and wondered what sordid past the weapon had experienced, and how it passed into the hands of Force 19. The gun was an M642, produced in Nazi-era Germany. Sly had seen them before, but never had hands on experience…until now. He pulled back the trigger and poured an unceasing barrage down the hatch of the conning tower. The barrel of the machine gun began to glow a murky red, and the belt whipped back in forth in a frenzy of explosive release that came to a sudden halt when the last spent shell clanked down against the metal of the conning tower.

A gunpowder haze wafted over the tower as Sly waded through the mounds of empty brass that spilled down into the smoking mouth of the hatch. Sly had rightly assumed that his attack had cleared this portion of the two-hundred-fifty-foot diesel-powered submarine. He pulled from his belt the same grenade that he had found wired to the Deck A dining room of the Achilles Lauro. He wrenched the pin free and released the spring-loaded mantle of the grenade as he dropped it below. The moment that the grenade had fallen into the open conning tower, Sly kicked the hatch shut and turned the wheel to lock it.

Without another moment of hesitation, he leaped free of the dark submarine. There was a muffled thump and the metal of the submarine bulged outward, throwing a hail of popped rivets. They sliced through the air around him, and Sly grunted as several caught him across his rib cage, breaking cartilage and cracking bone. He spun into the sea amid a downpour of rivets that ricocheted from the side of the Achilles Lauro, and fell into the ocean.

The blows forced the air from Sly's lungs, and he struggled to resurface, pain shooting through him each movement that he made with his arms. He reached air and refilled his lungs, but the mere act of breathing left him grimacing in pain. Turning in the water, he saw the submarine slowly rolling over as the sea poured in through the seam created by the explosion of the grenade within the claustrophobic confines of the craft.

Sly didn't know how severe the damage was, but he hoped that it would be enough to keep the sub from being in any position to fire its torpedoes. The terrorists within the submarine might be able to close off portions of their vessel and keep it airtight, staving off the impending sinking and drowning, but he hoped they couldn't.

Mitz watched the action from the deck of the Achilles Lauro, and when he saw that Sly had returned to the water, he began lowering a life boat to the sea below. Sly climbed over the edge of the wooden boat, and sat on its floor, noticing that his blood was mingling with the salty waters that drained from his body. He saw that his tank top was soaked with blood, and he painfully lifted it off, throwing the gory rag aside and examining the dripping gashes on his rib cage.

He had been wounded many times, and despite the mental fuzziness that crept in around the edges of his mind, he realized that this was not a serious wound. As long as he could staunch the flow of blood and keep from going into a state of shock, he would be able to function.

Mitz raised the lifeboat and as soon as he had helped Sly to the deck of the Achilles he pushed him down onto a bench. He stripped off his own tank-top and pressed the fabric of the shirt against the wound to stifle the blood that poured down Sly's craggy abdomen.

"Bullet wounds?" he asked.

Sly shook his head. "Rivets, and they didn't even penetrate. It's nothing."

The sound of battle rose from the back of the Achilles Lauro, and Fritz's heavy battle cry could be heard rising above the din.

"Let me up," growled Sly. He pushed at Mitz who determinedly pressed back on Sly's shoulders.

"You stay here and stop the blood," ordered Mitz. "I'll go give Fritz a hand."

"Like that's gonna happen," spat Sly.

Mitz was successful in holding back Sly for only a moment. Even weakened by loss of blood, Sly's strength was of titanic proportions. Because of Mitz's uncanny forearm strength he could beat Sly at arm wrestling, but over all Sly's strength was almost as irresistible as a force of nature. Sly heaved his body erect, throwing Mitz back a few feet.

The blonde drummer realized the futility of arguing with his older brother. "Have it your way," he conceded. "Keep up with me if you can." Mitz turned and sprinted down the arcing walkway and sped down its railed length to the rear of the ship.

Sly lunged along, attempting to keep pace, but finding that he was having some difficulty keeping his legs beneath him. His vision reeled around him, but he doggedly trailed Mitz, determined to help his older brother who was engaged in battle somewhere at the rear of the boat.

Curious as to what the terrorists were loading aboard the Achilles Lauro, Fritz slid over the upper railing and quietly dropped to the deck below. He did this several times until he stood just one deck above the men who feverishly loaded the sinister crates aboard the cruise ship. Arabic was not one of the languages that Fritz spoke, but now that he was closer he was able to lean over the rail and clearly see the moonlit markings emblazoned on the crates. They were filled with explosives.

Fritz quickly reconstructed the terrorists' activities. They had attempted to board in large numbers and all had been heavily armed. Fritz suspected that they had planned to quickly sweep the decks and kill every passenger that they saw. Meanwhile their cohorts to the rear of the boat would be setting explosive charges that would sink the Achilles Lauro to the bottom of the sea. By the time bodies were dredged and the facts came out, the submarine would be safely away, hiding out in the waters of a country friendly to the Palestine Liberation Organization and their terrorist activities.

It was probable that they were reluctant to torpedo the boat. Probably Force 19 wanted to keep the fact that they had obtained a submarine quiet, so they could use it for surprise attacks in the future. Using standard explosives wouldn't leave any trace to suggest that a submarine had disgorged the terrorists that had destroyed the Achilles Lauro.

Fritz's mind had precisely ordered the facts and produced a likely scenario, but he hadn't been idle during this thought process. The sheer amount of explosives that were being brought aboard made it dangerous to use a gun. Depending upon the stability of the explosives within the crates, the slightest spark might ignite the entire lot, obliterating Fritz and a huge portion of the ship. Fritz smiled; this gave him the opportunity to use an often less practical, but eminently more elegant weapon; one which he had trained with intensely.

His katana was worn in an unorthodox manner, on his back, but this was necessary in order to avoid being tripped up by the lacquered scabbard while engaged in any of the strenuous activities they had undertaken since leaving the tugboat which they had hidden themselves on board.

Fritz slipped the gentle arc of the blade slowly outward, minimizing the rasp of the black-lacquered sheath. Then he leaped, the Mediterranean wind pushing his wavy hair away from his craggy features. As he descended, he swung the blade, the tip biting through the shoulder and cutting deep into the chest of the terrorist who had been unfortunate enough to be standing below. The man bellowed, falling to his knees and clutching at the tip of the katana, which was immersed in a crimson wash.

Though his surprise attack had been thus far successful, Fritz's landing did not go equally well. The attack had thrown him off balance, and he slipped to his knees, still grasping the hilt of the katana.

The terrorists' surprise lasted only for a moment, and Fritz heard the sound of steps behind. At any moment he expected to feel a bullet burst through the back of his head. Still, Fritz's intensive training had prepared him to react with precision in even the least advantageous of positions. He yanked the blade free, and pivoted on his left knee, lashing out with his katana. The blade cut through the tendons behind the terrorist's knee. Cursing, the man pitched involuntarily backward as his leg gave beneath him. His finger jerked back the trigger of his Kalashnikov, and angry belches spit erratically from the muzzle and into the star-studded sky. Before the unfortunate hijacker could fall to the deck, Fritz's follow-up attack disemboweled the man.

As Fritz came to his feet, he faced the last terrorist on board the Achilles Lauro. In the raft below, two more men balanced in the rocking inflatable boat from which they had unloaded the crates of explosive, but at this moment it was just the two of them alone. Red rivulets dripped down the razor arc of Fritz's katana, which he held centered in front of him, leaking over the hand guard and across his callused fingers. The terrorist stared back, wild-eyed—with perspiration beaded on his tense brow. In the thick fingers of his left hand he held a miniature detonator, his right hand trembling as he held it over the plunger.

Without daring to take his eyes far from the target, Fritz saw that a wire fell from between the fingers of the Palestinian's hand, it trailed down past the worn knee of the man's pants and into a thick coil at his scuffed boots. From here, the wire wound its way through a fist-sized gap in the top of the nearest of three crates. Each of these crates had a similar gap in their lids, and Fritz imagined that they were meant to be linked together before detonation. From the type of detonator that the man held, and the fervent expression that his visage wore, Fritz guessed that for this zealot, the action to destroy the Achilles Lauro was also a suicide mission.

Fritz's sudden attack had prevented the terrorists from hooking up all but one of the crates, and from properly placing any of them. As it was, even this one crate would likely destroy a large chunk of the rear superstructure of the Achilles Lauro. Perhaps the passengers would be spared from death or injury, but Fritz had no desire to end his short ride on planet Earth quite this early.

Briefly, he considered leaping across the crate and cutting down the terrorist, but he worried that the fraction of a second that it took to bridge the gap between him and his adversary might prove too long, and allow the terrorist to trigger the explosives by pressing the plunger. There was another way to deal with the threat at hand, but it, also, was not without its risks. Fritz considered the dilemma no longer. He knew that the more time he took to decide on his course of action, the more resolve the Palestinian would muster, and the quicker the plunger would be depressed.

Fritz struck out with his blade in one quick decisive movement, bringing the sharp edge down upon wire, just before it disappeared into the darkness of the crate. The katana bit through the cord, and imbedded in the stained slats of the crate, at the very moment that fanatical zeal urged the hijacker to slam down the plunger, which sent an electrical impulse surging through the detonation wire. But the trigger was pressed just a scant moment too late, and the current sparked futilely at the end of the severed wire.

Letting go of the sword, Fritz leaped across the crate as the frustrated terrorist grasped for the pistol at his belt. The oldest Gantlet brother might have, likewise, reached for his Colt Anaconda, and it would have become a classic battle of gunfighter speed at very, very short range—but the distance between them was so minimal that Fritz instinctively decided that a hand to hand assault might prove faster, and just as effective.

The terrorist was so involved in reaching for his pistol that he offered no defense against Fritz's brutal assault—he was banking on his pistol as being the deciding factor. Fritz slammed the Palestinian hard against the metal railing of the cruise liner, and he heard bone crunch. This was hardly the finesse move that years of martial art training had taught Fritz, but it was merely the set up.

Fritz grabbed hold of the terrorist's elbow and wrist as the terrorist began to lift his pistol from his holster. He twisted the elbow joint back up and toward the man's scapula. The Palestinian, realizing that his arm would be broken if he didn't change his posture, whirled, and as his face was turned toward the sea, Fritz wrenched the arm upward and pushed the man up and over the railing.

Tottering in the inflatable craft at the stern of the Achilles, two baffled terrorists listened to the screams of their accomplices above. Each of them cautiously lifted their assault rifles and pointed them toward the railing, but because of the steep angle of the ship's hull they could not see what was conspiring above them. When a dark form flew over the railing, they opened fire, hot bullets slicing through and around the shadowy shape that flailed through the air toward them.

A horrible scream emitted from their target, and the barely living corpse of their compatriot fell into the center of their raft, capsizing it and throwing the two remaining Force 19 soldiers into the murky waters where they abandoned their rifles in their efforts to stay above the waves.

On the Achilles Lauro, Fritz drew his gun as he heard footsteps pounding up the walkway toward him. He turned and saw Mitz sprinting to his side, followed by the reeling form of Sly. His brothers took quick stock of the carnage on the rear deck, then stepped to the rail to watch the two men below attempting to right their boat in the swells that continuously pounded them up against the stern of the cruise ship.

Mitz holstered one of his Double Eagles, and with the other, carefully drew a two-handed bead on one of the figures below.

Fritz waved him off from his efforts. "Don't waste your bullets. They'll drown before long."

The screeching of nails from wood prompted both Fritz and Mitz to turn. They saw Sly tossing aside the top of crate and reaching into the shadowed recesses of the box. His hand emerged with a bundle of dynamite held tightly in his grip. He cut the fuses loose, and began twisting them together.

"This will help them along a bit," he said, his eyes glazing over as he spoke. Before he passed out, he produced a lighter, lit the fuses, and tossed the three stick bundle over the back of the ship. The dynamite splashed into the Mediterranean and it blew a massive dome of water into the air. Before the concussion died, Sly slipped to the deck, clutching his bloody ribs.

Mitz shook his head as he began to walk away. "I told him that he should stay put."

"Where are you going?" asked Fritz.

"I promised someone I'd get them a snack."

Matthias produced a silver-plated lighter and triggered the flint. A two-inch flame sprang to life, quivering in the belly of the Boeing 737 and spreading its feeble rays toward the corners of the plane's baggage compartment. Though Matthias was an adamant non-smoker, he habitually carried the lighter, and had found more than one use for its flame in years past.

Fortunately, he found that the hold of the jet was both pressurized and comfortably heated. Still, he hoped to make a move on the terrorists above while the plane was still in flight. On the ground they might be expecting some sort of resistance, and even if they weren't, they would certainly be much more wary and alert. In mid-air they wouldn't be expecting someone to burst from the hold to attack them.

He crept along the scuffed floor of the hold, feeling as though he were crawling through the ribbed belly of some mythological beast. He examined the ceiling above him as he moved toward the head of the plane, and finally he found a small hatch. Reaching upward he carefully tested the hinged panel, and found that it was securely locked from above.

This didn't surprise him, but he was faced with dilemma of opening it quietly enough so that the passengers above weren't immediately alerted. And even if he were to quietly open it, he faced the risk that someone might notice his entrance into the passenger portion of the plane. If this were to happen, he would immediately lose the advantage of surprise, and he knew that he was outnumbered.

Matthias pulled loose a hunting knife from within his black leather jacket, and began probing the seam of the hatch until he located the latching mechanism. Once he found this, he began cutting into the resin of the ceiling around the area that contained the extended locking bolt. It was slow and painstaking work to quietly saw away the area, but once it was completed, he had access to the dead bolt that locked the hatch. He inserted his knife between the ceiling and the dead bolt, and after several concerted efforts the bolt snapped free, clanking across the baggage hold.

The breath hissed from Matthias's teeth, and he hoped that his quarry above hadn't been alerted by the sound. He waited, listening, for sometime. However, he could hear little above the roar of the plane's engines. The hold was not insulated from sound and he couldn't hear any of what was going on in the passenger compartment over the whine of the jet's engines. He hoped that the same noise that prevented him from hearing had masked the sound of his crude, but successful, attempt to bypass the locking mechanism of the hatch.

He could hear, however, occasional foot treads as someone passed by the hatch way. This didn't mean that there wasn't someone standing over the hatch, but Matthias knew that he must take a chance sooner or later. He decided to make it sooner, and slowly eased the hatch upward. Carefully he hoisted himself through the undersized hatch, and found himself in a small alcove that contained racks of serving trays, a refrigerator, and a microwave. The 'kitchen' was really only big enough for one person to stand, but a curtain was drawn half way across the miniature alcove, and Matthias eased it closed a little further, to help shield him from sight.

Now he could plainly hear the voices of the terrorists. Matthias slipped the shiny surface of his lighter out beyond the edge of the kitchen walls, and watched the reflections on its face. The images were small and blurred, but he could see a group of men gathered together at the center of the plane. Matthias could smell cigar smoke, and he could see them lifting jugs of khamsin. Wine was forbidden by the Muslim faith, but these members of Force 19 obviously didn't feel it necessary to abide by every admonition of Muhammed.

Although his brothers occasionally partook of alcohol, Sly in particular, Matthias's past experience with it had led him to immediately swear off its use. He liked being in control and applied rigid discipline to himself to accomplish his goals and aspirations. Alcohol made him lose his focus, and made him feel curiously disjointed from reality. He didn't like the feeling. He hoped that the khamsin that the terrorists drank would blunt their senses. Matthias needed every advantage possible if he was going to come through this alive.

The reflection in his lighter revealed at least five men at the center of the plane. Matthias rotated the lighter, searching for more. There had been four hijackers, and in addition to Abul Abbas, there had been two other PLO representatives that had met them on the tugboat. It was highly possible that in addition to the men he had spotted thus far, that there were two more Palestinian terrorists somewhere on the plane.

Suddenly the door to the cockpit flew open, and a man came barreling past Matthias's hiding spot, shouting to the men who were laughing and singing near the center aisle of the 737. "We are surrounded by fighter planes!"

The men broke from their huddle, going to the windows, as four F-14 Tomcat fighter planes lit up, showing their gleaming feral lines and racks of wing-mounted missiles. Two tomcats flanked the EgyptAir jet on either side and lunged erratically toward, then away, from the jet. They repeated this threatening movement, and the fighter planes appeared hungry for the kill.

"They've contacted us. They want us to change our course and follow them," shouted the Egyptian captain from the cockpit.

"Contact Cairo and inform them of the American's interference," ordered Abul Abbas.

"I've tried, but there is static on every frequency."

"They are jamming us," cursed Abul Abbas. "American dogs! We know how to deal with them!"

Suddenly the plane began to drop, falling hundreds of feet per second. Matthias found himself momentarily floating above the floor. He shoved himself off the ceiling and came back to the floor, the plane rocking as it dissected a pocket of turbulence.

As they leveled out thousands of feet lower, Matthias heard the sound of a crate being pried open. The velocity of the plane was slowing when a sudden gush of wind howled through the passenger compartment, tearing at the curtains that hid Matthias and whipping them back so that they flapped and strained at the slender metal rod that sustained them. Had someone opened the passenger hatch of the plane?

Matthias was exposed now, and anyone who passed the small niche toward or from the cockpit would be sure to see him. Fate had played his hand for him, and now was the time to make his move. The lowered altitude had solved one problem for him. Now he could use his guns without fear of a bullet hole causing rapid decompression. However, the same thing went for the terrorists. Now they could unload on him.

Boldly, Matthias stepped from his erstwhile hiding place, his massive .44 magnum Desert Eagle gripped in his right hand. As he emerged, a hijacker stepped from the cockpit to relay some further information to his compatriots. Matthias aimed high, his gun jumped and a bullet smashed through the skull of his target, splattering the cockpit door with gray matter and leaving a crimson haze hanging in the air.

Blasts of cold air pushed against Matthias as he leaped from the narrow corridor, through the flapping curtains of the small first class cabin and into the main passenger compartment. Matthias's hair formed a writhing halo of darkness around his head as he emerged from the rent veils of first class. The laser site mounted beneath the barrel of his magnum flashed a red line across the wind-swept panels of the passenger cabin, bullets exploding from the muzzle of the gun as it crossed the scattering targets.

Terrorists screamed as the magnum bullets sliced into them, mushrooming and tearing through their insides. Blood swirled in the air as bullets bodily picked men up and threw them down the aisle or felled them across the three-wide seats in dying agony. Four bullets took three men to their death, but even as Matthias made the shots he realized why the terrorists of

Force 19 had thrown open the two hatches of the plane.

Fifteen feet from Matthias a swarthy terrorist squinted against the wind as he lifted a British-made Blowpipe anti-aircraft missile to his shoulder and sighted in on the F-14 fighter that flanked the jet. Toward the tail of the jet, another man disappeared behind a wall bearing a similar missile. These were remote-guided missiles designed to down aircraft from on-the-ground troops. Matthias guessed that they would prove equally effective from the air.

The nearest terrorist bearing the anti-aircraft missile fired the same time that Matthias did. The .44 magnum bullet shattered the terrorist's spine, pushing him out the open hatch of the 737. A plume of smoke wreathed from the back of the Blowpipe, and the eight-bladed missile leaped from its rack. But the hammer blow of the bullet ruined the aim of the terrorist, and the toggle-guided missile went awry, spiraling toward the night-clad waves, vaporizing water in a ball of fire that illuminated the ocean with angry light. The falling terrorist plunged into the midst of the roiling explosion and was lost forever.

Matthias turned the muzzle of his gun toward the second man whom he had seen with a Blowpipe, hoping to fire through the wall at the now concealed terrorist, and wound or kill him before the deadly missile could be fired at the US fighter flanking the jet's opposite side. As he looked, though, he heard the hiss of the missile, and saw a flash of propellant through the dark windows of the 737 as it hit its second stage of propulsion. Smoke filled the cabin of the jet, only to be grabbed by the wind and sucked through the cigar-shaped body of the jet in long eddying streams of murky gray.

The F-14 veered, going into a steep dive in a desperate attempt to escape the wrath of the anti-aircraft missile. With more time, the pilot might have lured the missile into a downward flight, and been able to pull up and away, escaping. But the Blowpipe had been fired at nearly point blank range, and it traveled at speeds approaching one and a half times the speed of sound. The fighter jet could not leap to that speed quickly enough, and the barbed missile burrowed into the back of the F-14, consuming it in an expanding sphere of blinding heat. Matthias saw the canopy of the fighter rip loose, then shatter in the explosive concussion. He hoped that the pilot had safely ejected, and hadn't suffered the same fate.

A few feet away, Abul Abbas pulled at the gun holstered to his waist. Matthias thrust the barrel of his gun into the PLO leader's crafty face. "Don't do it!" he warned.

Matthias didn't know if Abbas could speak English, but the muzzle of a gun seemed to be the universal language, and the terrorist desisted, raising his hands above his head in acquiescence. Turning Abbas around and removing his pistol, Matthias put the hot barrel of his gun to the terrorist's temple and walked him down toward the rear of the plane.

"What is it that you want from me?" asked Abbas calmly in German.

Abbas's switch to German told Matthias that the terrorist had recognized him. "I want you to tell your man behind the wall to close up the hatch and come out here with his hands over his head."

Calling out in rapid Arabic, Abbas appeared to relay the information to his cohort behind the wall. Momentarily the slip stream of air ceased, and the terrorist came out with his hands over his head.

"What now?" asked Abbas.

"We're going to tell the pilot to land wherever the F-14s order him."

Hours later the EgyptAir jet limped into Sigonella Air Base on the island of Sicily. Immediately, the American commandos of Seal Team Six boarded the airplane. They found four dead bodies and a long-haired rock musician stretched out across three seats, training a .44 magnum on two PLO terrorists.

As Abbas was taken into custody, he turned his steel gaze on Matthias. "Next time," he said in German, "things will be much different."

"Next time, I won't waste my time with your lackeys," answered Matthias. "I'll shoot you first."

A pilot had to be hired for the flight home. Though he insisted it wouldn't be a problem, Sly wasn't in condition to be piloting the Concorde. The hired pilot, however, didn't seem to be much of an improvement. His bone-jarring landing bounced the Concorde down the Fort Lauderdale runway in less than impressive style.

Sly groaned as pain lanced through his side. "I hope this guy isn't expecting a tip."

Mitz and Carna rounded out the roster of passengers on the return trip to Fort Lauderdale. Otto had taken a liking to the statuesque Erena, and extracted her approval to escort her back to Greece. Meanwhile, Fritz heard reports that the terrorists had been intercepted and forced down; he flew to Italy to see if he could find Matthias.

Sly reclined in a seat, a permanent grimace on his face. Mitz had spent some time stitching the wound closed, bandaging the area, and then taping Sly's ribs to keep movement to a minimum. Carna stood by with the antiseptic and gauze. The beating she received at the hands of the hijacker left her face swollen and bruised, but from the moment they had left the Achilles Lauro she had been in excellent spirits.

"I can't wait to see Aaliyah," she said brightly.

As they stepped from the plane into the brilliant sun and humid air, a call came in on Mitz's cell phone. He halted and let Sly, who was in front of him, take his time as he stiffly descended the stairs to the tarmac.

Mitz answered and spoke briefly. He hung up and easily caught up to Sly. "Looks as though we need to go straight to the hospital," he said.

Sly waved a callused hand, passing off the suggestion. "I'm not in that bad of shape. I'm feeling pretty good. I could handle about anything right now."

"Good," said Mitz. "Because I just talked to Aaliyah. She's a little tired right now and little Jacobbe Gantlet needs a diaper change."

"Diaper change?" said Sly, a perplexed look crossing his rugged face.

"You're a father now," explained Mitz more slowly.

For the first time in the last three days, Sly felt scared.

Epilogue:

Much of the previous incidents were suppressed in the press. The second assault on the Achilles Lauro, and the Gantlets' involvement, were not made a part of public record. Likewise, reports of the successful interception of fleeing hijackers did not include the loss of one F-14 jet fighter (the pilot survived the ejection). News reports suggested that four hijackers and Abul Abbas were apprehended in Italy, but three previously incarcerated PLO terrorists were used to replace those that Matthias Gantlet killed. This was done to reduce the backlash that might occur if other nations knew of the involvement of the Gantlet brothers, who are wanted in several countries, and whose presence in the situation might provoke further diplomatic problems. Abul Abbas escaped prosecution by donning the uniform of an EgyptAir employee and slipping out of the country. It is believed that he had help from at least one sympathetic Italian official. Abul Abbas was apprehended eighteen years later by US troops on the outskirts of Baghdad after Iraq was liberated from the totalitarian regime of Saddam Hussein.

The Hard Luck Killers

When at long last the homing beacon began to moan, Chul-Moo Kung pushed the wild-haired blonde away, her bare limbs flailing. In confusion, she tried to extricate herself from the twisted tangle of sheets and pillows. "What's wrong, baby?"

Chul-Moo leaped out of bed and pulled on a pair of expensive Italian pants that were laid neatly across a nearby chair, so as not to disturb the razor-pressed creases. "I've got work to do," he grunted, the livid scar from cheek to mouth creasing as his face tightened. "Your money's on the nightstand."

Honey shrugged and shoved a trio of counterfeit bills into her Gucci purse. "Easiest three bills I ever made. Request me again when you've got a little more time to kill, and we can finish what we started."

Chul-Moo didn't respond, but dialed a three digit sequence on the large cellular phone that he had for three months kept within arm's reach. Instantaneously, the phone contacted the pagers of five different professionals on retainer and standing by in the case that the homing beacon should be located. He had begun to think that the device had been deactivated and that he would be waiting interminably in this miserable hotel.

The Korean shrugged on a fresh white shirt and buttoned from navel to collar in a few seconds. He looked out the window and watched a glistening Boeing jet descending through the blue Nevada skies toward the runway at McCarran Airport. With nimble fingers he knotted a silk necktie around his collar while he strode to the closet. A row of thousand dollar jackets hung from the hotel hangars and he reached for the black pin-striped jacket. Tucked inside a sewn holster was a nine-millimeter Belgian pistol, with a stubby silencer screwed onto the barrel and a cartridge already in the pipe. Though hardly necessary at this range, out of habit, he thumbed on the laser sight and turned, putting the red dot of the laser on the center of Honey's chest as she struggled into her blouse.

Honey saw the red dot wavering on her freckled and sun-darkened skin and glanced up, uncomprehending of the danger she was in until she saw the dark maw of the pistol and the grim, scarred face behind it. She opened her mouth to scream, but the silencer squealed as it released suppressed gasses, and her cry was aborted as three bullets cut into her. Then she crumpled on the blood-spattered sheets, the dying rattle of her breath leaving her body.

"Sorry, Honey," said Chul-Moo, his voice cold as a winter grave. "I can't leave any witnesses."

With leather jacket unzipped, Matthias Gantlet lounged beneath the Luftanza Air sign in the McCarran Airport, back against the wall, long brown hair flowing around his bulging shoulders, and bullet-proof Gargoyle sunglasses pushed on top of his head. He checked the giant digital clock upon the wall. He didn't wear a watch himself because he didn't want to feel like he was a slave to some arbitrary measure of time, but he wasn't even fooling himself. There was no escaping the rigors of time, whether it meant an appointment to be kept or whether it meant the ravages of old age creeping upon him and slowly sapping his youthful strength and vigor.

Even now he was concerned that his appointment was running twenty minutes late. His brother, Sly, had been very cryptic in the short note that Matthias had found among his effects and the character Matthias was meeting was on the kill list of as many countries as Matthias. Old enemies had a way of catching up with one in the most unexpected of moments.

Matthias spent the next five minutes watching the airport patrons rush to and fro, pulling trains of bags and suitcases behind, before he spotted a towering black man with close-cropped hair and a distinctive widow's peak kissing a chocolate-skinned woman farewell. He watched them reluctantly part, and then the tall man turned and walked directly toward him with an easy, athletic stride. His torso was shaped in the form of a wedge and his physique was similar to that of a swimmer's—not as heavily muscled as Matthias but still possessing a power and symmetry that caused both men and women to turn their heads. He was dressed in casual attire, but impeccably, in custom-tailored Christian Dior slacks and a tight-fitting polo shirt that displayed his form to advantage.

"You're late," said Matthias.

"Affairs of the heart," said the man, and he turned to watch the curvaceous strut of his departing companion. "She's mighty fine, isn't she?"

"She's certainly easy on the eyes," agreed Matthias. "But I'm a happily married man, and I find it best to keep my focus on the matter at hand, instead of letting my mind wander and become distracted."

Dillon seemed surprised. "You're not much like your brother, are you? Corri's an actress," said Dillon. "She has a substantial part in the latest Bruce Willis, Damon Wayans movie. I think she's got the talent to go all the way with it."

"Corri's got the talent and the looks—but if you're dating her you've also got to be willing to put up with the attitude."

"What in the blazes you talking about?" said Dillon.

"It's not just her," said Matthias. "It's actresses in general. I've dated enough of them to see that they almost all fall into the same category."

Dillon craned his neck to get a final glimpse at Corri as she disappeared into the throng of the airport rush, but he was obviously irritated by Matthias's proclamation. "Well, you're definitely as irritating as Sly. Maybe you're related after all."

Matthias frowned.

"Go ahead," urged Dillon. "I'm curious now. Illuminate me with your wisdom about life, love, and actresses."

"Well since you put it that way..." said Matthias, the sarcasm heavy in his voice. "Look, it shouldn't be any revelation to you or anybody else that they tend to be self-centered, needy, and egotistic. Besides that, you never know if they're genuine..."

"Genuine?" said Dillon, making an hour glass shape with his hands. "Believe me, Corri's the real deal."

"That's not what I'm referring to. I'm talking about their emotions and their interactions. If they are good at their craft—and Corri is, I've worked with her—then who's to say that their real-life interactions are anything more than just...acting? What's real and what is pretend?"

Anger flashed in Dillon's copper eyes. "You've worked with Corri? What do you mean by that?"

"I mean that at one time I thought maybe being a rock musician wasn't good enough. I wanted to be a movie star, too—and I made a couple of studio movies. They didn't make as much as Die Hard, but Corri was the lead female in one of them."

"So you've never..."

"I'm a married man, Dillon. Get your mind out of the gutter."

"You plan on doing any more movies?"

Matthias shrugged. "The acting is fun, but sometimes you wait for hours while the shots are being set up. I like the end product, but I'm not so sure if I care for the process. Sometimes I think I might be content fading into obscurity. Being famous has a lot of drawbacks. It's hard keeping a low profile when people keep asking for autographs."

"Really," snorted Dillon. "How many did you sign while you were waiting for me to show?"

"Three," said Matthias. He lifted a dangling key into the air and tossed it to Dillon who reflexively caught it. "The fourth was a woman who insisted she give me the key to her hotel room. She might be your type—she said she was an actress."

A tall glacial blonde sat at the bar tucked behind an archway flanked by potted palms. Here the incessant clatter of the slot machines and the ringing of bells was somewhat diminished. She wore large diamond earrings on her lobes, and diamond encrusted tennis bracelets of gold upon each wrist, and after she stubbed out her cigarette she immediately withdrew a pack from the flap pocket of her shaped herringbone blazer and expertly lit another.

The handsome man that sat nursing a beer next to her was at least five years younger than she, but her cool beauty seemed an irresistible challenge. His gaze lingered on the embroidered lapels of her blazer, and drew upward along her open neckline, past the coiled gold necklace around her slender neck and then met eyes so blue that they might freeze the marrow of a man less bold. "I've never seen that brand of cigarettes before; do you always smoke them?"

She nodded and blew out a plume of smoke. "I can't stand American cigs. These are Turkish."

"Where do you buy Turkish cigarettes?" he asked, spinning on his bar stool so to fully face her, and he was gratified when she didn't spurn his attention.

"In Turkey," she said. "If I'm not in Turkey I have them imported by the case."

"That must be expensive."

"Very expensive," she confirmed. "But I have an insatiable taste for them, among other things."

"Are the other things as unhealthy as the cigarettes?"

"Hmm, some less...some moreso. But given my line of work it probably won't be cancer that kills me."

The younger man put his arm on the bar so that his hand rested a few inches from hers. "Is your line of work stressful?"

"Very stressful," agreed the woman. She pushed a business card across the bar to the younger man.

He took it up and read the inscription printed in basic black type. "Monica Killingsworth: Conflict Resolution Specialist."

"What exactly does a Conflict Resolution Specialist do, Monica?"

She reached over and placed a slender but callused hand upon his. "I'm afraid you have me at a disadvantage. You know my name, but I don't know yours."

"Allen Kessler," he replied with a grin. "I'm here at the Mojave for a real estate convention. I'll be here for a couple of days."

"I've been here for three months," laughed Monica. "I'm here on retainer—but what about you? I've always thought that real estate would be a fascinating field."

"It can be," Allen agreed, "but fortunately the stress doesn't seem to be as overwhelming as your job—whatever it is..."

She smiled with her mouth, but her eyes were still cold. "It's exactly like it sounds: I do whatever it takes to resolve conflicts between people with goals that run counter to each other."

Allen was about to reply when the pager in Monica's pocket gave a loud buzz.

"I'm afraid," said Monica, "that there is a conflict that needs resolving."

"Maybe we can continue our conversation later?" asked Allen.

"You've got my number," said Monica as she slipped from the bar stool. "Call and leave a message. If I'm still in town tonight we'll get together."

"You might be going somewhere?"

Monica straightened her jacket so that it covered the brace of pistols holstered at the small of her back. "That all depends."

Dillon scowled. "So now that you've thoroughly dissed my taste in woman, would you like to tell me what I'm doing here?"

"I was hoping that you could shed some light on it. We were going through Sly's effects and found..."

"What do you mean his effects? Is Sly dead?"

Matthias pulled himself upright and hoisted himself out of the airport seat. "You didn't know?"

"I thought he was too ornery of a cuss to die. I'm sorry, I had no idea. No wonder you're busting my chops for being late. What happened?"

"He blew a Russian attack chopper out of the air and it came down on him."

"That's a turn of hard luck. At least he took his enemy with him," said Dillon. "Still, it's a cruel twist of fate."

"A blessing really," said Matthias. "He'd been suffering from a brain cancer brought on by exposure to a North Korean nerve agent."

Dillon shook his head. "Sly had a way of getting on my last nerve and every time we got together we barked and complained at each other, like an old married couple, but the truth is I trusted your brother. I'll miss him. Not that I'd ever tell him that..."

Matthias retrieved a duffel bag from beneath his chair and unzipped it, revealing a safe around four inches high and about twenty across. On the top was a scan pad for fingerprint identification. "Apparently, Sly was giving some thought to your friendship before he died. He left this safe and a note saying that it was keyed to be opened only with your thumb print and my thumb print—and that we should open it at the McCarran Las Vegas Airport."

"That was it?" asked Dillon.

"There was also some kind of gibberish about paying off a bet."

"Really!" Dillon's eyes brightened. "He would never admit that I bested him that night in La Esca. Maybe his conscience was wearing on him?"

"I doubt it," said Matthias. "The version of that arm wrestling match which I heard from Sly involved putting you down so hard that your wrist shattered."

"Why, that son of a..."

"Watch what you say about my mother," warned Matthias. "And don't worry about it; Sly has been known to exaggerate from time to time."

"Exaggerate! Why that's nothing but a bald-faced lie!"

Matthias ignored Dillon's outburst. "Since you don't seem to know anymore about the contents of this safe than I do, why don't we open this sucker up and kill the suspense?"

Igor Nekrasov watched the slot gobble his last silver dollar and pulled the lever of the slot machine. A moment later he saw a trio of mismatched shapes roll onto the screen. He cursed viciously in Russian and spat on the controls before kicking over his stool and stalking away. The long-legged serving girls saw him coming and steered a wide berth around the Russian. For the last three months he had been a permanent fixture at the gaming tables and slot machines of the Mojave Casino and Hotel, and his foul temper and tirades were becoming fodder for break-time story swapping among the employees.

Still, his hotel room was always paid for a week ahead of time and he dropped nine or ten thousand dollars in drink and gambling every month, so the hotel management felt it was worth the bruised egos of a few disgruntled employees to keep the Russian around instead of rousting him out the hotel and casino.

A slender Italian wearing a turtle-neck sweater, and holding a half-finished Bloody Mary intercepted him next to the roulette wheel. "You lose the last of your monthly retainer, again?"

"I tell you, Dominic, the casino's crooked," raged Igor, clenching a meaty fist. "I'm going to find the thieving sooka that owns this shack and feed his guts to the crows."

Dominic paused to empty his glass and put it on the top of a nearby slot machine. "All casinos are crooked. Do you think they run these things to make you rich? The slots are the worst odds—they are computerized and the casinos set them to pay out as much or as little as they like. You've got better chances playing at the cards."

"See!" rumbled Igor. "I'll find the owner and slice him open."

"Not in public, you won't," said Dominic, and he steered the Russian toward the buffet at the back of the casino. "Why don't we grab a bite to eat and make some plans over a juicy steak?"

Igor rumbled some minor protestations, but food was about the only thing that could satiate him when he was angry. Dominic had worked with Igor once before when they had been hired to kill a Brazilian drug lord. Once the hit had been accomplished, Igor cut the throats of the drug lord's wife and children just for the pleasure of it.

Halfway to the buffet both their pagers began to buzz, and a wicked smile spread slowly across Igor Nekrasov's face.

Matthias and Dillon pressed their thumbs against the matching plates on the miniature safe and after a moment's hesitation they heard a click. Matthias pulled back the lid and revealed a single car key and an attached note.

Check the trunk of the Blue Maserati on Parking Level 5, Slot G23. You'll find three satchels. One is marked for Dillon and contains a hundred G's which are a token of my esteem to his claims that he beat me arm wrestling that night we first met in Alphabet City.

The second bag and its contents must be destroyed.

The third bag is for Matthias to dispose of as he sees fit.

By the way, if you're reading this I've already gone on to my eternal reward. Dillon, the Devil and I get together every evening and roast marshmallows over the pits of hell. We think of you frequently and the Devil appreciates all the scum and lowlifes you've been sending him. We look forward to the time that we'll be enjoying your company, too.

-Sly

Dillon gave a low chuckle. "It seems that Sly couldn't resist getting in one last jab."

"Oh, I doubt if it will be his last," muttered Matthias, and he wondered if he was unwittingly participating in some elaborate practical joke that Sly was playing on Dillon from beyond the grave.

In the subterranean parking lot of the Mojave Casino, Jock Anderson sat behind tinted windows in his chrome-edged Ford F-150 and he finished wiring a pack of C-4 plastic explosives to a timing mechanism. His brother Bill sat next to him, lanky and unkempt in the same pair of overalls he'd been wearing for the last three days. Bill alternately loaded a thirty-two round magazine of nine-millimeter UZI ammunition with fragmenting, incendiary, and steel-jacketed rounds.

"You never know which bullet is going to serve you best," he explained to Jock, who had heard the speech many times before. "Sometimes you need a mushrooming bullet that is going to rip as big a hole as possible in flesh, but sometimes the target has got hard cover and the steel jackets have the penetrating power that you need to tear right through the cover, and as for the incendiary bullets—well all that hogwash you see on movies and TV about cars exploding when a bullet hits the tank, that just don't happen without a spark. The incendiary bullets provide that little spark that can make such a satisfying bang."

Jock pushed his homemade C-4 bomb beneath the seat as he caught sight of the hotel security cruising the parking garage in a modified golfcart. "Blue at three o'clock."

Bill dropped the ammunition magazine between his feet and lifted a map of the casinos on the strip, as if intently studying just where to blow his paycheck. The security guard cruised on by, either finding nothing suspicious in the actions of a couple of farmland tourists or noticing nothing behind the heavily-tinted windows of the roll bar-equipped truck.

Jock's pager began to buzz inside of his glove compartment and he reached in front of his brother to retrieve it. He briefly examined the code on the LED screen. "It looks like we're on."

Bill pounded a fist against the ceiling of the truck and grinned. "Hot dang! The Korean must've located the homing signal." He reached down and finished loading the last few shells into his ammunition magazine then removed an already loaded miniature Israeli-made submachine gun from a case behind the seat.

Jock started the Ford's motor and Johnny Cash's Bad News blared through the speakers.

Parking Level 5 was eerily silent as Matthias approached the dusty blue Maserati with his towering dark-skinned companion; they heard only their own footsteps on the concrete floor of the parking garage. Though Matthias was broad and muscular he seemed dwarfed by the much taller Dillon. He walked with a slight limp; he'd never fully recovered from the gunshot wound in his calf.

"I always thought the Maseratis were a bit boxy," said Dillon. He drew a finger across the windshield and painted a streak in the thick layer of dust. "It's been here for at least a couple of months."

"They don't look like much," agreed Matthias, "but they've got great acceleration." He circled around to the back of the vehicle and used the key to pop the trunk. Three battered canvas satchels lay inside, each with a numeral scrawled on the side.

Dillon hoisted out the bag marked with the number one, set it the top of the car and cracked the latch. He pried open the satchel and saw ten bundles of one-hundred-dollar bills jumbled inside. He chuckled. "Well, I guess my trip out to Nevada was well worth my while—besides spending some quality time with Corri I've got a little extra spending cash for the casinos."

"You're not a gambler are you?" asked Matthias.

"I make a living out of dodging bullets. When you gamble with your life on a regular basis, what's the harm in gambling a few dollars, or a few thousand?"

"You've been lucky so far," said Matthias. He produced a flashlight from a jacket pocket and played the light into the shadowed corners of the trunk. He handed Dillon the two other satchels and he placed them in a line upon the roof of the Maserati.

"We've both been far luckier than any of us has a right to be," continued Matthias. "There's been a hundred times when I could have zigged when I should have zagged and I might have caught a bullet in the head."

Dillon closed the satchel. "So, what are you getting at?"

"I mean, angels must be watching over us for either of us to have survived this long. How long is it going to be before one of those angels has a lapse of attention and we get a turn of that hard luck that killed Sly, or for that matter Otto and Fritz?"

"You feeling your mortality?" asked Dillon, and he shrugged his broad shoulders. "Live by the sword, die by the sword—and I'm going to live by the sword until the reaper cuts me down. In the meantime I'm going to enjoy life to the fullest. I'd rather go in a hail of bullets than rotting away from old age."

"I'm not so sure, anymore," said Matthias, still examining the interior of the trunk. "I'm sick of the killing—ready to plant my guns in the garden and spend the rest of my life puttering around the orchard and playing croquet with the kids. I've got so much blood on my hands...rivers of blood."

The rock musician lapsed into uncomfortable silence, and Dillon hoisted the first satchel. "Well, it's been loads of fun hanging with you, but if I get going I can get some more one-on-one time with Corri before I go blow this hundred grand on roulette and Demerara."

Matthias bit his lip and squinted, casting a hard gaze at Dillon. "I thought maybe you, of all people, might be able to understand. You can only revel in the death and destruction for so long."

Dillon turned and waved a massive hand. "I don't revel in it, Slick. But I've accepted it as a byproduct of the life I've chosen. Or maybe it chose me. Some days I think I had a choice about the course my life took, and some days I think it was set out for me before I was born. I don't think about questions like that anymore. Now, if you'll excuse me, I've got a good time planned, and you'd only drag me down with all your moping. Take some Prozac and look me up when you're ready to party."

With a chuckle, Matthias straightened. "There's some kind of radio trigger mechanism around the lip of the trunk, Dillon. Looks similar to the sort of the thing the banks place at the exits."

"You mean Sly put a dye pack in my money?"

"That would be my guess."

"That skeevy son of a gun! If he were still alive I'd give him a beat down he'd never forget."

"Tough talk," said Matthias. "Are you always this brave when you're talking about the dead? Maybe you can prove your manhood by threatening my dear departed grandma next."

Dillon whirled, his copper eyes hard. "You ain't dead...yet. Maybe you want to try me?" He tossed aside the satchel, and a muted explosion sounded from within, orange dye spurting from the seams.

His handsome face twisted in irritation, and he cursed—his fists balling into dark hammers. "I'm going to take that out of your hide, little man."

Matthias waved him off with a dismissive gesture and undid the clasp of the second satchel. "Don't bother. I know the secret to cleaning the bills— learned it from an FBI man."

"Turn around and face me!" demanded Dillon. "I don't have a problem sucker-punching you."

Matthias slowly turned to face the advancing giant. He was dwarfed by nearly half a foot in height, and anyone could see that the advantage of reach belonged to the taller man. "That wouldn't prove much, would it? Listen, if you really want to do this I'll oblige—but it's a pointless battle. I've got better things to do than beat on a friend and ally. Sly said you saved his life in Hunjiang."

Dillon relaxed his fists and the tension went out of his shoulders. "Hah, I'd run into him in the strangest of places. I was chasing this Chinese girl, Ah-Lam Lim, slender as a willow with these bewitching green eyes. Turns out her father was importing endangered animals from North Korea and selling them to collectors all over the world and was cohorts with some rather unsavory and quite deranged—

Matthias ducked and thrust with his legs, driving his shoulder hard into Dillon's solar plexus. Dillon gasped and bent over as the two of them tumbled to the ground. Behind them, the windows of the Maserati exploded into a spray of shards, and bullet holes stitched across the door panels.

The fluorescent lights of the parking garage gleamed against the chrome trimmings of a cherry red Ford as it careened through the parking lot. Bill Anderson leaned out the passenger window, wind tearing at his bedraggled blonde hair and his miniature UZI spitting hot lead. At sixteen rounds a second it took him all of two seconds to empty his magazine and he released it, so that it tumbled across the concrete floor.

While his brother, Jock, steered the truck through the parking lot at a headlong pace, Bill slapped the magazine with alternating ammunition into his UZI. "See," he yelled. "This is the perfect opportunity to flush them from cover using the steel jackets!"

Jock grunted a reply and, with one hand driving, he set the timer on his C-4 bomb to five seconds, long enough to reach the hiding men and toss it out the window.

While Bill Anderson reloaded, Matthias shook his head forward so that his sunglasses slipped over his eyes. His hand dipped beneath his jacket and emerged bearing a .454 Cassul revolver that carried five rounds of the most powerful handgun ammunition in the world. He zipped his leather jacket and rose behind the hood of the nearby station wagon, using the engine block as cover. A two-foot gout of flame licked from the Cassul each time that he fired. His first shot tore off the massive side view mirror and ripped a bloody gash across Bill Anderson's face. The second and third shattered the windshield and tore gaping holes through Jock Anderson.

Jock dropped the C-4 bomb down by the brake pedal and he slumped to one side, his foot getting stuck in the crease by the accelerator. The massive trucked veered left and plowed into a line of parked cars, that crumpled and bucked with the impact. Bill Anderson was thrown free from the passenger window and flew like a rag doll, spreading a web of stress lines when his body smashed into the windshield of a Toyota sedan. Still, through all this, he doggedly clung to his freshly-loaded UZI.

As the Ford rocked forward on its front wheels and then settled back to the ground, the C-4 pack at Jock's feet detonated. The truck disintegrated into scraps of glass and shrapnel that flung through the parking lot. Shards of metal sprayed Matthias's leather jacket, and one ricocheted off his bullet-proof Gargoyle sunglasses and left a slice across his forehead.

Dillon threw up a forearm to shield his eyes as flying glass cut through his shirt and nicked his body in a half dozen places. A chunk of flaming chrome roll-bar impacted on the roof of the car next to him. As the explosion died, Bill Anderson came staggering out of the inferno, his body aflame and his parched throat unable to form a scream. Blinded by the smoke and stench of his own burning clothing and flesh, he tried to aim at Matthias and Dillon but his shots went awry and he sent bullets spattering, cutting, and burning through a group of automobiles parked about fifty feet away.

One of the incendiary bullets punched into a gas tank, and even as a second, less powerful, explosion rocked the parking garage, Matthias fired the last two rounds in his Cassul and put Bill Anderson out of his misery. Flame and fumes continued to rise from the wreckage even after the explosions had subsided, and the thick black smoke gathered at the ceiling blotted the light of the surviving fluorescents so that the garage was plunged into an artificial twilight.

Matthias opened the cylinder of his Cassul and shook out the five empty shells of the .454 magnum ammunition. He reached into one of the many pockets within his jacket and came out with a speedloader, a plastic ring pre-loaded with cartridges that could be pressed into the cylinder of the gun so that it could be reloaded all at once instead of cartridge by cartridge. The rock musician inserted the cartridges, peeled away the plastic ring and snapped the gun shut.

Only now did he notice that Dillon was beside him shouting into his ringing ears. The soldier of fortune held a nine-millimeter Glock pistol in his fist. "What happened to all that jive about you burying your guns in your backyard garden? It looks like you're carrying an entire arsenal in your coat pockets."

"I said I'd like to bury my guns in the backyard," replied Matthias. "The problem is that people keep trying to kill me."

As if to punctuate the point, three bullets stitched across the back of Matthias's jacket, and he fell forward to his knees. Dillon went into a roll as hot lead cut by him, and he came up firing at a blonde beauty who had crept upon them during the turmoil of the explosions and was firing at them with double-fisted .45 caliber pistols. By the time that Dillon returned fire from behind the hood of the Maserati, she had ducked behind the engine of a maroon Mercedes, but Dillon put a few bullets into the engine just to let her know that he was watching.

Matthias crouched beside him with the Cassul in his hands.

"Shouldn't you be bleeding to death?" asked Dillon.

"This jacket is about fifty pounds of leather, Kevlar, and ceramic plates. It's hot as hell on a warm day, but it's saved my life more times than I can count."

"Listen," said Dillon. "Besides the hot blonde, I've spotted three other professional killers. They've got us boxed in. I recognized one of them, Igor Nekrasov, ran into him once in Prague. He's a sick puppy; I saw him tear the arms off a woman with his bare hands. Any ideas what they want?"

"Unless it's related to your work in Prague, I suspect it has something to do with what's in the satchels sitting on top of the car."

"Don't grab them," advised Dillon. "They'll shoot you down the second you show your face. In fact, they probably think you're dead. Let's let 'em think it."

"Got it," said Matthias. "But take this Desert Eagle .44 magnum. You need some more firepower than that nine-millimeter." He laid the gun down on the concrete and placed three loaded magazines next to it. Then Matthias dropped down to his chest, and with bruised back stinging from the sledge-hammer blows of the bullets, began to work his way along the garage floor, past the edge of the Maserati and then beneath the golden Humvee parked across from it.

While Matthias was painstakingly working his way out of the trap, Dillon took up the .44 magnum pistol and switched the nine-millimeter to his left hand, then he held down the fort. Whenever he saw a face peering from behind a car or a flash of movement as one of the hired killers tried to move into a more favorable position, he fired a shot to keep them pinned down or to let them know he was watching, and to distract them so that they wouldn't notice that Matthias's dead body was steadily crawling out of the crossfire that they were setting.

This maneuvering went on for a couple of minutes, and Dillon realized he was at a severe disadvantage. Without eyes in the back of his head, he was eventually going to be blind-sided by one of the killers. One killer would distract him and another out of his line of sight would move into a better position to take a shot at him. Dillon was a sharp enough tactician to real-ize what was happening, so when the blonde killer popped up from behind a Volkswagen and took a trio of rapid fire shots that punched through the pas-senger windows and windshield of the Maserati, Dillon did not return fire.

Even though he felt the hot breath of the bullets as they whined by, he turned the opposite direction, with his back against the side of the Maserati. He was rewarded by catching a glimpse of Igor Nekrasov as he dodged between vehicles.

It was nigh on impossible to aim and hit such a fleeting target, but Dillon often accomplished the nigh on impossible and he fired with well-honed instinct. The Desert Eagle jumped in his hand, and Igor spun to the ground, his throat ripped out by the bullet. While the Russian gagged on his own blood, Dillon turned and evenly stitched six bullets across the body of the Volkswagen. The Desert Eagle had enough power to punch all the way through the vehicle, and though he heard no screams to indicate he'd hit his hidden target, he did notice gasoline leaking onto the pavement—evidence that he'd punctured the fuel tank.

Dillon pondered whether to toss over a lighter, to see if he could flush out the blonde—but while he was pondering, a voice accented with Korean shouted out. "Enough of these games! We've got you outnumbered and pinned down. Eventually we'll kill you, unless you throw us the satchel."

"Which satchel do you want?" shouted Dillon.

"The one with the plates," answered Chul-Moo from concealment. "You can keep the other satchel, and whatever it contains."

"Sounds like a good deal to me," said Dillon. "I never had much interest in kitchenware, anyhow. Now how we going to do this, without you shooting me the second I stand up to toss you the satchel?"

There was a moment of silence as Chul-Moo pondered the logistics, and it was obvious to Dillon that they certainly had intended to shoot him the moment they had him in their sights. Now that he had pointed out the obvious, they had to formulate a way that he could actually deliver the satchel and feel he could safely do so.

"Monica will leave her guns behind and come out to retrieve the satchel. We get it and we leave. If any of us make a suspicious move you can shoot her."

"Fair enough," said Dillon. "Send her out."

Monica arose from behind a black Chevy not far from the Volkswagen that Dillon had riddled, and he realized that as soon as he had fired at Igor she had wisely changed her position. She had her hands high above her head, and in each of them she held a pistol. "I'm setting them down," she called. Slowly she lowered the guns and left them on top of the Chevy's hood.

Then she strode out into open, maintaining an even pace that was not dawdling, but not too brisk to be interpreted as threatening. Her nerves seemed as steady as ice and her step did not falter. A smile flickered on her lips as she saw Dillon hunkered down by the tire of the Maserati. "Hey, handsome."

She stepped by him and opened the satchel that was marked with the numeral two. She seemed satisfied with the contents. "What's in the satchel marked number three?"

"Search me," said Dillon. "I didn't even know what was in the second bag."

She raised an eyebrow. "Do you now?"

"Printing plates manufactured in North Korea for counterfeit US C-notes."

"Very good. Sly Gantlet shot the forger and absconded with them a few months ago. The tracking device malfunctioned and the last signal triangulated to McCarran Airport. Moving it out of the trunk must have jogged the circuits and got it working again."

"With the forger dead, I can understand why North Korea wants to retrieve the printing plates. The North Korean forgeries are supposed to be so good that they are indistinguishable from the real thing."

"Indeed, and North Korea has been printing at least 25 million worth of them a year," said Monica as she closed the satchel. "No hard feelings, handsome. Next time maybe we can get to know each other under more amicable circumstances."

"Wouldn't be the first time I've had a viper in my bed," said Dillon.

She began to stride away then paused. "Where's the man I shot?"

"He's on a tight schedule," said Dillon. "Couldn't stick around, but I'll let him know that you inquired about his welfare..."

A gunshot boomed through the haze of the parking garage. Somewhere, Dominic slumped against a vehicle that was spattered with his own blood and brains.

"That must be Matthias now," said Dillon. He moved quickly and wrapped Monica up in his brawny arms. She was strong and lithe, but many men stronger than she had been overcome by Dillon's strength. He turned her, feet dangling, in the direction of the Korean's voice, and even as he was doing so, Chul-Moo rose from hiding and fired his Belgian pistol. The first bullet bit through Monica's shoulder, and Dillon felt the sting as it sliced into his own flesh.

The Korean's second and third shots went awry as bullets from Matthias's .454 pounded through glass and steel, and tore gaping wounds in Chul-Moo's body. Matthias stopped firing when all five cylinders of his pistol were empty. Chul-Moo's gory corpse slowly slid from the side of a sports utility vehicle where the gunshots had temporarily pinned him.

Blood seeped into the embroidered lapel of Monica's herringbone blazer, and she collapsed in a dazed heap. Then with a groan, she began to drag herself toward the black Chevy and her brace of guns, but her limbs had lost their strength and she lapsed into shock before she pulled herself ten feet.

With grim face, Dillon clutched at his shoulder and watched Matthias approach, emptying and reloading his revolver as he walked.

"I guess," said Dillon, "that it was inevitable I'd eventually be on the receiving end of that hard luck that's been going around."

"Nah," said Matthias. "You've come out with lady luck smiling on you. If you hole up for a week or two with Corri tending to your every need, you'll be as good as new. Today, it's these killers who were the ones on the receiving end of the hard luck."

Sirens sounded in the distance, the smoke began to settle, and Matthias fired his pistol into the bag of printing plates until they were so shattered and punctured that they'd never be of any use to a printer again.

Dillon nodded at Matthias's smoking pistol. "So you going to bury those guns, now?"

Matthias shook his head and motioned to the carnage and the bodies strewn around them. "How can I, when scum like this are roaming the earth?"

"See!" said Dillon. "That's what I've been trying to tell you. Some of us have a calling...and we'd be shirking our responsibility if we didn't stand up and fight when evil rears its ugly head."

Matthias smiled. "The bullet that killed Igor...that was a one in a million shot. A real beauty."

"Nice of you to notice," said Dillon. "Do you want to check that third satchel before the police get here?"

"Nah, I'm sure it's loaded with counterfeit bills. I'd rather not be up to my armpits in them when the police show up."

"Counterfeit!" said Dillon. "That dirty rat. So that's what Sly meant when he said that the hundred thousand was a token of his esteem to my claim of beating him at arm wrestling. He paid me with counterfeit bills."

"...Implying that your claim of beating him was counterfeit as well. You should know better than to ever hope for any satisfaction from Sly—dead or not."

Dillon smacked a meaningful fist into his meaty palm. "If he were here I'd give him a token of my esteem."

Dead Beat in La Esca

Written with Derrick Ferguson

New York

It wasn't quite the fickle hand of fate that led world adventurer and fortune hunter, Dillon, and the famous German guitar player, Sly Gantlet, to walk into the La Esca tavern on the same night, only about fifteen minutes apart from each other. But rather it had to do something with the beautiful women that escorted each of them, their subtle machinations being not so much of the feminine variety, but closer to the diabolical. Given the separate careers of the two men, each infamous in their own way, it was perhaps inevitable they meet at sometime. However, none could have anticipated the circumstances that their first meeting would have taken place.

The entrance to the La Esca was obscured at the end of a Manhattan alley in Alphabet City well away from the red-carpet clubs with high-wattage signs and brightly-lit entryways located further uptown in the Village and along Broadway. Sly parked his Ferrari and let the headlights extinguish and drop into the hood of the canary yellow high-performance sports car before he stepped out and stared dubiously at the run down tenements that were intermittently lit by the few working street lights. Alphabet City was a part of New York that the casual tourist just didn't go strolling through day or night since it was infested with violent drug gangs. But the clubs located in Alphabet City were among the hottest in the city and for a man like Sly Gantlet who had partied in the fleshpots of cities such as Morocco, Cairo, Isthmus City, and Casablanca, the least of his worries was the denizens of the neighborhood.

A woman slipped out of the passenger seat after applying a second coat of bright red lipstick. Sly admired her form as she bent to straighten her too short and too tight dress. There was nothing subtle about her. She was the definition of blonde bombshell—all curves, slink and strut. The kind of woman a man might kill for. Sly had spotted her in the crowd at that night's show at Webster Hall, and made sure that she received a backstage invite.

"Hey babe, you sure you've got the right place? It looks pretty dead around here."

Holly stopped and the corners of her fire engine red lips turned upward in a coy smile. "You think that because I'm blonde, I don't know my way around this town?" She pointed a long red-nailed finger down the alley between two tenements. "La Esca is right down there."

As she finished speaking, the thump of bass speakers came to Sly's ears. "I think I hear the music from the club."

Holly took his burly arm as he came around the low front of the Ferrari. "It ain't the band Gantlet, but since I've got Gantlet's lead guitar player as my escort, I think that I'll be able to make do with whatever second rate music they're playing tonight."

In a room with bare cinder block walls, a slight man with a shaved pate hunched over a bank of monitors and a computer screen. His face was unshaven and his eyes a piercing black. At the end of the table, just within his reach rested a 9mm MAT-49—a French made machine gun—the magazine handle momentarily folded forward to reduce the amount of space it used on the edge of a table already crowded with surveillance equipment.

A gruff voice crackled across the intercom. "Target One is approaching in south alley entrance."

Moricz Mortoni reached a hand over to the keyboard and slapped a key, bringing up the target's profile for one last review.

Target 1: Slatko Gantlet

Name and Aliases: Sly Gantlet, Ten Fingers of Destruction, Slats Gantlet, The Foot.

Cover Occupation: Lead guitar player for the rock band Gantlet.
Covert Operations: Forays into the Mid-East to destroy nuclear caches, foreign anti-terrorist activities, assassination of domestic drug lords, CIA work for hire and numerous other activities.

Confirmed Kills: 245

Reported Kills: 1,200+

Contracting Parties: The Conglomerate

Contact: La Maitresse D'or

Total Bounty: Dead-$3,400,000 Alive-$10,675,000

Weaknesses: Family, Women, Alcohol, Ego
Assault Assessment: Capture. Certain members of the conglomerate want him for torture. Only surviving family members are brothers Matthias, Mitko, Otto, and Fritz, and are too dangerous to use as bait. Use out-side party of feminine pulchritude...

A smile crept across Moricz's face and he switched cameras so he could view the burly rock guitarist escorting a curvaceous blonde into the alley.

Sly accompanied Holly down the narrow alley, raising a dubious brow at the Dumpsters and the mangy cats that scrounged through them. He wore heavy spandex pants that did little to disguise his thick thighs, and his waist was wrapped with a studded leather belt, the silver buckle embossed with a G. A fringed leather jacket was tossed over a tank top emblazoned with the logo of the rock band Condemner. Sly's blonde hair was nearly as long as Holly's, but hers was teased and sprayed into curly waterfalls. He stood six foot two inches, nearly half a foot taller than his date, and his barrel chest nearly burst the seams of his shirt, just as Holly's generous proportions strained at the confines of her dress. He certainly didn't look like the lead guitar player of one of the world's most famous and top selling rock bands. Sly Gantlet looked more like an ancient barbarian or mythological Norse warrior transported to the 20th century and turned loose on an unsuspecting civilization. There was something elemental and wild in his eyes and, despite his heroic musculature, he moved as lightly as a dancer.

At the wall at the back of the alley, Sly could see a small blue neon sign that read La Esca. A battered, rusty metal door stood next to the sign and, as Holly seemed incapable of any sort of normal stride, she strutted up to it on those four-inch five-hundred-dollar Blahnik stiletto heels and knocked three times on its peeling face. A small hatch in the door slipped open.

"What's your business?" asked a gruff voice.

"No business, just pleasure," purred Holly as she put one slender hand on Sly's chest.

Apparently this was a good enough answer because the door opened up and a seven-foot-tall bouncer the color of mahogany let them inside. Sly glanced at the bouncer with the disdain he reserved for anyone that appeared to have a powerful enough physique to match him in a fight. This cocky disdain was meant to dissuade potential challengers, although it sometimes had the opposite effect of goading them into a rage. Either reaction was perfectly okay with Sly as he enjoyed a good fight as much as most other men enjoyed a gourmet meal. And it most certainly was always good to know that he could back down an opponent with just a stare. In his other line of work it was a talent that often came in handy.

A cover band played on a small stage at the far end of the club, while lights flashed and strobed across the gyrations of the sweaty crowd bumping and grinding away on the sunken dance floor. They were doing a pretty good cover of Squeeze's Black Coffee In Bed. The drummer seemed determined to throw in his own little personal riffs that gave the song a nice little twist and the lead singer had a professional level voice, Sly noted with pleasure. Tables were clustered around the dance floor, and a long glass bar, softly illuminated from the inside with cool blue and indigo lamps, stood along the left hand side of the club, up a couple of steps from the dance floor.

"Let's dance," said Holly. She tried to drag Sly to the dance floor but found herself instead being pulled to the bar.

"After we get a drink," said Sly. "I'm parched."

The rangy bartender had an old purple scar running along his left cheekbone and he appraised Sly for a long moment, and then spared a brief glance for Holly. "What's your poison?"

"Whiskey," said Sly and he looked toward Holly for input on her drink. "The lady will have..."

"A kamikaze," said the bartender with a sort of bored familiarity. "She never drinks anything else."

Holly slipped onto a barstool, and so, naturally, Sly took the one beside her. "So you're a regular here."

"I come in two or three times a month," she said. "I like to dance." Indeed, even while sitting on the stool, her shoulders and hips were twitching in a delightful manner that was most pleasing to Sly's eyes. She flashed him a grin that had more than flirtation in its promise.

"And what do you do when you're not dancing?"

Her chocolate brown eyes seemed momentarily innocent as she gazed into the steel gray hiding behind his slitted lids. "Oh, I like to do lots of things—but I work as an account specialist."

The bartender slipped a blue drink in front of Holly and filled a shot glass for Sly. He downed it one gulp. "Does it pay well?"

"Very well," said Holly, "but I work freelance, so I sometimes have dry periods between jobs."

"But you make enough when you work to cover the bills when you're looking for the next job?"

"It's a booming economy," said Holly, "and it seems that there has been no shortage of messed up accounts that need balancing." She raised her glass and sipped her drink, looking at Sly over the rim of the glass. He was looking back at her in a new light.

"That's interesting," said Sly. "I took you for just another empty-headed bimbo, but you intrigue me."

"Is it my body or my mind that intrigues you, Mr. Sly Gantlet?"

"I was referring to your mind," said Sly, "...err, not that your figure isn't plenty intriguing. So tell me more about your occupation; what sort of companies call you in, and just how messed up are their accounts?"

Holly seemed distracted by something that was happening at the front entrance of the club. She squeezed Sly's arm and nodded toward the door of the La Esca. "Have you ever seen that man before?"

"Target Two entering building," reported the gruff voice on the intercom.

Moricz Mortoni rubbed his hands together and settled back in his chair to watch his handiwork, while profile information scrolled slowly across the third screen at his left.

Target 2: Dillon

Name and Aliases: Carrick MacFhearghius, Chan Carson Henry Peace, Henri Cross, Jasper Dillon, Jake Dillon, Dillon Jakes, The Ghost, Black Ice, Raymond J. Johnson, Jr. and a dozen lesser used aliases and identities.

Cover Occupation: None (ostensibly a soldier of fortune)
*Covert Operations: Raids into Ceylonese area countries at behest of
foreign powers, mercenary and bodyguard work for dozens of offshore
entities. Wanted in 23 different countries. Possesses classified knowledge
of great value to particular parties.*

Confirmed Kills: 117

Reported Kills: 1,300+

Contracting Parties: The Conglomerate

Contact: La Maitresse D'or

Total Bounty: Dead-$2,495,000 Alive-$15,000,000

Weaknesses: Friends, Women, Ego
Assault Assessment: Capture as per plan C of Gantlet package.

A black man a couple of inches taller than Sly walked through the door, giving the bouncer a condescending sneer as he did so. His simple yet elegant Versace suit gave him an aura of respectability that Sly's rocker attire most definitely did not. However, the muscular arms, wide shoulders, and tapered back shattered the illusion that this man was some sort of banker or stockbroker. Sly noted the casual way the black man sized up the room. To anybody else it appeared as if he was merely checking out the room but Sly noticed the way that the man's eyes rested for the briefest of instants on the various exits, making sure of their location and then going on to scan the crowd, picking out possible threats.

The woman that was on the newcomer's arm warranted at least as much examination as he did. She was a Nubian princess with a long graceful neck that was accentuated by the fact that her long black hair was tied at the back of her skull, dropping in wavy rivulets that did not touch her neck. She was nearly six feet tall and she moved as gracefully as a gazelle. Together the two of them made a striking pair that turned heads as they made their way through the club toward the bar.

Holly punched him in the shoulder when his eyes lingered over long on the long legs of the Nubian princess. Legs that seem to go on and on… "Don't forget just who it is you're taking home tonight."

This snapped Sly's attention immediately back to Holly. "Mama Gantlet warned me against women like you."

"Do you always listen to your mama?"

"Not always," admitted Sly, "but I've always regretted the times I haven't, God rest her soul."

The Nubian princess perched next to Sly on the bar and glanced coldly at him and Holly. She gestured to the blue beverage in front of Holly. "What kind of drink is that?"

"A Kamikaze," said Holly, in equally chilly tones. "I haven't seen you in here before, but you look familiar. What's your name?"

"Andrea Ross," answered the woman with a toss of her head. "I've done three Vogue covers," she added, as if slighted that Holly didn't recognize her. "Right, Dillon?"

Dillon shrugged his broad shoulders. "I'm not a big reader of Vogue myself, but I'm sure those three covers were well worth examination."

Andrea Ross turned her attention to Sly. "Aren't you famous or something?"

Sly seemed a little annoyed by this, not so much by the fact that he was recognized in public, but by the idea that she couldn't put a name to him.

Holly came to Sly's defense. "He's Sly Gantlet, world famous guitar player. His last record only sold like a million albums."

"Actually, it was 6.7 million albums," Sly corrected with a twinge of pride in his voice. Now Dillon paid sharper attention to the bearded blonde man in fringed leather and spandex that he had dismissed as some sort of eccentric hippy throwback. Sly looked into Dillon's penetrating eyes that were the copper color of freshly minted pennies and Sly could swear that he could see the man thinking. Sly's name had tripped some kind of mental Rolodex in Dillon's mind he was flipping through. A fact that was confirmed when he said easily; "From stories I've heard here and there, he does a little more than play guitar."

Sly picked up a shot glass and gazed mournfully at its emptiness. He motioned to the scarred bartender. "Get me a Sly Beer, and get the rest of these folks whatever it is they're drinking." He reached into a pocket and withdrew a well-used leather wallet held together with old brass rivets and withdrew a crisp new hundred dollar bill that he slipped onto the bar top and plunked the empty shot glass on top of it.

"Give me a shot of Demerara," ordered Dillon. "You do have some, don't you?"

The bartender didn't answer, gave him a knowing smile as he reached under the bar and produced a bottle of Demerara rum. He slapped a fresh shot glass on the bar and poured it to the rim. "You want a chaser for that?"

Dillon downed the fiery liquid as if it were plain water and slammed the glass back down on the bar. "Yeah, give me another shot—and keep 'em coming. After all, it's on Daddy Big Bucks' tab."

Sly pulled the tab on his beer and tossed it into an ashtray.

"Oh, wow!" said Holly. "Your picture's on the can."

"I've got a merchandising deal with Anheuser-Busch," explained Sly. "They license my name and brew extra potent German-style ale. I negotiated a slice of the sales. Last month they cut me a check for thirty grand. It's peanuts compared to the record royalty and concert fees, but it's icing on the cake."

Holly dipped a red nail in a puddle of condensation on the bar and began doodling. "What is it that you do for a living, Mr. Dillon?"

"Just Dillon, please. Every time somebody calls me "Mr. Dillon" I look around for Dennis Weaver. As for what I do…I suppose you could call me a troubleshooter. Firms bring me in as a specialist when their full time staff doesn't have the necessary skills."

Sly's eyes narrowed and he looked to Holly. "Really? That sounds a lot like how Holly describes her profession—except she calls herself an Account Specialist."

"I'm sure our areas of expertise are somewhat different," said Dillon as he moved on to the next shot of Demerara. "My hourly fees are quite exorbitant."

Though Dillon had arrived a few minutes later, he was rapidly catching up to Sly in the quantity of drinks that he had consumed. Sly took a large swig from his beer; as a point of pride he was determined not to let the newcomer out drink him.

"Just how exorbitant?" he asked, and for a moment he imagined that he saw a smile flicker across Andrea Ross's chiseled features.

"I probably pull down about as much for a day's work as you do per concert; more for certain jobs."

Sly scoffed at this suggestion. "I'd like to see your client list."

"I'm afraid that wouldn't be possible," replied Dillon as he pushed away his empty glass. The bartender was right there to fill up another. "My clients are rather touchy about their privacy. They prefer that news about my employment not get out to certain parties."

"I see," snorted Sly. "How convenient. I would guess from the clothes and ghetto fabulous smooth that most of your work is done while sipping champagne while you tell bored housewives how beautiful their eyes are. What are you, some sort of high-priced gigolo?"

Moricz Mortoni watched this exchange on his video monitor and couldn't help but laugh. The two fools were playing right into his hands. Already they were each sitting with half a dozen drinks in their bellies, and whatever good sense they had begun the night with was oozing away as the heady buzz of intoxication set in. If he could keep them drinking, and too wrapped up in their rivalry to notice they were being force fed alcohol, they would soon be three sheets to the wind and easy prey.

"Why don't we step outside and resolve this matter like gentlemen?" said Dillon, a dangerously deceptive grin on his face that belied the calm suggestion.

"What? You don't want your woman to see me mop the floor with you?"

"Actually, I was trying to spare you the humiliation of having your woman watch me beat you down."

The bartender poured a shot of whiskey and it somehow found its way into Sly's hand. Sly gulped it down as he stood from the bar. "Let's do this right here—in public—but let's make it interesting. You see, if I beat the tar out of you I don't get anything out of it. I want to see if you'll put your supposed money where your big fat mouth is."

Another shot of Demerara appeared in front of Dillon on the bar and he slammed it down, and then stood to face Sly toe to toe. "You're on. Just name it."

"Arm wrestling," challenged Sly. "Best of three wins the pot. You name the stakes."

"Ten Gs," said Dillon. "Andrea and Holly hold our bets."

Sly sneered. "Weren't you just telling me about how much money you make in a day? I wipe my butt with thousand dollar bills. Ten grand is a pathetic wager."

"Fine. If it's not too rich for your blood we'll call it a hundred G's."

"It's a bet," said Sly. He whipped out a platinum American Express card and handed it to Holly. "Don't go running off with this, baby. There's no credit limit on that sucker."

"Really?" said Holly turning the card over and over in her hand, examining it with interest. "Well maybe after you take care of this jerk we can rent the best room at the Cobalt Club and celebrate."

Andrea examined Holly with the sort of irritated look that one gave a silly little puppy that's piddled on the floor. "You're rolling with a character who looks like Fabio after a three day bender and you're calling my man a jerk?"

"Ladies," said Dillon as he pulled a platinum card from his own wallet, "Mr. Gantlet and I are going to resolve our differences, and there is no reason for two beautiful women such as you to berate each other." He handed Andrea the card and smiled. "It shouldn't take more than a few seconds for me to put this dim bulb in his place."

Most of the tavern's occupants had paused in their activities to witness the stand off between the two men. Either one was a prime specimen of manhood, bulging with muscles, and oozing spare testosterone through every pore. And neither man looked like someone you might want to run into in a dark alley. The very air between them seemed charged with tension as they sized each other up. It was as if a magnificent Bengal tiger had turned a corner in a dense jungle trail and bumped heads with a sleekly lethal black panther.

As Sly and Dillon chose a table and pulled up chairs, the cover band ceased playing and the excited customers crowded around, jostling for a good view of the upcoming match. One enterprising young man began to take bets and the scarred bartender quickly negotiated the club getting a cut of the action.

Sly grinned. "You may wanna take off that fancy suit. Hate to see your fine threads get messed up."

Dillon returned the grin. "Ah, you'd be surprised at how much I can do in this suit and never lose the crease."

Before the two rivals locked hands, a long-legged waitress bustled up with another shot of poison for each of them. In unison they emptied their glasses and slammed them down on the table. They looked into each other's eyes and gripped each other's callused palms with fervent intensity.

The bartender counted down and shouted for the match to begin, but neither Sly nor Dillon moved. Their muscles bulged and writhed, they gasped with intense effort, and sweat began pouring down their faces, yet the locked hands wavered neither to the left nor to the right.

They sat as statues for long minutes and someone in the crowd yelled. "Well, start wrestling!" But neither combatant could seem to get the advantage. Every muscle in their bodies, from their toes to their necks was locked rigidly, unable to budge the other man from his position. They might have been gripped with some kind of weird paralysis, so immobile were they. The only way one could tell they were actually wrestling was the sweat dripping from their chins and noses and the occasional blinking of their eyes.

"This is insane," whispered Holly. Andrea, who stood next to her, nodded in mute agreement. "What have we gotten ourselves into?"

As Sly concentrated every fiber of his being in driving his opponent's hand through the table top, he noticed a peculiar lethargy washing over him as if he was just too tired to continue with the match. He averted his eyes from the locked fists at the center of the table to look at Dillon's dark face, and noticed that he was blinking hard as if trying to fight off the effects of fatigue.

It didn't come to Sly in a flash or an instant, but slowly, as if through molasses, the idea pushed until it emerged fully formed. "It's a set-up, man! We've been drugged! We've got to get out of here now!"

With great effort he wrenched his hand away from Dillon's grasp and staggered to his feet. He glanced at the crowd and saw hands reaching for weapons hidden in pockets and purses.

"Tasers!" shouted Dillon, as it worked through his fogged brain just what was happening. It was all a trap, and the two beautiful women had suckered him and Sly in here. He threw up the table in front of him and charged past Sly, even as three or four taser units were raised and fired. Double wires unspooled from the weapons, the darts sticking in the wooden tabletop which Dillon wielded as a shield. Fifty thousand volts of energy sparked from each taser, and Dillon could feel the tingle in his palms as the current conducted through the wood.

The tasers had a range of about fifteen feet and if the darts hooked you, the high voltage stimulated your muscles to produce massive quantities of lactic acid which locks up the muscle fibers and makes the victim incapable of moving. Dillon had taken a hit with a taser on more than one occasion and knew how nasty they were. He was already sluggish from whatever drug the bartender had slipped into his last Demerara, and a hit from a taser just might put him out for the count...if the drug didn't do its job first. He didn't know how long he had before that narcotic knocked him unconscious...it could be a matter of minutes.

Moricz swore in Hungarian at the monitors. "Someone shoot a taser into their backs!" As he spoke a couple of his hirelings in the crowd attempted to do just that, but Sly leaped, twisting aside with deceptive grace as the sparking darts whipped past him, and then he pounded down the offenders with two mauling fists.

Dillon used the table as a battering ram, knocking down seven or eight people before abandoning the table and turning to find Sly, bloody-fisted, rising up from two unconscious forms.

"Sly!" pleaded Holly, "what is going on?"

Sly grabbed Holly's arm and started dragging her toward the door. "It's a trap; we've got to get out of here!"

Andrea approached Dillon, her hand reaching out for him as he moved toward the door with an agility that seemed impossible for a man of his considerable height. "Get me out of here, Dillon."

Dillon scowled and straightened his arm, sending her graceful form staggering and sprawling in a most un-gazelle-like manner. A stun gun fell from her left hand and spun across the floor. "You're not a model, and you ain't that good of an actor," said Dillon. "Get lost before I give you some of what you deserve."

Andrea scrambled across the floor, heading for one of the back rooms. It became clear to Dillon that some of the crowd were merely hired as extra bodies to fill in the club, because these scampered for the four corners of the tavern, anxious to be out of the way of the conflict at its center. Those who were in on the scam were tangled in the sparking wires of their compatriots' tasers, beneath the splintered remains of the table, or lying mauled and unconscious. The sounds of crashing tables, breaking glass, cursing and yelling echoed in the smoky confines of the club.

As Sly dragged Holly to the door, the gigantic bulk of the bouncer moved between them and the exit. Sly's feet felt leaden and his brain was swimming in a mist of fatigue. The bouncer slapped a sledgehammer fist into an open palm. "Which way you want it, Mr. Gantlet? You can make it easy on yourself and come with me, or I can break a few bones."

Sly swayed as he looked into the face of the giant. "I'm going to pick the hard way."

When Sly Gantlet served in the US Navy, for a few extra bucks, he had taken part in non-sanctioned kickboxing bouts that provided a way for the Navy men to gamble and lose their wages. He'd been champion for three years before he knocked out the wrong person and had been discharged from the Navy. Now, because of the alcohol and drugs in his system, it took every bit of concentration he could muster, but he spun around and leaped into the air, laying a boot across the jaw of the bouncer.

The bouncer's head snapped to one side, then his eyes rolled up in his head and he crashed backward, caving in the sheet rock on the wall, before sliding down into a massive, but limp, heap.

Sly staggered and fell after he landed the kick. He tried to stand, but his legs were rubbery and they went out from under him twice before the blurry image of Holly leaned over him, her long blonde hair brushing his cheek.

"Good night, Sly," she whispered. "I wish it could have been different, but I'm an account specialist, and I'm being paid very well to even accounts with you." Sly felt something bite into his neck, and then felt a rush of narcotic bliss as sleep rushed in to claim him.

Dillon saw Holly plunge a syringe into Sly's jugular and push the plunger. She looked up at him, but her eyes momentarily glanced to his left. Dillon wheeled and found the bartender rising from behind his bar, a sawed off double-barreled Winchester shotgun in his hands.

Throwing himself to one side, Dillon heard one of the barrels let loose and felt a slug rip past him before tearing a fist-sized hole in the cinder block wall. It was probably only the fact that the shotgun barrel was sawed off to a nub that had saved Dillon's life. That reduced the accuracy of the gun considerably, and since the bartender was firing a slug, there was no pellet spread— but who knew what the second barrel was loaded with?

Moricz let loose with a string of Hungarian profanity as a shotgun slug tore through his wall and blew apart a bank of monitors, sending glass and plastic scattering across the room. Moricz reached for his MAT-49 machine gun, scooping it off the table as he ran for the door, all the while yelling into his headset. "Team Four close the alley, now!"

As Dillon dodged he reached for the holster in the small of his back and his fist emerged carrying a .44 magnum Desert Eagle pistol. The drug in his rum made it appear that there were three bartenders firing at him, each with a double-barreled shotgun. Dillon didn't know which one was real, so he fired three shots, one into the chest of each.

The bartender pitched backward with a gurgle as his heart was blown out through his back. Holly was long gone, fled out the front door, Dillon presumed. He took three strides and leaned over the unconscious Sly Gantlet. He repeatedly slapped the rocker hard on alternating cheeks, thinking that it would be more satisfying if Sly were awake to react to it.

With a sudden start, Sly's eyes opened up, wild and uncomprehending. He grabbed Dillon's wrist. "Matthias?"

Dillon wrenched his gun hand away. "Who's Matthias?"

Sly shook his head in a futile effort to clear away the cobwebs, and pushed himself to his feet with one brawny arm. "Matthias is my brother. He's the only one I know besides myself that carries a .44 Desert Eagle."

Dillon gave Sly a shove toward the door. "Is Matthias black? Or has that drug addled your vision as well as your brain?"

Sly turned around, leaning heavily against the wall beside the exit. "Wait, did you steal my gun? Let me see the grips, because mine has a silver inlaid G on both sides." To emphasize his adamancy on the point he balled up his bloody hands into fists.

Dillon did a double take and showed him the grip of his automatic, only because he figured it would be quicker than starting a fist fight with Sly, displaying the silver-engraved D on his own gun.

"What in the...?" bellowed Sly. "You engraved your gun grips, too? What are you? Some Sly Gantlet wannabe like that Hal Alden[3] guy?"

"Not hardly," said Dillon with obvious disdain. He felt his limbs sag and his eyes began to flutter closed. It was only the adrenaline in his system that was keeping him from keeling over. He doubted that Sly would last much longer, either—especially with a double dose of sedative pumping through his system. "Let's get out of the area before we both drop unconscious."

"Right," said Sly. He tried to open the door, but fumbled with the handle, the mind-numbing cocktail in his system somehow making it beyond his mental capacity to work the simple mechanism. With frustration he threw his body against the door and wrenched the door free from the wall, frame and all, so that it collapsed into the alley. Sly staggered through, followed by the reeling Dillon. The two of them wobbled on unsteady legs, looking more like a pair of drunks attempting to demonstrate The Hippy Hippy Shake than two desperate men trying to escape a death trap.

"My car's around the corner," said Sly with a half-hearted effort to point the way. At that moment three men in flapping jackets, silk shirts and neckties came barreling around that same corner at the end of the alley. The first was a rail-thin fellow with an emaciated face and a Mac-10 submachine gun in his hand. The other two held magazine-fed 9mm pistols. Sly and Dillon managed to process these facts despite the drugs that slowed their minds and reflexes, and while Sly fumbled for the gun inside his jacket Dillon sent a hail of hot lead down the alley. The most dangerous of the men, was of course, the one holding the Mac-10. The gun could put out 1,145 rounds per minute, and with a thirty round box shoved into the handle, that meant the machine pistol could be emptied in about a second and a half.

Under normal circumstances Dillon or Sly might have beaten the machine-gunner to the trigger. As it was, with their minds befuddled, Sly was still pulling out his pistol when Dillon fired, and the machine-gunner was already pulling back the trigger when two of the five rounds Dillon fired punctured his chest. The Mac-10 sprayed the alley as the machine-gunner fell to the ground, stitching Sly across the torso with nine-millimeter bullets.

Sly flinched but didn't fall. Instead he seemed oddly invigorated by the

3 Read more about Hal Alden in the Gantlet Brothers novel, The Nuclear Suitcase

blast of lead. Dillon's gun was empty now, but Sly took up the slack and his .44 belched fire and lead, dropping the two remaining members of Team Four to the ground, dead or dying.

Sly grimaced. "Oow! That stings like a son of a gun!"

"You have a vest on?"

"The jacket is Kevlar lined," explained Sly. "Those bullets sure woke me up, though. I thought I was going to fall asleep until all that lead hit me."

They raced down the alley as fast as their plodding legs would take them, and as they rounded the corner Sly's yellow Ferrari came into view. It sat low at the curb, sleek and gleaming in the dim street light. In this part of town, Sly was surprised that it hadn't been stripped for parts by now.

Sly pulled out his keys and tripped over the curb, falling flat on his face. The keys fell from his hand and Dillon scrambled over the back of the barrel-chested guitar player and scooped up the keys.

"I'm driving, you can't even stand up," said Dillon as his knees sagged beneath him, and he reached out with one arm to steady himself on the Ferrari. He found the key, opened the door and fell awkwardly into the driver's seat.

Sly muttered a curse under his breath, but he heard the sound of screeching tires and he knew that whoever it was that was orchestrating this evening wasn't quite done with them yet. He crawled from the street and to the passenger door, yanking it open as Dillon reached over and unlocked it for him. Before he had even finished pulling himself into the seat Dillon gunned the Ferrari out onto Houston Street, nicking the Chevy Malibu parked in front of them so that it slammed Sly's door shut.

With a groan, Sly stuck his head out the window and examined the massive dent in the car door. "You're going to pay for that. This is a hundred thousand dollar car!"

"Deduct it from the bet money you owe me," said Dillon as he did his best to keep the car on the road, which was difficult because his vision kept blurring into four or five indistinguishable lanes. He headed in the direction that he judged was east. If he could just make it to FDR Drive and head uptown to a safehouse he had on 74th Street maybe he and Sly could get out of this alive.

"Are you crazy? I'M the one that won that match!"

At the cross street ahead a Ford sedan cut across the lane and screeched to a halt. The doors flew open, disgorging three heavily armed men. When Sly saw the car pull across the lane he was already acting. He pulled a secret lever beneath the glove compartment and it rolled open revealing an Israeli made UZI submachine gun and a half dozen thirty-two round magazines. Chuckling deliriously, Sly leaned out the window and began firing. Nine-millimeter casings spewed from the UZI, clattering on the pavement to intermingle with the banshee whine of the Ferrari as Dillon took the speed of the car up to one hundred miles an hour.

It took two seconds for Sly to empty the first magazine of the UZI and this wasn't long enough for the occupants of the Ford sedan to clear their car and began firing at the Ferrari. Holes erupted in the sheet metal frame of the sedan, glass shattered, the driver took a bullet through the temple, and a machine-gunner dropped to the ground as a pair of bullets took him in the abdomen.

In a yellow flash Dillon veered the Ferrari around the blocking sedan. The tires screeched and a billowing cloud of burning rubber erupted from the pavement as Dillon spun the car around in a complete 360. By then, Sly had gotten a fresh magazine into the Uzi and was freely spraying the Ford sedan. Windows burst and the hood flew off as something in the engine exploded. Machine gun fire rattled after them, but Dillon slammed on the brakes, straightened out the Ferrari and fishtailed around the corner, getting them safely away from the ambushers.

Sly eased back into his seat and closed his eyes, momentarily dreaming that Holly was sitting in his lap, running her fingers through his hair. He suddenly awoke. "What happened to Holly? We have to go back and get her."

"She jabbed a syringe in your neck and took off running, you moron. She and Andrea were in on the whole thing."

"Oh yeah," said Sly, the vague memories coming back to him. In his drugged state it all seemed some insubstantial dream. "Someone must have really wanted us bad to go to all that trouble setting us up."

"I knew it was a trap all along," said Dillon.

"Yeah, right—and you took that rum shot full of sedative just to lull them into a false sense of security."

"Did you know that La Esca is Italian for the bait?" asked Dillon. "The name couldn't have been more of a dead giveaway. And it wouldn't be the first time I've walked in and out of a trap."

"Yeah, well I guess we took the bait alright." His grin was rueful, but tired. "Too bad about Holly, though. She was awfully hot."

"She had nothing on Andrea." Dillon squinted, trying to ascertain what color the traffic light ahead was. It was blinking hypnotically. It seemed to be telling him to go to sleep. Blissful sleep.

Sly slugged Dillon in the shoulder and Dillon snapped back into consciousness, yanking on the wheel so that the Ferrari left the sidewalk and skidded back onto the roadway.

"We've got two cars following us still," said Sly. "I don't know if we're going to be able to lose them. Pretty soon both of us are going to fall asleep at the same time and we won't be able to wake each other up."

"If I could only concentrate," said Dillon. "In this car I should be able to lose just about anything else on the road."

Moricz Mortoni gripped his French-made MAT-49 as his driver did his best to keep pace with the yellow Ferrari that veered wildly across all lanes of traffic. "What is going on? Dillon has enough sedative in him to tranquilize a bull elephant, and Gantlet has twice that much; what's keeping them awake?"

The cellular phone at Mortoni's belt rang and he picked up the hefty module and lifted it to his ear. "Is the capture proceeding according to plan?" asked a voice that was colored with a French accent.

"We're having a few hiccups," answered Mortoni.

The voice on the other end became as cold as ice. "The Conglomerate requested you because of your reputation as a detail man, and a planner that gets the job done without any muss or fuss. If I wanted wetworks I would have hired The Ten or The Pistol Men."

"The targets are both tranquilized," said Mortoni. "It's only a matter of time before the drugs take their toll and they drop. In the meantime we're trailing them at a respectful distance."

"C'est Bien," replied the voice, and then the line went dead.

Sly let the Uzi's magazine drop onto the floor and he slapped a full box into the handle. He leaned out the window and waited for the headlights of the sedans to grow closer, but they never did. The waiting seemed interminable. Sly closed his eyes for a moment of rest, and the clatter of his UZI careening away down the middle of the road awoke him. He realized that he had fallen asleep and let it drop from his fingers.

Barely conscious, he slipped back inside the cab of the car and as he settled into his comfortable seat he noticed that Dillon had both arms folded across the wheel, his head resting on them and his eyes closed. A rattling snore escaped his lips.

The last reserves of Sly's willpower were gone and he was fading fast. Even the pain of his massively bruised torso was no longer sharp enough to keep him conscious. A donut shop drew up fast on their right, and two police cars were parked side by side, with their officers standing a few yards away, chatting while they chewed on pastries and washed them down with coffee.

Sly pushed his foot down on top of Dillon's left shoe so that the brakes of the Ferrari locked up. He grabbed the steering wheel and sent the car hurtling directly at the pair of police units. Then he fell into the sweet embrace of Morpheus.

Moricz Mortoni goggled as the yellow Ferrari plowed into two parked police cars, rending metal and shattering glass. The surprised police officers acted with only a moment's hesitation. One called in for backup using the radio at his belt, and the other rushed to the mashed and shattered Ferrari and began pulling out the limp and bloody forms of the two occupants.

Mortoni's driver pulled to the side of the road and adjusted the police scanner, eavesdropping on the report that was called in. Moricz Mortoni swore when he heard the details: both victims unconscious, but with minor wounds

"Mission aborted," said Mortoni. "Begin clean up phase." In a couple of hours La Esca would disappear as if it had never existed. Dead bodies would be burned in previously arranged furnaces and every last piece of evidence would be destroyed. It was his worst failure yet. It had seemed like the perfect set up, put two men in the same room that couldn't stand the idea of being second best to anyone and watch them self destruct while trying to get the upper hand on the other. It had started out perfectly, but how could he have known that they would instantly put aside their differences and cooperate at the first sign of danger? Even so, Sly and Dillon had narrowly escaped death.

Red lights splashed the streets as ambulances pulled up and paramedics hoisted the heavy bodies of Sly and Dillon onto separate stretchers.

"What happens to them now?" asked the driver.

Moricz thought of the massive payday that had just slipped through his hands and then he shrugged. "We're off the job. If I were a betting man I'd say that the Conglomerate will hire The Ten to take a shot at them."

The driver shuddered at the mention of The Ten, and then he cranked the wheel and made a quick U-turn away from the scattered wreckage and flashing lights, leaving behind the messy results of the evening's misadventures.

Sly Gantlet awoke with a start, sitting straight up in the bed he was lying in. He blinked and took in his surroundings. The antiseptic smell told him he was in a hospital but the room looked more like a luxury hotel suite. Fresh flowers were on his nightstand and on the coffee table in the foyer he could see through the open door. His bed was a marvelously soft king-sizer and soft music was playing from hidden speakers; sounded like early Fleetwood Mac.

There was a man sitting next to his bed. A tall rangy man wearing a good suit but it looked the worse from too much wear. His deeply suntanned skin and cowboy boots gave him a vaguely Western air but the badge clipped to his handcrafted belt was that of a New York Special Inspector. The man stood up slowly, unfolding long legs and his eyes were sharp, bright and suspicious. "Mr. Gantlet? I'm Demetrius Wright, NYPD Special Inspector. You've had quite the close call tonight, haven't you?"

"Where's Dillon?"

"He's gone. Dillon's not welcome in New York. As soon as he regained consciousness and his wounds were treated I gave him an hour to get the hell out of my town. You see, he and I have had dealings before. He's not good for tourism, let's say." Demetrius Wright smiled slightly. "You on the other hand are a member of a world famous rock band. You've also got quite the bit of juice. After I contacted your brothers they got in touch with some…friends of theirs who said that you were to be treated as an honored guest of the city."

"So why are you here?" Sly was examining himself. He was sore and stiff but that was to be expected after a car crash. He was more interested in knowing what had happened to that smug son of gun Dillon.

"Just to give you a message from me to you: if you're a friend of Dillon, don't bring your problems to my city. New York's got enough trouble as it is. And here: he gave me this to give to you." Demetrius Wright passed over a long white envelope. Having done so, he headed for the door. Only pausing long enough to turn around and say; "By the way…I don't care what the critics say…I thought The True Blue Chariot rocked. Wasn't bad for a first time solo album." Demetrius Wright left and Sly Gantlet tore open the envelope and the only thing that fell out was a business card.

Bronze in color, on one side it had a black, raised stylized letter D and on the other side a short note:

Pay me when you see me again.

For the next two minutes the luxury hospital room was filled with the booming voice of Sly Gantlet as he gave vent to exactly what he thought of Dillon and for the sake of our gentle readers with gentle dispositions and even gentler constitutions, we will not relate exactly what was said in this narrative….

Authors Note: *Be assured that Dillon and Sly Gantlet did indeed meet again but that is a story for another time. Until the day of his death, Sly Gantlet swore that he won the arm wrestling competition in La Esca, and that Dillon still owed him a hundred thousand dollars. Dillon however, still maintains that it was he who won the contest. No other reliable witnesses were found, however portions of this account were based on the verbal recounting on the incident by one Francie Brink, who was known to Sly and Dillon as Holly on the night of the occurrence. Francie now lives with a menagerie of cats in an Iowa trailer park.*

Trouble at the Whisky

The Whisky a Go Go was packed with big-haired women in tight spandex and loose bangles, and young roughnecks in tattoos and denim jostling for position in front of the stage. Strychnine finished the last of its set with the bang of flashpots and glitter that coruscated in the stage lights before drifting into obscurity. The crowd began to disperse to their tables and drinks and the lead singer, Brent Mickelson, staggered off stage and into the arms of a voluptuous blonde wearing his own garishly-colored leather jacket emblazoned with the band's logo.

At the bar, Sly Gantlet tossed back his fifth shot of whiskey that evening and chased it with a swig from a beer bottle that was branded with his own name. "That was some of the crappiest bubblegum music that I've ever heard," he grumbled. "I'll have to scour my ears with some Condemner just to get that idiotic chorus out of my head."

Sly's brother Mitz sat next to him nursing his lone beer of the night. When he really wanted to cut loose he'd drink two beers, but he knew that his secondary line of work didn't allow much room for inebriation. He seemed aloof in the midst of the drunken revelry of the tavern, not acknowledging the other tavern patrons, even though the eyes of several women were upon him. There was something about this crowd that bothered him, too—something that he hadn't quite yet defined; perhaps an undercurrent of vigilance or expectancy, as if something were about to happen. "I told you we should have gone to another club."

The oldest Gantlet brother did a double take as he caught sight of the woman draped on Brent Mickelson's arm. "Yeah, the band's a washout but check out that babe."

"Hmph," said his brother. The term pneumatic blonde had been invented for this woman. Long-lashed, full-lipped, with a deep bosom and narrow hips, she was certainly easy on the eyes. "That's Andi Eisley—I'm surprised you haven't seen her before. She's on that TV show Lifeguard with all the slow motion montages; major groupie—after our gig in LA she showed up at Matthias's hotel room wearing nothing but a trench coat and holding a bottle of champagne."

Sly laughed. "Really? She obviously didn't do her research. Still, she doesn't need to dangle champagne as bait. Did he bite?"

"You've got to be kidding," said Mitz. "She's been around the block more times than a taxi cab. You know Matthias has got higher standards…"

"Sure," said Sly. "But look at her! Matthias is only human. He can succumb to temptation just like the rest of us."

"Remember what Mom used to say? Forge your own path. Stay away from the commonplace and the paths often trod."

"What's that got to with anything?" asked Sly. "I'd hardly classify her as commonplace."

"Think about it. My advice is to stay away," said Mitz. "She's nothing but tr—" He glanced over to find that his brother was already gone, pushing his way through the crowd toward Andi. Brent Mickelson had left his pneumatic arm candy unattended as he made a trip to the restroom and Sly had seized the opportunity.

Sly inserted himself directly into Andi's line of sight and thrust out a hand of introduction. "I'm Sly Gantlet, lead guitar player of the band Gantlet."

She shook his hand and gave him a vibrant smile that was not without interest as she examined his muscular frame and the dark-bearded features offset by a lion's mane of long, blond hair. "I'm Andi Eis…"

"I know your name and your public image," said Sly. "But I'm betting there's more to you than meets the eye. What do you say we get out of here and go some place quieter?"

Andi hesitated, her eyes wandering towards the men's bathroom and Sly knew that she was reluctant to leave Brent high and dry.

"Don't worry about your friend," said Sly. "I'm sure he'll find someone to keep him company this evening. I'll even write him a personal letter of apology. Once I explain that I was so entranced by your beauty and charm that I couldn't help myself, he'll be forced to forgive me."

All this time Sly hadn't let go of her hand and she gave him an appraising glance that included an arch of her pencil-thin brows. "Okay, Sly. Where are you going to take me first?"

"I understand Mulholland Drive has a great view," said Sly and he felt someone tapping on his shoulder.

"That's my woman, you overgrown freak," called a voice from behind him.

Sly frowned, apparently Brent Mickelson had returned from his potty break all too quickly.

"A woman is no one's property," replied Sly with uncharacteristic diplomacy. "Andi is a living breathing human being, not your chattel. What are you, some sort of Neanderthal?"

"Chattel?" repeated Brent, a confused expression on his face.

"Personal property, possession, slave or servant," defined Sly. "I'm surprised that you'd treat a woman like Andi with such disregard."

Suddenly Andi was feeling more than a little outraged. "Yeah, Brent, I'm not cattle and I'm more than a set of double D's. I'm an independent woman with thoughts and feelings...and right now I feel like taking a drive with Sly."

Sly's ploy to make Brent look bad in Andi's eyes seemed to have been more successful than he ever could have imagined, and he couldn't help but let a self-satisfied grin cross his bearded face. As he took Andi by the elbow and they started toward the door of the Whisky, he glanced over his shoulder and added insult to injury. "See you later, loser."

A strangled cry of inarticulate rage rose in Brent's throat and his fists tightened. He threw his body into a round house sucker punch that Sly didn't see coming until it was too late. However, Sly was turning away when the punch connected and it bounced off his thick skull nary causing the German guitarist any discomfort, but causing Brent to fall back, clutching a broken and bloodied hand.

Sly was inclined to ignore him, seeing that Brent had already succeeded marvelously in making a fool of himself, but Andi looked at him with hazel eyes and batted her dark lashes. "You're not going to let him get away with that, are you?"

"I guess not," replied Sly, who suddenly found the tables turned. Now it was him being goaded into a certain course of action, and he was no longer the one pulling the strings. Instead, Andi was the puppet master. Sly suspected she was quite good at persuading men to do things they might later regret.

However, Sly had to admit he found no little satisfaction and little cause for regret when he spun and laid the bottom of his boot across the side of Brent's face. Brent sank with a groan, knocking over stools, bar patrons, and a full stein of beer.

Sly clucked as the contents dribbled off the bar and splattered over Brent. "Waste of a good beer."

Andi arched a pencil thin eyebrow. "You didn't hurt him too badly, did you?"

"Just a love tap," Sly assured her as they made their way to the Whisky's side exit. "He'll wake up in about five minutes with a bruise and a bad headache. I received far worse when I was kickboxing in the Navy."

She wrapped an arm around Sly's waist. "Really? I didn't know that kickboxing was part of military training."

They emerged into the alley at the side of the Whisky, strolling past a pair of men passing a cigarette of dubious legality. "It was more a hobby that turned into a heap of trouble. I knocked out a superior officer during a grudge match, and that was the end of my military career."

"Oh!" she said, her hand dipping beneath his shirt and running down his muscular chest. "I like bad boys. Are you a bad boy?"

"You have no idea," said Sly.

When Sly and Andi disappeared out the back, Mitz realized that he was on his own for the rest of the evening. That was nothing new. It wasn't the first time that Sly had ditched him for a woman. In fact, it had happened so often that Mitz had grown to expect Sly to gallivant off after a woman on their evening excursions. If Sly hadn't found a woman that caught his fancy, Mitz would have been surprised.

A crowd had gathered around Brent Mickelson's unconscious form, the inner circle consisting of the rest of Strychnine and their roadies, but the outer circle composed of a number of inebriated fans who were very displeased that the lead singer of their favorite band had been assaulted and they were looking for someone to vent their anger on. Fortunately, the majority of Strychnine's fans were women, but a few had already pointed Mitz out as being a friend of the bearded ruffian that had knocked Brent cold and walked away with his girlfriend.

Mitz didn't mind mobs of admiring women, but mobs of angry women made him extremely uncomfortable. He'd had groups of crazed groupies rip the shirt from his back while he exited the tour bus, so he could only imagine the damage that a mob of not-so-friendly fans of a rival band might inflict. He shoved away his unfinished beer and began to rise, thinking it a wise time to take leave of the Whisky. This is when he noticed an even uglier undercurrent—something that he had sensed before, but hadn't been able to pinpoint.

A man at the end of the bar with too neat a haircut for the Whisky crowd lifted the tattered lapel of his jean jacket and spoke a few words. Mitz couldn't decipher the sounds of those words over the music piped into the PA system and the clamor of the growing mob of angry Strychnine fans, but he read the man's lips—a talent he'd acquired after many years of being behind the rest of the band and not being able to hear a word they said unless they turned and mouthed the words to him.

"Sly Gantlet is located and incapacitated. Acquire target now."

In most states it was illegal to carry a firearm into an establishment serving alcoholic beverages—for some reason inebriation and handguns don't mix well—but Mitz had duly ignored such arbitrary injunctions since he found his life to be at risk just about anywhere he went, whether it was a tavern or convenience store for a Slurpee.

He habitually carried a brace of Double Eagle Colt .45 semi-automatics. They held eight rounds in the magazine and Mitz liked to cheat in an extra round by keeping one in the pipe. Before the imposter in the frayed denim jacket—undoubtedly picked up a day earlier in a Salvation Army foray—could pull loose the Glock Pistol concealed beneath his armpit, Mitz had both pistols out. He fired the pistol in his right hand, flame belching and the sound of the bullet cutting through the canned music and the outraged cries.

The bullet took the imposter through the skull and he pitched off his stool. When the woman next to him saw blood begin to leak onto the uneven floor she began to shriek. As if by magic, gun-wielding men seemed to emerge from the crowd, throwing off their disguises as patrons of bubblegum rock and converging on the fallen form of Brent Mickelson, shoving groupie and roadie aside and firing a barrage of bullets into the ceiling.

People began to stampede for exits, shrieking groupies trampling each other in an effort to escape. Mitz rolled over the top of the bar, knocking over steins of beer as he found some cover. Even amidst the noise and mayhem his shot had attracted some attention and one of the gunmen had noticed his fellow infiltrator go down from Mitz's shot. The gunman turned and fired at the colorfully-garbed rock musician as he disappeared over the top of the bar.

One night in 1966 Jim Morrison had come into the Whisky high on acid and brandishing a single-action Belgian-made Nagant pistol he'd borrowed from the collection of a girlfriend's father. Legend had it that it was Morrison's profanity-laced version of the Doors' 'The End' that had led to their firing from their slot as the Whisky's house band. In truth, it had been the pistol incident that had inspired the firing and had also inspired co-owner Elmer Valentine to install a sheet of plate steel behind the face of the bar.

Now that sheet of steel saved Mitz's life as nine-millimeter rounds pounded and flattened against the steel. A few bullets splintered through the bar top and skimmed over his head. On his hands and knees he scrambled toward the end of the bar and then poked around the corner, both guns blazing. He caught the gunman barraging the bar looking in the wrong direction as he slapped a new magazine into the handle of his pistol. Mitz planted three bullets in his chest before he could turn.

The gunman pitched backward, firing his freshly-reloaded pistol into the ceiling and then he lost all will to fire—instead gasping for breath that his punctured lungs would not take in. A haze of loosened plaster drifted down and through the haze Mitz could see that the interlopers had scooped up the unconscious Brent Mickelson by the arms and legs and were hustling him out the back passage of the Whisky.

Mitz had no particular fondness for Brent Mickelson or Strychnine, for that matter, but it was obvious to him that the kidnappers thought they had Sly Gantlet and had absconded with the wrong blonde long-hair. Sly had made plenty of enemies over the years and apparently they had chosen this not too terribly strategic moment to snatch him. That they kept their kidnappee alive meant that either they thought that Sly knew something very important which they wanted to extract or that they wanted him to die in a very slow and very painful manner. That they had grabbed the wrong person instead of Sly meant that they were also morons. Sly Gantlet weighed about one hundred pounds of solid muscle more than Brent Mickelson. Any kidnapper worth his salt would have immediately noticed the difference, especially once they picked him up.

As smoke rose from the barrels of his pistol and as the kidnappers disappeared from sight, Mitz noticed a dark-haired girl sprawled beneath a table next to him, her long legs, encased in lace stockings and thrusting from the faded fringes of an artfully-aged mini-skirt, splayed out behind her. She seemed vaguely familiar to Mitz, but he couldn't immediately place her face or her figure.

"Aren't you Mitz Gantlet?" she asked.

"Yes," he answered, and then he placed the woman, though he hadn't ever expected to see her anywhere outside of fashion magazines or MTV guest hosting. "Aren't you Cindy Warner?"

"Not actually my real name," she said. "But my agent thought that Cynthia Wachowski wouldn't sell in Hollywood."

"Are you here alone?"

She made a wry expression. "My date went screaming for the door once the gunfire began." Cindy paused. "Well, what are you waiting for?"

"What am I waiting for?"

"Aren't you going to go after Brent Mickelson? Saving people—isn't that what the Gantlet Brothers do—besides cranking out rocking tunes, I mean."

Mitz sighed. "Yeah, I suppose I'd better. Did you know that this bar was lined with steel?"

"Heck, no!" she exclaimed. "Or I would have crawled behind it, too."

"Nice meeting you," said Mitz, and then he was on his feet and running toward the front door. He still had a few moments in which he might be able to intercept the kidnappers' getaway vehicle. He vaulted over a number of bar patrons who were still lying on the floor, fearing it might be too early to stand, or suffering from bruises and contusions from the initial stampede toward the exit.

The bright lights of the Sunset Strip washed over Mitz as he emerged onto the sidewalk and threaded between the parked cars. The screeching of tires alerted him and Mitz saw a blue van barreling out of the alley behind the Whisky a Go Go. The van veered into the street, heading in Mitz's direction and so he started pumping his legs, sprinting in the same direction to match the trajectory of the vehicle.

For a few moments he was almost within touching distance of the van and he reached out to grab hold of the back door handle and pull himself onto the rear bumper. Then the engine of the van roared and the vehicle lurched forward and out of his reach—leaving him in a haze of blue exhaust illuminated by the gaudy neon of the strip.

Mitz came to a lurching stop and jerked a Double Eagle from its holster. With both hands he took careful aim at the receding target and snapped off two shots before a crossing Volkswagen Bug interfered with his aim. He thought he'd hit the rear tire of the van, even saw a splatter of goo as the bullet struck—but this indicated that the tire was probably constructed with gel-filled compartments. One bullet might take out a compartment or two, but enough of the tire would remain intact that the vehicle could continue on unimpeded.

Thanks to Sly, the DeLorean sports car they had arrived in was no longer parked at the curb, and Mitz had no way to chase the van. He cast about for some possible alternative—even a cab. Most cabdrivers were half crazy, anyway. It might be possible to find one that was willing to chase down a van for the right price...if only there were a cab in sight.

Each second that passed it became more and more unlikely that Mitz would be able to catch or even find the escaping van. By the time he managed to break into and hot wire a vehicle, his opportunity would be past. He thought he caught a glimpse of the van passing Tower Records, where West Sunset Boulevard split away from Sunset, and veering past Spagos.

A cherry red sports car with an open top pulled up alongside Mitz and he recognized the driver whom he had met on the floor of the Whisky.

"Do you need a lift, stranger?" called the dark-haired beauty from the cockpit of the Dodge Viper.

"Do I ever," said Mitz.

Cindy scooted up and over the manual six-speed gear shift into the passenger's seat. "Then you're doing the driving. I've had this beast for three weeks and I haven't dared take it over sixty miles per hour. You do know how to drive, don't you?"

Mitz grinned and climbed into the driver's seat without bothering to open the door. He'd had the opportunity to take a Viper for a test drive when the line had been released three months earlier. Car and Driver had accurately referred to the Viper as the 'world's largest Fatboy Harley.' It didn't have much in the way of the niceties of luxury or anti-lock brakes, and even the steering was tricky. It was heavy on blunt power and short on finesse.

Still, that translated into a car that could do zero to sixty in 4.6 seconds with a top speed of 195 miles per hour. Mitz cycled smoothly through the gears leaving a strip of smoking rubber in front of the Whisky. He threaded through the traffic, chasing the elusive ghost of the kidnappers' van past the yellow canopies of Tower Records and past the stuccoed walls and tiled roof of the shabby Spagos. He sent the Viper barreling through the Y-intersection, narrowly avoiding a collision or three.

Cindy breathed a sigh of relief and locked in her seat belt harness as her dark hair whipped in tangled streams about her lovely features. She looked ahead and thought she saw a glimpse of blue van. "They're turning left on North Crescent Heights!"

Mitz knew that North Crescent Heights went past the Laugh Factory on West Sunset. If he cut through on North Olive he could get on West Sunset and possibly intercept the van before it reached the intersection of North Crescent and West Sunset. Before he had time to fully mull over the decision, his huge forearms sent the Viper wheeling around the corner in a 1G turn that they could feel in the pit of their stomach.

Threading the traffic as best as they could they emerged onto West Sunset and blew through two stoplights at one hundred twenty miles an hour. They shredded past the palm-flanked Argyle Hotel and as they approached the Laugh Factory they saw the blue van they were pursuing pass through the intersection heading north.

They were close now and Mitz laid into his brake, wrestling with the wheel to keep the sloughing beast under control as they rounded the corner and dropped back six or seven cars away from the van.

"What are you doing?" asked Cindy. "We're close enough to catch them now! That van can't outrun this car!"

"I'm trying to remain unobtrusive," said Mitz. "Something that is quite difficult in a car as flashy as this."

"You're from Germany, right?"

"Yes," confirmed Mitz. "What does that have to do with anything?"

"In Germany maybe a car like this would stand out like a sore thumb, but we're in Hollywood. Everybody owns the flashiest car that they can or especially that they can't afford. Only the cars that aren't flashy end up standing out."

"I hope you're right," said Mitz. "If you are, then maybe we can tail the van and find out where they're taking Brent."

"I don't get it," said Cindy. "What do they want with Brent?"

"They think that he's my brother, Sly," explained Mitz. "A lot of folks would love to torture him for a few weeks before dumping his body in the ocean."

"A lot of folks?"

"He has a way with people," shrugged Mitz. "It's just a gift he has."

"But Brent looks nothing like your brother—except for the long blond hair."

Mitz shook his head. "I never said that the folks who hate Sly were smart."

"What do you think they'll do when they find out that they grabbed the wrong person?"

"They'll probably kill Brent," said Mitz. "He's seen their faces. They won't want witnesses."

"But there were hundreds of witnesses in the Whisky," protested Cindy.

"They might have caught glimpses between flashes of gunfire, but how many of them really got a good look? Most were too busy ducking for cover or getting trampled in the rush for the door. Can you tell me what they looked like?"

"No," admitted Cindy. "I was on the floor. The only thing I can identify is that one of the kidnappers wore a pair of Lester Dentini leather wingtips. I recognize them because I worked with a photographer who owned a pair. He bragged that they set him back a thousand dollars and that they were only available at an exclusive shop in Beverly Hills."

Mitz pulled a bulky cell phone out of his leather jacket and handed it to Cindy. "See if you can get my brother on the horn."

"Which one?"

"Sly's the only one in the state. But he's with Andi Eisley. Let's just hope that he picks up the phone."

***

As the silver DeLorean wound its way up Mullholland, slipping through the pools of light shed by the overhanging street lamps, Andi Eisley unbuckled her seat belt and moved onto Sly Gantlet's lap so that she was facing him, and so that he could scarcely see the road given the expanse of cleavage blocking his view. This distraction made it difficult to drive so Sly began to pull over to the side.

"You just keep your eyes on the road, Mr. Gantlet," Andi cooed in his ear. She began to unbutton his shirt, running her fingers through the hair on his chest. "Get us to the top of Mullholland."

"I understand it's quite a view," said Sly.

"Oh, it is," said Andi as she began to kiss his neck, the hot wind streaming in from the window made a writhing halo of pale hair around her head.

The phone in Sly's jacket began to beep, but before he could free a hand to answer it Andi reached past the holstered Desert Eagle pistol and fished the phone out of a pocket. She glanced at it.

"Who's calling?" asked Sly.

"I don't like interruptions," said Andi and she dropped the phone out the window so it broke into a half dozen pieces as it cartwheeled across the pavement. "Now where was I?"

Finally Cindy gave up trying and set the phone on the console near the shifter. "I've tried about a hundred times. No one's picking up."

Mitz pulled the Viper to rest in the shadows outside a long row of Hollywood back lot warehouses which contained the relics of movies and picture shows past. They watched as the blue van pulled into a dark corridor between warehouses. The kidnappers turned off their lights and glided down the alley until they no longer could be seen. "Looks like we're on our own, then."

He left the keys in the ignition and began to climb out of the car. "I'll go in on foot and check out the situation."

"I'll be right here waiting for you," said Cindy. "Unless you think I should come with you."

"Right here is a good spot," said Mitz. "Thanks for the offer, but I don't know what I'm going to run into. If there is any sign of trouble I want you to take off."

"But what about you?" asked Cindy. "I can't leave you hanging."

"I've been in tight spots before," said Mitz. "I can hot wire a car if I need a lift."

"So, you've got other skills besides percussion?"

"Minor hobbies," said Mitz. "Percussion is my only marketable skill."

"But what if they catch you?"

Mitz patted his jacket in the spots where his pistols were holstered beneath. "At least I'll go out with a bang."

"Very funny," said Cindy. "I'm worried about you and all you can do is make jokes."

"If I don't see you again tonight I'll give you a call tomorrow morning to let you know that I'm alright," said Mitz.

Cindy stood and rested her arm on the top of the windshield while she fished for something in her purse. "And how are you going to do that without my phone number?"

Mitz pulled back the cuff of his sleeve and extended a forearm as big as a ham. Cindy inscribed her phone number with a pen.

"It's unlisted, so don't take a bath until you've transferred the number onto something permanent."

Mitz flashed a smile and trotted across the street and his form was soon lost among the mingling shadows of the night after he climbed the chain-link fence and sprinted toward the looming warehouses. The drummer crept through the darkness, his eyes adjusting to the wan moonlight and the pale beams that filtered between the roof lines of the great warehouses.

Using the darkness as cover, Mitz was able to reach the blue van without being discovered. He put his hand on the hood and felt the warmth that confirmed this was indeed the same van he had been trailing from the Whisky a Go Go. He ducked low and swung around the front of the van. With his left hand he brushed off the mud-obscured numbers of the license plate and committed them to memory. He had a keen mind for numbers and rhythms and the license would be an easy thing for him to recall. In truth, Cindy Warner could have just told him her phone number and he would have been able to remember it the next day or even next year.

Mitz heard a rustle of movement on the other side of the van and he glanced beneath the van and found a pair of feet standing next to the door of the warehouse. He watched the placement of the athletic shoes until the feet pointed in the opposite direction, and then he slipped around the edge of the vehicle.

The kidnapper was tall and lean, wearing an ill-fitting Strychnine t-shirt that had served to help him blend in with the crowd at the Whisky and to conceal the bulge of the Heckler and Koch pistol at his waist—the same gun that was now in his hand as he looked down the alley between the warehouses and toward the cars on the opposite side of the street.

From behind the kidnapper, Mitz had the same line of sight and as a car roared by the high-beams swept the red Viper and briefly exposed the dark-haired woman that sat behind the wheel. The kidnapper started forward as if to discover why a supermodel was staking the location that he and his fellows were holding their detainee, but Mitz took a few quick steps and caught up to him. He wrapped one massive forearm around the kidnapper's neck and tightened with a sudden jerk.

Despite what cinema would lead someone to believe, it was very difficult to snap a man's neck with bare hands and the larynx is not as easily crushed as some martial 'experts' might have one believe. Still, it was easily collapsible and Mitz gave the kidnapper a stunning shot in the throat even as he applied a choke hold. A choke hold required a matter of seconds or even minutes to knock a person unconscious, and the kidnapper began to struggle with all his might, attempting to break Mitz's vice-like grip. Before the kidnapper could start pulling the trigger of his pistol, Mitz wrenched him to the left and smashed the kidnapper's skull against the frame of the van. The body went immediately slack in Mitz's arms and he let it fall to the ground next to the .45 pistol which had already fallen from the kidnapper's nerveless grip.

Mitz picked up the pistol and shoved it into the back of his waistband. If the kidnapper regained consciousness, he preferred that he remain unarmed. He popped open the driver door to the van and noticed the keys still dangling from the ignition. Drummers weren't usually noted for their subtlety and though Mitz could be subtle when needed, he figured blunt force might serve just as well any other approach.

He climbed into the driver's seat, put on the belt, backed up the van clear across the alleyway, revved the engine, and slammed the shifter into drive. The van lurched into and through the door frame in a splinter of wood and torn metal. It burst right through the wall and Mitz kept the vehicle moving as it entered the warehouse, jouncing over sheet metal and pushing aside bent wall studs that had been torn from their concrete moorings.

Once the debris cleared from the windscreen, Mitz saw a lone kidnapper turn and fire at the barreling van. A shot punctured the radiator and a plume of hot steam spumed from the grill. Another shot punctured the glass a foot away from Mitz's head, webbing the windscreen. Then Mitz spun the wheel and accelerated the van over the top of the unfortunate gunman, his body becoming tangled in the undercarriage and then caught beneath the back wheels as Mitz braked the vehicle to a stop just before colliding with a massive temple backdrop from Big Trouble in Little China.

Mitz disengaged his seatbelt and rolled out of the van, guns out and ready for action. However, no one else fired a shot at him. The open area of the warehouse was empty except for a lone chair that had, perhaps, been intended for the kidnapping victim. Temple sets and mock-ups of underground passageways surrounded this empty area and Mitz expected a flurry of shots from hidden gunmen at any moment, but nothing came.

He found the mangled kidnapper he'd run over still caught beneath the rear tire, hacking blood.

"Where's Brent Mickelson?" demanded Mitz.

"Who?" coughed the kidnapper.

"The man you think is Sly Gantlet," said Mitz.

The kidnapper seemed to understand this and he knew he was a dead man already. "Promise to put me out of my misery if I tell you."

Mitz shrugged. This seemed an easy enough promise to keep. "I'll make it quick and painless."

"We spotted the red Viper following us, so the minute we got Gantlet here they hustled him into a car they had waiting in back of the warehouse."

"Where are they taking him?" demanded Mitz.

"Don't know exactly," groaned the kidnapper. "They said they have a safe house on Mullholland. That's all I know."

Mitz frowned and stood. He couldn't exactly go bursting into every single house on Mullholland hoping to find Brent Mickelson.

"That's all I know," choked the kidnapper. "You promised you'd kill me!"

"Who are you working for?" asked Mitz.

"We never met him—just an altered voice we heard over the phone. The man called himself the Condemner."

A cold chill ran up Mitz's spine. "Condemner's a band and they're all dead—every one of them except for Legion Tate."

"I don't know anything about that," said the kidnapper, and again he began to cough blood. "Please, I'm telling you the truth."

Mitz fired one bullet through the kidnapper's skull, a spatter of blood and brains spreading on the concrete floor beneath him.

Sly was halfway up Mullholland and Andi was halfway to proving her reputation as an exhibitionist when her phone began to ring insistently. She ignored it for awhile, letting it go to voice mail at least three times, but the phone began to ring yet again. Sly reached for her Gucci handbag intending to provide a similar fate for the cell phone as Andi had doomed his phone to.

Andi slapped his hand away and answered the phone. "This better be important. I'm right in the middle of..."

Sly overheard a feminine voice on the other end of the line.

A line creased Andi's forehead. "Cindy Warner? How did you get my phone number?"

Now Sly could overhear the response. "It's written on half the bathroom stalls in the Whisky. Can you put Sly Gantlet on the phone for me?"

Andi's lips quirked into a frown. "Find your own man, honey. Sly's mine."

"You can keep him," said Cindy. "I'm just calling to let him know that his brother's in some trouble."

Sly grabbed away the phone before Andi could hang up. "This is Sly, what's going on?"

"I'm following a black Mercedes up Mullholland. They've got Brent Mickelson in the trunk."

"They, who?" snapped Sly.

"Some kidnappers that broke into the Whisky just after you left. They grabbed Brent and took off with him. Mitz and I followed him to a row of warehouses, but after Mitz went in to investigate I saw the kidnappers coming out the back with Brent. They stuffed him in the trunk and I followed, but I've lost them now."

"Where's Mitz now?"

"Back in the warehouse."

"Turn around and pick him up," ordered Sly.

"What about Brent?"

Sly saw the headlights of a black vehicle sweeping up the lane. The vehicle swished around the curve at fifty miles an hour, rushing by Sly's DeLorean which was parked at the curb. "Does the Mercedes have New Mexico license plates?"

"How did you know?"

"I'm on Mullholland and they just passed by," answered Sly. "I'll pick up the tail and you fetch Mitz. I'll give you a call to let him know where to meet me."

"Be careful," said Cindy. "These guys have guns and aren't afraid to use them."

"No worries, darling," growled Sly. "I can take care of myself."

He hung up the phone, shoved a perplexed Andi aside and eased the DeLorean back onto the road, trailing the Mercedes at a respectful distance.

"What are you doing?" she demanded.

"Your ex-boyfriend is the trunk of that car. I may not have any qualms about stealing his hot girlfriend, but I'm not such a jerk that I'll sit by while he gets kidnapped."

Andi straightened her disheveled clothing and checked her make-up in her compact mirror. "Kidnapped? Why would anyone kidnap Brent?"

"Beats me," said Sly. "Maybe they can't stand the idea of another Strychnine album? I know I've considered kidnapping a few times myself."

"What?"

"Just idle thoughts, baby. Just idle thoughts."

The DeLorean had no trouble keeping pace with the Mercedes but Sly hung back until the black sedan extinguished its lights and swung into the drive of a stilt-legged home that hung over the crest of the hill. He continued on past the home, peering into the open garage as a quartet of hard-eyed men wearing ill-fitting rock and roll paraphernalia and Strychnine shirts disgorged from the Mercedes, casting suspicious glances at the silver DeLorean that slipped past.

The garage door began to slide closed but Sly, Andi and the DeLorean were already far past the home.

"That was the car!" cried Andi. "Why are you still driving?"

"Occasionally, retrieving kidnapping victims requires some subtlety," said Sly. "If I pull into the driveway with guns blazing, Brent's going to end up dead. Instead, I'll park out of sight of the house and approach on foot."

Andi considered this for a moment and it seemed to make sense to her. "There are four of them and only one of you. How are you going to get Brent away from them?"

"I'm playing it by ear," said Sly.

"Maybe I should call the cops," said Andi.

Sly shrugged on his kevlar-lined leather tour jacket and shoved Andi's cell phone into his pocket. "You do that, baby." He dropped the keys to the DeLorean into her hand. "In the meantime you get yourself home and out of the way of any stray bullets."

"Not so quick, tough guy." Andi grabbed the lapel of Sly's jacket and laid a long kiss on his lips. "That's for luck."

She pushed something into the pocket of his jacket. "Look me up when you're done here. I'll have a reward waiting for you."

Sly smiled. "Then I'll see you a bit later. Out of curiosity, what kind of reward are we talking about?"

She slid into the driver's seat and gave Sly a wink. "You'll just have to find that out, won't you?"

Sly's thoughts began to run rampant but each step he took toward the stilted house where Brent Mickelson was being kept prisoner took him further from his idle imaginations and focused him on the task at hand. Besides that, the words of his mother niggled at the edges of his conscience so that he wondered at the wisdom of taking up with a woman like Andi Eisley.

The house had a flat roof top with a hot tub, and was built of great glass panels to better take advantage of the view of the Hollywood Bowl and the great panorama of lights that spread as far as the eye could see. Hollywood Babylon, mused Sly. He certainly seemed ready enough to throw himself headlong into the excesses and indulgences of Tinsel Town. He wasn't exactly standing on the moral high ground.

Only a few dim light glowed from within the house, and these from inner chambers. Likely, they were keeping Brent sequestered in the lower level of the home, which had glass panels only on the front of the building. Sly's task was to figure out how to break in. The garage seemed as good an entry as any. There was a man door built onto the side, and Sly crawled through the shrubbery on the steep hill side, risking a nocturnal encounter with a rattlesnake or scorpion. This brought him to the concrete pad of the garage and he climbed alongside the door and thrust a lock-pick gun into the mechanism of the door. It was just a matter of a few moments before the lock yielded and Sly traded his lock-pick gun for the Desert Eagle magnum that weighted a holster inside his jacket.

The pistol deserved its reputation as a hand-cannon. The ten-inch barrel made the gun a bit slower on the draw, but much more accurate at longer distances, and the .44 magnum rounds carried quite a wallop. The garage was dark and Sly eased himself inside, groping his way to the hood of the Mercedes, the hood warm to his touch.

Sly produced a miniature flashlight to illuminate his path to an inner door. He paused to shine the beam through the windows of the car and noted that the keys were still sitting in the ignition. He pondered slashing the tires with the punch dagger hidden beneath his belt buckle, but decided the car might come in handy if he needed to make a quick getaway.

He listened at the door but heard nothing. Sly was about to try the knob when a sudden cry of pain came to his ears. It seemed that the kidnappers had begun their interrogation or torture of Brent Mickelson. Using the cries of pain to cover his approach, Sly opened the door and began to ascend a long flight of stairs which carried him into the lower story of the two story home—the garage being on a distinctly separate level below the living quarters.

He reached the top of the stairs without meeting any opposition. Sly peered around the corner and to the left he found a spiky-haired kidnapper at the end of the hall, watching the street through a great glass panel. Sly counted himself fortunate that he had chosen to creep through the rocky shale and scrub brush of the steep hillside instead of approaching from the road.

Sly tended to prefer brute force, shock and awe, as opposed to the subtle—but he reigned in his natural instincts and ducked back onto the stair. He carried a few extra magazines of ammunition inside his jacket, but nestled in a pocket among these he found a suppressor. He screwed this onto the threaded barrel. Sly had lost the gun sight when he'd modified the barrel and cut the threads and so he'd mounted a laser site below the barrel.

Though the suppressor significantly cut the sound of the Desert Eagle, it carried a supersonic round so it was still fairly loud. In order to keep his presence a secret he would have to time his shot to coincide with Brent's shrieks of pain. There were a few moments of blessed silence and then Brent began to scream again. Sly ducked around the corner to fire at the spike-haired kidnapper, but at the sound of the scream the kidnapper turned and caught sight of the gun-toting musician just as he came into view.

The kidnapper reached for the nine-millimeter pistol thrust into the waist of his designer stone-washed jeans, but even though Sly's gun was unwieldy with an extra ten-inches of suppressor, his pistol was already drawn and Sly beat the kidnapper to the trigger. He fired just one shot and it came before Brent's shrieking subsided. The bullet punched through the kidnapper's chest, the hollow point mushrooming and tearing a hole through his back, before webbing the glass wall that overlooked Mullholland Drive.

With a groan, the kidnapper staggered back, striking the webbed glass before sinking to the floor. Sly had been keenly aware of the sound of the Desert Eagle as it fired, but Brent's scream had been loud and piercing and he hoped that it had been enough to mask the shot.

The sound of Brent's screams seemed to originate from a room down the hall to the right and now that the spike-haired kidnapper's eyes had glazed over, Sly crept down the corridor. His feet sinking into the soft carpeting and masking the sound of his footfalls as he approached the door from which the cries of pain were emanating.

"The great Sly Gantlet sure does scream like a girl," spoke a man with a voice that sounded like whiskey and three packs of cigarettes a day.

"I'm telling you," pleaded Brent. "I'm not Sly Gantlet. Sly Gantlet is a guitar player for the band Gantlet. I'm the lead singer for the band Strychnine. I'll prove it to you—sing you a few lines from 'Every R—"

"Gag him," growled Three-Packs. "Screaming I can handle, but not his singing."

"Gladly," replied another of the kidnappers, the voice lilting and tinkly tones that seemed incongruous to the situation. "Then perhaps you'll let me break out my knives? Your methods are so crude compared to my knife work."

"Just don't make it quick. Damian says that he should suffer three days before we put him down—and he wants to be here to gloat. Seems that he and Sly Gantlet have some sort of history."

Sly's eyes narrowed and he wondered if he might have misheard the words through the door. He hoped he had been mistaken. It had been three years since he and Legion Tate had ended Damian's string of grisly murders by sending him plunging off the Sobre La Zanja bridge in South America[4]. The height of the fall had pancaked Damian, shattering every bone in his body, the mangled remains of which were dragged from the Sao Paulo River twelve miles downstream by the policias. It seemed impossible that Damian had revived from the grave, so perhaps it was someone else going by the same name. But if so, why refer to a history between him and Sly—unless the torturer knew something of the conflict between Sly and Damian Van Hellstrom[5] and was trying to elicit a reaction from his victim.

---

4 *Details of Trouble at the Whiskey were passed to the author by Mitz Gantlet who was not present when Damian plunged from the bridge. He said that Legion Tate referred to the bridge as Sobre la Zanja and thought that it existed in Brazil. The Pravda confirms these facts of Damian Hellstrom's demise, even showing pictures of the bridge and river and stating them as being located near Sao Paulo Brazil—even going so far as to show pictures of the bridge. However, the Pravda is not known for its accuracy in reporting and Brazilian bridge directories don't list a Sobre la Zanja bridge. It is possible that Sobre la Zanja is a sobriquet given the bridge by locals and that it is listed by another name, but this author has had difficulty matching the images with those provided by the Pravda. In Spanish Sobre la Zanja roughly translates to 'upon the ditch' but Brazilian locals speak Portuguese so this calls into question the accuracy of Tate's and the Pravda's account. So for the moment, without living eyewitnesses, the exact location of Damian's plummet remains in question.*

5 *There is a similarly named Marvel Superhero character who goes by the name Son of Satan. The similarities in name between the serial-killer and former lead singer of Condemner and the comic book character may not have been entirely coincidental. Research into Damian Van Hellstrom's past suggest that the name he was known by was probably not his given name, and was a name he assumed later on as he embarked on his*

If so, he failed horribly. "Who's Damian?" cried Brent from the torture chair. "And what does he want with me?"

"How am I supposed to know?" rasped Three-Packs. "Maybe he finds your music a personal affront. Aren't you some sort of famous guitar player?"

"No, no, no," pleaded Brent. "I keep telling you. I'm a vocalist for the band Strychnine."

"Right, right. Just wait until Lanny starts in on you. You'll be singing, all right."

Lanny gave a lilting chuckle as he opened his instrument case and lovingly gazed at the plethora of torturer's implements that were laid out before him on the velvet lining. "Do we have to gag him? I do so like to hear my subjects scream."

"This place is virtually soundproof," said Three-Packs, "but listening to him scream might affect my delicate sensibilities."

Another of the kidnappers snorted. "Weren't you the one that pulled out Bonnie Von Elsa's intestines inch by inch until she agreed to tell you where she kept her diamonds[6]?"

"It's my job to get results," said Three-Packs. "Torturing for pleasure—that's not my thing."

---

dabblings in Satanism. This self-given name may have been inspired by the comic book character, though clearly his actions were not.

6 Bonnie Von Elsa was a 1940's movie star who headlined several high profile films but then had a falling out with the studio heads (or more specifically Maurice Standish who was said to be so infatuated with Bonnie that when she spurned his advances he saw to it that her contract was revoked). Once she was released from her contract she found work in a number of B-Movies such as Mole People Unite, Terror at Party Beach Too and The Blob Returns Again. She was a favorite of socialite columns and was known for her ostentatious collection of diamonds necklaces, broaches, bracelets, and earrings.

In April of 1982 thieves broke into Von Elsa's home, brutally tortured and murdered her, cracked a hidden safe and absconded with that collection of diamond jewelry. Sadly, it was entirely unnecessary. A close friend of Bonnie's confided to the police investigators that Bonnie had long ago sold off whatever real diamonds that she had in order to pay for her home and living expenses. Any time she made a public appearance she wore imitation gems and that was all that she kept in her safe. Bonnie had so closely guarded this secret that she refused to tell the thieves where her safe was until they had tortured her—because she felt if word got out it would ruin her reputation.

The perpetrators of these crimes were never found by the police investigators.

"And such wonderful results you got," replied Lanny as he chose a curiously hooked implement. "But a fistful of paste or not, sadism is its own reward, I always like to say."

Sly coiled his legs beneath him and was about to throw his weight against the door, when he heard the a distant thrum in the air. The thick double panes of glass and the insulated roof did much to mute the noise, but Sly recognized the sound—the beating blades of an incoming helicopter. The muted resonance of the blades vibrated through the stilted home, but still Sly could hear the voices in the room.

"What's that?" growled Three-Pack.

"Must be Damian coming to gloat over the prisoner," said Lanny. "He'll be very upset if he gets down here and sees that I haven't already started the knife work."

Even as the skids set down on the roof, Sly heard Brent Mickelson scream. Suddenly Sly's resolve faded. He felt an unaccustomed fear in his belly and the ice water in his veins began to melt. Was it really Damian on the rooftop? Between he and Legion Tate they had put a dozen .44 and .50 caliber slugs into the man before he had toppled, laughing maniacally as he plunged off the Sobre la Zanja. Even now he could feel the coldness of his presence, a sinister evil that was as palpable as the smog in the Los Angeles skies—and Sly knew in his heart that Damian Van Hellstrom had indeed returned from the dead.

He imagined he heard footsteps on the roof, then booted feet crunching down the stair and entering the room where Mickelson was being tortured.

"Damian!" cried Lanny. "I'm a genuine admirer of your work."

"We've started torturing Sly Gantlet as you requested," said Three-Packs.

The voice came as cold as an arctic wind and at that moment Sly knew that Damian Van Hellstrom was indeed in the room beyond. "You fools! That isn't Sly Gantlet."

"What?" said Three-Packs. "He's got long blond hair, just like you said he would."

"You've failed me," said Damian. "I don't abide failures well..."

Screams echoed within the confines of the room and finally Sly found the will to move his limbs. He barreled into the door, smashing it aside and he found a tall figure dressed entirely in black—from jack-booted feet to trench coat—and holding a pair of bloodied knives. Three-Pack lay at Damian's feet, his carotid slit and blood pooling. Lanny lay a few feet away amid scattered instruments of torture. His eyes were gouged out, and he convulsed sporadically. The third kidnapper was slumped against the wall, clutching his stomach.

Brent Mickelson sat on a chair a couple of feet from Damian, his eyes wide in terror, and blood trickling from a fingertip where Lanny had driven a slender steel spike. Damian blinked dark eyes that were rimmed with black liner and then he laughed maniacally.

"Why, it's Sly Gantlet! Just the man that I was looking for. What a strange, strange coincidence. Unfortunately, you're standing in the wrong spot. You should be sitting right where this imposter is. In fact, I'd like you to exchange spots with him right now."

"You forget who's holding the gun," croaked Sly, and he hovered the laser sights on Damian's forehead. "A bullet travels much faster than one of your knives. Drop them or I'll give you a .44 magnum frontal lobotomy."

"Did you stand in front of the mirror and practice that line?" asked Damian. "Because you deliver it very convincingly—such passion and determination." Even the sound of his voice brought chills up Sly's spine. There was something dark and utterly evil about his very presence. Other cold-blooded killers that Sly had met seemed jovial and kind in comparison.

Sly tightened his finger on the trigger and began counting down. "Three, two, one…" Damian made no move to drop his dripping knives and on the count of one Sly pulled the trigger. The Desert Eagle rocked in his hand, but Damian jerked his head aside on the count of one, and the bullet buzzed by him, blowing a fist-sized hole in the wall at the back of the room.

Before Sly could adjust his aim a series of sledgehammer blows caught him in the back and pounded him to the floor. The blows were accompanied by the sound of gunshots and as Sly struck the ground he knew that he had been shot from behind. The Kevlar that lined his leather jacket had dispersed the impact of the bullets, so they hadn't penetrated, but the force of multiple impacts sent his pistol flying from his stunned fingers.

By the time he managed to get back to his hands and knees, Damian was holding the Desert Eagle to Sly's forehead. "You're getting sloppy, Sly. Have you made so many successful head shots that you've started to believe that you're an exception to the rules of gunfighting? Every gunfighter knows that you shoot for center body mass." He snickered. "And you did the favor of giving me a countdown so I knew just when I needed to move out of the way. You're a bigger fool than I thought."

"Apparently so," agreed Sly through gritted teeth. He saw that a trio of black-clad Goth gunmen had joined Damian. Their pistols were still smoking and Sly was sure that these were the gentlemen who had snuck up behind him and shot him in the back.

"Besides, you and Legion Tate put at least a dozen bullets into me on the Sobre la Zanja. If a dozen bullets couldn't kill me, how did you expect just one to do the job?"

Sly's back was a fiery mass of pain. "I never saw your body when they pulled it from the Sao Paulo."

"That's right," said Damian, his face was chalk white and his eyes dark as the pits of hell. "That body belonged to a fisherman. I killed him, exchanged clothes, and shot him a number of times to simulate the wounds you thought you gave me. Then I dumped him in the river for the police to discover."

"The coroner must have been blind not to notice that a Brazilian was laying on his slab."

"It was still fairly obvious," agreed Damian, "but I thought it best to stay dead. It's easier for me to enjoy my various illicit pursuits when everyone thinks that I'm rotting in the grave. I merely threatened the coroner with the death of everyone he loved. To make my point I slaughtered his dog and hung the dripping corpse over his doorstep. After that, it took very little persuasion for him to positively identify the corpse as belonging to Damian Van Hellstrom."

"You're a piece of work," said Sly.

"You have no idea," said Damian, and he grinned bleakly. "I've gotten the band back together. Well, not the original band—I killed all of them, except for that slippery guitar player, Legion Tate. Do you have any idea where he might be hiding?"

"I haven't heard from him since we parted ways in Brazil," said Sly. "You might have noticed he keeps to himself."

"As well he should," cackled Damian. "The Devil knows I've made his life a living hell. I expect he quavers in fear every time he thinks of the old days, all those years in a tour bus—a serial killer right under his nose. Heh, for the longest time the police thought it was a deranged Condemner fan that was committing a murder in every town that we played. You've got a deranged fan...don't you, Sly?"

"Hal Alden," said Sly, wondering how he could escape Damian and his three Goth gunmen, and not coming up with any scenarios that didn't end up in death.

"Yes, strictly an amateur in my estimation. Why settle for a deranged fan when one can be a deranged musical genius?"

"I'd hardly call your screaming rants musical genius," said Sly. "More like musical torture. Even Brent Mickelson's got more vocal chops than..."

With a snarl Damian lifted the Desert Eagle to pistol whip the blonde-haired guitar player that had dared levy an insult, and that's when Sly found the opening that he was hoping for. He lunged forward, bearing Damian to the floor. The pistol descended weakly upon his shoulder instead of delivering the brutal skull-cracking blow that Damian had intended. Sly pinned Damian's gun arm to the floor and the pistol belched out bullets that flew in random directions.

Damian didn't look like much, but his lanky physique was deceiving. He possessed a wiry strength and a maniacal fury that gave him the power of three normal men. It was all Sly could do to keep the serial killer pinned and the gun controlled so that the spewing bullets wouldn't hit him or Brent Mickelson.

Bullet after bullet plowed through walls, floor, and ceiling until the slide of the Desert Eagle gaped open, the gun emptied of cartridges, the scent of gunpowder in the air, and a ringing in Sly's ears. Seeing that the gun was empty, Sly smashed a leather-clad forearm into Damian's jaw, forcing the maniac's face against the oak planks of the floor with a satisfying crack. Blood spurted from Damian's mashed lips and he ceased to struggle, instead laughing hysterically.

Sly reached to his belt buckle, pressed a secret catch and pulled loose a punch dagger that had been secreted behind the buckle. He pushed the point to the corner of Damian's right eye. "What are you laughing at? Call off your men or you're a dead man."

"I'm already a dead man," laughed Damian. "You killed me once and I came back. What makes you think I won't come back this time?"

"I'm willing to take my chances," said Sly. "Now call off your weirdo friends!"

"Take a look," said Damian. "I believe that my 'weirdo' associates have the upper hand."

Sly looked and saw one of Damian's Goth henchman standing behind Brent Mickelson, holding a .25 caliber pearl-handled Raven to Mickelson's skull. A .25 caliber certainly didn't have the punch of a .44 magnum, but at that range it would make a mess of Mickelson. He'd certainly never strangle a note again.

There was another little known fact about low-caliber guns. They didn't have the sheer flesh-rending potential of larger caliber weapons, but because of their lower velocity they had a way of slipping through the Kevlar strands of body armor, like the plates that lined Sly's tour jacket.

"What do I care if Strychnine loses a lead singer?" bluffed Sly. "A hobo off skid row could fill in and no one would notice the difference."

"Yet, here you are trying to save his life," replied Damian. "What about your own skin? Maybe you care more about that?"

Sly felt the barrel of a pistol being pushed up against the base of his skull. It would be foolhardy for the Goth gunman to pull the trigger, because the bullet might easily hit both Sly and Damian—but it was convincing enough to Sly that he slowly withdrew the point of the punch dagger away and dropped it on the floor. "I guess I'm outmatched on this one."

"You guess?" mocked Damian as his henchman grabbed Sly by his golden mane and wrenched him to his feet. "You don't have the cranial capacity to know for sure? You're little more than a baboon trained to play the guitar, and I've finally proven it."

Damian wiped away the blood from his face and licked it from his finger. "Cut the imposter loose and strap Sly to the chair. It's welded steel and lag-bolted to the floor. It should be enough to restrain even a baboon like him."

One of the Goth henchmen unstrapped Mickelson and he staggered to his feet, rubbing at his wrists. "You're going to let me go?"

"Of course not," said Damian. "I can't go around leaving witnesses can I? It's just that I plan on torturing Sly for a good long while and you happen to be sitting in his seat of honor. How those morons I hired to kidnap Sly mistakenly grabbed you I'll never know."

"So what are you going to do with me?"

Damian rubbed his chin. "I have yet to think of something suitably spectacular." He paused as if in deep thought. "Perhaps I'll tie a rope around your neck and drop you over the Golden Gate Bridge. It's a ways from here, but I think it would be worth it just to read the headlines when the lead singer for Strychnine is found dangling, his neck snapped like a twig."

Mickelson's Goth escort threw the hapless singer in the corner of the room and trained a gun on him, even while Sly was led at dual gunpoint to the steel throne. Both gunmen were very wary and alert for any sudden moves that Sly might make. In fact the gunman who had thrust a pistol against his skull had backed off a few paces so he wasn't within easy reach of the burly guitar player.

One of the Goth gunmen strapped Sly into place with thick leather bands while the other trained a gun on the musician. Damian also made a point of drawing a Ruger Vaquero, the handle of which was inlaid with golden skulls and the barrel scratched with numerous marks that tracked the maniac's kills with the weapon. "I do prefer knives," he admitted. "A gun seems so distant and impersonal. I like to do my work up close and intimate...but I admit there is something primal about the feel of a big pistol going off in one's hand. Wouldn't you agree, Sly?"

"Keep me out of your sick little diatribes," growled Sly.

"You may notice that I carry a caliber that you prefer," continued Damian. "Vaquero's are produced in a .44 caliber as well as for 44-40 and .45 rounds."

"Enough with the talking," said Sly. "Aren't you going to start torturing me or something?"

"Oh, I think I already have," said Damian. "I'm going to describe each and every one of my murders in loving detail: how they pleaded for mercy, how they screamed in pain, how I violated them before they died, and you're going to listen."

"I'm not a shrink or a priest," grunted Sly as a leather band was cinched around his neck. "I already know what you are. Confess to somebody else."

Damian leaned over Lanny's leaking corpse and chose an implement from the glittering selection on the floor—a small knife with a hooked snout.

He brandished it in a hand that displayed his black-painted nails. "You mistake my intentions, Sly. I'm not looking for absolution. I just need an ear so that I can brag about my exploits—and when I'm through bragging, I'm going to cut that ear off. Both of them, in fact."

Now that Sly was secure in the throne of torture, Damian drew nearer, and he traced the edge of the knife across Sly's cheek, slitting a long thin line in the ruddy skin. "When I'm through with you not even a coroner will be able to identify the remains."

He took the point of the knife and cut open Sly's shirt, exposing the musician's burly chest. Sly grimaced, straining futilely against his bonds as Damian began to carve his initials—D.V.H.—into his flesh. He roared in pain and anger and the three Goth henchmen stared at the grisly scene with sadistic fascination.

That's when Brent Mickelson wrenched the pearl-handled Raven away from his Goth captor and began pulling the trigger. The pistol popped three times and the Goth gunman sagged with a groan.

"You'll never take me alive!" shouted Brent, and he swung around and began firing at Damian, but he was no marksmen and the remaining three shots in the pistol went wild. One of them notched Sly's ear and two poked holes in the far wall.

Sly strained to break free, pushing his feet against the floor and wrenching at the chair. He was rewarded with only the slightest bit of movement and the lag bolts that restrained the chair held firm. Perhaps, if he had more time, he might eventually be able to rip the chair from the floor, but he didn't have the strength to tear it wholly from the oak planks in one titanic effort.

With the Raven empty, Brent suddenly found himself fruitlessly pulling the trigger. One of the other Goth gunmen moved in and clubbed him in the skull with the butt of an Army Outlaw pistol. The savage blow drove Brent to the floor and his scalp began bleed from a gash in his head. This was enough to take the fight out of Brent and he dazedly crawled to the wall and used his headband in an attempt to stanch the flow of blood.

Damian seemed unmoved by the loss of his henchman, whose glassy eyes stared blankly at the ceiling. One of Brent's shots had punctured his heart and killed him almost immediately. "It seems our accidental kidnappee has more spunk in him than I expected. Put some cuffs on him so he doesn't get any more bright ideas—but make sure he doesn't bleed to death. I want him alive when we hang him from the Golden Gate."

He turned his cold, cold stare upon Sly. "It seems I have yet to finish carving my initials. Before I finish, perhaps you'd like to hear the story of sweet little Anya Mcyntire—an innocent young girl of seventeen who thought it was exciting to flirt with the appearance of danger and, against her parents' wishes, she put on a pair of spandex tights, a leather belt that hooked with handcuffs, and her best rock t-shirt. She waited outside the backstage door after the show, hoping she just might have the opportunity to meet her hero..."

"Does this story end up with Anya dead and you the murderer?" interrupted Sly. "Because, if that's the case, I've already heard it."

Damian's calm, cold demeanor suddenly turned to fiery rage. He leaped to his feet and brandished his bloody knife. "I will not be mocked! I'll carve out your heart!" He thrust his blade forward as if he might, indeed, perform his threat—and Sly feared that he might have pushed the psychotic murderer over the brink, short trip that it was.

He pushed the point of the blade into Sly's flesh, but stopped short. "But I won't kill you, yet. Tell me where Legion Tate is hiding!"

Sly grimaced as Damian twisted the blade. "Are you deaf? I've already told you, I don't know where Legion Tate is. The last time I saw him was when we chased you down in Brazil. What's your obsession with him, anyhow?"

Damian withdrew the blade and watched crimson rivulets roll down its stainless surface. "It was Legion that turned me over to the police. He was my brother. We made a pact of loyalty and he sold me out when he discovered that I was the one committing the killings—my sacrifices to Satan."

"Of course he sold you out. You're a murderer. If I was running around carving up innocent people I'd expect my brothers to turn me over to the police—or put a bullet in me themselves. Loyalty has to be earned."

"A pact is a pact," frothed Damian. "He has to pay for his betrayal. And you're going to tell me where he is."

Sly realized that the only way that Damian was going to stop his knife work is if he told the maniac where he could find Legion Tate. The fact was that he didn't know. He had a phone number, but it went straight to an answering machine that said, "You have not reached Legion Tate. Leave a message at the sound of the tone."

Every message that Sly had left over the past year had been duly ignored. Legion might have reverted to his old ways and crawled inside a bottle. He might be back in the asylum trying to get past the horrors he'd witnessed, or he might be enjoying a sabbatical away from the cares of the world. He might already be dead. Sly didn't know.

Sly could create some story for Damian or he could resist to the last drop of his blood. Either way he was going to end up dead and Brent Mickelson was going to end up hanging from the Golden Gate. A quicker death would be easier, but from the day Sly was born he had a perverse streak running through him.

"I know where he is," said Sly. "But I'm not going to tell you."

Damian gave a tight-lipped grin and glared at Sly past the bloody tip of his knife. "Then let the games begin. Which eye do you want to lose first?"

"I've always been partial to my right eye," said Sly. "Why don't you carve out the left one first?"

"My pleasure," said Damian. He pushed the hooked blade into the cheek bone just below the socket of Sly's eye.

A sudden staccato of gunfire broke the quiet and Damian stiffened as a half dozen bullets spattered across his back. He dropped his knife and crumpled to the floor, his long leather trench coat folding around his lanky form.

Sly caught a glimpse of Mitz standing in the doorway, twin Double Eagle Colts in hand. As soon as Mitz saw Damian fall, he switched targets, firing simultaneously at the two Goth gunmen, even though they stood on opposite sides of the room. Flashes of gunfire lit up the room as Damian's henchmen began to fire, but they had, again, been distracted by the prospect of grisly torture and Mitz's entrance had taken them by surprise.

Mitz emptied his guns, feeling a bullet tug at his curly blond hair as plaster spattered and spumed into the air next to him. He watched with satisfaction as both gunmen dropped to their knees and keeled over in concert. Mitz released the emptied eight-round magazines and they clattered to the floor. He took turns slapping full magazines into the hollow handle before coming to Sly's side.

"How did you find me?" asked Sly as Mitz began to loosen the leather straps that kept him bound.

"Cindy Warner picked me up and we started cruising Mullholland looking for you. When I saw the black copter I wondered if this might be the place. Then I saw the bullet hole in the tinted window and I took it for a sign that I was on the right track."

"Cindy Warner—the super model?" questioned Sly.

Mitz grinned. "If it wasn't for her I never would have found you."

"Yeah, but how do you rate a super model while I'm getting tortured?"

Mitz heard a rustle behind him and he turned to see the flapping form of Damian Van Hellstrom retreating toward the door. In a flash Mitz had a Double Eagle in his right hand. He fired off four shots before Damian was out of the room and tearing down the hallway. The shots staggered Damian, but none seemed to hurt him more than superficially.

"What? You didn't hit him in the head when you came in the room?" asked a dismayed Sly.

"I took out three gunmen and you're complaining that I didn't hit him in the head?"

"He's wearing Kevlar with ceramic plate inserts," said Sly. "I could tell when I was wrestling with him."

"Well, how was I supposed to know that?" protested Mitz. "You might just be grateful that I saved you from getting your eyes cut out."

"Go after him!" demanded Sly. "Don't let him get away!"

Already they could hear the sound of the copters blades as they began to rotate and pick up speed. Mitz abandoned his efforts to unstrap Sly and left him mostly bound to the torture throne. He could hear Damian's feet pounding up the stairs toward the roof, and he gave pursuit, leaping up the stairs as fast as his legs would carry him.

An ill smog-laced wind greeted Mitz as he emerged on the tiled roof of the home, the wash of the copter's quadruple rotors washing over him. It was a Bell 412 painted midnight black, its thirty-six-foot-long body nearly stretching the length of the rooftop. Damian stood shadowed in the mouth of the copter, his long leather trench flapping obscenely in the churning winds.

Damian whirled and began firing his Vaquero. The first shot took off the hinge of the door through which Mitz had exited onto the roof, and as the copter began to lift, the second shot passed over the drummer's head.

Mitz returned fire with the Raven he had scooped from a dead Goth's hand as he exited the torture chamber below. It seemed outrageous that someone would spend so much money putting pearl-handles on a seventy-nine dollar gun, but Mitz knew that the low-caliber bullets might have a chance of sliding through Damian's Kevlar suit.

He pulled the trigger twice and swore he could hear the sound of the .25 caliber slugs smacking the leather of Damian's trench coat. Mitz thought he saw the serial killer's frame sag in the mouth of the copter, but then the Bell 412 tilted away from the roof, so that Mitz's only clear shot was at the black belly and the landing skids of the copter.

The tail rotor of the copter was still exposed but the Raven would be worthless against the body of the Bell 412, so Mitz tossed away the pearl-handled pistol and reached for his fully-loaded Colt Double Eagle. He fired six, maybe seven times, before one of his shots penetrated the gear box and shattered the rear rotor. A fragment of sharp blade came spinning off, ricocheting across the roof top.

Mitz hurled himself to the ground and the shard of rotor passed over his head, slicing away a lock of his curly blond hair. He looked into the air and saw the helicopter spinning wildly, losing its altitude and then finally plunging against the rocky slope that was studded with spindly pines.

The drummer went to the edge of the roof and watched the mangled body of the helicopter roll down the slope, snapping tree trunks and bounding over precipitous drops until it finally came to rest against a massive boulder. Mitz could see fuel leaking out of the smashed fuselage.

Mitz heard his brother's voice at his shoulder. "This seems like a good time to take up smoking."

The drummer nodded. "Brent, do you happen to have a light on you?"

Brent patted his pocket and handed Mitz a chrome Zippo emblazoned with a skull's head.

"Most appropriate," grinned Mitz. "Let me get down there before Damian manages to pull himself from the wreckage."

Brent was still bewildered. "What are you going to do?"

Sly regarded the wreckage with grim certitude. "Aircraft fuel and a lighter make for a spectacular view."

"Are you coming with me?" asked Mitz as he headed toward the sagging doorway.

Sly winced as he opened his jacket and exhibited the bloody wreckage of his chest. "I'll be along in just a second. I need to have a chat with Brent."

Mitz nodded and disappeared down the stairwell.

Brent blanched as he looked on Sly's ruddy visage. "You're not going to kill me are you?"

"No, I'm not," said Sly. "I'm going to apologize. I've said a lot of nasty thing about you, Brent—but from now on whenever anybody maligns you or Strychnine I'm going to tell them you're a stand-up guy. You killed a man trying to save me."

Brent shrugged. "Maybe, or maybe I was just trying to save my own hide."

"Don't undersell yourself. If ever you need a favor from me—anything— you give me a call."

Brent nodded and swallowed hard. "About that man I killed: are the police going to haul me off to jail?"

"That's a clear-cut case of self defense if I've ever seen it," said Sly. "Besides, the government and the Gantlet Brothers have an understanding. We don't kill anybody that doesn't need killing and they overlook the minor details."

"How does that work?" asked Brent.

"America is the best country in the world," said Sly. "Believe me...I've been to most of them. But there's still some bad men ensconced in very powerful positions. It so happens that we've amassed a bit of evidence on some of America's less savory operations. If the government crosses the Gantlets, that information gets released to major press agencies."

"So the police won't do anything to you?"

"The police won't exactly be happy when they find a room full of bodies and they might even arrest us—but then they'll get a call from their bosses telling them to kick us free."

Brent Mickelson paused as if considering the wisdom of broaching a touchy subject. Finally, his bravado overcame his trepidation. "You owe me big time, dude. Not only did I get my skull laid open for you, but you made off with my girlfriend."

Sly raised an eyebrow. "Andi?"

"Yeah, Andi."

Sly fished about in his jacket pocket, found what Andi had shoved inside when they had parted. He dangled a key with a plastic tab engraved with the logo of the Argyle Hotel and stamped 211. "Andi's waiting for you in room 211 of the Argyle Hotel. She told me to give this to you when I tracked you down. Seems she had second thoughts."

"Yeah, right," said Brent, but he took the key anyway and eyed Sly suspiciously. "Andi doesn't seem inclined much toward second thoughts. So why are you really giving this up?"

"I owe you." said Sly. "And, also, when a person is about to have their eyes carved out it's a good time to think about life and what's most important."

"So Andi's not important?"

"She's a glitzy distraction," said Sly. "And I'm easily distracted. It's a personal weakness of mine."

"You're only human," said Brent.

"So I've told myself, but I made some promises when I was sitting in that chair."

"You didn't seem too concerned," said Brent.

Sly's lip turned up at the corner. "I didn't want to give Damian the satisfaction, but I was praying like crazy. God followed through on His end of the bargain, I guess I'd better follow through on mine."

Brent gripped the key and smiled, apparently not affected in the least by Sly's torture-chair epiphany. "Your loss is my gain. Can you drop me off at the Argyle?"

"I've got to make sure that Damian's dead...and I don't think you want to stick around for that. There's a car in the garage with the keys still in it. Take that, but before you visit Andi, you may want to stop in at the hospital and have your head checked out."

"Yeah, right," said Brent.[7] He waved a farewell to Sly. "Next time you're

---

[7] *It seems that Brent Mickelson ignored this piece of advice. Besides some dizziness and headaches, the effects of that brutal blow to the head wouldn't entirely manifest until many years later. In 2010 Brent Mickelson was rushed to an L.A. hospital and found*

in town the drinks are on you."

"The drinks are on me," agreed Sly.

The force of a massive explosion impacted Sly's body and ruffled his mane, and he turned to see a great fireball rising from the flaming wreckage of the helicopter. He could see Mitz's distant form limned in the fiery light as he climbed from behind a boulder and watched the burning cabin of the Bell 412, a Colt Double Eagle cradled in his hands lest Damian Van Hellstrom should rise like a phoenix from the ashes.

---

to have subarachnoid hemorrhage, or bleeding onto the surface of the brain. Doctors surmised that this was caused by an old brain injury which had never entirely healed. Mickelson did recover from the injury and is still recording music and starring in various 'reality' TV shows.

Thank you to best friends and consultants Joe Benson, Scott Irey, Steve Mitzel, Steve Mrowiec, and Damon Orrell who remain the heart and soul of the Gantlet brotherhood.

Books from Pulpwork Press:

Derrick Ferguson

Dillon Series:
Dillon and the Golden Bell
Four Bullets for Dillon
Dillon and the Pirates of Xonira
Dillon and the Voice of Odin

Joel Jenkins

Dire Planet Series:
Dire Planet
Exiles of the Dire Planet
Into the Dire Planet
Strange Gods of the Dire Planet
Lost Tribes of the Dire Planet

Tales from the City of Bathos Series:
Escape from Devil's Head
Through the Groaning Earth

The Gantlet Brother Series:
The Nuclear Suitcase
The Gantlet Brothers Greatest Hits
The Gantlet Brothers: Sold Out by Joel Jenkins

Damage Incorporated Series:
The Sea Witch

Denbrook Supernatural:
Devil Take the Hindmost

Children's Books:
The Pirates of Mirror Land

Arthurian Fantasy:
Island of Lost Souls

Biography:
One Foot in My Grave

Collections:
Weird Worlds of Joel Jenkins

Josh Reynolds
Dracula Lives!

Percival Constantine

Infernum Series:
Love and Bullets
Outlaw Blues

Myth Hunter Series:
Myth Hunter
Dragon Kings of the Orient

Anthologies
How the West was Weird, edited by Russ Anderson
How the West was Weird 2, edited by Russ Anderson
How the West was Weird: Campfire Tales, edited by Russ Anderson

Coming in 2014
How the West was Weird 3
Lone Crow Collected by Joel Jenkins

For more information on these and other titles or for online ordering
visit us at PulpWork.Com or find our titles at Amazon,
KoboBooks.com, and BarnesandNoble.com

Visit the author's blog at JoelJenkins.com

www.ingramcontent.com/pod-product-compliance
Lightning Source LLC
Chambersburg PA
CBHW052025020726
47501CB00004B/1258